LEAGUE OF ELDER
Against the Druries

THE BELMONT SAGA

Ren Garcia

Loconeal Publishing

Amherst, OH

Against the Druries

Copyright © 2013 by Ren Garcia
Cover Art by © 2013 by Carol Phillips
Title Page Art by © 2013 by Eve Ventrue
Listed copyrighted interior image art is provided in the 'List of Illustrations'
Edited by Barbara Taft Verducci

Loconeal books may be ordered through booksellers or by contacting:
www.loconeal.com
216-772-8380

Loconeal Publishing can bring authors to your live event. Contact Loconeal Publishing at 216-772-8380.

Published by Loconeal Publishing, LLC
Printed in the United States of America

First Loconeal Publishing edition: March 2013

Visit our website: www.loconeal.com

ISBN 978-0-9885289-3-2 (Trade Paperback)

ALSO BY REN GARCIA

The League of Elder Series:
Sygillis of Metatron
The Hazards of the Old Ones

The Temple of the Exploding Head Trilogy:
The Dead Held Hands
The Machine
The Temple of the Exploding Head

The Belmont Saga:
Sands of the Solar Empire
Against the Druries

The Shadow Tech Goddess (2014)

For more on The League of Elder, please visit:
www.theleagueofelder.com

www.loconeal.com

TABLE OF CONTENTS

Part 1—The Sisters' Fist

Part 2—The Woman in Gray

Part 3—The Pilgrims of Merian

LIST OF ILLUSTRATIONS

CRONYN WORLD MAP

League Shipping Lane

To:
Nu Torriander
(Onaris, Bazz)

DRURIES BELT

CRONYN WORLD

Seeker's path as laid out by the lantern

Windward

Seeker intercepted by
Demophalon John

Path of Demophalon John

Edam
(Hell)

Merian Lookout
Point

The Solar Wind

Path of Seeker

Seeker traveling
by the stern

THE SWARM

X

Seeker returned
by Sisters

Leeward

To: Beta Terrigrin
(Kana)

PART 1

THE SISTERS'

FIST

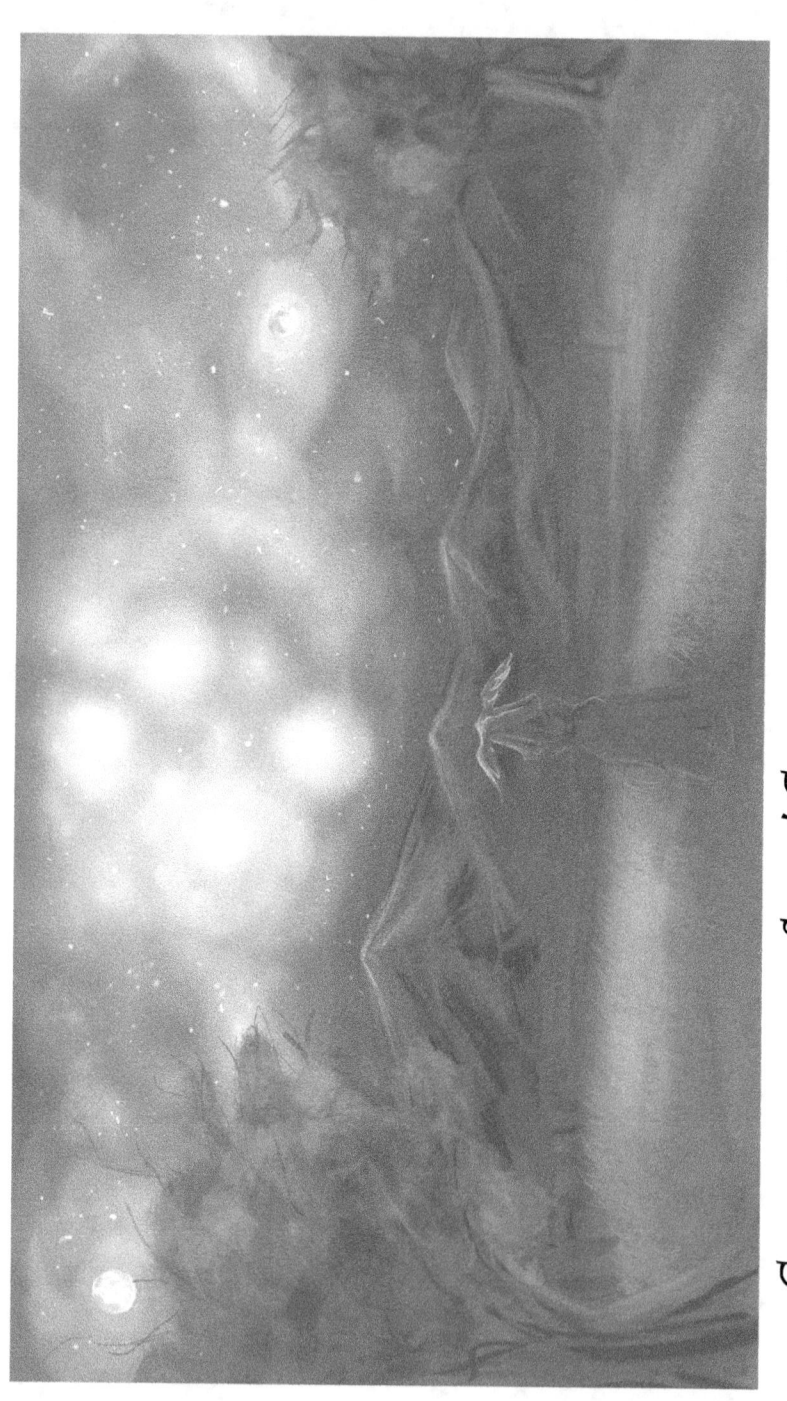

CAMALOPARDUS, THE SISTERS' CONSTELLATION, AS SEEN FROM KANA

1

—The Deep Sea—

Three souls huddled in the dark of the great, airless ship flying backwards through the deep sea to Bazz.

A fabled ship with a proud history, the *Seeker* had seen better days. She was designed decades prior to be fast and strong, to be agile, to inflict damage upon the enemy, and to comfortably house several hundred souls deep into the empty cradle of space, the "Deep Sea" as the Fleet sailors called it. The MFV *Seeker* had done that and more. A veteran of such classic battles as Sorrander-quo, Mirendra I and II, Two-pitch Nebula, Hardee and Xandarr, she had survived them all, had sunk many enemy ships, and was feared among them.

But, as in all things, time passes, the new becomes old and the state-of-the-art becomes obsolete. The glory days of the past become footnotes on withered pages in a forgotten history book and the *Seeker*, old and worn, in need of costly repairs and refits, ought to be barge-towed to the boneyard, smelted, and remade into something fresh and useful. Many great ships had taken that sorry trip.

But, the right people favored the *Seeker*. The Sisterhood of Light, beloved of the Fleet Admiralty and of the League, was fond of the old Warbird. "How is the *Seeker*?" they often asked, and those casual asides, frequently posed, helped save her. The Admiralty could not simply smelt the Sisters' favorite ship; that would not do. So, they decided to raise the *Seeker's* chair for debate one last time, and appoint a captain with vast sums of money to donate and demonstrate to the Sisters once and for all that the *Seeker* was simply too old and unsafe to continue flying. Why, they could melt her down, sell the refined metals to the Sisters, and they could build a new convent from it if they wished. That would be a bold irony.

So, the Admiralty put the *Seeker's* captain's chair on the blocks and they appointed a captain, an odd man from Tyrol wearing a hated HRN coat and a mask of all things: Lord Stenstrom of Belmont-South Tyrol, a self-styled eccentric and a Paymaster to boot. He had been the only person to make a serious offer for the chair, and he had privilege, he had Programmability, and best of all, he had money. Lots of it.

Giving a Warbird's chair to a Paymaster, a civilian clerk, was unheard of, and, not only that, Lord Belmont was a clown as well in an HRN coat and mask. Such an appointment would make the Admiralty a laughing stock—if such a man could take a Warbird's chair, why not anybody? Soon every peg-legged Diddy from Calvert would be storming the Admirals' Hall demanding a chair. What would become of the Fleet?

PAYMASTER STENSTROM, LORD OF
BELMONT-SOUTH TYROL

So, they kept the appointment quiet, out of the Posts and usual gossip and intended Paymaster Stenstrom not sit on the *Seeker's* chair for long. Admiral Derlith of the 3rd Fleet devised a wonderfully devious plan to ensure just that.

They Admiralty went in and gutted the *Seeker*, had her huge SM coils ripped out, her thermoplant dismantled, her battleshot batteries and canisters hauled away, and her bridge partially disassembled. They took everything: carpeting, tables, chairs, beds, they even took food from the pantries, stationary from the drawers, and toilets from the heads, leaving bare, knurled metal and gaping holes where toilets once resided. As for the crew, they were allowed to conscript onto other vessels and were encouraged to do so.

As per tradition, a newly appointed captain was obliged to perform a mission at the pleasure of the Admiralty. Normally, this mandatory mission was something simple and easily accomplished; however, if Lord Belmont were to fail in this mission, then his chair would be lost and his money forfeited.

Lord Stenstrom's mission for Admiral Derlith: Deliver brandy to a ball being thrown at the Fleet HQ annex Teflegar-Martin II on Bazz in twelve days hence. It was more of an errand than a mission. Bazz was barely a full day's hard sail away, unworthy of a once great Warbird.

But, with the *Seeker* disemboweled in a steadily decaying orbit, with no crew to man her, no engines to propel her, and with his orders specifying that the *Seeker* herself be the one to deliver the brandy to Bazz, Admiral Derlith and the rest of the Admiralty couldn't conceive of any way Paymaster Stenstrom could possibly succeed.

In one devious stroke, Admiral Derlith would take Lord Stenstrom's money, humiliate him in the process, and prove to the Sisters that the *Seeker* was done as a Main Fleet Warbird—why, it couldn't even make an easy trip to Bazz; the fact that she was scuttled and without propulsion was irrelevant.

In sporting terms, the plan was the Cinco Pass. It couldn't fail.

✳ ✳ ✳ ✳ ✳

One small thing Admiral Derlith didn't plan for or anticipate: great ships are said to have a soul and a will of their own. Like a champion race horse that refuses to lose though its competition might be stronger and faster, the *Seeker* had never failed a task it had been assigned, not in decades and after hundreds of engagements. Its current task: deliver brandy to Bazz, a demeaning, worthless task, but, regardless, that's what was set before it, and if it had to make the trip to Bazz on its knees, gasping, crawling every inch of the way with stolen parts and a misfit crew, then so be it.

Great ships found a way.

And events were set into motion. Lord Stenstrom needed help, and somehow, someway, he managed to secure the assistance of two unlikely people, one a worthless Marine private known for her sloth and lack of discipline. The other was shocking: Lt. Josephus, Lord of the tiny House of A-Ram, Admiral Derlith's own personal adjutant. A modest, rather milquetoast young man of limited skill outside of the office, and rather grounded in his aspirations; a man who feared his own shadow. The Admiral always felt he was doing Lt. Josephus a grand favor keeping him safe and secure in his office at the 3rd Fleet.

But look! Josephus turned out to be a rather accomplished pilot, and flew the three of them aboard the *Seeker* in a Sub-Orbital of all things—a very bold and dangerous thing to attempt.

Josephus had done that?

Furthermore, Paymaster Stenstrom and his crew of two mismatched and unskilled personages somehow managed to correct the *Seeker's* decaying orbit and, by means of a stolen scouting ship, the *Westminster*, blasted out of orbit using her engines and were on their way to Bazz at slow speed with the brandy.

Great ships have a soul and find a way.

Annoyed by this turn of events and careful to keep things under control, Admiral Derlith saw to it the "*Seeker* Situation" was kept under tight wraps. Paymaster Stenstrom, though a buffoon and eccentric, had powerful friends in the Fleet Captaincy and beyond—namely his venerable and well-liked father, Stenstrom the Older of the Warbird *Caroline*, and his mentor and sponsor the famed Captain Davage of the *New Faith*. Fleet captains loved to stick it to the Admiralty whenever possible, and this situation was tailor-made for such an intervention. They just might swoop in from all over, tend to the Paymaster's scuttled ship in flight and give him a grand escort to Bazz, all the while laughing in the Admiralty's face. Such a spectacle would be unacceptable and never lived down. Paymaster Stenstrom also had an impressively high Programmability with the Sisterhood of Light, and, should they become involved and dissent in his favor, this game would end . . . immediately. But, until that time, the game was afoot.

Admiral Derlith used his influence and kept things nice and quiet. He ordered standard communications in the shipping lanes between Kana and Onaris/Bazz blacked out for "maintenance purposes." He then summoned his niece, Lt. Gwendolyn, Lady of Prentiss, to intercept the *Seeker* in space with her scouting ship, the *Demophalon John*, board her, clap Paymaster Stenstrom and Private Taara in irons, and return Lt. Josephus to the Fleet. He gave her carte blanche in her assignment, to do whatever she needed to get the job done. Period.

Ever dutiful, Lt. Gwendolyn agreed and, even now, was nearing the *Seeker's* position, her small guns run out and ready to fire on the unarmed, unpowered Warbird should they be needed. And, if she had to kill Paymaster Stenstrom in the process, then so be it.

So be it.

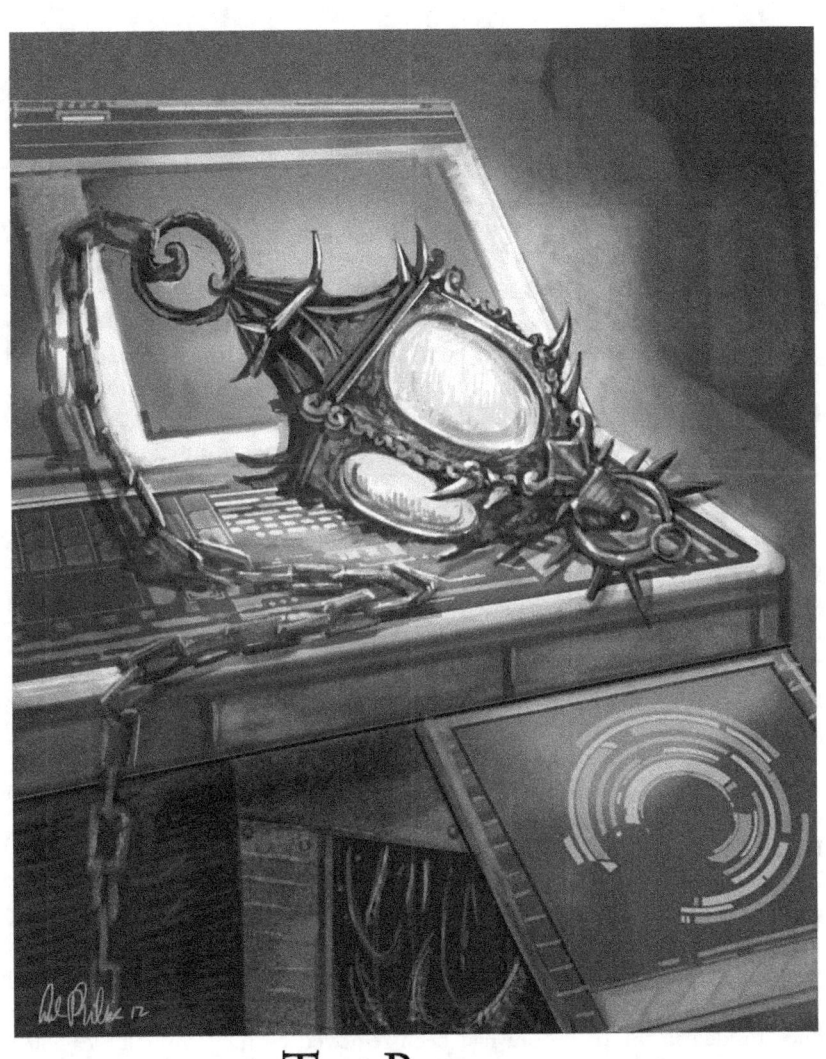

THE PARAMEL

2

— THE LANTERN —

"**G**oddammit! This piece of goddamn shit!" came an echoing voice. A-Ram covered his ears and Stenstrom shook his head. Such language, truly shameful.

✳   ✳   ✳   ✳   ✳

All things considered, they weren't doing too bad on the *Seeker*. They'd been through quite a bit since boarding the tumbling, silent hulk of the ship several days earlier, crashing through a large window in their gasping Sub-Orbital, praying to Creation that the ship's emergency shutters would close and seal the hole they'd made.

Fortunately for them, it did.

They'd gotten used to the stale air and slightly stuffy interior of the ship due to the excellent insulation of the *Seeker's* armor. They were amazed how quickly they could learn to do without such essentials as running water, hot meals, clean clothes and a warm bed. The lack of a comfortable place to sleep was rather trying. Taara did fairly well curled up at the padded Missive's station's chair, while Stenstrom, and A-Ram had to make do with the unyielding floor.

There was one thing, however, they couldn't live without.

They were in Stenstrom's office just off the main bridge, the place glittering with fresh stars and steady lighting. The bridge and the office were like home using all the improvised bits they'd collected, the only thing they lacked was running water and a working toilet. As answering the call of nature was a long inconvenient process walking through the unlit, noisy bowels of the ship, which none of them really wanted to do, getting the bathroom in Stenstrom's office working was a top priority, and they'd been hard at it all afternoon since the last *Westminster* engine burn. The pristine commode that once resided in the bathroom had been removed by the Admiralty leaving a bare, surprisingly large hole and unappealing smells.

The three of them, under Taara's direction, had managed to get the water lines to the bathroom working by sacrificing a bit of generator power and connecting up a condenser on Deck Six. Of course Taara had no knowledge of engineering or shipboard plumbing. She was wearing A-Ram's MOLLY, a mystical charm that allowed one to know things one shouldn't know and to do things one shouldn't be able to do. A-Ram was too afraid to use it himself, as the Sisters required registration before using it, so Taara, unafraid, was game to try, and the knowledge it gave her was invaluable. The price for using it, A-Ram said, would be a demon hungry for her soul.

It had been a great deal of grungy work, crawling through the maintenance shafts, hooking up lines and hoses and turning valves. The plumbing system on a starship was a complicated tangle of positive and negative piping, relief hoses, valves and nitrogen tanks to aid in maintaining pressure, and so on. Taara sometimes got a little cross and impatient as Stenstrom and A-Ram fumbled around and started yelling. People from Bazz had a reputation across the League for coarse language and raised voices and Taara was proving the notion to be true. She yelled at A-Ram when he miss-connected a hose, calling him some choice Bazz names and hurt his feelings.

"Hey, hey," she said. "I didn't mean anything, that's how we talk on Bazz. We do a lot of yelling. I didn't mean anything by it. You know I love you guys. If I make you mad, just yell back, that's all." She hugged him and the matter was forgotten.

Later, they crowded into the bathroom, the three of them staring at the fine pewter faucet like it was some sort of pagan altar ready to spew fire.

"Well, come on, let's do this," Taara said and Stenstrom opened the faucet, they listened to the network of pressurized pipes groan and then marveled as clean water gurgled into the basin. It was cause for a celebration, lots of hugging and splashing of water.

Now, for the star of the show: the commode. The Admiralty had done a smashing job of removing every toilet, head and potty trench they could find from bow to stern. Taara, with her MOLLYed up smarts, had worked up plans for connecting a sink to the head and supplying it with a trickle of water to flush it out, but then Stenstrom had a mindwave.

He remembered Lt. Kilos, the former First Officer of the ship, once talking about a secret head near the main mess, installed for the captain's private use during important functions when excusing one's self for protracted periods might not be possible. It didn't appear on the blueprints for the ship and was a custom addition built specifically for Captain Davage, as Lord Milos of Probert, the ship's designer, was a close personal friend of his. Ki used to say she'd hide out in the "Secret Potty" from time to time when she wanted to be alone, sneaking in when nobody was looking and she'd have a long, relaxing constitutional free of people bugging her.

Such a prize, if it was still there, was worth a plunge into the dark, and they made the long, disturbing trek through to the unlit back section of the ship to the mess, the place of their initial entry days ago. The trip was like walking through a haunted wood at midnight, the inky black of the ship alive with ghosts and noises.

Stenstrom remembered the last time he'd plunged into the darkened reaches of the ship.

Taara and A-Ram missing. The corridors over-run with Soul Devourers.

Their horrid touch . . . Their tittering . . . Starving for his soul which his Mother had promised them.

And then Lilly appeared from the dark. Lilly, his Lilly, a talented but mundane girl from Gamboa his Mother had selected for him years earlier. His Mother had wanted a distinctly non-arcane girl to balance his forays into the mystical realms, and Lilly fit the bill perfectly.

PRIVATE TAARA DE LA ANDERSON

But then there was Lilly, emerging from the dark in the bowels of the ship carrying an arcane lantern, smiling as if there was nothing odd or unusual about appearing from nowhere when she should be thousands of stellar miles away back on Kana.

"Bel, don't I always arrive when you need me most?" she said.

Once they arrived in the mess, they found the remains of their destroyed Sub-Orbital mangled in the corner, along with the all-important case of brandy bottled at the home of Admiral Derlith himself.

The brandy was his "cargo", he had to deliver it to a ball at Teflegar-Martin II on Bazz in twelve days, otherwise, his appointment to the chair of the *Seeker* would be lost. Given the barely habitable condition of the ship, the brandy had been largely forgotten in the last few days, they had left it where it sat.

There was a disturbing display waiting for them when they arrived. There were fresh footprints dotting the mess, scampering along the floor and even up the walls.

"What are these?" A-Ram asked with trepidation.

Stenstrom inspected them: bare feet with hints of claws. "Soul Devourers," he announced. They had been all over the ship, conniving in the dark, starving for his soul.

. . . YOUR SOUL!! they had screamed.

"Do you think there are more of them hiding about?" A-Ram asked, somewhat panicked.

"I doubt it. Not much for hiding and stratagem, Soul Devourers. If they were here, they would attack. We would know it by now."

"What happened to them?" Taara asked.

Lilly, she had killed every one of them and pushed their bodies into fanciful positions. Always the artist, Lilly. Hundreds of their corpses turning to ash . . .

"Don't know," Stenstrom lied.

Taara quickly discovered the secret head off in a corner, and there it was through the hidden door: a pristine commode the Admiralty had missed, a wondrous prize worth its weight in gold. Wringing her little hands, Taara fell on the commode and had it disconnected in minutes, scooting it out along the floor leaving a trail in dust. Heavy, the three of them hoisted it up and lugged it back to the bridge, so intent they were with their prize they barely noticed the voices from the dark cajoling them along the way.

"What happened to Lilly? Where did she go?" A-Ram asked.

Where had she gone?

Standing on what appeared to be Kana, Lilly was about to reveal all to him when a horn sounded and Lilly shrieked in frustration, tearing at her golden hair. And then Stenstrom had been returned to the airless dark of the Seeker.

"No, no! It's not fair!" Lilly cried. *"I thought I'd have more time! Remember, you just extended me your hand, and I'm not giving it back!"*

"She was called home," Stenstrom said.

"Hey Lilly!" Taara cried out. "We could use a hand! This thing's awkward and heavy!"

A-Ram was alarmed. "Don't call out for her, Taara. She's a demon."

Stenstrom took momentary exception to A-Ram calling Lilly a demon, but then, after all that had happened and been done, what else could she be?

"Why, Bel, of course I'm of the arcane . . ." she had said.

Lilly . . . a demon.

They hauled the commode up the low gravity of the lift shaft and into Stenstrom's office. Taara double-checked all the connections before they seated the toilet in place. She quickly got flustered.

"What's wrong?" Stenstrom asked.

"Damn thing. I can't get pressure. I don't get it. This should be ready to go."

A-Ram leaned over and placed his hand near the mouth of the hole. "I don't feel anything."

"Well, that's just it, there should be negative pressure. You should be feeling a slight breeze sucking everything down the hole to the pipe junction below. All right you two, out of the way!"

Taara set back to it and soon was swearing up and down, making both Stenstrom and A-Ram blush.

"Why don't we take a break?" Stenstrom suggested.

"No way, Bel—no damn way! This thing isn't kicking my butt! I want this commode working, and then I'm going to celebrate by having a nice, long poop!"

Taara stared at the hole in disgust and pushed her black hair and dangling sideburns from her face. "It's like there's something stuck in there. There's got to be a blockage or something gumming everything up." She removed her Marine coat and boots.

"What are you doing?" Stenstrom asked.

"I'm going in. I'm going to fix it."

A-Ram gazed down the tight hole. "Down there?"

"Yep. See what things I do for you guys, huh?"

She smiled up at Stenstrom and he gave her trademark Mollock sideburns, a mark of being unmarried on Bazz, a yank for luck. Without a hint of fear, Taara shimmied into the hole and squirmed down, reaching a T-bend about two feet below. She moved her legs into one end of the T-bend and carefully stretched out on her stomach into the other side. Stenstrom watched, fearing she might get stuck.

She squirmed around for a minute or two, and then she reacted violently, her body tensing up. They heard the muffled sound of a scream.

Stenstrom reached down and grabbed her by her shirt. "Taara!" he yelled. He pulled back, revealing her head and shoulders and she clambered out, hanging onto him.

"Taara, what happened? What did you see?"

She sat there a moment and collected herself. Stenstrom drew his NTH pistols and gazed down into the hole, seeing nothing but the pipe leading down and the T-bend.

"Let me get you some water," A-Ram said running out of the office.

"Taara, what did you see?" Stenstrom asked again.

Taara composed herself. "I saw somebody down there, stuffed into the pipe."

"Down there? You mean a body?"

"It was alive, a lady, I think, with blonde hair and blue eyes—I remember the eyes." She regained her composure and laughed. "Wow—that ... that was a rush!"

Blonde hair, blue eyes, it sounded like Lilly.

"She looked really, really pissed, like she wanted to get at me or something. She reached out and that's when I freaked."

A-Ram returned with a bottle of water and gave it to Taara and she accepted it with trembling hands. As Taara drank, Stenstrom leaned down and listened for sounds coming from the hole.

He heard a tiny noise issuing from the pipes: "... *teehee* ..."

"Lilly?" he asked.

No answer.

"Lilly!"

No reply.

Her final words to him before she disappeared rang through his mind.

"*I ACCEPT!!*"

"A-Ram, I'm going to give you one of my NTHs. I want you to go down there and have a look."

A-Ram swallowed hard. "Me? You want me to go down there?"

"I do. I won't fit, and you'll have my NTH's. The NTH's can slay anything."

A-Ram didn't want to go. "Well, perhaps Taara can ..."

"Taara's a girl, she can't use the NTH's. They only work for men." He tried to lighten the mood with a bit of levity. "You are a girl, right, Taara?"

Lilly? What was Lilly? Not a woman.

"V-very funny," she replied.

With great uncertainty, A-Ram took off his coat and gingerly lowered himself into the hole, taking Stenstrom's pistol in his little hands. Stenstrom also gave him a yellow Holystone to see. He shook it and was bathed in warm yellow light,

"Cock the hammer, A-Ram," Stenstrom said. "And, don't worry about damaging anything—the NTH's don't affect inanimate objects. Oh, make sure you don't shoot upwards in our direction, the NTH-shot will go through the floorboards."

A-Ram gulped and worked his way into the T-bend.

"See anything?" Taara called down.

He wiggled around a bit and then came back out. "There's nobody down here, not that I can see," he said with relief. He waved the Holystone around.

"You don't see anybody?" Taara called down.

"I don't, and thank Creation for that. I do think I see something wedged in the pipe a fair distance away."

"Can you get it out?" Taara asked.

"I'll try."

He plunged back into the pipe and worked his way in. A minute or two later he re-emerged, backing out inch-by-inch and holding the end of a glittering golden chain. Stenstrom and Taara helped him out and pulled on the chain; whatever was on the end of it moved easily.

"Look at this thing," Taara remarked. "This is real gold. What's it doing stuffed up in the plumbing? And look how clean, it ought to be crusted with filth."

They continued pulling on the gold chain until something large and prickly like a pinecone emerged from the T-bend.

"What is that?" A-Ram asked, moving the Holystone around.

They hauled it up. Dangling at the end of the surprisingly lengthy chain was a brass lantern, about a foot long sporting four ovular lenses, one on each side, and a steeped top. The lenses were dark and full of mystery.

"Bel, is this the thing you were talking about?" Taara asked, pointing at the lantern.

Stenstrom stared at it. "Looks like it, sure enough. This is the lantern Lilly was carrying."

"Lilly? You mean the angry lady in the pipes?"

"I saw no one," A-Ram said.

"Oh, she was there all right."

Taara brought the lantern out of the office and set it on the Missive's Panel. Its flawless lenses were dark and inscrutable.

A-Ram approached and leaned in, adjusting his glasses to get a good look at it. "Seems sinister to me. And you say your lady was carrying this contrivance?"

Stenstrom agreed. "Lilly called it the 'Paramel'. It's an arcane object of some sort. I'm not certain how it works. It seems to function when it wishes."

"So what's it doing stuffed up our pipes?" Taara asked.

"I've no idea."

A-Ram was nervous and backed away. "We shouldn't have this, Bel. The Sisters keep a tight hold on such arcane things. They might have something to say about it."

"The Sisters have something to say about everything."

"We should put it back where we found it."

"Back in the pipes? No way, I want my toilet working!" Taara cried. She inspected it, tinkering with the lenses and tugging on the fittings. She knocked on its steeped cap.

"What are you doing?" A-Ram cried.

"I'm just tinkering," she said. "The MOLLY's not telling me much about it."

"That confirms it's an arcane device. Don't dally with it, Taara, for Creation's sake."

"Relax, will you?"

"Taara!"

Taara turned from the lantern sitting innocently on the Missive's Panel.

"Ok, ok! Whatever! Now, let's get back to that damn toilet. If What's-Her-Name wants to hang out in the plumbing, then I've got a nice little gift coming her way real soon."

They went back into the office and installed the commode, muscling it into place, inflating the ring, attaching the lines, and screwing it down. It only took a minute or two. Taara turned the valves and it filled with water. They flushed it with grand celebration, both Stenstrom and A-Ram patting Taara on the back. "Well done," Stenstrom said. "This working commode will serve us well and save us a lot of steps."

She couldn't help but bask in their praise.

As they stood there admiring the commode, Stenstrom noticed something out the windows of his office. "Hey, look at this!" he said.

They turned to the windows. Outside was a dramatic view of the aft of the ship, the long neck and the swan-like rear section with its cranked wings far away. Had the ship been fully functioning, the *Seeker* would have been lit up in a cityscape of sparkling lights: random windows burning in a yellowy glow, blinking white-light runners mounted dorsal and ventral, and cones of scanner light moving like spotlights along the length of the ship looking for imperfections in the hull, including the massive main sensor throwing out a great funnel of light ahead of the ship into the night of space. With the ship dead, the lights were all out, the bulk of the *Seeker* was like a blackened piece of driftwood in a midnight sea dappled with stars.

At that moment, however, the ship was blinking and flashing like a wild carnival: window lights snapped on and off, spotlights panned and went out and runners came on and went out in an insane, grid-like pattern.

"What's going on out there?" Stenstrom asked, taking it all in. "Taara?"

She wandered to the window sill and watched the ship as it lit-off like a rolling thunderstorm. "It's like power has been restored but isn't being properly controlled. I don't get it."

A-Ram peeked out onto the bridge and pointed. "Taara, Bel—look at this!"

They stepped out of the office onto the bridge. The Missive's Panel was lighting up like a sky full of fireworks. Taara seated herself at the panel and punched buttons.

"What's wrong?" Stenstrom asked.

Taara's eyes moved up and down the panel, her face lit up in a mosaic of reds, blues and yellows. "It's . . . got full power. The Missive's Panel is now fully operational. It's a little messed up without the Com Panel to control everything. The Com Panel is sort of like the 'spinal cord' of the ship while the Missive's Panel is like the right side of the brain—it can control much of the higher functions of the ship such as turning on and turning off lights, but without the Com Panel, it's not very coordinated."

"So it's is turning on and turning off lights all by itself?"

Taara punched buttons in a flurry, the MOLLY in her head working overtime. "Yep. I'm trying to see if I can get it under control here."

A-Ram watched Taara work. "How is the Missive's Panel fully-powered?

We don't have the energy to do that, do we?"

"Nope," Taara replied. "With the *Westminster*, we have just enough spare power to turn on a few sub-systems."

"So, where's the power coming from?"

Stenstrom turned to the lantern. It quietly sat on the Missive's Panel, its four lenses dark and mysterious. "What about Lilly's lantern here?" he asked.

"What about it?" Taara replied.

"Could it be somehow imparting power to the ship? I've seen this lantern do some amazing things," Stenstrom reached out and tentatively lifted it from the panel. It felt cold and bare metal in his hands.

The Missive's Panel immediately went dead. "Hey!" Taara cried lifting her hands. "I had this baby accepting data!"

Stenstrom put the lantern back down and the panel sprang to life again. "Sorry," he said. "So, that confirms it—Lilly's Lantern is an arcane device of immense power."

"Yes," A-Ram agreed. "Which is why we should not be making use of it in any way. The Sisters will find ill-favor with this."

Taara clacked away. "The Sisters can bill me, A-Ram. I don't see the harm of making use of a tool that's been given to us."

"Who gave it to us?" A-Ram asked.

"Lilly did, I guess, the lady in the pipes. She stuffed it up our plumbing."

A-Ram crossed his arms. "Lilly clearly has nothing to do with the Sisters and her having it must be illegal. Bel, we need to get rid of this lantern immediately. We risk the Sisters' wrath."

"Oh, screw the Sisters. A-Ram! You touch that thing and we're fightin'."

He turned to Stenstrom. "Bel!" he pleaded.

Stenstrom thought about it. He rubbed his chin. "Taara, what can you do with the Missive's Panel powered up? What is there to be gained?"

"All kinds of things! I can route power from the *Westminster* and get the lights turned on, I can get the ship's intercom system running and the security monitors as well. I can also get sensor data going. It'll just take me a little time to get all the kinks worked out of it. I can make this trip a lot easier for all of us, Bel, trust me."

He thought it over some more. "Well, I think there's no harm in making temporary use of this device. If it belongs to the Sisters then we'll give it back to them once we arrive at Bazz, no harm done."

A-Ram wanted to protest, but Stenstrom cut him off. "I'm certain the Sisters will be pleased to learn their device, assuming it is theirs, helped safeguard the lives of League citizens while in peril at sea."

"All right!" Taara cried. "That's what I want to hear. Give me a few hours and I'll have this baby humming."

The matter settled, they sat down for some lunch, eating cold insta-meals that they'd stolen from Dry Dock 275. Taara took her meal and returned to the Missive's Panel, engrossed in what she was doing. She called up several screens and punched buttons in between bites of food.

"Making any progress?" Stenstrom asked from his chair.

"Yep, slowly but surely. I'll have this ship flying right in no time."

"When's our next burn due?"

"Couple hours." She turned to Stenstrom and gave him a wink, her face framed by her sideburns. "I love this, you know, being up here with two handsome guys all to myself and doing all this crazy stuff with the ship. I hope it never ends."

A-Ram cracked into his lunch. "You won't be liking it so much when the demon comes for your soul. You can't just use the MOLLY all you want without expecting severe consequences."

"Yeah? I'm not worried."

They finished their lunch and, with full bellies, got sleepy, except for Taara who was deep into it at the Missive's Panel. She sat cross-legged in the seat in her socks, playing the controls like a grand organ. A-Ram collected their empty insta-meal boxes and took them away. He wandered into Stenstrom's office, and, a few minutes later, came the merry sounds of the commode flushing. He returned to the Navigator's position, folded his hands over his chest and was lightly snoring minutes later. Stenstrom sat back in his chair and wanted nothing more than to have a nice long nap. He hadn't had a regular sleep since being aboard the ship.

"I'm feeling sleepy, Taara. Stop for a while and rest," he said.

"I'm fine. I want to get this done. Go ahead and sleep, Bel. I'll yell or something if I need you."

He resisted the urge to sleep. The last time he'd fallen asleep Taara and A-Ram were abducted by Soul Devourers. He laid his NTH pistols out on his lap and struggled to keep his eyes from closing. Taara padded out of her seat and came to him in her socks. She balled up her coat and put it behind his head as a pillow. She lovingly adjusted the silk mask over his eyes and situated the folds of his coat.

"I've been waiting my whole life to get here," she whispered. "This ship is a long way from digging for clams on a Bazz delinquent farm. No time to sleep now."

She went over to A-Ram and removed his hat and adjusted his coat, doting on him in a motherly fashion. Sitting in his chair on the verge of sleep, Stenstrom felt very close to Taara and A-Ram. She returned to her seat, got comfortable and continued manipulating the Missive Panel, Stenstrom could only guess what she was doing.

It didn't take long for sleep to take him. The last thing he saw was Taara leaning over the panel lit up in color, her sickle-like sideburns hanging down near her collar.

3

—THREE LETTERS . . .—

"Bel! Bel, wake up!"

Stenstrom opened his eyes. Taara was leaning over him, her sideburns tickling his chin.

"Did I sleep?" he asked, rather groggy. He sat up and rubbed his eyes.

"Bel, I need to show you something," she said.

Still in her socks, Taara led him over to the Missive's Panel. Before he'd nodded off, the panel had been a confusion of random lights and strobe-like flashes lighting up the bridge like a gaudy dance hall, now it was tamed and orderly, lighting up with calculated precision with Lilly's Lantern sitting innocently in the center giving life to it all. "Did you get the system under control?" he asked.

"Sure did. I had to re-master it from scratch and get it away from the Com Panel, but I did it."

"Great work, Taara. You deserve an 'E' degree in engineering."

"Thanks. I managed to get the lights working on key decks on the ship— not many, but we can turn them on and turn them off from here now. I also got the cameras and ship's archive going."

"That's great news, well done."

Taara wasn't happy. "I was going over the ship's old records, they're still in the archives. They go back a pretty long way. Look here ..." Taara manipulated the controls. On the screen, many people appeared, mostly crewmen, all apparently vacating the ship, many dragging luggage and other assorted personal items with them.

"What we're seeing is the final service day of the previous crew a couple of months back. This is Deck Six, Central Section. Everybody's heading to the Ripcar bays to fly on down to the surface. The captain had given up his chair, the engineer and boatswain were gone by this point and the ship's Priory was closed. The crew was vacating in favor of other vessels. Look at all the hugs and thumps on the chest."

Taara pointed at the screen. "Look! Look there! See that?"

On the screen, mixed into the throng of departing people, was a blond-headed woman, a civilian, wearing a festive pink gown carrying a small handbag.

Stenstrom was astonished. "Is that . . . Lilly?"

"Looks like her to me, and I got a nice long gander at her in the plumbing."

The image of Lilly waded through the passing crewmen until the crowd thinned out to a trickle. Finally, as they watched, Lilly was alone in the now deserted corridor. She reached into her bag and pulled out a tiny white envelope, which she placed on the floor in the center of the corridor. She looked up at the camera for a moment, smiled and slowly walked away.

"Look at that—what's she doing?" Taara asked.

"Seems to be an envelope of some sort. Yes of course! Remember when we first came aboard and we found that odd letter lying in the central corridor?"

Taara rolled her eyes up, thinking back. "Seems like a long time ago. Right! I remember. It was sitting there on the floor in the central section of the ship just after we boarded. Wait! Wasn't it addressed to me?"

"That's what you thought and A-Ram thought it was addressed to him. We had a lot of work to get done, so I put it in my little case here to prevent it from distracting us. I had assumed we were all a little oxygen deprived due to our upload and were seeing things."

"And, your lady Lilly left it there for us. Why?"

"One way to find out." Stenstrom waved his hands and produced the case. He opened it. Inside was an innocuous white envelope lying face down. He picked it out and tossed the case aside. He held the envelope and flipped it around, reading the heading to himself. He held it out and showed it to Taara. "What's this say?" he asked.

She squinted and looked at it. "It's made out to me. It says: 'TO: PRIVATE TAARA DE LA ANDERSON, 110 MARINES'. Pretty handwriting."

"You're certain that's what it says?"

"Yes, Bel, I'm from Bazz but I can still read LC, you know." She puzzled at the envelope and fiddled with the golden charm of a fish hanging at her neck. "The MOLLY's not telling me much. The thing's giving me the creeps."

Stenstrom produced several Holystones, a prism and a polyhedron. "What are you doing?" Taara asked.

"I'm checking the envelope for the arcane. This olive Holystone here shall determine if this is actually a letter or some sort of arcane object disguised as a letter."

"Is that possible?" Taara asked, fascinated.

"Anything's possible."

He moved the Holystone along the face of the letter. The Holystone did nothing as it touched the surface of the paper. "Well, the letter is not Astral."

"What's that mean?" Taara asked.

"The Astral Plane is a sort of pocket dimension that is all around us, the Xaphans sometimes make use of it to travel great distances very quickly, though that's a dangerous proposition. The thing about the Astral Plane is that it plays havoc on your perceptions, you can't trust any of your senses. You say the envelope is addressed to you, but when I look at it I see it as being addressed to me, and, if A-Ram were to look at it, he'd see it as being addressed to him—that's what the Astral Plane does."

"Were you expecting such a thing?"

"I had a notion. When we arrived on ship, the bridge was contaminated with the Astral Plane."

"It was?" Taara asked. "You didn't say anything."

"I didn't want to alarm you, and, while incursions of the Astral Plane can be intentionally created, they can also happen on their own and are more common than you might realize."

The bridge studded with steel-jaw traps, waiting to bite . . .

"So, you were hoping the Astral Plane just happened to be here on the bridge by itself and not put here by somebody on purpose?"

"I suppose so, yes."

"You're more of an optimist than I would have been. How did you get rid of it?" Taara asked.

"How? Blue Holystones. They're full of certain metals and solutions that block out the Astral Plane. They are fairly effective at short range and I used then to clear the bridge. I have a few more here. So, I think this is probably the safest place to trigger the letter and deal with whatever happens afterwards. Then, it'll be done."

He waved his hand and produced a white Holystone. He rolled it across the face of the envelope. It rattled with a fuss. "Arcane. The letter detects as arcane."

The same Holystone detected Lilly as being arcane as well. She had quietly sat and allowed him to roll the Holystone down the length of her arm, rattling the whole time.

"Why Bel . . . of course I'm of the arcane . . ."

"I guess that's bad," Taara said as she pulled her boots on and wiggled into her coat. "What do we do?"

Stenstrom put the Holystone back into his coat. "We open the letter and face whatever is inside." He shook A-Ram, who was still sound asleep at the Navigator's position. "A-Ram, wake up."

He muttered and opened his eyes. "What? What is it?"

"We're opening that creepy letter we found the other day. It's all hexed-out. Bel's lady left it for us."

"So, why in the Name of Creation are we opening it?"

"We're going to discover its intent and be done with it. Taara, go ahead and open it."

Without fear or trepidation, Taara seized the letter and tore it open. "So far, so good," she cheerfully said. She pulled out three slips of scented paper. "Looks like a couple pieces of paper to me."

Taara laid them out on the panel. "Now what?"

While A-Ram held a few steps back, Stenstrom examined the slips. Continuing his bizarre examination, he rolled his Holystones over top of the paper, taking note of the results. He ran his finger across one of the slips. "I'm looking for grit, for minute scents and hidden writing on the paper, all of those things can be significant."

Taara sniffed the slips. "Smells like nice flowers to me."

"Lavender—that is Lilly's favorite scent, and lavender can be an ingredient in arcane tinctures."

"Perhaps that should have been a clue that your love wasn't all she seemed," A-Ram said, disconcerted by all of this. "There shall be nothing odd about my love, whoever she might be. Are you finding anything?"

"No," he stated flatly. "I'm not. The envelope reads as arcane, but the slips within seem to be just that: paper."

"Well, that's a relief."

Taara leaned in. "Looks like there's one for each of us. Here's one for me, the one in the middle is yours, A-Ram, and that one on the right is yours, Bel."

"How can there be one for me and you, Taara? We just met Bel a few days ago, and neither one of us know Lady Lilly from Lacerta."

"Who's Lacerta?" Taara asked. "Never mind, probably some crazy Kanan lady. Well, 'Rammy', I don't know. Apparently, Lilly isn't quite right, is she? She was all nice and snug up in our plumbing not long ago." She turned to Stenstrom. "Bel, what the heck is Lilly? Is she a demon?"

"The word 'demon' can be applied to most any creature or entity not of a standard classification, so, in that reckoning, yes, she is a demon. As to the exact nature of her arcane status, I have no idea. She was about to tell me and got 'summoned' by her masters, whomever they are, before she could finish. I'll say she had me and my mother completely fooled all these years. Mother thought, and I did as well, that Lilly was a highly talented, intelligent, but otherwise mundane woman from Gamboa. She even revealed to me that she's not from Gamboa, so all of the things I thought I knew about her were incorrect. In any case, she walked the planes between our little ship here and Kana and was powerful enough to kill literally dozens of Soul Devourers all by herself without so much as breaking a sweat."

"Dang!" Taara exclaimed. "Now, that's a girlfriend. You should suit her up and put her in the arena or something. The most I've ever done was fight two corporals, a slut, and an MP in a bar once."

Stenstrom picked up the paper made out to him.

"Read it, Bel—even the mushy stuff. I actually sort of like that," Taara chirped as she settled down to listen.

He cleared his throat and read. "It says: 'To my dearest Stenstrom. As it is no doubt obvious at this point, I have not been entirely honest with you these past years, about myself and other things as well. For various reasons, I have been compelled to lie to you, to not be forthright as to my true nature and purpose, though it pained me to have to do so. I have dreamt of the moment when I can reveal all to you, to allow you to see me as I truly am. I'm certain you have many questions, however, all I can do at this time is to state that my love for you has never been greater or more complete. Please know that, as you read this note, I am taking steps to ensure we are never parted again.

'I've watched you for most of your life, from afar, and long before our 'introduction' a few years ago. I've protected you too. I will inform you that your ship was heavily contaminated with the Astral Plane purposely placed there by parties unfriendly to you. I have cleaned the ship out as best I can, though pockets of Astral material might remain, and I do bade you to be careful. I have sought to locate these parties and deal with them, however, they have eluded me to this point. Once matters at hand have been squared away, you may rest assured that I shall discover and dispense with them.'"

They all looked at each other. Stenstrom continued.

"'And now I see you sailing alone into peril. Given my current situation I might not be able to help you directly, therefore, I have left you the Paramel, an Elder device that illuminates many things. It has agreed to help you and I have secured it at great risk to myself. I beg you use it well. I have determined that, on your present course and given the diminished condition of your ship, you shall soon sail into great danger. The old mariner tales that abound in this lonely region of space, whispered stories of the devil and missing people and of bad dreams seem, at least in part, to be true and I have seen your death in a dark place hidden from sight. I do not have time to fully explain myself, I will say only to beware Druries Belt and, most importantly, the leeward side of it. I have plotted you a safe course through the deep sea where you will not be detected. Please trust in me, follow Paramel's beam and you shall be safe, I promise.

'Please allow your companions to read their notes, and, when they are finished, place this paper into Paramel and you let it guide you to safe shores where I hope to be waiting.

'How I long to stand at your side.

'Follow Paramel's light and `ware Druries Belt.

'Your Betrothed.

'Lilly"

Stenstrom put the note back down onto the Missive's Panel. "And, that is all," he said.

A-Ram stood there, contemplating what was said. "Beware Druries Belt? I don't understand, it's just a cloud of gas. I've heard of old pirate stories and rumors of raider activity and the like near the Belt, but, in our modern League, the Fleet ensures safe passage for all. There are no more pirates or raiders, we're in the heart of the League, after all."

"That's not what we say on Bazz," Taara said, picking up her note. "Old timers used to call the route to Kana 'Nightmare Way'. Lots of nasty dreams and a whole lot of bad out there."

"But, the Fleet, the Marines . . ."

"What about them? How can you stop a bad dream?"

Stenstrom sighed. "What does your note say, Taara?"

4

—A Curse . . . —

Taara scooped her note up with vigor. "Let's see here. Mine says: 'To Private Taara de la Anderson, 110th Marines, Armenelos. Private: It is indeed fortunate my Lord is such a charitable and goodly man, otherwise you would still be . . .'" Taara paused a moment as she read the note. ". . . rotting at your post at Fleet Headquarters, merely a few swills away from total inebriation, both literally and figuratively. Had I a say in the matter, that's where you would indeed still be.'"

Taara looked up. "Wow! Ok, Lills', let's hear how you really feel, babe. Don't hold back or nothin'."

"Continue on please, Taara," A-Ram said.

Highly annoyed, Taara continued. "She says: 'Please note that I have allowed you into my Lord's presence . . .'" Taara was aghast. "*Allowed me?*" she cried. "Who does this dame think she is?"

"Lilly has demonstrated a jealous and rather uncharitable side at times," Stenstrom agreed.

"I wouldn't antagonize her, Taara," A-Ram warned. "She killed a hundred monsters via arcane methods."

"So?" she stated, unimpressed. Taara read on. "And then she says: 'I have observed that you are cursed . . .'" Taara did a double-take. "I'm what?" She was getting more flustered by the moment. "'You have carried this curse with you for over thirty years and it seems to have somehow infected Lord A-Ram and my Stenstrom as well. I do not fully understand barbaric Bazz medicine at this time, however, I shall thank you to do whatever is necessary to break this curse as soon as possible. Please remember, your presence at my Lord's side is by my leave, and should you anger me, should you attempt to impose your unclean Bazz self upon my Lord, the consequences shall be swift and severe. Place this note into Paramel's cavity and you shall see the curse I am referring to.'"

Taara was red in the face. "*By her leave? Impose myself?* I'll show her 'by her leave'!" She thundered forward and gave Stenstrom a good swift kick to the shins, her Marine boot clanging off of his metal Tyrol boots. "How about that, huh?"

"What in the Name of Creation was that for?" Stenstrom asked, astonished.

"Shin kicking!" Taara replied, having regained her usual humor. "It means a girl likes you on Bazz. I love you Bel, I love both of you, and I don't give a Toot what Lilly says!"

A-Ram shook his head and laughed. "A girl likes you and then kicks you in the shins? Creation you have some novel customs on Bazz."

"Gets your attention, doesn't it?" she replied. "Girls where I come from don't like to be ignored. And, I'll bet you two have had your shins kicked a lot." She turned to A-Ram to give him a kick too and he hopped away.

"Don't you dare! I don't have metal boots to protect my shins!"

Taara read through the note again. "So, I guess I'm supposed to put this inside the lantern or something?" She looked around, the MOLLY failing her in this case. She fumbled with the lantern, trying to get it open.

"Now, just a moment," A-Ram scolded. "This is an arcane device, and you really shouldn't manhandle it. There could be repercussions." The two of them probed the surface, having no luck getting it open.

Stenstrom came in. "I recall seeing Lilly open it here, I think . . ." He located a hidden switch and one of the lenses swung outward, revealing a hollow interior with a curious trapezoidal prism mounted in the center in such a fashion that it could spin freely if rotated. They placed Taara's slip of paper into the cavity and closed the lens.

"So, now what's supposed to happen?" Taara asked.

After a minute or so, the three of them heard the sound of movement within the lantern, followed by the crinkling of paper.

"I hear the prism moving," A-Ram said.

Slowly, the lantern came to light, the lens awash in a soft yellow glow that focused into a great, meaty beam. The beam of light issued from the lantern and played out on the far wall of the bridge.

Images formed, uncoiling in 3-D tableau.

In the beam of light four figures emerged standing back-to-back in a rough circle all bound at the waist by a common golden band like a group of shackled prisoners awaiting execution. There was Stenstrom in his green HRN, A-Ram in his blue coat, Taara in her vivid red Marine jacket and a fourth person—female, tall, brown-hair pulled tightly into a bun under a small hat and wearing a ladies Fleet *Tremblar* uniform. A handsome rapier-like weapon hung at her side. All four figures were completely lifelike and motionless, as if frozen in time.

"So what's all this?" A-Ram asked.

"Appears to be the three of us, and a tall Fleet lieutenant," Stenstrom said. "All bound together."

"It's Captain Gwendolyn. I've served her coffee many times in the Admiral's office. This sword here at her side is a FEDULA, her family's LosCapricos weapon."

Stenstrom rubbed his chin. "So, this is the woman who wants to knock my block off? You were right, Taara, she is pretty tall, and . . . Taara?"

Taara stood there silent and ashen. "Taara, what's wrong?" Stenstrom asked.

She said nothing.

"Taara!"

She shook her head and blinked. "What? What . . ."

"What's wrong?"

"Bel, don't you see it?"

"What?"

"The circle! Look at the circle around us. We don't like circles on Bazz. We're afraid of them!" Seeing the circle sent Taara into near hysterics.

"Why?"

"Vendetta. Vendetta Circle."

"What's that?" Stenstrom asked.

"It's something we believe in on Bazz. It's a weird curse that starts with one person and tends to spread out and suck people in. You know you're in a Vendetta Circle when you see yourself or your name in a circle. You never see circles at eye level or placed near a mirror or window that you might possibly see yourself in—it's a big taboo on Bazz. Want to start a fight, write down somebody's name and draw a circle around it and see what happens."

A-Ram inspected the image of himself in the lantern light, running his hand through their immobile bodies like a hologram. "What does this curse imply, from a Bazz perspective?"

"It implies that we're all going to die. That's what it implies."

"Die?"

"That's what the Vendetta Circle Curse does, it pulls you in, messes with your freakin' life, and then kills you all at once."

Stenstrom joined A-Ram and closely examined the figures in the Lantern's beam—the two of them figuring this to be some sort of Bazz nonsense and unconcerned with Taara's discomfort. He looked over Lt. Gwendolyn in particular. "She's a handsome lady: strong face, square jaw, thoughtful eyes. So tall, very un-Zenon-like. Most Zenon-girls I'm acquainted with are rather petite."

Taara hugged herself and fearfully observed the circle, taking in every detail. "Then she can be fitted for a nice big coffin once she's dead."

"Taara, it's going to be ok," Stenstrom said.

"No, no . . ." she moaned.

"Listen, we all have our regional beliefs and they mean a great deal to us, don't they? If I told you some of my personal beliefs you'd probably laugh. And, one thing I do know is this: your belief in a thing can fuel it, give it power, can make it real. I know the arcane, and I can tell you there is nothing that cannot be undone or unmade. Nothing—that is a constant. You said you're cursed, if that's the case then there must be a way to break it—Lilly even said so. How do we do it? You're the expert here."

"I don't know. There's these ladies back home, Ganaadas they're called, they prowl the streets waving their Cred Sticks around demanding money and claim they can either curse you with the Circle if you piss them off, or they can cure you."

"All for a fee, of course," A-Ram said.

"Yeah, yeah, their Cred Sticks are never far from empty. Too much Zemuda drinking. They certainly don't use the money they collect for bathing."

Stenstrom was cheerful. "Well then, when we get to Bazz, we'll simply hire one of these Ganaadas, you'll submit yourself to whatever rituals are required, endure their foul smells, and that will be that. Price is no object. Will that make you feel better?"

"What? No—the Ganaadas? I wouldn't trust those dirty cows to do anything but take your Creds and run to the nearest bar. And, Bel, it's not just *me* stuck in the Circle—look at it, we're *all* in it." She pointed at them and then at herself. "You, you and me are cursed!"

"And Lt. Gwendolyn as well?" A-Ram asked.

"Yep—her too. We probably won't even make it to Bazz. Maybe I'll get to watch her beat the hell out of you before we croak."

"Please . . ."

"And," Taara cried. "You know what? This means we're all related to each other, all three of us."

"Umm, Taara, you're from Bazz and we're from Kana, Lt. Gwendolyn as well. We're not related," A-Ram said.

"I don't mean by birth, Ignaz!" she snapped, calling him some obscure Bazz name. "I mean we're related by something, by events, by circumstance, by random encounters that seem innocent at first but have monumental effects later on. My aunt on my mom's side, she was stuck in a Vendetta Circle. She was hopping into the sack just about every guy in town, and one of the dudes had a jealous wife. She got really mad, and that's what triggers a Vendetta Circle—strong emotion from one person, and it just grows and grows from there."

"I don't understand," A-Ram said. "It's clear how a messy love triangle can generate ill will, but what's that have to do with us? We just met a few days ago and had no contact prior to that. I certainly didn't sleep with your aunt. How did we get pulled into a Bazz curse?"

"But remember what Bel's crazy demon girlfriend said—that this Vendetta Circle has been running for thirty years. Thirty years! That's a long time for all sorts of things to happen."

"Are you over thirty, Taara?" Stenstrom asked, noting her youthful appearance. It was always difficult to determine just how old an Elder person was as they remained youthful throughout their lives no matter how old they got, and it was a topic generally left undiscussed. In Taara's case, her jittery demeanor implied tweener youth.

She blushed. "Yeah, I am. And don't ask, because I'm not telling you how old I am."

"I'm not over thirty," Stenstrom said. "I'm only twenty-seven."

A-Ram was adamant. "I myself am over thirty as well, but, again, we just met. The three of us have no connection—zero—prior to our meeting at Fleet a few days ago."

Taara shook her head. "No, A-Ram, no, no. This curse walks around, it's subtle and it's sneaky to boot. This curse isn't stuck on Bazz—whoever started it could easily have taken a transport to Kana or anywhere else and brought you two into it. The Vendetta Circle curse tends to throw people stuck in it together, it plays with them, taking years to develop making you think you're safe, giving the people involved a subtle glimpse of each other every now and again, and then WHAMO!! It constricts and brings everyone together where they die! My aunt—she and all the people stuck in her Circle all died together in a bloody restaurant by the Endax Sea."

"How?" A-Ram asked.

"How? They were having a reunion dinner and a big freakin' wave thirty feet high took them out, restaurant, pier, beach, diners and all. And, you want to know what caused the killer wave?? The Endax Sea is just a big crater full of water, right? The angry lady who began the Vendetta Circle finally had had enough of her cheating husband, so she poisoned his breakfast. He didn't die until he got to work. He worked at an antimony mine on the other side of the Endax. When he finally died, he somehow set off a massive explosion, which caused a landslide into the sea which triggered the killer wave which took out the restaurant and everybody inside it. See, that's how Vendetta Circle curse works."

A-Ram considered that for a moment. "Poppycock," he finally said.

"Oh yeah? The more I think about it, the more I'm convinced we're all stuck in a Vendetta Circle, Lt. Gwendolyn as well. It makes sense, look at how we ended up here, look how circumstances seemed to push us toward each other. You needed a helmsman, Bel, and look who turns up in a virtually empty Fleet HQ building: A-Ram. You needed an engineer, and A-Ram's got his MOLLY that he's too scared to use, but here I am, and I couldn't care less, so I use it and get us out of our terminal orbit. We need an engine to break Kana, well there's the *Westminster* just waiting to be stolen and converted into a drive engine."

"And Lt. Gwendolyn?"

"I don't know, but she fits into this too, somehow. She's only out there in her scouting ship coming to get you right now."

"So, if I'm following your aunt's analogy correctly, since we're all together now on the ship, with the exception of Lt. Gwendolyn who is en route, that the Circle is near to running its course and we are soon to die?" Stenstrom asked.

She nodded and mumbled into Stenstrom's coat for a bit, trying to sort herself out.

"And, you're also saying that this Vendetta Circle we find ourselves in is caused by one person who has ties to all of us across two worlds?"

She nodded again. "I mean this is probably my fault. I got into a big fight with a Ganaada once. She was running around spouting off about my uncle who ran the local pharmacy, and I told her to shut up. She wrote my uncle's name down and drew a circle around it and then we were going at it. Maybe that's where it started?"

"How does that involve us, then?" A-Ram asked. "You're most certainly the only person from Bazz I know."

Taara sobbed. Stenstrom took her gently by the sideburns and she looked up at him in rapt attention, cheeks shiny. "All right, Taara. Obviously this is a belief you take a great deal of stock in, and we appreciate that. You say that this curse is something that's probably been brewing for some time now, yes?"

She nodded.

"Fine. Once we get to Bazz and deliver the Admiral's brandy, we will stay on until we get this sorted out. Our first priority will be to get out of this death curse, our second will be the refitting of the ship. We'll perform research, we'll prowl every library and sage's sanctum, we'll consult with the learned and the local shamans, we'll purchase whatever goods need to be bought, and together we'll determine a way out of this. Time and money is no object."

Hope filled Taara's eyes. "You promise. The three of us will do all that?"

"I promise. Right A-Ram?"

"Oh yes, absolutely," he replied.

"I've never been much in a library," she said.

"No time like the present to catch up." Taara gave Stenstrom a grand hug. She broke away and went to A-Ram, embracing him in the same fashion. "Hey, A-Ram, I'm sorry I called you 'Ignaz', ok? I didn't mean it."

"It's quite all right, Taara. I don't believe I know what it means."

"Good, that's good." Taara then pulled back and gave him a swift kick to the shins, just like she had Stenstrom, only A-Ram didn't have metal Tyrol boots to ward it off. He hobbled about in pain on one foot.

"Gods that hurt!"

Taara recovered from her funk. "So, what I think we need to do is figure out who started this Vendetta Circle, confront them, and . . ."

"And what?' A-Ram asked rubbing his shin. "Kill them? Murder them?"

"Well yeah, I guess. We have to deal with this person and change this Vendetta Circle Curse up."

Stenstrom spoke up. "I don't like the idea of murdering someone, Taara."

"It's them or us, right? We have to change the circumstances of this curse, I think that's how we can get out of it."

"Like I said, when we get to Bazz, we'll sit down and puzzle this out. I'm certain we'll not need to resort to something as crass as cold-blooded murder. And, I suppose, as you mentioned, our primary task will be to determine who this 'central person' to all three of us is. At this stage I have no idea who that might be. I also suppose that keeping Lt. Gwendolyn off the ship is more important than ever, to prevent the circle from closing."

"Ok, now you're thinking! Right now our primary task is to survive until we get to Bazz in the first place. Your demon lady said there's great danger out there, and we better listen to her," Taara said.

"We'll follow her advice and stay well clear of the leeward side of Druries Belt as dictated by the solar winds."

"That'll add some time to our trip," Taara said. "Staying windward of the Belt is the long way around."

"Will it cause us to miss our deadline for the brandy on Bazz?" Stenstrom asked, still fascinated by the images in the lantern's beam.

Taara thought a moment. "Nah."

CAPTAIN GWENDOLYN

5

—. . . And an Apparition—

One note remained unread on the Missive's Panel: A-Ram's note. Taara scooped it up and held it out. "Here's yours, A-Ram. Go on, read it. I've got some course correcting to do, but first I want to hear what Bel's lady said to you."

Tentatively, A-Ram accepted the note. He glanced at it and cleared his throat. "Ahem, it says: 'To: Josephus, Seventh Lord of A-Ram, St. Edmunds. My Lord: Though I do not approve of my Lord Stenstrom's current situation, I am pleased he has made your acquaintance and calls you his friend.'"

Taara interrupted. "How come she's all nicey-nicey with you? I got the 'by my leave' bit."

A-Ram continued on. "'I must say, though we have never met, I feel a kinship with you. I feel I understand your heart. You are like a beloved brother to me, and I look forward to the occasion when my Lord may properly introduce us. Steer the ship well and bring to me my Lord. You have my favor and I wish to offer you a gift. Place this note within Paramel and it shall reveal to you your future love—such power it has. You have often felt lonely, and unworthy, spurned by the Sisters and by members of your own family. I felt for you, and I wish to assure you that a fine love awaits. See her, please, and know, with my compliments, that great things are in the offing.

'I leave you with a warning, and pray you heed it,'" A-Ram swallowed and continued reading with dread. "'Your love is in danger and could easily fall to a terrible fate. She lives at the mouth of Edam and tempts death every day. She is very brave, and you would be most proud of her.'" A-Ram paused. "What's Edam?"

Stenstrom replied. "It's the Vith word for hell."

A-Ram pondered that for a moment. "'Follow the course I have set and you need not fear, your love will be safe, though a chance meeting with her will be lost. You would otherwise never meet her. When I am rejoined with my Lord on Bazz, I shall lead you to her side.

'Remember, beware Druries Belt.

'Your sister in spirit

'Lilly.'"

A-Ram puzzled over the note. "Well, gee, A-Ram," Taara said. "Looks like Lilly just loves you."

"She seems like such a kind person, I feel enchanted . . ."

"Yeah, yeah, you got the muzzle, I got the horns."

"My love?" A-Ram asked holding his note. "I've never really had a love before. I was always too awkward and shy for such things. What should I do,

Bel? Should I do as directed, or should I leave my fate to the unknown?"

"Must you ask such a question? Don't you know?"

"Well, I . . . I mean, who wouldn't want to know such a thing, but then there's always the joy of chance and circumstance."

"Whatever you choose, A-Ram, hurry it up. I've got to get the course corrections laid in," Taara said.

He considered the matter a moment further, and then fumbled with the lantern. "Lilly said my love's in danger, she might need me. Bel, can you get this open for me, please?" Stenstrom touched the lantern to open the lens. The images displayed in its beam reacted to his touching the lantern. The golden band trapping the figures together disappeared and, freed, they capered about in a demented fashion.

"Wow!" Taara cried as she watched.

The A-Ram image staggered over a far wall and placed his hands on the bulkhead. He pounded on the wall and reared back in apparent anguish before vanishing.

The image of Taara transformed before their eyes. The MOLLY hanging at her neck dug itself into her flesh and she grew, blossoming into a goddess-like woman with luminous violet eyes.

"Hey—look at that!" Taara cried as the image faded away. The Stenstrom image collapsed to the floor on all fours, his body seemingly broken under his HRN coat. His right hand fell away from his arm leaving a stump, as if chopped off. "What happened there?" Taara asked as the sad image vanished.

The Gwendolyn image lingered. She looked around with crazed, lamp-like eyes, her face sunken-in and pocked with insane suffering. She stumbled forward toward Stenstrom, drawing her FEDULA.

"Captain?" he asked. "Can you hear me?"

She reacted a little, her head turning, darting eyes trying to make sense of her surroundings. She dropped her FEDULA and raised her arms in a teetering zombie-like manner. A clean, straight cut formed on her right cheek, as if from a sabre strike. A curtain of fast flowing blood raced down her face and dripped off her chin.

"Captain, you're bleeding," Stenstrom said, trying to assist her.

She opened her mouth, not to speak, but to scream. She fell back and was gone as Stenstrom tried to catch her.

"What in the Name of Creation was all that?" A-Ram asked still holding his note. "Was that the future we were seeing? It was terrifying."

"I'm not certain, but I'll agree it was disquieting," Stenstrom said. He took A-Ram's note and placed it within the lantern's cavity, closing the lens back up. Inside, the prism turned and the paper crinkled.

"You sure you want to see this?" Taara asked. He didn't answer.

The lantern came to life again. Appearing before them in a whirling column of rising fog like a clay pot taking shape on a wheel, was a solitary figure bathed in greenish lantern light. A-Ram gritted his teeth and watched.

The figure appeared to be a small female clad in an emerald hooded cloak made of shimmering brocade lined and sleeved with gold fabric. Under the cloak was a white linen smock made of coarse thread. She wore a number of red and green beaded necklaces around her delicate neck and, around her waist, a loose belt made of red and green shells. She was quite attractive with a pearly sort of smooth complexion and delicate features, slender hands and a pretty face. Her hair was thick and black held back in a loose bun with several sticks and combs. She didn't appear to be wearing any shoes, though her feet were wreathed in fog.

"Wow, pretty cute," Taara chirped. "What do you think, A-Ram? She's a looker."

A-Ram stood there and stared at the figure, taking in her features. He seemed quite speechless. "Hello?" he stammered. "Dearest madam?"

The figure didn't speak. She looked back over her shoulder. Her features were etched with concern.

"This woman looks like a Pilgrim of Merian, the white smock, the red and green beads, the green cloak. That's what they wear, all homemade stuff." Stenstrom said.

"What's a Pilgrim of Merian?" Taara asked, A-Ram too stunned to speak.

"It's a religious order on Kana and elsewhere preaching an alternate view of the Elders. They're very benign, simple people. My family manor is an old Merian monastery and I used to play with my sisters in their abandoned hermitage near Merian's Hill. They are good, honest people."

"Hmmm, I've never seen this woman before, nor do I recall ever seeing one of her order," A-Ram said. He approached the woman. "What is your name, ma'am?"

She reacted and turned in his direction. When she saw A-Ram, her face lit up in delight—how pretty she was when she smiled, full lips and straight, well-tended teeth. Her blue eyes sparkled. She said something, though her voice could not be heard.

"What did she say?" Taara asked.

She said it again. Stenstrom read her lips. "It looks like she said 'Whammy' or something like it."

"No, no, she didn't say 'Whammy', she said 'Rammy'," A-Ram said. "She's saying my name." He took another step forward. "Ma'am, do I know you? What's your name? Please tell me."

The apparition appeared concerned. She pointed to Stenstrom's office. "Do you want us to go in there? What are you trying to tell us?"

A-Ram went into Stenstrom's office, followed by the silent apparition of the Pilgrim of Merian. She pointed at the windows. Outside was the usual carpet of quiet stars, the darkened bulk of the ship, and the long yellowish band of Druries Belt drifting off toward the Onaris/Bazz system imperceptibly fluttering in the solar wind.

"She's pointing at Druries Belt!" A-Ram said. "Remember the warning! 'Ware the Belt!"

Alarmed, Taara flew back into her chair at the Missive's Panel. "I think I can get the some of the ship's sensors working. I'll bet we've got a visitor out there!"

"A-Ram, get to your post!" Stenstrom said. He ran out of the office with the apparition slowly following.

Stenstrom opened the lantern and placed his note, the one Lilly said would guide the ship, into the cavity.

"Don't jostle the lantern!" Taara cried. "It's what's powering the panel right now."

For a third time, the lantern lit up, this time in a tight, bluish beam. The beam went out into Stenstrom's office toward the aft of the ship, floating like the needle of a compass moving steadily in a clock-wise motion.

"I think it's giving us a heading," Taara said. She burst out of her seat and followed the beam into the office. She picked up her sextant and, using the beam as a point of reference, took a reading. "A-Ram, give me five pegs hard a starboard, Z plus 260 degrees. Hurry!"

A-Ram kicked the floor levers and strained as he turned the wheel, the female apparition in green silently watching him. Outside, the thrusters ticked and the ship banked. The lantern skittered to the right as the ship's bank deepened, threatening to slide off the panel. Stenstrom held it fast, preventing it from moving further.

Taara thundered back into her seat and continued with the panel, furiously manipulating the screens.

"Five pegs starboard, Z plus 260 degrees, aye!" A-Ram said from behind the wheel.

"Ok, ok, hold that," Taara said staring at her screens and watching the lantern's beam change direction. She stared at her screens. "Whoah!"

"What, what is it?" Stenstrom asked.

Taara rechecked her screens. "For a minute we were reading something big out there."

"Big like a passing ship?"

"No, I mean big like a planet. I'm serious. It filled up the screens, but it's gone now." She crunched more data. "I don't see it anymore, must have been a glitch. Ok, A-Ram, now, go three pegs hard a larboard, Z to level and hold."

The helm groaned as A-Ram turned the wheel. The lantern's beam moved slightly.

"Got it—three pegs hard a larboard and Z to level, aye!"

"Are you seeing anything out there, Taara?" Stenstrom asked.

She was engrossed, crunching data fast.

"Taara? Talk to me."

"A moment . . ." She pulled up another screen, her eyes moving up and down the data. "Contact!" she announced.

"What is it? What are we reading?"

"Something small this time, moving fast."

"Is it a Fleet ship?"

"Unknown, reading motion only. Our sensing capabilities are for shit. Not seeing any hoisted flags or other forms of identification. But it's out there, dead away at 9:45AM."

"No flag?"

Stenstrom went into his office and gazed out the windows, seeing nothing but stars and the glowing yellowish band of Druries Belt—Lilly's warning fresh in his mind.

Beware Druries Belt . . .

"Should we burn the *Westminster*, Bel?" Taara asked. "We're going to have to do it sooner or later."

"No, let's wait. Let's keep the ship quiet for now and stand fast."

The apparition gave A-Ram a warm smile and slowly faded away. "Wait!" he cried holding the wheel. "Don't go! Please!"

A moment later, she was gone.

"I wonder what—"

"Shh!" Stenstrom commanded from the office. "Stand your post."

"You see something, Bel," Taara asked.

Through the windows he squinted out at the vast glowing ribbon of Druries Belt. For a moment, a distant black silhouette, like a speck of dust, appeared, back-lit by the Belt, and then was gone.

6

—A Friend From Prentiss—

Working the wounded *Seeker* kept the three of them busy for the remainder of the afternoon, putting gloomy thoughts of arcane Vendetta Circles aside in favor of more immediate issues such as the *Seeker's* tendency to drift and roll. Eventually, the unknown contact they had just managed to avoid drifted off the scopes and Taara was permitted to perform a long burn of the *Westminster's* engines, following the meandering course laid out by the lantern's blue beam. She announced they would have to burn-correct every seven hours. For now, they were safely windward of Druries Belt. It was good to be busy.

A-Ram was dour behind the helm. His thoughts were riveted on that woman in green.

"I wonder who she was?" he asked. "Wasn't she pretty?"

"She certainly was. You've never seen her before?"

"No, no, I'd remember a lady like that. What would she want with the likes of me? That's what my brother would say."

"Your brother's a jerk," Taara replied.

The lantern sat on the panel near Taara, its lens issuing the long, tight beam which had become a comfort for them. They had lashed it down to the panel with disused optical cabling, keeping it from sliding.

"Perhaps you'll see her again," he said. "I think the lantern knows our fate to some extent."

A-Ram cheered. "You think so? You think she's tied to me somehow?"

"That's what Lilly said."

"Then perhaps our paths shall cross at some point in the future, as Lilly promised. I . . . I hope she'll like me."

Taara laughed. "You know, 'Rammy', I don't think now's a good time to be fixing yourself up a date. She didn't even have Mollocks or anything."

"Well then, Taara, I suppose she's not from Bazz." A-Ram held the helm wheel, his eyes distant.

As far as they could tell, they were on their way to Onaris following the ever-changing lantern beam. Once there, they would use the planet as a sling-shot to pick up speed and continue on to their final destination, Bazz.

A-Ram stood there, the helm in his hands. "I feel a lot better now that we're underway. It'll be nice to get to Bazz. Once again, where on Bazz are you from , Taara?"

Taara was sitting in the Missive's chair, her favorite place to sit, eating another insta-meal. "Dyson Clampton, in the western continent. I'll show you around when we get there—you'll love it. You guys like spicy food?"

"No," A-Ram said flatly.

"Oh, come on, A-Ram, you Master Helmsman you. Stick with me; I'll have you loving it. You and your lady can try it. That's the one thing I really wish I had right now was a little hot sauce to give this insta-meal some life."

A-Ram let go of the helm and walked to the box of meals. He rummaged around. "I thought there was a chicken meal in here."

"There was, A-Ram, I just ate it," Taara replied.

He sighed and selected a beef concoction.

Stenstrom thought a moment. "Taara, you say everything on Bazz has two names, right?"

"Yep."

"Then how come the name of the place is just Bazz? Shouldn't the name of the planet have two names also?"

Taara gazed back at him from the Missive's chair—for a second he thought she looked a lot like Crewman Kaly, only with sideburns. "I wasn't around when they came up with all that stuff, Bel. When I become the Queen of Bazz, I'll fix that problem. We'll call it Bazz Bazz, how about that?"

Stenstrom laughed. "Taara, how long before we get to Bazz Bazz?"

"About ten days—depends on this lantern here and how much speed we pick up around Onaris."

"Ten days—that's really going to be cutting it close."

"That's the best we can manage. What are we going to do once we get there?"

"I'm hoping, once we fulfill the Admiral's mission, we can get our various legal issues sorted out in earnest, and then we can look to the ship."

"Don't forget the Vendetta Curse," Taara said.

"Right, right. Once we get our 'Curse' issues corrected we'll refit the *Seeker* and press in a fresh crew. We'll first need an engineer and a boatswain—those shouldn't be hard to get, I'm hoping, if we make enough noise."

"Can we prowl the docks, Bel, scope out people, beat them up, and bring them aboard?" She popped her small fist into her palm.

"I'm certain we'll have no trouble finding a willing group to fill our needs, Taara. No need for the hook or for rough stuff."

"It'll be nice to sleep in a real bed once we get to Bazz Bazz," A-Ram said. "Oh Creation—now you two have got me calling it that too."

"Addictive, isn't it?" Taara said.

"Bel?" A-Ram asked, "those Pilgrims of Merian? Can you tell me about them? I'd like to hear."

"Well, they're . . ."

The Com chattered, interrupting him. "Incoming message, Bel, you want it?" Taara asked at her lit-up Missive's Panel.

"Who's it from?"

Taara looked into the viewer. "It's your friend, Captain Gwendolyn."

Stenstrom sighed. "Are we certain it's her this time? No more mirages?"

"Looks like a real Com to me."

"Sure then. She probably wants to yell at me again. Put her on. Go ahead."

The bridge's central Holo-cone jumped to life, though the image was still poor at best. There was Lt. Gwendolyn, standing tall in 3-D. This time her eyes were not sunken and crazed, no gushing blood on her cheek.

"It appears I'm not where I'm supposed to be, Captain," Stenstrom said from his chair. "Is this your declaration of war between us?"

She stood there a moment in the cone. "Paymaster, I would appreciate a word with you in private if possible."

"Whatever threats you wish to make to me, you may say in front of my crew."

"I would be more at ease speaking to you in private, sir."

Stenstrom stood. "Taara, please send the Com to my office." She casually pressed a few buttons.

"Hey, Bel! Don't lock the door, I might want to use the toilet in a bit."

"Fine."

He walked across the bridge and went through the door. Taara's strut-metal sextant sat on the ledge. He seated himself behind Captain Davage's old desk and opened the Com, which, thanks to one of the stolen generators, had power. Captain Gwendolyn appeared on the screen.

"Paymaster, thank you for giving me this opportunity to speak with you in private," she said in her cultured Zenon accent as he sat down.

He regarded her—a sturdy-looking lady, as before. On the tallish side as with her mirage, dense, but not unattractive in the least, her long brown hair tucked into her hat. Rather like Private Taara, she was deceptively good-looking. "Of course, Captain," he said. "You scared several days and nights worth out of me earlier."

Lt. Gwendolyn was puzzled. "Sorry? I what?"

Stenstrom laughed. "Never mind. So, Captain, still wanting to beat my brains in, are you?"

She smiled. "No, Paymaster. I want to apologize for my outburst earlier. It was unprofessional, and rather rude of me. I suppose I've been known for having a hot temper, and perhaps I justly deserve such a reputation. Please forgive my previous lack of manners, and if you wish to file a formal complaint against me, I encourage you to do so."

Stenstrom laughed. "Oh, please. My first officer doesn't seem to think that I would have stood much of a chance against you, should we have come to blows."

Gwendolyn lifted her eyes and looked at him through the Com. "Well, sir, if I am to base my response on your appearance, I should say that I think you would have fared quite well."

"Thank you. So then, Captain, what's on your mind?"

She continued. "I want to clear the air between us. I want to make it plain that I, like you, have been forced into this situation and I find it rather uncomfortable. I have no desire to cost you your chair—though the essence of my mission is to do just that. Rather, I must say that I have been most impressed with what you have accomplished to date. I simply want to say that I have my orders and I must carry them out, but that doesn't mean that I have to like them, or to agree with them for that matter. Furthermore, I want to say that it is my hope that, after all this is over and matters have been sorted out, we could sit down, like two civilized people, have lunch, and shake hands."

"Are you trying to say, Captain, that you want to be friends?"

"I would like that, sir, yes. I just want to assure you that what happens over the next few days is not of my making. I'm just following my orders, such as they are."

Stenstrom glanced out the windows. The stars appeared to not be moving. Far away was Druries Belt, glowing and ominous. "Are you still intending to arrest Private Taara and forcibly return Lord A-Ram to his slow death at the Fleet?"

Lt. Gwendolyn shook her head. "No, Paymaster. I have done as you previously suggested. I have sent word to the Fleet of your conscription of Lord A-Ram as helmsman and your appointment of Private Taara as your first officer. The movements have been logged at Fleet and duly noted. There are no further penalties awaiting Private Taara. Her unit appeared to be rather glad to be rid of her, truth be told; however, the Fleet office and Admiral Derlith demand payment for Lord A-Ram—it is their right to request compensation."

"Fine, whatever they want, I will pay it. I'll let Taara and A-Ram know. It will be a load off their minds."

Gwendolyn looked at the floor for a moment. "Now, Paymaster, I wish to know what your feelings are on this matter. As I have said, I have no desire to cost you your chair, yet I must do my duty."

"My feelings, Captain?"

"Yes, as you touched upon, I was hoping we could be friends, and that is not simply idle talk; that is my genuine position. I must say I admire your tenacity."

"How about this, Captain? If you bag me fair and square, you may rest assured that I will sit and lunch with you. You may do your job in the knowledge that I harbor no ill will toward you or any of your crew. If you get me, you get me, and that's that. However, I am not going to make it easy for you. I intend to fulfill my mission and deliver Admiral Derlith's gasp-inducing brandy to Bazz Bazz."

"Sorry," Gwendolyn replied. "To where?"

"Oh, forgive me; it's a habit I've acquired. I am going to deliver my cargo to Bazz. You will not step on my ship until I have fulfilled my mission, and that is the simple truth."

Gwendolyn lit up. "So it's settled. I can't tell you how much better I feel having had this conversation with you, Paymaster—now that we understand and appreciate each other properly. I am certain that you will give me all I can handle and then some—I had better be on my top game. Do you enjoy playing cards, sir?"

"I'm afraid I don't know any games. And please, Captain, you may call me Bel, short for Belmont. All my friends call me that."

She looked at the floor and smiled. "Thank you, and you may call me

Gwendolyn, or simply Gwen if you prefer—my family calls me that. I would like to teach you a game or two. Playing cards is a passion of mine that I wish to share."

"I thought boxing was."

"I like to box as well. If you want to box instead of playing cards, we can do that. I have a famous right hook." She smiled and seemed to be enjoying the conversation as it advanced from business to more personal matters. "Bel, I have heard that you can make items appear from thin air. Is that simply a story, or can you actually do such things?"

"Who told you that?"

"Oh, various people. My uncle, for one."

Stenstrom raised his hands and showed her his palms. "Watch carefully." In a blur he waved his hands and produced a MARZABLE between his fingers. Another wave and it was gone again.

Gwendolyn clapped. "Oh, well done, Bel. Now, to prove my good faith, I'll inform you that I expect to arrive at your position, after our course correction, in four hours. I have a fully functioning *Tekel*-class scouting ship at my disposal, and I have been authorized to use whatever means necessary to board your vessel, including disabling it. You have my word, I'll not do such a thing."

"Thank you Captain . . . I mean, Gwendolyn. But, you needn't hold back because of me—do what you feel you need to do, and I shall do the same."

Gwendolyn looked at him over the Com screen. "So, Bel, can you assure me that your life support and other critical systems are functioning well enough to sustain you and your people? Both myself and my Hospitaler, are genuinely concerned about you."

"I can. The items we borrowed from Dry Dock 275 are working rather well. We have fresh air and a fair amount of power , we even have a fully functioning bathroom."

Gwendolyn seemed surprised. "Shipboard plumbing requires extensive training and experience. I am amazed by your industry."

"Necessity begets industry."

"Do you have any engineering skills, Bel—that's a fairly complicated procedure."

"I don't. Private Taara did it."

"She did? That's very impressive—she must have some experience in that area. I have a degree in engineering from the University of Arden and I'd hoped to sit on the Engineer's chair of a larger Fleet ship some day. See, my pin here?" Over the screen she pointed to a tiny pin on her lapel—it was the same kind of pin his sister Lyra now wears on her gown.

He recalled the circle Taara had mentioned. He'd seen Gwendolyn there in Lilly's lantern light. She was in it too.

He recalled her mirage on the bridge: sword drawn, eyes sunken and crazed, face hollow, blood gushing, full of delirium.

"That's a very difficult degree to achieve, so I'm told. You've cause to be most proud. I believe my sister is currently matriculating at the University of Arden as well, though not in engineering."

She sat down and appeared to relax a little; she even took off her hat. "Belmont is a Zenon House, yes? I think, geographically speaking, that we are neighbors. I am from Prentiss, just a ways north from you I think."

"I grew up in Tyrol near my mother's holdings—my cousins still live in the Zenon region, however." He had a thought. "Captain?"

"Gwen, please."

"Gwen, may I ask an odd question of you?"

"Certainly."

"Thank you. Have you sustained an injury to your right cheek lately, as if from a sword cut?"

Gwendolyn appeared puzzled. She reached up and touched her cheek. "My cheek? No, not that I'm aware of. Why do you ask?"

"I . . . had a dream recently where your cheek was injured and bleeding."

She laughed. "You're dreaming of me, are you, Paymaster?"

"Yes, apparently so."

Gwendolyn's panel lit up and she glanced at it. She pressed a few buttons and then resumed the conversation. "Well, I look forward to putting this business behind us, and I am certain that we'll laugh over it someday soon. I have to return to my duties. As we are now friends, will you promise me that you will contact us immediately should your life-support situation change?"

"Sure, I promise."

"Good. So, Bel, until we meet again—and we shall meet again, make no mistake—I bid you good luck and fly safe."

"And to you, good luck, Gwendolyn, Lady of Prentiss, for you shall need it."

"Oh, Bel, one more thing?"

"Yes?"

"You posed an odd question, and now I have one for you. I . . . I must know. That mask you wear . . . Why, why do you wear a mask?"

"It's a long story. I say, after this is over, and I've delivered my cargo on Bazz Bazz—I mean Bazz, we'll sit down, have a nice dinner, and I'll tell you all about it—the whole sorry story. How does that sound?"

Gwendolyn lit up in a smile and put her hands together. "I look forward to it."

"You should do that more often."

"Do what, Bel?"

"Smile. How your face fills up when you do so."

7

—Standoff—

It had to be the slowest chase in League history, the huge, but limping Warbird *Seeker* against the fully functional but much smaller *Demophalon John*. The *Seeker* was big and swan-like, graceful and menacing, but she was darkened and mostly dead. She was flying backwards, her lone motive power being supplied by the *Westminster*, strapped down in forward facing Ripcar Bay 5.

Stenstrom saw the jumpy, blurry image of the scouting ship on the holo-cone. "Right on time," he said. He went into his office and gazed out the windows to get a clearer look. "Taara, get in here!" Taara joined him.

There she was, swooping in from 12:45pm: the *Demophalon John*. She was a standard *Tekel*-class scout ship, about three hundred feet long. Its structure consisted of an elliptical disk five decks high, buttressed by three evenly-spaced convex cylinders roughly shaped like bananas—hence the *Tekel's* long standing nick-name: the Banana-Boat. The upper conning run was shorter than the lower two and flashed-out with a tail assembly.

She was nimbly orbiting around the length of the *Seeker*, looking it over. She was lit up with service lights, scanning cones, and glowing windows. Stenstrom thought he could see occasional movement in the windows, people passing by—and he wondered if Lt. Gwendolyn was looking out of one of them even now.

She, stuck in Taara's closed Vendetta Circle, just like he was … maybe.

"Taara," he said. "What are we looking at here?"

"It's just a run of the mill *Tekel*-class scout ship. It's a fairly fast boat, got four J-400 Stellar Mach coils, but those are pretty small. If we were normal, they couldn't keep up with us at full sail—but we're not normal right now, are we?"

"What's its armament?"

"It has six X-MaSS rim-fired chain guns mounted forward."

"Those are 'Christmas Guns', right? I remember hearing about those."

"Yep. Just a fast-firing light gun. Got punch, but we're pretty heavily armored."

"How badly can that type of gun hurt us?"

"They can do a fair amount of topical damage, but that's all. A Christmas Gun's not going to put a Warbird out of commission. Why, are you afraid Captain Gwendolyn's going to shoot us up?"

"She might. I'm thinking she's going to do the following: I'm thinking she's going to try and land several Ripcars first, then she's going to try and dock, then she's going to go for the *Westminster*, light it up and shut us down.

That's what I'd do."

He looked over his shoulder. "A-Ram! Do you have a good reading on your Helm displays?"

"I do. I see her orbiting around, trying to casually lock on and dock using automated signaling. Won't work, as we don't have power to those automated systems. It'll be like making love to a dead man."

"Don't knock it 'till you've tried it, A-Ram," Taara replied.

"Keep her at bay," Stenstrom said, "and feel free to give her a little love tap if she comes in too close."

He gazed at the *Demophalon John* floating around outside. "You once said there was somebody aboard that ship that I care deeply over, Taara."

"I don't recall saying that."

"You did, back when you first put the MOLLY on."

"Hmmmm, maybe I was talking about the Captain. Maybe she likes you. She might as well, for she's going to die in the Vendetta Circle just like we are."

They returned to the bridge. "How're we looking, Bel?" A-Ram asked.

"Slow. How are we doing for maneuverability?"

"We're fine—we can maneuver with a scout ship any day; we just can't outrun her."

The Com crackled on the bridge. "Paymaster Stenstrom," Gwendolyn's voice said, "So, here we are, sir. Are you feeling thirsty? The sooner I board, the sooner I'm buying you an ale back at Fleet," she said in a good-natured manner.

"Nah, Captain, I'm good, I think," he replied.

"Well then, fair hunting," she said.

"A-Ram, the only two places she's going to be able to dock is dead forward and to the starboard off the neck, right?"

"Right!" Taara answered for him.

"Very well, keep the nose and the starboard side away from her—you are free to maneuver however you see fit."

"Gotcha,' Bel," A-Ram said, tugging on the wheel.

"Just remember, keep clear of the damn Belt. No need to test fate."

"Agreed."

"She doesn't sound mad or anything, Bel," Taara said with a hint of disappointment. "Not like before."

"We smoothed things out. She doesn't seem like a half bad person really, but I'm still not letting her on the ship."

"So, you're not going to fight?"

"I rather doubt it."

"I was hoping to watch a good fight, and I think she would have beaten the daylights out of you, if you really want my thoughts."

"Thanks, Taara."

A-Ram looked into his screen. "Reading four small vessels exiting the ship. Ripcars, Bel, and they're coming in fast."

Stenstrom saw the flickering images on the holo-cone. "Which one is she in, Taara? Can you tell?"

"The one that's heading for Ripcar Bay 7."

"Right. A-Ram, track the one heading for Number 7 and keep her from docking. Don't worry about the rest of them. The other ones are just decoys."

A-Ram spun the wheel.

The Ripcars from *Demophalon John* chased the *Seeker* around for a while. Though the small ships were relatively fast and maneuverable, they weren't as fast as the *Seeker* with its *Westminster* drive engine. Even though the *Seeker* had no Stellar speed available to it to fare the deep stars and was flying backwards, she was faster at maneuvering speeds than the *Demophalon John's* Ripcars; it was like a pigeon being chased by a slightly slower swarm of bees. A-Ram kicked the bar, and the *Seeker* outpaced them. After a time, the Ripcars gave up and returned to the *Demophalon John*.

"That had to be humbling for her," Stenstrom said. "Now that her Ripcar gambit has failed miserably, I think she's going to try and hard dock the ship."

Sure enough, the *Demophalon John* tried to slide in, first to the front of the ship, and then to the starboard. But, even in a diminished state, the *Seeker* was fairly light on the helm and A-Ram, with a bit of doing, kept the scouting ship at bay, matching it turn for turn. The two ships performed a swirling dance, the scouting ship moving one way and the *Seeker* matching.

"You didn't think I'd let you just up and knock on the front door, did you, Captain?" Stenstrom asked.

Gwendolyn's voice came back on the Com. "You can twist away all you want, Bel; where are you going to go? I can out-run you with one coil in lock. At this speed, you've got a ten day trip to Bazz ahead of you, and you have to sleep sometime—me, I've got the night bell to take over when I get tired. You might just wake up and find me smiling down at you. You said you liked my smile—why not see it in person?"

"A-ha!" Taara said. "See."

Stenstrom laughed as A-Ram pulled on the wheel. "Ah, but haven't you heard, Captain? I've got Tyrol sorcery. I don't need to sleep."

"Tyrol sorcery isn't real."

"Oh, yeah—think so?"

There was a silence over the Com. Then: "Bel, is everybody on the bridge?"

"Yes, why do you ask?"

"Because I'm thinking about running out a Christmas Gun and shooting out your engine. I just wanted to make sure everybody is safe and whole on the bridge before I do it."

"Thought you said you weren't going to do that,"

"I thought you said you wouldn't mind if I did."

"You might want to think twice about shooting my engine. My engine is the tach-scout ship *Westminster*. If you shoot her out, you'll be willfully destroying a Fleet vessel."

"Ah, just a couple of rounds, just a hole or two—she'll be fine after I board and patch her up."

Stenstrom laughed. "But, Captain, you're not giving me enough credit for having a devious mind. I figured you'd try such a thing, so I rigged the *Westminster* with a shaped charge of Shaddout. You run out a Christmas Gun and light her up, she'll blow hard."

"I see, and where did you get a shaped charge of Shaddout? That's not usually to be found in any quantity on a half scuttled ship."

"I borrowed it from Dry Dock 275—a virtual grocery store, that one."

On the Holo-Cone, Gwendolyn put her hand to her chin and thought. "Hmmm,"

The two ships continued spiraling around each other, the *Demophalon John* darting in, and the *Seeker* matching the move.

After an hour or two, Gwendolyn Commed back in. "So, what are we going to do here, Bel? You can't get away from me, and I can't dock. I don't want you to exhaust yourselves. May I please make a suggestion?"

"Shoot."

"Why don't we dock, and you come aboard my ship—I promise I won't try to board. Then, you and I can, between ourselves, see if we can come up with a fair way to settle this."

"How do you propose we do that?"

"We'll have a contest of some sort. We'll play cards."

"I don't know how to play cards."

"I'll teach you a game. Something simple. I'm certain you'd be a natural, and I should think you'd have beginner's luck on your side. You win, you get to go to Bazz. I'll even help pull your ship, allow it to pick up a little speed. And, if I win, then you let me dock and we head back to Fleet."

Taara shook her head and butted in. "No, no, no, you don't settle something important with a game of cards. Got an issue to settle, you fight it out, and let me watch. Come on, Captain, you can take Bel here."

Gwendolyn looked at Taara, somewhat incredulous. She seemed for a moment like she was going to get mad, then she composed herself and smiled. "Quite the little thing, aren't you, Private?"

"I am. So, are you two going to fight or not?"

One of her crewmen handed Gwendolyn a report. She looked at it and appeared concerned. "Bel, in all seriousness, we've drifted off the shipping lanes. I ask that we bear to 3:45PM and get back into the patrolled regions. There's a whole lot of nothing out here, moving this slow and all, and drifting off the lanes is dangerous. That's how ships and people end up missing."

"Sorry I'm cramping your style, Captain."

Taara muted the Com and pointed at the lantern. "Fun and games aside, Bel, she's right. We're drifting awfully close to the Belt."

Gwendolyn continued. "It's all right. Come on, follow me back into the lanes—and for Creation's sake, stop calling me Captain—we're past that already. Once we're back in the lanes, we can continue this. And I really think we should dock, and you come aboard my ship. If you don't want to play cards, we can box, as your first officer suggested. Then I'll knock you out fair and square and this will be over. If you don't board, I'm still thinking about using a Christmas Gun on you, so keep that in mind. In the meantime, follow me!"

Taara looked into her sensing visor. "The *Demophalon John* is turning away to 3:45PM, Bel."

"Very well, A-Ram, go ahead and follow her—just make sure she doesn't try anything funny along the way."

A-Ram adjusted his stance and began turning the wheel. "Hey, Bel, something's resisting me. I'm having trouble with the helm."

"Are we breaking down?" Stenstrom asked.

"I don't know, I don't think so. It just doesn't want to turn."

Taara looked at her visor. "Bel, I'm reading a large gravity well forming to our ventral. It's pulling us down."

Gwendolyn's voice filtered back over the Com. "What are you doing, Bel? Quit loitering back there. I'm not going to try anything until we get back into the shipping lanes."

"I'm not certain where it's coming from, Gwen, but we're falling into a gravity well forming at our 6:00am."

The Com Holo flickered. Gwendolyn was alarmed. "I'm reading it too. I don't see anything on our charts indicating the presence of such an irregularity in this region of space. Look, Bel, you need to let me dock and take you out of there. It might not be safe."

The lights on the bridge flickered and went out for a moment except for the lantern which burned steady and true.

They all heard a cold voice from nowhere that chilled them. "*Taara . . .*" it said.

"Oh, not now, for Creation's sake!" Stenstrom yelled.

There was a clank and the lights flickered. "Bel, the *Westminster* has just shut down!" Taara said.

"The Helm has gone dead right along with it!" A-Ram added.

"Bel!" Gwendolyn cried, her voice crackling over the flickering cone. "Your ship is fading from my screens. Enough of this, Bel. We're boarding to get you three out of there! We've played this game long enough! I want you out of there, now!"

Something enveloped them.

"Bel!!"

And the *Seeker* vanished.

8

—THE WOMAN OF SAND—

S tenstrom shot out of his chair. "Taara, what happened to the *Demophalon John?*"

"I don't know. According to this half-working viewer, we're on the other side of the damn League right now." The lantern light spun.

"What? How'd that happen?"

"I don't know, Bel."

"What's our exact position?"

"Near 0, the *Camalopardus* area. Uninhabited space."

He turned to A-Ram. "Do we have helm control?"

"Yes, it's back, Bel. And I agree with Taara. According to my helm screens, we're way over on the other side of the League, near Xaphan space.

The Holo-cone suddenly came to life.

Something moved. A voice spoke. *"Paymaster Stenstrom, Lord of Belmont. Welcome, we have been expecting you."*

Stenstrom stood up. "Who's there? Identify yourself!"

"Please come to the ship's Priory as soon as you are able. We will be waiting."

"Who is this?" he said. "Lilly? Is that you?"

No answer.

"I am not going anywhere until you have properly identified yourself."

"We have known you all your life. We held you aloft when you were a baby, barely a few moments old. We watched over you, and we protected you. We returned you to your mother's arms. And, we have known you . . . intimately, many times."

'Sisters?" Stenstrom asked.

"The Priory. We are waiting for you, Lord Belmont."

The lantern moved of its own accord. It wrenched itself free from the Missive's Panel and floated in mid air, its golden chain moving like a silk ribbon. Its guiding blue light went out, replaced by a purplish one.

"Hey!" Taara cried. "What's happening to our lantern? All my shit's dead now!"

The voice spoke again. *"The Paramel is our property. We forgive you its unauthorized use. We await you in the Priory."*

"Umm, we sort of need that?" Taara piped. The voice did not reply. The Holo-cone then went out and died.

"Taara, what do we have left?"

"Nothing right now. The panel's shot without the lantern."

A-Ram held the wheel. "I don't like the sound of that, Bel."

"Me neither," Taara said. "The Sisters give me the horrors and they're stealing our bloody lantern."

"I told you we'd get into trouble using it," A-Ram said.

Stenstrom stood and checked his NTHs. "Let's go, what are we waiting for?"

Following the floating lantern they slowly made their way out of the lit up bridge once again into the dark, stuffy interior of the ship.

They climbed down the Lift shaft and into the lower reaches of the "neck" of the ship. The dark halls of Deck 7 seemed even darker than before as they made their way down the corridor; the metal walls and looming shadows were alive with noises, rattles, and half-seen movement.

"Taara . . ."

"Belmont . . ."

"A-Ram . . ."

"HAHAHAHAHAHA!"

Shadow figures darted about in the lantern's purple light. Stenstrom drew his pistols.

They reached the Priory and the lantern drifted in, its beam throwing all the tossed furniture and fallen pieces of art into bloody, jagged relief. Taara drew her huge SK and cocked it. They made their way through the antechamber to the forbidden rooms beyond.

"Lilly was in there," Stenstrom said, pointing to a side room.

A-Ram poked his head in. "There's nobody in there now."

Stenstrom looked around. "Lilly?" he called out, not expecting to hear a reply.

Wait . . .

". . . *Bel* . . ." came a soft voice from the depths of the Priory.

"Did you hear that?" Taara asked. "Is that Lilly?"

"Sounds like her." Stenstrom quickened his pace. "Lilly!" he called out again. They reached a great oaken door and an adjacent open archway leading out into what looked like a dense wooded space that was slightly lit up in soft purple, joining the lantern's beam. "This archway was filled-in when I was here before; it was just a blank wall. Through this door is a passage leading to the bottom of the ship. That's where you two were being held."

"That's where all the bodies were, right?" Taara asked, holding her SK.

"Yes. The lantern must be opening a gateway, just like Lilly had done."

Through the archway, Lilly's voice drifted out again; only this time it was anguished and sorrowful. ". . . *Bel* . . ."

"Lilly!" Stenstrom cried. "We're coming!" He turned to A-Ram and Taara. "Come on, let's go!" They continued through the arch and down the path. Trees and low brush were everywhere. An obvious path led away to a bend through the trees. Grass and dry leaves crunched under their boots, and the temperature changed. Looking up, there was sky, purplish and dusted with starlight.

"Where are we?" A-Ram asked. "Is this the Astral Plane?"

Stenstrom checked his gear. "No, no it's not. Lilly said that the Sisters Priories are connected to some sort of pocket plane or dimension that they have free access to. That's how the Sisters always seem to escape a doomed starship," he said. "Lilly led me through here to Kana, just like we're doing now. Only this time it's not Kana. The sky's the wrong color and I don't recognize the stars."

"They can't have the lantern back, we need it, Bel!" Taara said. She reached for its chain, but it moved away, easily avoiding her grasp.

They continued down the path until they came to a clearing. In the center of the clearing were two structures. One was a large gray building made of stone, squat and dome-like rising up about a hundred feet. The other was a narrow, cylindrical tower composed of lacy, purplish-blue metal. A-Ram craned his neck—the tower went up and up until it broke the clouds and faded from view—a rather dizzying sight to behold.

"What's that?" A-Ram asked.

"That tower looks high enough to enter orbit. I'm going to puke," Taara said.

"Oh, come on, where's the pluck I've come to expect from you?" Stenstrom said. He took a good look at the gray stone building ahead and stopped. "I've seen this building. Lilly showed it to me."

A-Ram was a little nervous. "I know the Sisters' protocols, Bel—entering the Priory is forbidden unless you've been invited. You were invited, Bel, not either of us—not me certainly as I'm a bloody Untouchable. The Sisters might get angry."

"Don't be silly—I'm certain the Sisters won't mind your presence."

"The Sisters have belittled me and my family for as long as I can remember," he said with a distinct touch of bitterness. "For those of us here who have *not* had the pleasure of their repeated attention, I find it most galling."

A door opened in the center of the dome-like building with a gritty slide. The darkened doorway invited them to enter.

"Lilly?" Stenstrom called out.

No answer. The lantern drifted in on its own.

Slowly, they approached the open door and went inside. They rubbed their eyes and struggled to see in the dark, the lantern's light lost in the vastness. Within was a modestly furnished open space, with the heights of the dome hovering and rustling overhead with over-grown ivy and nesting birds. Dead leaves littered the floor.

Four figures sat in the center of the dome. Stenstrom remembered seeing them also

"They did it all, Bel," Lilly had said.

"Who are you?" Stenstrom called out. The figures didn't answer. They continued toward the center.

Four Sisters sat on small couches in the center of the dome. They had no Marines with them, which was an odd sight for Stenstrom who honestly couldn't recall a time in the past when he saw a Sister without one in attendance, even when he was participating in their Program. As usual, they sat with perfect posture and grace, their hands placed properly in their laps.

"They did it all . . ."

"Sisters?" he asked.

In addition to the missing Marines, the Sisters seemed a bit odd in other small ways as well. Though they were sitting, they appeared abnormally elongated, and Stenstrom guessed they might very well be freakishly tall if they stood up. As per usual for the Sisters, they were quite pretty—in a motherly sort of way, though one of them had a rather ovoid, somewhat reptilian face; Stenstrom imagined that, if she were to open her mouth, she might have a forked tongue and possibly snake's fangs. Also, their complexions, though perfect, appeared distinctly green, although that was probably a trick of the dim lighting of the dome.

Their dress was also a little off from most of the Sisters Stenstrom had ever seen. They had the usual white robes, wrapped-up arms to the wrists, and large, cornet-like headdresses, but instead of the usual sky blue traveling cloaks the Sisters always wore—a very comforting color—these wore either dark blue or black cloaks over their white robes.

Under the heights of the dome, the two opposing sides stared at each other for an agonizingly long stretch of time. Leaves crunched underfoot, birds overhead rustled about and chirped.

Finally, Stenstrom spoke. "Great Sisters, it is with profound relief that we find you here today. Your presence is comforting, as always."

The Sisters smiled and then turned to Private Taara. She gulped and took a few steps forward. "I am honored that the Sisterhood of Light would grace me as the vessel of their thoughts," she said in a quiet, practiced manner.

She spoke again, this time with words not of her own making. The Sisters barged into her head and took her over.

"Lord Belmont," Taara said, suddenly carrying herself in an alien demeanor. "It pleases us to see you safe and unharmed. You have caused quite a stir in the Fleet Admiralty, so we have been told."

Another Sister barged into Taara's head. Again she spoke. "You have shown great ingenuity and tenacity in this matter, Lord Belmont. We are most impressed."

Again, there was a bout of silence as the two groups stared at each other, Taara trying to clear her head.

The lantern floating high overhead came to life, throwing a strong yellow beam down on the Sisters. Bathed in its living light, they suddenly no longer seemed green or reptilian or overly tall. They appeared as fair, flawless ladies. "Yes," Taara said, "we ought to be more careful with our things. The wonders the Paramel shows true."

There was another bout of silence, then Taara spoke again. "Lord A-Ram," one of them said through her mouth. "We are curious—why did you choose to join Lord Belmont in space? Certainly, you knew there might be consequences. We had you decided as a hopeless wretch, a spineless coward and progeny of bad chefs and bad Brandtball players not worth another look. You and your family."

A-Ram slightly reacted.

"Why not just Stare him and find out for yourself?" Taara said, momentarily regaining control of her mouth. Just as quickly, the Sisters wrenched it back.

"Because that is so uncivilized, Private," she said responding to herself.

A-Ram looked at the floor and answered. "I thought what the Admiral was doing to Lord Belmont was unjust, and most cruel. I thought the Admiral was cheating Lord Belmont out of his money, and for no good reason. And I thought he was a decent fellow and deserved help. I wanted to help him. I wanted to be his friend."

"And, you've no regrets?"

"None, Great Sister."

"Ah, true friendship. You shall be rewarded, Lord A-Ram, for your unexpected display of courage. We appreciate and newly admire you, sir. Perhaps we, like everyone else, were wrong about you, and failed to see the heart beating within your frail chest."

The Sisters moved on to Taara. It was odd hearing her speak about herself in the third person. "And you, Private Taara. Always the little rebel, are you not? So lonely and starving for attention, and, like Lord A-Ram, not near the hopeless wretch your people thought you to be, are you? You too shall be rewarded for your bravery. And yes, you are correct, Private, we are dangerous. We are savage and brutal, truth be told. which is why we have asked you three to come to us. We have work for you all, and, you shall be suitably rewarded."

"Work?" he said. "I don't understand."

The Sisters were silent.

"I heard Lilly's voice. Lillian of Gamboa. Is she here?"

Taara approached him, fully under the Sister's control. "Yes, she's here."

"May I see her? She needs me."

"Does she? Ah, young love. Yes, you will see her, but first, allow us to ask a question. That mask, Lord Belmont. Tell us, why do you wear it?"

Stenstrom struggled for words. "I . . . admired the exploits of Lord Terrance of Walther."

Taara gazed up at him, her eyes alien and unfamiliar. "Ah, we understand. The Mad Lord of Walther. How interesting. Certainly you know our official policy regarding the Mad Lord of Walther was public dismissal, seizure of lands, censure, banishment, and, his eventual execution. And, is that the only reason?"

Stenstrom stood there.

"You feel shy," Taara said. "You needn't feel shy with us—of all people, after all we've shared together." Her hand, controlled by the Sisters, wandered to his chest and moved down past his sash. "Allow us to answer for you. Could it also be that be that you wear a mask because you believe that your late mother once cast a spell that will tear your soul apart should you choose to engage in dangerous activities and that the mask, and the magical items you have hidden within it, protects you? That, in trying to save you, your mother has a knife poised at your throat—just like she always had, a knife at your throat, at your sisters' throats? In your chest, perhaps? Ah, the price of love. And now, being deceased, there is no way to remove the spell—that you have a stain on your soul, is that correct?"

Stenstrom answered: "Yes, Great Sisters." What was the point in lying?

"Clearly, we know all about your mother's former activities, and could have acted should we have had a mind to do so. We did not, for your sake. Tell us, how do you feel about your mother?"

"I love my mother, to this day. I would have her no other way than what she was. I failed her. I didn't come home when she asked."

"Spoken like a true son. It will interest you to know that your mother did not cast the spell that has imperiled your soul. Your mother, throughout your life, loved you very much—to the point of madness. She set no demons against you. She put no stain on your soul."

Stenstrom considered that for a moment. "Then where did the Soul Devourers come from?"

Taara's eyes grew wide. "We did it, Lord Belmont," she said. "It was not your mother who put the curse on your soul . . . it was us."

Lilly and the scene at the pool came flooding back to him.

"They did it!" she said. *"They did it all!"*

The Sisters did it.

Stenstrom stood there. "I don't—I don't understand . . ."

"Do you not remember seeing us in the mirror aboard your old ship? Do you not recall feeling our hands claw at your chest? Yes, we have been lending our influence into your life for some time now, since you were a child. It was through our efforts that you survived your birth, for you nearly perished. We have been always near, guiding you with a firm but loving hand."

Stenstrom didn't know how to take any of this. "Sisters, I do not understand your continued interest in me. Who am I but a Lord of Belmont?"

They looked at each other and smiled. "Who indeed? Across the League there are whispered tales of solitary men who are of exceptional quality. On Kana there are tales of the Star that does not Fall. On Onaris, the Lone Rider. On Bazz, there is the "It" Man—the man who comes and goes. You, Lord Belmont, are the "It" Man, the Lone Rider. You are the Star that does not Fall."

The Sisters paused for a moment. Stenstrom didn't know what to do or what to say. A-Ram shuffled uncomfortably. "Sisters," A-Ram said quietly, looking at the floor, unable to meet their gaze. "Those are children's stories."

The Sisters ignored him. Taara continued in their voice. "These special men have the genetic ability to receive and utilize our power without being destroyed they are no child's story, Lord A-Ram. There have been others like you through the centuries: Homma of Telmus Falls, Atrajak of Want, Billus the Knave, Darius Jones of Bazz, and, most recently, Terrance, the Mad Lord of Walther. Normally, the birth of these "It" Men, using the Bazz reference, are rare—perhaps once in the passing of centuries," another Sister said. "We had our Lord Terrance of Walther and did not expect, per our calculations, to see another "It" Man for three hundred years—and he was to be born in the

Barrow region according to our charts. We do manipulate things a bit with our Celebrants. And then, there was you, the "It" Man we never saw coming. A very happy surprise."

Taara held her hand where it was, her eyes burning. "We checked our calculations—certainly we'd made a mistake." Her fingers tightened. "No, no . . . we made no mistake, there was to be no "It" Man from Esther for another thousand years, yet there you were. How could this be? How, how?" Taara spoke in a dreamy, breathy sort of fashion. "We were quite determined to find out, so much so that a Grand Abbess gave your case her personal attention. And, eventually we had the answer: you are a manufactured "It" Man. You came to be via chemical methods, not genetics. Your departed mother used chemical tinctures to enhance her body for years to prevent the creation of a male child, to blackmail your father into quitting the Fleet and staying home with her. Her internal chemistry, we found, had changed because of the prolonged exposure to these chemicals, creating a unique situation in her womb. And then your father, craving a son after twenty-nine daughters, took the so-called "God-Sperm" potion from Bazz. These two tinctures collided in your mother's womb, creating quite the spectacle.

"And there was yet a third element to this odd puzzle. We found, in our analysis, that the potion your father took on Bazz was tainted with an unknown substance of caustic properties. We believe the potion he drank on Bazz was poisoned. The exact nature of this poison remains a mystery— clearly, an extraordinary set of circumstances conspired together to create you, Lord Belmont,—the "It" Man who nearly slipped through our attention. We are vigorously studying this situation, even to this day. The mystery of your accidental creation shall not be a mystery for long, we promise."

Stenstrom opened his mouth to pose several questions, and Taara, under the Sister's control, cut him off.

"We are fortunate to have you, Lord Belmont, for there is work to be done. Please attend. The recent Kestral Affair revealed to us that we are arrogant, and possibly out of touch with the happenings of the League. It is our responsibility; all the people who died—they are on our hearts. We are here to protect the people, and we failed. In light of this, we feel it is time to resurrect an old custom—for the good and safety of the League. Your hero, the Mad Lord of Walther, was our Fist—he performed our bidding. Homma, Atrajak, Billus, Darius Jones—they were all our Fists too."

Another Sister barged into Taara's head. "We of the Sisterhood are in an unusual situation, Lord Belmont. We have power—it is largely understood that we have power; yet, if we openly display too much of it, the people begin to fear. The people fret for their freedom, and we suppose there is validity to such a feeling. Therefore, we cannot allow the people to see us unchained, unfettered. We, in times past, have granted some of our power to select male individuals—the "It" Men with extraordinary qualities—the Lone Riders. A heroic male figure doing extraordinary things seems much less threatening to the masses at large than we of the Sisterhood doing it—appearances are everything, are they not? You, Lord Belmont, possess those exceptional qualities—we have steered you to this task throughout your life. You, like those select men before you, are our Fist."

A-Ram found his voice and spoke up. "But, Great Sisters, all the men you mention—Homma of Telmus Falls, Atrajak of Want, Billus the Knave, Darius Jones, and even the Mad Lord of Walther—they were all lunatics. Homma was a cannibal, the Telmus area of Vithland still reeks with the ghosts of the devoured he made. Atrajak was a Slayer of Sisters and has been erased from the history books, Billus the Knave nearly committed genocide on Hoban, Darius Jones was a raving madman running nude through the streets, and the Sisterhood burned Lord Terrance of Walther's holdings to the ground and publically called him out and executed him."

All four Sisters were suddenly pained—heartbroken.

"In the case of Lord Walther, that was a carefully crafted public ruse. As his name implied, Lord Walther truly went mad toward the end of his life. We took too much from him. We cherished Lord Walther—he honored us, he did his service to the League well, though at great cost to himself. Behold . . ."

Floating high overhead, the lantern cast a beam to the far end of the dome.

A crypt appeared. Standing over the crypt was the large statue of a man. Hat, pantaloons, spurred boots, the handsome face behind a jeweled mask—Stenstrom had seen this man before when he was a child—it was the Mad Lord.

"We keep his remains here, close to us, for we loved him so. As he inspired the hearts and minds of the League, so too he did for us as well. To keep our secrets safe, we had to destroy him, to take everything he had, though the penance we pay in grief continues to this day. You, Lord Belmont, can only hope to be half the man he was."

The Sisters let Taara go for a moment. They all turned to the crypt and looked at it with longing and reverence.

They then turned back and continued. "To properly honor that man, we are not going to repeat our past mistakes with you. We of the Sisterhood are not perfect. We have failed several times with the "It" Men of old. Homma had access to our power all the time, and it tore through his soul; he went mad with the power we gave him. Atrajak too, showed the same degeneration. We hit upon the idea of limiting the "It" Man's access to our power, and Billus seemed to thrive much better than Homma or Atrajak, but he too eventually fell into madness. Darius Jones was simply unhinged from the start, we had no idea what to make of him. With the Mad Lord, we used Sisters who were genetically compatible with him to fill the tower, and he thrived for years and years."

Another Sister spoke. "And hence, our coming to you, Lord Belmont, as often as we did. Many of the Sisters slumbering in the Great Tower outside are of your blood—are of your seed."

And another. "It wasn't our power that drove Lord Terrance mad. It was something else. Someone introduced a poison into his system, and that's what drove him mad. Additionally, Lord Terrance, as Homma and Atrajak and Billus before him, was alone. Alone with the weight of the League on their shoulders, alone with our power. We have made mistakes with the "It" Men of the past. We shall not repeat our mistakes with you. At last, the Lone Rider shall be alone no more. Those who have chosen to stand at your side shall guard your soul, your sanity, and keep you well. You shall be surrounded by people who love you. Look, Lord Belmont, look what we have given you."

Stenstrom found himself rather mesmerized by all of this. He struggled to speak. "What . . . what have you given me?"

"We've given you everything, Lord Belmont. We gave you the desire to long for the stars, to want to be a part of something larger than yourself. We gave you your thirst for knowledge and adventure. We gave you your membership to the Bones Club, and the IBBAANA, and we gave you the *Seeker.*"

"The *Seeker?* You gave it to me?"

"Yes, we wanted you to have it. Captain Gona, hearing those troubling noises—thinking his ship was haunted, went fleeing into retirement. The Admiralty wanted to decommission the ship, and we pressured them not to. We kept our thoughts plain to the Admiralty regarding the *Seeker*, leaving the ship open, for you."

"Captain Gona might be correct regarding the haunting, Sisters. This ship appears to be infested with demons, as we heard them as well," A-Ram said, finding his voice after some time.

The Sisters smiled. "Is it?"

From behind Stenstrom came a chilling voice: ". . . *Taara* . . ." He turned and, of course, nobody was there.

Another voice came. ". . . *Where is your Mother, Lord Belmont* . . ."

He turned, but again, nothing was there.

"We are the demons besetting this ship, Lord Belmont. It is we who haunt it," Taara said. "We needed certain things of you. Your training as a sorcerer, we assisted with that. The Soul Devourers who pursued you across the face of the League, we did that as well, to drive you in the direction we wanted you to go. We could not allow you to simply join the Fleet and become another officer. We had to make you something else—something novel. The HRN coat you wear, your mask—we wanted to self-style you as an eccentric, as with the Mad Lord before you. Great men are always eccentric, are they not? We had to turn you into the fool, into a cad, so that we could publically dismiss and laugh you off as a mere oddity not worth a second thought. Who would suspect that the masked fool actually wields the Sisters' power? And then, to top things off, we gave you this ship."

Stenstrom took exception. "No, no, Great Sisters. I am sorry, you did none of that. My coat, my schooling, my admission to the Bones Club, my occupation as Fleet Paymaster, that was all Lilly's doing."

The Sisters smiled. "And we gave you your Lilly as well."

"Come again?"

"You refer to Lady Lillian of Gamboa, of course. Lillian of Gamboa does not exist, Lord Belmont."

They paused a moment to allow Stenstrom to drink in the information.

Then, they continued: "Oh, there actually is a Lillian of the House of Gamboa, a small, insignificant woman your mother once fancied, and she did come to your home on two occasions to meet you, but not a third time, for she developed a powerful dislike of you. The woman you met and came to know is not her."

Stenstrom, from his previous meeting with Lilly in the bowels of the ship, knew all that, but it was still odd to hear out loud. "I don't understand. You must be mistaken."

The Sisters smiled. "Are we? Look, Lord Belmont," one of them said pointing to the far end of the dome near the Mad Lord's crypt. "See your Lilly . . ."

There, in the far distance, he saw a blonde-headed woman in a pink Gamboa gown emerge from the shadows. He saw her holding a parasol.

"Lilly?" he said. "Lilly!"

"Stand fast, please, Lord Belmont," The Sisters said.

Not hearing them, he sprang over the Sisters' couches and ran toward her, his HRN coattails flapping. "Lilly, Lilly!" he cried.

The possibilities registered through his mind as he sprinted toward her. The question that had been festering in his mind, "What is Lilly" was about to be revealed.

Was she an enchantress?

Was she a Sister?

????

As he approached, she glanced at him and backed up into the darkness near the crypt. After a few more steps, he was there, the statue of the Mad Lord towering over him.

In a corner next to the crypt, Lilly stood. She was pressed into the wall, the back of her hand demurely covering her face. Her expression was that of sorrow and anguish.

"Lilly?"

No answer. She didn't move.

The radiant beam from the lantern floating high overhead panned down and shined on Lilly.

Lillian of Gamboa transformed in the light—in her place was a perfectly formed pillar of sand in her image; pink gown gone, blue eyes gone.

Just sculpted sand in human shape.

He gazed at it in horror. ". . . Lilly . . ." he managed to stammer.

The sand glistened back at him. The molded face in sand looked sad, like she had just lost something dear to her.

"You have loved a woman of sand, Lord Belmont, all these years," the Sisters said from far away. "She was our gift to you—your protector, your tutor . . . your lover, arming you for battle, sending you in the direction we wanted you to go. That was her purpose and it has come to an end, as has she."

Everything spun—he felt his brain short-circuiting. All the truths of the world were suddenly gone—now there was chaos.

Lilly emerged from the darkness, Lilly slayed hundreds of Soul Devourers.

"*I accept!*" Lilly had said, taking his hand.

Everything he had done, he had done for her, for Lilly. She suggested he go to school, and so he went to school. She suggested he join the Bones Club, so he did it. She gave him the idea of becoming a Fleet Paymaster; she selected his HRN uniform for him.

She wound him up and set him to it . . .

She did it . . .

She did it all!

How could this be? How could he have not known? Even his mother had been fooled.

Rooted in normalcy. Talented, but mundane.

Sand . . . All this time.

Alitrix. Lady Alitrix knew. *"I don't know what she is, but she's not a woman . . . It's as if she is steering you to some pre-determined destination."*

And Kaly. What had Kaly seen? *"Who was that you ditched me for?"*

"How do you mean?"

"I don't know; she seemed kind of strange . . . like a mannequin . . ."

And here was Lilly, and she was naught but a woman of sand. There was a word scraped into the sand above her breast:

"I ACCEPT"

He reached out to her, his mask becoming damp. "It's . . . it's all right, Lilly, I'm going to take you home ..."

He touched her face and she fell apart. He watched the sand slip through his fingers and fall to the floor in an uncaring hiss. There was something hidden in the mound of sand as it fell away, many thin, squarish objects stacked together in the center. He probed the mound with his hands.

The square objects were letters, dozens of them. All the letters he'd written Lilly over the years, here they were, unopened, unread—intercepted, discolored in sand. His love's discourse stacked up and kept hidden near the heart of an artificial woman.

"LILLY!!" he choked. The letters slipped out of his hands and fell to the top of the Mad Lord's crypt.

He fell to his knees. The loss, the feeling of total loss. He openly wept.

The Sisters were unimpressed. "Come now, Lord Belmont, do get a hold of yourself. You are making a scene. Please, attend to us at once."

His eyes flashed in anger.

The Sisters!

How could they?

HOW DARE THEY?

This was all their fault!! They murdered his Lilly!

"They did it all . . ."

He drew his NTH's, ready to slay the four of them.

Before another moment passed, he was TK'ed off the ground, his pistols pointing toward the dome above, and was carried back in attendance to the Sisters. They spun him around and forced him to face them.

"What is the point of this, Lord Belmont?" Taara asked for them in a stern voice. "It is done. Cry over your phantom love another time, and face reality. We tried to give you love, albeit temporarily. We tried to guide you, to do you a favor."

He hung there in their TK and wept, uncontrollably.

One of the Sisters appeared perturbed. "Really, Lord Belmont, this display is most unbecoming. You should . . ."

A-Ram watched and stirred. He spoke up. "And so, this is the Sisterhood of Light, is it? I spent my youth believing there was something wrong with me and my family: 'See the A-Rams,' they said in Calvert. 'Look at how the Sisters shun them. Look at them—they are fools.' And we were humbled and shamed, not worthy of the Sisters' attention. Here you are, tormentors, manipulators and inflictors of pain … little more than Black Hats without the masks. Look what you've done to him, and all on a whim!"

One of the Sisters rose to rebuke A-Ram, but another one seated nearby raised a hand, and the first sank back into her seat.

The Sister in the center couch watched Stenstrom weep and her expression changed. She pulled him close to her, reached out, and wiped away one of his tears.

She appeared sad. "We meant to give you love, safety and guidance. We did not mean for you to become devoted to her—we expected your long departures to prevent that. What do you want, Lord Belmont?" Taara said in a kind voice after a moment.

"I want Lilly! I want to kill you!"

Taara walked up to Stenstrom, reached up, and took his sobbing face into her hands. "Perhaps we have underestimated the effect our woman of sand would have on you. Perhaps we underestimated you as well. We have used similar tactics before, and our fellows did never respond in quite this fashion. Perhaps we underestimated the capacity of your heart to love—to cherish the woman of sand, to truly love Lillian of Gamboa. Perhaps our hearts are so old that we have forgotten what that is like. If that is the case, then we repent what we have inflicted upon you. We do not mean to be cruel."

The Sister lifted her hand, and his hat and mask were gently TK'ed off his head and face. "We wish to offer you a gift." She took the hovering mask and unwound it. The three silver hermelins he had fashioned to protect himself from the Soul Devourers came out of the fabric and floated on air. Taara spoke. "Were we truly cruel and uncaring, we would simply give you back the woman of sand, the phantom of Lillian of Gamboa that we made all too well."

His treasured golden locket Lilly had given him as a gift floated out of his HRN pocket. It hovered near his face and opened.

There was Lilly's beautiful face. He wondered if she had actually painted it herself, or if a Sister somewhere in one of their strongholds had done it. He was racked with anguish.

"But, you would be living an illusion—a lie," Taara said. "She is not real, her love for you fabricated, pre-programmed. A heart such as yours deserves a heart in kind. She was simply a tool we used—a touch of jasmine, a hint of rose, and a pile of virgin sand is all she ever was. We would not have you trapped in such a fantasy. Your fine heart is broken, and it is our fault—fear not, for we shall repair your broken heart. Yea, we shall strengthen it. You deserve a real love, one that is earned and cultivated with time. You, It Man, will not be alone as was our beloved Mad Lord. You will be surrounded by your friends and those who love you, your soul kept safe. You shall love another and forget all about Lillian of Gamboa."

With a flick of her wrist, the three hermelins and his golden locket clattered away and fell to the floor. "You won't have a need for those anymore—we take back the curse on your soul," Taara said. In a flash of blue light, a new hermelin formed, spinning in mid-air. It formed into the shape of a man in a long coat holding his hands to his heart. "We replace the old magic with a new hermelin, one that shall tend to your broken heart and shield you from all the torments that go with it."

The hermelin floated into the loose folds of the mask. It returned to him and settled back over his eyes, the cloth damp from his tears. "Wear this and be protected, until your true love comes to steal your heart afresh. Your true love shall unmask you, Lord Belmont, our It Man and Lone Rider. Through you, we shall atone for our mistakes of the past."

Stenstrom stopped weeping and the Sisters released him from their TK. His hat floated back down onto his head. He stood up, wiping his face, catching his breath. A-Ram put his hand on his shoulder.

"You all right, Bel?" he asked.

He tried to speak. "I'm all right, A-Ram." He turned to the Sisters. "Why, why have you done this to me?" he asked wiping his eyes.

"To groom you to serve the League, as all the It Men before you have done. You have work that is bigger than us all. Dedication to the League is the hallmark of the Sisterhood. Everything we do is for the good and safety of the League. That tower you were admiring on your way here. It contains over two hundred and fifty thousand Sisters, many of which are of your blood, all of whom have dedicated themselves to this task. They sleep within it, adding their power to the service of the League. You shall have occasional access to this power. We shall allow you to borrow it when we see fit."

Another Sister grabbed into Taara's mind. "Likewise, to protect you from the prolonged exposure that damned Homma and Atrajak, we shall take the power back when we see fit. As long as you can see *Camalopardus* in the sky, the constellation of the candle flame that is the center of the Solar Empire—the Elder's universe, you will have access to the League's power. All under its light is the domain of the Solar Empire the Elders founded long ago, that which we keep in trust from ages past. You will be our Fist. You will follow our command, searching the League in your *Seeker*, looking for signs of the Kestral, and where you find them, you will destroy them. That is your ongoing task.

"Protect us from evil, Lord Belmont. The Kestrals are intertwined in the fabric of the League, and you shall save us from them. We have prepared you to protect us. There are others serving this cause as well. Your new friends—they are at your side. There is this great ship, which we have given to you. And look, there is another . . ."

From out of nowhere, a slim female appeared before Stenstrom. She was about 5'7 in height, slender and silent. She wore a loose-fitting scarlet robe that ended just above her knees. Her legs were covered in black wrappings, and her arms and hands were also covered in black. She wore a nimble pair of black shoes. On her head was a featureless black sash, completely covering her face.

"Who is this? A Black Hat?" Stenstrom asked.

"Allow us to introduce Knife, a Shadow tech female who is in the service of the Sisterhood. Not a Painter, not a Hammer, she is of Knife-class, mobile, solitary and deadly. It is through her that we shall command you. Where she goes, you will follow. She is your enemy. You will pursue her, dog her every step, flush her out time and time again, and it is there you will find signs of the Kestral and destroy them. Our Lord Walther had his Sedgwick of Kold, his constant enemy; you shall have your Knife, your ready Knife."

"I will not do this," Stenstrom said.

"It is done, Lord Belmont. And, you will notice that we have not asked you—we are telling you. We have not labored this long to be denied. You are our Fist, square with it or not. Your flesh belongs to the League, as do we all."

"You cannot compel me to do something that I do not choose to do."

"Oh, can we not? We are dedicated to the preservation of the League, and in that task we are prepared to do what needs to be done, even if that includes sacrificing ourselves, Knife, and you in the process. Consider the scores of Sisters asleep in the tower outside—your flesh and blood. Consider Knife. She has given her life in this effort as well—look what she has sacrificed, no hearth, no home, no loving Lord at her side—she would have made you a fine wife. But, instead, she is alone and she is your Knife, and all out of love for the League. She is a hero, though none but you three will ever know that. She shall be a dark spirit, despised, her name reviled in the posts, forever your enemy. Where she goes, you will follow, else she will create chaos and shed blood, all on your hands should you choose not to follow and stop her."

Knife stepped forward. She pulled her mask off. Underneath, there was the face of a pretty young woman, blue-eyed, sandy haired. She looked at Stenstrom hard.

"I wanted you to see me," she said quietly. "You will never see my face again, nor hear me speak. My service to the League begins now, and there shall be no mercy—for neither you nor me."

She put her mask back on, turned and vanished.

"Sisters, this is barbaric," A-Ram said.

"I shall not participate in this," Stenstrom said.

The Sisters smiled. "Ah, how nice—suitably outraged and demure. You play your part well. Now, to your reward. And we do not simply offer a single reward—our rewards are ongoing. We can offer you most anything you desire."

"I told you, I want no part of this."

They ignored him. "Do you want this little girl here? We will give her to you if you wish, in place of your Lillian of Gamboa. You may do what you will with her—love her, cherish her, abuse her . . . kill her; it's your choice."

"Taara is my friend."

"Yes, indeed . . ." One of the Sisters waved her hand and, before Stenstrom, an image appeared in mid-air. In it, he could see Lt. Gwendolyn walking around on her bridge. She seemed concerned.

"How about this one," the Sisters asked. "Is she your friend too? She's looking for you, and she is frantic, though she'll not find you, not here. She's a firm, strapping girl—will provide you with many fine children."

"I've never even met Captain Gwendolyn in person."

"Well then, look . . ."

On the bridge of the *Demophalon John*, Stenstrom could see Gwendolyn and the crew busily moving about.

And there was Knife, red-robed and black-masked. Apparently Cloaked in some fashion, she walked up behind Gwendolyn unseen and raised her hands, clenching them into claws.

"It begins Paymaster," the Sisters said through Taara. "Knife is on the prowl."

"What is she doing?"

"She is doing her duty—she is forcing you to act, to follow her, just as Sedgwick of Kold forced the Mad Lord to follow him. No telling what she might do on that ship. Might find the Captain in pieces—might find them all in pieces, the ship that became a ghost ship, its crew mysteriously slaughtered. No telling how many people she will be willing to sacrifice to compel you to do your duty. Do you wish that on your soul, Lord Belmont, that you could have stopped her and did nothing?"

"She is moments from death, Lord Belmont," another Sister said through Taara.

Stenstrom stared at the image in horror. He saw Knife move her gloved fingers and a small cut appeared on Gwendolyn's right cheek. It began gushing blood—the Captain, apparently not aware she'd been cut, continued doing what she was doing. Somebody pointed at her and she reached up and touched her face, horrified.

Knife's hands went to Gwendolyn's throat.

Stenstrom couldn't take it anymore. "Sisters, you said I was to have a reward . . . then I wish Captain Gwendolyn as my reward. Safe and unharmed, along with her crew."

"And why, Paymaster? This woman, as you say, means nothing to you. And, if we are not mistaken, she threatened to physically assault you earlier."

"We got off to a rough start. It was my fault—I insulted her. She had a job to do, like it or not. Do not harm her, Sisters, I am warning you."

The Sisters eyes widened. Then they smiled. "Very well, be it so."

On the *Demophalon John's* bridge, Knife disappeared and Lt. Gwendolyn turned away her face bleeding, unaware of the death she had just avoided.

"A fine choice, sir," the Sisters said. "She will bear that cut upon her face as a scar for the rest of her life. Again, she is a fine, strong woman—your match in many ways. She is yours, now and forever."

Stenstrom shook his head. "I simply did not want Gwendolyn or her crew harmed."

"You love her, Lord Belmont," the Sisters said.

"I do not know Captain Gwendolyn. I love Lilly, though your sorcery has currently drained it from me," he replied.

"As we said, Lillian of Gamboa, as you know her, does not exist. Your fate is with Gwendolyn, Lady of Prentiss—Gwendolyn the Scarred. She will remove the mask and its protective hermelin from your face."

Stenstrom made to object, but Taara cut him off. "And you, Private Taara, what do you want?"

The Sisters released Taara and she staggered to the floor. Stenstrom knelt over her and took her hand. She wheezed for a moment. "Taara," he said. "Say nothing—you needn't be a part of this."

She spoke, this time with her own voice. "The lantern . . ."

"Out of the question!" the Sisters snapped in return. "The Paramel is a Noab artifact of terrible power, not for general use in the League. Pick something else."

"Then, I . . . want to keep doing what I've been doing. I like knowing things that I shouldn't know and doing things I shouldn't be able to do. I want to continue."

The Sisters took her back over. "Ah," she said. "Most practical. Look, you shall have your wish."

As Stenstrom watched, the MOLLY around her neck somehow began to melt into her flesh. After a moment, it was gone. "There, now you may continue as you have been."

"But, demons will come for her soul," A-Ram said.

"As we have established, Lord A-Ram—we are the demons. We take exception when mystical objects such as the MOLLY are used too much, and we punish the practitioner, sometimes with death. As Private Taara is in the service of our Fist, we will waive that punishment. As long as she serves our Fist, she need not fear."

A-Ram stepped forward. "Sisters," he said quietly. "You said I too was to have a reward?"

Taara, fully possessed by the Sisters, smiled and sauntered up to him. "Indeed we did, Lord A-Ram. You showed great spirit in assisting Lord Belmont—we've not seen that from you before. Therefore, you will have a reward—the first of many. What is it to be?"

A-Ram stood there. "I—I would like you to Stare me for the answer. I'll not say it out loud."

The Sisters, sitting on their couches, tittered. One of them leaned forward, eyes-wide and Stared him.

Stenstrom watched. The Sister's eyes were big and fixed on A-Ram. They were the eyes of a beast, a wild animal. He noticed A-Ram twitching under her Stare. He was in pain.

After a few more moments, the Sister leaned back and gave him an open-lipped smile. "Oh, really . . ." Taara said under her influence. She snorted. "You feel ignored? You feel slighted, do you? You showed us nothing, Lord A-Ram. You were a cowardly simpleton not worth our time, as was your whole family. Bad chefs, bad Brandtball players and you. Again, perhaps we misjudged you—underestimated you, just like Admiral Derlith and everybody else, seeing nothing but the frail little man with morbid hobbies. You hide your admirable qualities well, but they are there, nevertheless, and, on your tiny shoulders rest the soul of our Fist. Very well, Lord A-Ram, make your choice."

The light from the lantern panned away. The fair guise the Sisters had been wearing passed with it. There they were again strange, elongated, somewhat sinister.

A-Ram stood there a moment, and then he walked a step or two and took his place in front of the Sister who had just Stared him. Slowly, her wild-animal eyes fixed on his, she stood up. Sitting there on her couch it was hard to tell just how tall she was, but, as Stenstrom had suspected, she, standing erect, had to be at least eight feet tall.

Towering over A-Ram, she pulled off her headdress and tossed it aside. Cinder black hair came spilling out of her wrappings. She opened and closed her fists, her fingers moving in a spidery fashion. She appeared to want to eat A-Ram. To his credit, he stood there and didn't flinch.

Taara hovered next to A-Ram. "Oh, we are going to enjoy this, Lord A-Ram. You have made an interesting and exotic choice. Again, you have impressed us with your unexpected bravery today, and we shall make it worth your while. Again, this shall be but the first of many rewards you shall enjoy."

Taara leaned into him—fully possessed. She started speaking in the first person—Sisters rarely did that, and the things she said gave Stenstrom considerable pause. Her voice was laced with savagery.

"*I am going to take you places seldom seen! And I am not going to be gentle—I am going to burn you, A-Ram. Burn you!*" The Sister reached out and grabbed him by the nape of his shirt. She lifted him off the ground and pulled him close . . . and she licked him slowly, passionately.

Stenstrom, shocked, couldn't look any further, he turned away.

Taara spoke. "The meeting is over; you two may leave. Lord A-Ram shall be returned to you tomorrow."

As commanded, Stenstrom began walking away, not really of his own accord. Soon Taara, released from the Sisters, joined him. "Bel!" she piped, out of breath. "What is A-Ram doing? That Sister, she's not just a Sister, she's one of the Grand Abbesses I think . . . and she's going to . . ."

"He's a grown man, Taara, and the Sisters aren't going to hurt him. If that's what he wants, then let him experience it himself."

"But Bel . . ."

Taara stumbled and fell to the floor, her sideburns touching the stone. Stenstrom helped her stand. One more time, Taara seized up and was possessed by the Sisters. "You will follow Knife and you will look for signs of the Kestral, and where you find them, you will destroy them! Your first assignment is at hand! Do not fail!"

As they exited the building, they heard the Sister speak in her own voice. It was harsh, tinny, like the voice of a demonic child. "*Come along, A-Ram . . . I'm ready for you . . .*"

9

—Parting Gifts—

Like two scolded children, Stenstrom and Taara returned to the bridge without A-Ram. The place was a darkened, flickering mess. "Well," Taara said, "I guess I better start getting this place back in order. It was nice having the lantern while it lasted. I guess the Sisters don't want anything to be easy on this trip, do they?"

"I suppose not. Better get a fix on our position." He felt dizzy and seated himself in his chair.

Lilly . . .

Where was his heart?

Where was his love? He searched for it. Not there to be found, just a confused empty spot.

His feelings ripped from him by the Sisters.

Taara went into the office and picked up her sextant. She looked the horizon over, full of stars.

"Well, we're still over *Camalopardus*. The good news is we're really, really far from Druries Belt. You can't even see it with the naked eye from here. The bad news is we're also really, really far from Bazz too. We'll never make our brandy deadline now. We'd be lucky to get to Bazz in under a year."

She popped back out onto the bridge still holding her sextant. "I suppose we'll need to set sail and get moving. We'll run into League traffic eventually and perhaps we can get a lift home." She passed Stenstrom and went to the helm, mumbling to herself. *"A couple of pegs larboard and a + 250 Z and that should get us pointed at Corvus . . ."* Taara kicked at the foot levers and struggled with the pegs.

"Creation, where's A-Ram when I need him? Messing with the helm is more art than science. I think we should be good. I hope he comes back soon."

"Me too."

She suddenly dropped her sextant and doubled over. Stenstrom flew out of his chair and went to her. "Taara, what's wrong?"

"Sick, I feel sick. The Sisters do that to me every time."

"Sit down and rest."

She shook her head. "No, no . . . Let me get some systems going first, then we'll adjust our orientation and take off." Taara stumbled to the darkened Missive's Panel and began making her calculations. "We're going to have to start . . . from scratch."

Stenstrom picked up her sextant. "Did you notice how quiet it was out in the ship as we returned?"

Taara, though sick, continued her work. "What?" she asked.

"The ship. I recall no groans, no oppressive noises or feelings of dread and cold breezes. No half-heard screams. I suppose what they said is true—they were the demons haunting this vessel, and now that they've announced their intentions they've cleared the ship of their influence."

Taara finished her calculations. "Told you, the Sisters are way creepy. Get ready for a jolt, I'm firing the *Westminster's* mains."

Stenstrom returned to his chair and felt the tug of the *Westminster's* engines pushing the ship ahead.

"How long's this burn, Taara?"

"Five minutes. That'll get us off and running at least."

Taara slumped over, holding her stomach, her sideburns dangling.

"Still not feeling well?" he asked. "What's hurting, your stomach?"

"My stomach, my head, everything."

"Well, as soon as this burn's over with, turn in and get some sleep."

"But, the bridge . . ."

"We can worry about the bridge later. I want you to rest, agreed? I think I can whip up something to help make you feel better."

"Thanks, Bel."

He stood and went into his office and produced a red, blue and yellow Holystone. Conjuring up a MARZABLE dagger, he scored them open and sorted through the dried ingredients to calm Taara's system. Through the window, he could see the distant, bluish glow of the *Westminster's* engines as it burned.

As he mixed the selected ingredients together, he noticed something. A large leather bound book sat on the sill.

The ship shuddered and the *Westminster* went out, the burn complete. He threw the book onto his desk, scraped the ingredients into an emptied Holystone shell, shook it up, and took it out to Taara.

She looked miserable slumped in the chair. "Burn's done, Bel," she mumbled.

"Here, hold this, it should make you feel a little better."

She took it. "What is it?"

"Just a little something to quiet your system. Go on, stretch out and get some sleep. When's our next burn due?"

"Ten hours. You think A-Ram will be back soon?"

"He should be."

Taara's voice was groggy. "I want him back. You, me and A-Ram, we're family."

She pulled her coat and boots off and situated herself on the padded Missive's chair. He took off his HRN and draped it over her; the large coat was easily big enough to serve as a blanket over Taara's small body.

"So, I guess I don't need to worry about demons coming to get me anymore," she mumbled, her words slurred.

"I suppose not."

"I didn't mind. I liked you watching over me. Made me feel safe . . ."

Moments later, still holding the Holystone, Taara was out.

Stenstrom returned to his office and got the book. It was a book about monsters, summoned creatures and other fanciful beings. It was elaborate and hand painted. It looked like a book belonging to the Sisters. A navy blue, silk bookmark was placed a quarter of the way through the thick book. He turned to the bookmarked page.

It read:

NARGAL

Nargals are any of a number of summoned, invoked, or otherwise artificially created creatures made for purposes of servitude and/or task fulfillment. Depending on the materials used in their construction, Nargals can be extremely powerful.

If this was a book belonging to the Sisters, what was it doing here? Did they leave it for him to find to emphasize the point that Lilly was not a real woman, perhaps attempting to appeal to his sense of logic? As Stenstrom read on, he discovered that Nargals could be made of gold, silver, or bronze. They could be fibrous, made of wood, rock or gemstones. They could be elemental, of earth, fire, water or air. They could also be made of dead flesh, offal, bones, and ashes. He then came to an interesting sub-heading:

SAND NARGAL

Sand Nargals are generally of least construction and least potency compared with other, more advanced types of Nargals. They are comparatively easy to assemble with common materials. They have a rudimentary intelligence and can be programmed to perform simple tasks with great reliability. They, unlike most Nargals, have multiple forms, the first being a free-formed rotating column of sand indistinguishable from a cyclone or dust storm, and secondly, their desired programmed form which can be plant, animal or human. Such versatility makes them highly desirable as guards, spies, and warriors; however, there is a great danger regarding the prolonged use of Sand Nargals as they tend to dream that they are alive instead of being a mere construct. At such times they can become spiteful and rebellious of their masters. They are also easily taintable and turned from their original task or intent. (See: BLACK SAND).

So, there it was. Lilly was a semi-intelligent, conjured woman of sand, who possibly dreamed she was alive but was not.

"Don't ever let anyone tell you what I feel isn't real . . ." she once said.

Despite the Sisters' hermelin suppressing his feelings for Lilly, he felt sad and somewhat lost. He fetched some paper and a marker from his coat and scribbled down a few notes. He put the book away and went back out to the bridge. He sat down next to the sleeping Taara and leaned against the chair. Before long, Taara's little hand came sneaking out from under the HRN and made its way to his shoulder.

Something small and golden rested in her hand. "I took your locket, Bel. I lifted it. I thought you might want it later. So I lifted it . . ." Half asleep, she mumbled. "Circles, people draw circles."

"Pardon?" Stenstrom asked.

"The curse, as it closes, people start drawing circles with names in them . . . they don't even know they're doing it. Can't write nothin'. Means the curse is drawing to an end." She faded back into sleep.

There was Lilly's locket, a gift he'd kept with him for years. He opened it. Inside was Lilly's smiling face painted with meticulous skill. There were also three small shards of metal rattling within—the hermelins from his mask. Taara must have lifted them too. Comforted, he closed the locket and slept.

10

—THE LADY IN GRAY—

S trange dreams. Voices.

"I've escaped . . ."

He felt himself being shaken awake. "Bel?"

A-Ram was leaning over him. Stenstrom rubbed his eyes and awoke, his dreams quickly fading to oblivion. "A-Ram, you're back."

"I am, Bel," he said in a rather dreamy way. He walked up to the helm, and surveyed the area. He adjusted the foot levers a little. "You don't have this set correctly." He moved in a light, boneless sort of manner.

"Are you all right?"

"I'm excellent," he said calmly.

"You certain?"

"Yes." He checked his helm screens. "Everything's dead."

"The Sisters took the lantern back."

"Ah. Are we still in the middle of nowhere?"

"Yep, though we've set sail for Corvus. We'll be there sometime next year at this rate."

Stenstrom was burning for information. Taara awoke, stretched and yawned. "Hey, Buddy, you're back!" She quickly asked the questions Stenstrom was too shy to ask. "So, how was it?"

A-Ram stood there a moment, his hands on the helm's pegs, and then he smiled. "It was worth the wait. I've never experienced such a thing. Remarkable. I—I feel like a new man."

"She didn't . . . hurt you?"

"Of course she didn't hurt me—quite the opposite in fact."

"She said she was going to burn you!" Taara said.

"Burn me, in a metaphorical sort of way. I think it was rather enjoyable for the both of us."

"Weren't you nervous?" she asked.

"No . . . no. It's remarkable really—considering how long I've waited for Programmability." He held the helm and thought back. "You know I found my thoughts going back to that beautiful woman we saw here on the bridge."

"The Merian woman?" Stenstrom asked.

"That's the one. I recall she looked rather sad. I was wondering why she was so sad?"

Taara put on her Marine coat and bounced over to A-Ram's side. She pinched his cheek. "Because she probably misses her 'Rammy'. You did all this fancy thinking while you were muff-mashing and carpet-banging with the Sister?" Taara asked.

A-Ram blushed. "Well, yes, I had a few moments of amazing clarity, especially as we came close to . . ."

"To busting a nut," Taara added.

A-Ram, and, to a lesser extent, Stenstrom, was shocked. Such frank language. He spun the helm a turn or two and thought a moment. "I recall reflecting on quite a number of things as we came together—my thoughts gained certain clarity and unprecedented speed. I could even hear the Sister's thoughts. It was incredible."

He paused a moment. "I believe that Taara is correct," he stated.

"About what?"

"About us, about how we are linked together. Whether the linkage is due to a Bazz curse or not I don't know, but I saw how tightly we're inter-woven—*how we have influenced each other's lives long prior to what we thought was our first encounter a few days ago.* It's all so clear. The closed Vendetta Circle that you mentioned, Taara, it really does appear to exist."

"See, I told you so," Taara said with a bit of triumph.

"I also believe I know who the common person that links us together is."

Stenstrom was curious. "That's remarkable. All right, so what did you discover on your introspective journey with the Sister?"

He began. "We are three separate people, four if you count Lt. Gwendolyn, all disjointed in not only geography, but in class and age as well. Bel is from a Tyrol Great House, Lt. Gwendolyn from a Zenon. I am a Calvert from a House Minor and Taara is a commoner from Bazz. We have minimal ties, no previous meetings, no familial connections, no nothing. But, search your thoughts, and be honest with yourself, I'm going to ask an odd question and just respond with the first thing that pops into your head."

"All right," Taara said. "Hit us with it."

"Who do you fear most?"

Stenstrom and Taara exchanged glances. "Pardon?" Stenstrom asked.

"Who do you fear most of all?"

He was stumped. "I don't think I really know. I can't pinpoint anything, and . . ."

"How about a woman dressed in gray?" A-Ram said jumping in. "How about that?"

Stenstrom thought a moment. "I . . . um, had a nightmare once about a lady dressed in gray who came to kill me. I was just a boy, and, looking back on it, I'm certain she was simply a manifestation of my fears. I've actually seen her many times throughout my life, usually during times of great stress or uncertainty. She's just in my head."

"And you, Taara?" A-Ram asked turning to her.

"I'm afraid of fire."

"Why?"

"Because my uncle's pharmacy burned down with him in it. I haven't liked fire much since then."

"Could it be that the fire you mention was most likely set by a foreign woman dressed in gray about thirty years ago?"

The three sat there silent.

"How do you know that?" she finally asked.

"I'll explain. I'm certain you all know I am most afraid of the Fiend of Calvert, that mad man who terrorized us in St. Edmund's years ago. He was like a ghost, prowling the alleys and wharves, leaving dead men behind. My brother used to try to make me believe he was the Fiend and that he was going to kill me. I spent a lot of terrified nights hiding under my covers, and then there was the evening I actually heard the sound of the Fiend's footsteps as he fled from the Mad Lord of Walther across our rooftop . . . bump, bump, bump. Bel, remember discussing the Fiend with me when we first boarded the ship? You said that a colleague of yours suspected that the Fiend was a woman dressed in gray, contrary to the popular opinion of a man in a gas mask? I recall I scoffed at the notion."

"Yes. A friend of mine, Grand Dame Miranda of Rossel, believes that to be the case, and she also believes that the woman I encountered as a boy, the one who tried to kill me, was herself the Fiend of Calvert. But, that cannot be, as I said she is . . ."

"Your colleague was correct. I was wrong. The Fiend of Calvert was a woman who dressed in gray. My encounter with the Sister has allowed me to remember everything for as long as I have served Admiral Derlith—every meeting, every idle word that was exchanged that I was there to hear as I served him coffee and buttered his bread. Years of disconnected comments and unexamined detail all came together, and from that, a new and somewhat sinister picture emerges. Much of what I previously assumed to be true, is not true after all. I now understand that Admiral Derlith's older sister, Lady Vendra of Cone, has had a long and varied life. I never gave her much thought; she's such a frail, unassuming person, and she visits the Admiral often. Her health is quite fragile. I have served her coffee and tea four-hundred and fifty-seven times in the Admiral's office."

"That's a lot of cream and sugar," Taara remarked.

Stenstrom interrupted. "Admiral Derlith's sister? Does she wear gray all the time?"

"Yes and no—I thought she always wore the colorful gowns of Cone—very vibrant colors of red, blue and yellow, and she usually wore a shawl to keep her warm—her health always an issue."

"Sounds like a parrot," Taara remarked.

"Yes, the colors are rather like a parrot," A-Ram agreed. "She never married, and that is because she gave her heart to a man who was stolen from her. That man was your father, Bel, and the stealer was your mother—and that's what started everything. That's what made her so angry. Maybe that's what prompted her to start killing all those men in Calvert, for revenge. Lady Vendra of Cone is the Fiend of Calvert."

"Where did you get that idea from?"

"From her own lips and from the Admiral's. Oh, not at once. I heard it in bits and fragments over a long period of time, whispered comments and the ends of sentences that I walked in on and didn't piece together."

"You said she gets herself up in parrot colors," Taara said. "Where's the gray?"

"That is what she wants you to think she's wearing. However, she actually wears nothing but gray; a hat, a conservative Remnath dress, and button-up boots. That's all she ever wears."

Stenstrom shrugged. "Ok, A-Ram, let's hear your logic."

"She appears to be adept at disguise, whether by Cloak or some other means, I don't know. I don't think she's using a Cloak—it has to be something else. She appears to have some sort of mastery over the senses—the sense of smell being particularly potent. I recall her leaning over my desk discussing, of all things, the Fiend of Calvert one day. I remember seeing her reflection in the Admiral's tea service that I had to keep so brightly polished, and her reflection was all in gray, though to my eyes she appeared to be wearing a bright Cone gown."

Stenstrom threw his hands up. "All right, A-Ram, let's say for the sake of argument that Lady Vendra of Cone is a woman who dresses in gray. You say all of this started because she thinks my mother stole my father away from her? That would have been, let's see, almost a hundred years ago. I would think she would have gotten over it at some point."

"The Cones are stubborn people. The Admiral is in love with a girl he met in passing during his young manhood and never forgot. Once they give their hearts, they do not take them back easily. I don't know the gross details, and, of course, all I know of the matter is from her perspective—she feels your mother willfully stole your father after she had declared her love for him."

"Oh, that's rotten," Taara said. "Matters of the heart are prime for kicking off a real sour Vendetta Circle, ask my aunt."

A-Ram continued. "Apparently so—she never allowed herself to forget the matter. She then declared Wirguild against your mother."

"She's the one who Wirguilded my mother?"

"She is."

"What's a Wirguild?" Taara asked.

"It's a formal declaration of revenge. If you have it in for somebody, you can go to the Sisters and declare your desire for revenge. If granted, then anything that person does to the other is perfectly legal."

"Gods," Taara exclaimed. "You Kanans make a big deal out of everything."

A-Ram continued. "Moving on, events then become fuzzy for a short time. The next significant thing that happened was that Lady Vendra received a short apologetic letter from your father, trying to make amends to some extent. The letter didn't work, and she tried to kill herself. She survived the incident and was declared insane by the Hospitalers and shipped off to a distant convent to prevent her diminished condition from scandalizing the family. Several years later, she returned from the convent apparently fully recovered—that was when she started wearing gray, and has worn that color ever since, though, again, she disguises that fact."

"What convent did she go to?" Stenstrom asked.

"I don't know—it was never spoken of; again, her madness was a family secret and hidden shame. Clearly though, the convent is the key—whatever happened to her there has influenced everything since. The Admiral recalls through quiet conversations and mournful correspondence that she returned from the convent a very different person—that the loving sister he remembered was gone, replaced by an outwardly smiling woman, but who inwardly was bizarre and remorseless and seething with rage. He recalls she often vanished, for days at a time without telling anyone where she went. He also remarked upon the strange assortment of gentleman callers she often had—dirty, unshaven, and seemingly in a trance of some sort. That was right around the time when the Fiend of Calvert was holding sway in the south."

"Are we assuming that she was somehow controlling these men?"

"We are."

"How?" Stenstrom asked.

"The Admiral never made a definite connection as to how she was doing it, but he was certain she was. He made a curious note, one that I think is significant. He once found a mysterious box in her room. He looked into the box and found a number of vials full of unusual chemicals. There was also some sort of device in the box, one with a long stinger or barb attached to it. The general shape of the device reminded the Admiral of an internal, female contraceptive appliance."

"With a stinger on it?" Taara said, shocked.

"Yes, and with that discovery, he became very afraid of his sister and left home to get some space from her, joining the Fleet and eventually becoming an Admiral. His sister often visited him in his office at Fleet—I saw her there many times. I had always thought they were simply close, brother and sister; however, I now see that she was constantly chiding the Admiral, pushing him to do this and that, and her visits weren't something he enjoyed. The Admiral believed that his sister somehow had a method of controlling men, of turning them into zombie-like slaves, and that he thought she was trying to control him as well, but was having a measure of mercy on him as he's her kin. They also had a long disagreement regarding the Admiral's niece . . . Lady Gwendolyn."

"Gwen? This Vendra of Cone, the Fiend of Calvert, is Gwen's aunt?" Stenstrom asked.

"Yes indeed. See how things are coming together, but I've only just started. The Admiral believed Lady Vendra was attempting to corrupt Lady Gwendolyn, to make her like herself, into an angry, hateful woman, and he was determined for that not to happen, as he loves his niece very much. He got her into contact sports, such as wrestling and boxing and managed to channel her aggression in a positive fashion. There's also Lady Vendra's involvement with your lady, Lilly."

"Lilly? How so?"

"The Admiral once sent me on a strange set of errands. These errands sent me all over the countryside, the purpose of which was unknown to me at the time. I am now convinced those errands were specifically to gather the materials necessary to attack Lilly, to taint her, to turn her into one of her slaves."

"Go on."

"The Admiral had me collect five parcels and deliver them to an undisclosed location in the city of Dee. I remember feeling all day long that I was being followed, that I was seeing glimpses of a figure in gray following me. Then, that evening after I'd completed my task and returned to Fleet HQ, the figure in gray came upon me and pulled me into a bathroom. I think she was going to kill me right there and then. In the bathroom was a Marine girl sitting on the veranda drinking from a bottle. The figure in gray was startled and I managed to escape. Taara, that Marine girl was you—I recall seeing your sideburns and thought at the time that you had a dirty face. You saved my life."

Taara thought back. "Oh yeah! Right! I remember that! I was having a nip of home brew when a crazy woman in gray smelling of bunny scent came in. I recognized her and got scared. I thought she was there for me I tore out of there fast."

"You recognized her?" Stenstrom asked.

"Yeah, she was dating my uncle . . ." Taara's eyes grew distant and she went pale. "The same one who got burned up in the fire."

"Yes," A-Ram said. "See how this Lady in Gray touched us all? Taara saved my life, and as I continue to give tongue to my thoughts, we shall see that Taara not only saved me from the Lady in Gray, she saved you too, Bel."

"Me?"

"To continue, Lady Vendra suffered a few setbacks about thirty years ago. There was a sensational story that hit the wires about a city of the dead under the old ruins of Woodward in Remnath—a place populated by zombies. The Mad Lord of Walther, who was being paid by Lord Catherbaum of St. Edmunds to investigate the Fiend, uncovered it, and, shortly thereafter, defeated the Fiend of Calvert. I think, the Mad Lord uncovered Lady Vendra's hidden place where she kept her men, within easy telepathic reach of her home in Jacarta, discovered the Calvert connection, and engaged her. Beaten and pursued by the Mad Lord across Calvert, she left Kana for a time, heading for Bazz of all places, giving herself an opportunity to recover and lay low. I'll mention she used a Fleet transport ship to return from Bazz to avoid the usual customs and the logging of her passage. The ship she took was none other than our very own *Westminster*. I booked her passage myself at the request of the Admiral. But, that's a side-oddity. To continue, to a stuffy, upright Kanan woman, Bazz no doubt seemed like a wooly, uncivilized place to hide in plain sight. I'm certain that's where the Vendetta Circle began, when she went to Bazz, and that's where you fall in, Taara."

Taara swallowed and listened.

"You've mentioned that you're a kid fairly often; however, I'm going to wager that you are much older than both Bel and me. I'm forty-three. How old are you, Bel?"

"I'm only twenty-seven."

"And you, Taara?"

She blushed a little. "Ok, I'm sixty-eight. So, I'm, the granny of the group here; what difference does it make? You guys better not tell anybody."

"Nobody here is old, Taara. I'm just making the point that you were around when Lady Vendra was hiding out on Bazz. From what I gather, while she laid low on Bazz, she attempted to lure your father to her, Bel, and snare him."

"How so?"

"I'll get to that. Taara, you mentioned seeing a lady in gray about your uncle's pharmacy, correct?"

"She was sleeping with my uncle, throwing money around, and renting those crazy guys who make air for a living."

"Atmospherics, you mean," Stenstrom added.

"Yeah, whatever. She bought one of those guys to keep her cool like most well-heeled Kanans do when they visit Bazz. I remember she used to sit at a cafe near his shop basking in the cool air. The Ganaadas used to pester her all the time because they thought she had money, and then my uncle's shop burned down and she vanished. We didn't see her again. My family figured since I was there that day the shop burned, I must have had done something, so I got sent to youth camp on the Endax, digging for nasty clams in the stinking mud."

"Think back. What exactly happened?"

Taara rolled her eyes back and thought, "What happened? Things didn't start off well. I got into a big fight with this crazy Ganaada. You're not supposed to fight Ganaadas because they'll put a curse on you, but she drew my uncle's name in a circle and was waving it around. The next thing you know we were rolling around all over the place. She just about pulled my shirt off, and I lost my shoes; it was a big mess. It was one of those fights where everybody's watching and hollering and betting Cred Sticks—sort of embarrassing, you know."

"So, who won?" Stenstrom asked.

"I'd say I did, and she'd probably say she did. I busted her lip and scratched the hell out of her, and she blackened my eye and tore my clothes to shreds. So, the next day, there I was wearing rags. I needed some Creds to buy some new clothes, so I decided to steal the Lady in Gray's bag. I was a thief back then well, I'm still a thief, sort of. I saw her sitting there at the cafe, this time without her Atmospheric and she was sweating it out. I thought she might be easy pickings, Kanan ladies never have a clue what's going on, so I gave it a go. She caught me, though, and bent my arm back. I thought she might have broken it or something. It really hurt, and so I was trying to get at some Lytol from my uncle's shop to ease the pain. My uncle caught me and we struggled, making a fairly big mess of spilled bottles and such. Once everything calmed down, he made me spend all morning helping him clean the place up. I didn't know what went where, so I just started putting things wherever."

"See, I think that's the key," A-Ram said. "I'm fairly well certain Lady

Vendra sent your father an unsigned note informing him of the legendary God Sperm potion Taara's uncle sold in his store. The potion is supposed to ensure the birth of an exceptional boy, right?"

"Yeah," Taara said. "It's a swirling gold color and it smells like sweat."

"She knew of his lack of an heir and played upon his fears of losing everything to the Lords of the City. So, she lured him to Bazz with a carefully crafted note. Her intention was to slip him a Bazz Love Potion, also sold in Taara's uncle's shop, and enslave him to her. On a side note, she also mentioned that, when she saw your father in the square, she decided to take him right there and then using whatever means she had available to her. Taara's little wrestling match with the Ganaada sorceress thwarted her attempt to get to him, so, she waited until the next day to slip him the Love Potion. Taara, I think your messing around with the bottles that day played a critically important role in what was to come—perhaps Bel's father, Lord Stenstrom the Older, didn't get the bottle Lady Vendra intended he get, the Love Potion. Perhaps the bottles got mixed together somehow, or perhaps he got something else entirely—we shall never know. In any event, you Taara—in fighting the Ganaada, in creating chaos in the pharmacy—are wholly responsible for Bel's existence as is and his status as an artificially created It Man; so, that's your connection."

Taara thought back a moment. "I did have his stuff all scattered around. You really think I helped bring Bel into existence?"

"I do."

She pondered it a little more and then looked a little teary-eyed. "Then, I guess I did something right as a kid after all." She gave Stenstrom a friendly pop on the shoulder.

A-Ram continued. "So, that's it. Also, Bel, as a side note, I caught a few glimpses into the Sister's mind as we came together. I saw some things. I'm pretty sure the Sisters let Lady Vendra try to kill you as a lad to see if you actually had the It Man capabilities. They knew she was exceeding the limitations of her Wirguild. They knew she was coming at you, Bel, as a baby. The Sisters can be remarkably analytical, and instead of revoking her Wirguild, they allowed her to proceed. They watched her men place a rather horrid-looking steel trap in the sand pit behind your manor where you and your sisters played and cover it up."

Stenstrom twitched.

Snap . . .

"That was just a dream," Stenstrom said, shuddering. "That's my old dream I have from time to time."

"It wasn't a dream. It happened. The Sisters were watching and saw you spring that trap and survive unharmed; then, they knew for certain."

Stenstrom felt the walls closing in on him. "Well then, here we are in a place where our deepest nightmares are actually real and the truths we've clung to are nothing but dreams."

"Are you referring to Lilly?" A-Ram asked.

"Of course. Of all the women in my life, other than my mother and my sisters, she was the most real, the most grounded. And now, look . . ."

Lilly, a fallen piece of enchanted sand.

"Well, I guess I'm a little creeped out, but this is actually great news," Taara said. "Now we know who we need to hunt down and kill—the Lady in Gray, and it's not like she doesn't deserve it."

Stenstrom sat there in his chair and pondered the notion. The Lady in Gray, the person he'd feared since childhood and had rationalized away as a mere phantom, was real.

She came at him in Fox Park, ready to kill . . .

He remembered the knife she carried. "I'm sorry," she had said as she raised it up.

She tried to abduct him at the reunion dinner years later in Rustam . . .

The Mad Lord had recognized him as a fellow "It" Man.

She came at him at the University of Bern . . .

A cyclone had burst through the clouds and distracted her. A Cyclone? Lilly in her true Sand Nargal form, protecting him as she claimed she did?

The Lady in Gray deserved to die, Taara had said.

His mother had stolen his father away from her years ago. A broken heart turned to murderous rage.

He wondered what he would do now should he come face-to-face with her.

He wondered . . .

"I'm sorry for your Lady," A-Ram said. "I had hoped to meet her."

"She's a Nargal, a Sand Nargal to be specific, some sort of conjured creature," Stenstrom said. "The Sisters left us a nice book on the subject."

"And, are you all right, Bel? Are you in pain for your Lady?"

Pain? After all he'd discovered, shouldn't he be in pain?

"No. The Sisters took it from me. I feel nothing. Remarkable, isn't it, how they can empty one's heart when they see fit?"

"I'm truly sorry, Bel. What they did to you is unthinkable, and even in making amends I'm horrified for you. To strip a man of his feelings, I think I'd rather be heartbroken."

Stenstrom remembered the stabbing anguish, the heart-stopping total loss. Now, he was just hollow and devoid of emotion.

The woman of sand standing before him.

"No, A-Ram, no you don't."

Taara tried to lighten the subject. "Hey, Bel, you still got me. I love ya'!" She threw her arms around him and gave him a big kiss on the cheek.

"Thanks, Taara."

"That book the Sisters gave you," A-Ram asked. "May I see it, please? I'm curious."

Stenstrom got out of his chair and fetched the book from his office. He brought it out to A-Ram. He took it and opened to the bookmark, admiring the detail and craftsmanship of it.

"Taara," Stenstrom called out. "What are those four bright stars to our starboard?"

She immediately answered: "Alcalla, Ecar, Savel and Penta, all big ole' magnitude 1 stars making up the constellation *Camalopardus*. *Camalopardus* is the brightest constellation as seen from Kana and is visible throughout the League. Xaphan space too. It's the Sisters' Constellation."

"Thanks."

A-Ram got out the paper with notes he'd written. "Hey, Bel, what's this?"

"What?"

"This paper?"

"Just some notes I made."

A-Ram showed it to him: hard scrawl, circles mashed in blunt violent strokes from a demented hand, unreadable names within it. Stenstrom didn't recall doing any of that. Taara saw it and gasped. "I knew it! This is it!"

As if by design, a blinding light flooded the bridge, and there before them was the lantern once again, star-like in its brightness and floating like an angel, this time guided by the Sisters' hand.

The lantern went to super nova in intensity. They covered their eyes and a voice filled their heads

"*Lo to thee, It Man, Lone Rider . . . It is not for you to walk the pathways of others. Your road is the road to perilhood, to damnation. We shall return you to where you are needed, and, ever after, you shall follow Knife wherever she goes.*

"*Find the Kestrals and Destroy the Kestrals and remember our light.*"

The lantern increased in intensity until it became overwhelming.

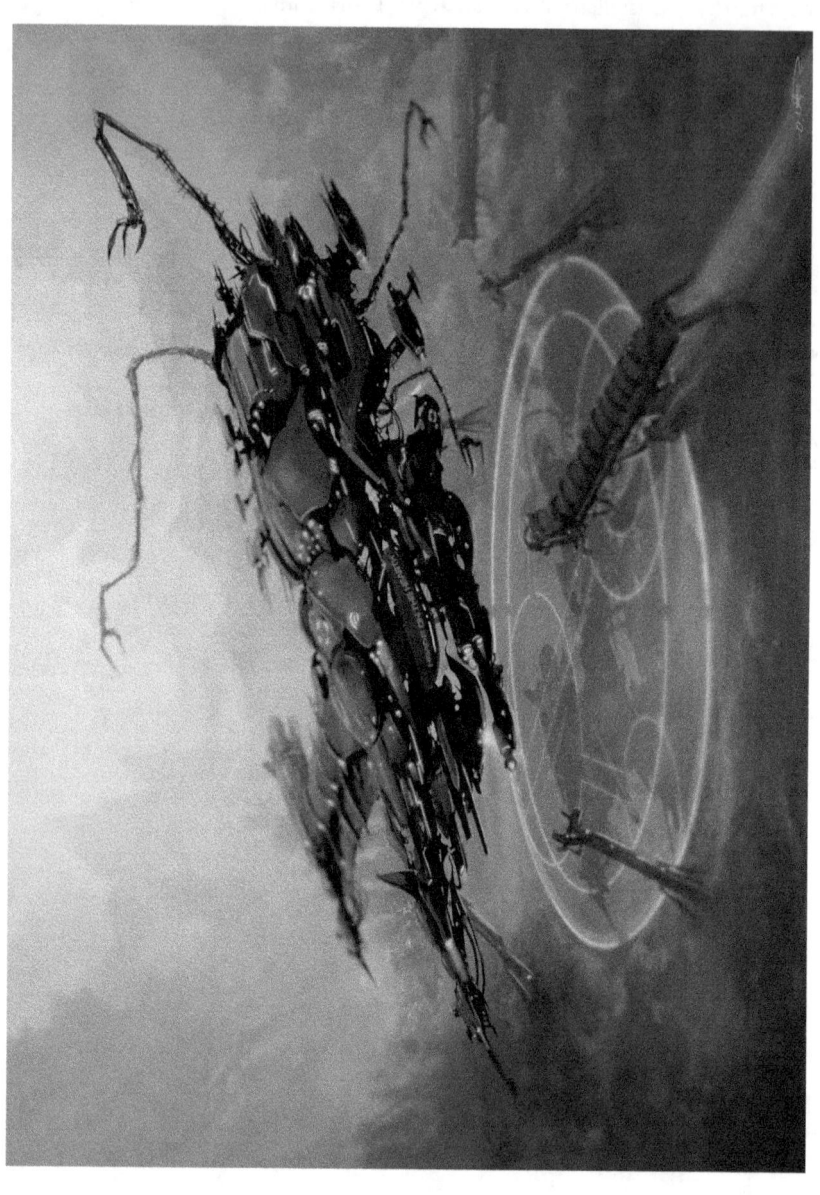

11

—The *Heade-on-the-Hearth*—

W hen the light subsided, the lantern had gone. They rubbed their eyes. "Hey!" Taara said. "I've got a little power on the panel here—must have bled some energy from the lantern. Probably won't last." She manipulated screens.

Through the windows in Stenstrom's office, he could see more familiar stars laid out around them, along with the shimmering yellow band of Druries Belt. "Looks like we're back where we started from," he said. "The Sisters are always full of surprises, aren't they?"

Taara stared at the panel. "Bel, A-Ram . . ." she said. "Remember what Lilly said in her notes, about making sure to avoid the leeward side of Druries Belt? Well, guess where we are? Guess where the Sisters put us!!"

Stenstrom stared at the stars, and at Druries Belt in particular, in horror. Before their encounter with the Sisters, the Belt had been roughly to the left of the ship, following the safe path Lilly had laid out for them. Now, it was far to their right. The Sisters had dropped them right in the very place Lilly said they needed to avoid.

Your road leads to perilhood, they said. Scrawled circles on the page. Taara's curse drawing closed.

"A-Ram, hard a-starboard! Taara, get us out of here, best possible speed!" A-Ram tugged on the wheel and the ship pitched around until Druries Belt was dead ahead.

"A-Ram, wait!" she cried. "I need to plot a vector and set our course, otherwise, we'll head off in the wrong bloody direction and we'll never get to Bazz."

"Hurry, Taara!"

She slammed the panel, moving screens around. "Hang on, hang on . . . Give me a minute!" She stood up. "I need my sextant! I'm not ready to die just yet!"

A light went off on the panel. She stared at it wide-eyed.

"What's that?" Stenstrom asked. "What's blinking?"

"Contact ..." she replied, somewhat breathless.

"What is it?" Stenstrom asked.

"Unknown, but it's coming in, and fast."

"Could it be Captain Gwendolyn?"

"I'm not reading her flag. The Contact isn't reading as anything, we're just seeing its motion. 5:00AM and climbing. We should be able to visually see it through your office windows."

"Hold Fast, A-Ram, and keep it at station should it try and get too friendly."

"Aye, Bel."

"Keep our thruster ticks to a minimum. Perhaps they won't notice us."

Stenstrom and Taara exited the bridge and entered his office. "Which way?" he asked.

"That way" Taara said pointing down past the wing to the right."

Through the windows Stenstrom saw a distant patch of black moving in, blotting out the stars. Lilly's warning rang through his head.

'Ware Druries Belt.

The patch of black came in, getting bigger and bigger.

Distant spotlights came on and honed-in on the ship.

"They got us made. They're scanning us," Taara said.

As they watched, the unknown vessel came in. They saw the latticed, partial hulk of an old *Webber* ship coming in fast and lit up in running lights, its superstructure loaded-out with capsules and decrepit add-ons.

"A *Webber?*" Taara snorted. "I got my knickers all up in a bind over a stupid *Webber* ship? What's an old beater like that still doing flying?"

It approached swiftly and then slowed, a node of strong spotlights eyeballing the *Seeker*. It moved in a deliberate fashion across the length of the *Seeker's* neck, the spotlights making round, lit-up circles on the hull, caressing it in light. It looked hodge-podge and pieced together in comparison to the sleek *Seeker*, rather like a hermit crab under a tin-can shell.

Stenstrom knew about the venerable *Webber*-class ships from his father. The venerable *Amazing* was a *Webber*. Once, they made up the bulk of the Fleet and were associated in a romantic light with the Golden Age of the League/Xaphan conflict, as the Xaphans matched up much better against the *Webbers* than they did against the *Straylights* and *Triumphs* that came later on.

This *Webber* was missing much of its starboard side, its classic "H" silhouette looking more like a toppled-over T. Its starboard engine was gone, it was bolstered with a series of smaller, capsule-shaped rockets that were strapped on with welded metal bands. It seemed to have a number of odd accessories attached to various quarters along its length. The whole ship had a vacant, rather decrepit feel to it.

"Who is that out there?" A-Ram asked.

"Dunno," Taara said. "Pirates, Raiders? It's got to be pirates, rocking an old beater like this one."

"In the middle of League space?"

The *Webber* spun around and focused its attention on the frontal section of the ship, the roving spot-lights greedily panning about, casting the silhouette of the *Seeker* in a passing whitish glow. It reached the forward main hatch just aft of the *Seeker's* frontal section. A flexible, tubular docking assembly snaked out of the ventral of the *Webber* and made its way to the *Seeker's* main docking ring. It moved in a sinuous fashion—it reminded Stenstrom of the sex organ of a male bird.

"What is that?" Taara asked. "Doesn't look like a standard piece of equipment a *Webber* would mount."

"She's trying to dock, A-Ram. Move us away."

He turned the wheel. As A-Ram rolled the *Seeker* away, several flexible arms, like the vast tentacles of a cuttlefish, shot out of the *Webber's* forward sections and wrapped around the neck section of the ship, holding it fast. The whole mass of the *Webber* seemed flexible and articulated in an advanced way; it was balling up and unballing, like the movements of a pillbug in a manner well beyond that of any ordinary *Webber*, which was a notoriously rigid class of ship.

Clinging fast, the odd ship latched on with a clank that they could hear all the way in the bridge, and its advanced docking assembly coupled with the *Seeker's*.

Taara stared at it through the window. "Look, the name plate reads . . . *Heade-on-the-Hearth*. That particular ship was listed as lost at sea decades ago," she said.

"We better get down there!" Stenstrom said heading to the lift. "Taara, can you route a little power from the bridge to that section of the ship. I want lights."

Taara stopped at the Missive's Panel and pressed a few buttons. "Ok," she said as the lighting in the bridge dimmed a little.

"Come on, A-Ram, let's go. We need all hands down below."

"Me?" he squeaked.

"Yes, you, let's go!"

They climbed down to Deck 4, which was dimly lit in unsteady light from the bridge, and made their way to the docking ring. They arrived and waited. Taara drew her SK and cocked it.

They waited a few minutes more. The docking ring clanked, and they could hear droll male voices chattering on the other side of the hatch.

'Ware Druries Belt, Lilly had warned.

Stenstrom wondered what sort of monstrosity awaited on the other side of the hatch.

Through the slim windows, hints of movement flickered by.

Finally, the docking hatch swung open.

Four men came in. They were smallish and skinny, though, in a side-by-side comparison, they were a bit bigger than the very small A-Ram. They wore a mish-mash of faded and out-of-fashion clothing, rather in the old Fleet style: washed out coats with dirty frills, seedy shirts that were clearly once white but now an unidentifiable gray, filthy knee britches with tarnished brass buttons, and worn black shoes. Their hair was straw-like and unkempt. They also smelled—not like body odor or dirt, but like innards, raw and stinking.

They appeared to be rootless scalawags in dire need of a shower and a nourishing meal, nothing more. He breathed a sigh of relief.

"Halt and identify yourselves!" Stenstrom said in a commanding tone, trying to sound authoritative. Taara hefted her SK and made sure they could see its gigantic barrel pointing at them.

Stenstrom found himself struggling a bit—he wasn't sure how to handle a situation like this—to be boarded in the Deep Sea. He recalled his father once mentioning that to board a vessel at sea without due sounding and invitation was the most provocative act one could commit, short of opening fire. His father said something about "should he ever be boarded" he would have to respond with deadly force.

Should he ever be boarded... That implied that, in his long career sailing the heavens, his father had never been boarded to that point.

And now here he was, on his maiden flight, and he was boarded. And he was warned as well.

And, of course, Stenstrom had no security detail, no Sisters, no Marines, no ship hands to hoist weapons and back him up, not to mention the fact that he had no able-bodied ship, no ship guns and no engines—he couldn't even tuck tail and run should it come to that. It was just he, Taara, and A-Ram, and there were four boarders, so he was down a man.

The boarders were surprised, standing there big-eyed and open mouthed.

"Great tap-dancin' gods!" the first man said in a gruff accent.

"Indeed," Stenstrom replied. "You know of course that boarding a flagged Stellar Fleet vessel is a capital offense. I am well within my rights to put the lot of you to the sword here and now, gentlemen."

The second man raised his knobby hands. "Hold up there, Gov—this didn't look to us to be no flagged Fleet vessel. We didn't detect no flag flyin'. We thought she was a derelict, adrift and towed out."

"Yeah, performin' a safety service we was," the third man said. "She's out the shipping lanes; this here's the backwater mate, the open country."

The fourth man saddled out of the dark. The smallest of the bunch, he had a shifty look, his goggle-eyes panning about, seeing everything. He wore a modest merchant's hat on top of his nest of messy hair. "Oh, *merde!* Who, pray, are you?" he asked.

"I am Paymaster Stenstrom, Lord of Belmont-South Tyrol, captain of the Main Fleet Vessel, *Seeker.* To my right here is Lord A-Ram, ship's Master Helmsman, and to my left is Private Taara de la Anderson of the 110th Stellar Marines, my first officer."

The fourth man looked about and then carefully studied Stenstrom. He had a groping, invasive sort of stare. *"¿Y qué tenemos nosotros aquí?* You have a Fleet adjutant for a Master Helmsman, and a Marine private as first officer? A novel bit of selection there, a-heheh. And you sir, that is not a standard uniform you are wearing, is it? What is your rank, Lord Belmont, pray tell?"

"You'll pardon us if we ask the questions for the time being," Taara said, jumping in giving her SK a shake.

The smallest man turned to her. *"Ah, ce qu'une petite fille délicieuse . . ."*

"What?" Taara replied.

The man chuckled. "Your pardon, I have a love of irrelevant and obsolete languages of old. A hobby of mine, a-heheh. I merely said what a handsome young lady stands before us." He waved his arms in an inviting manner. "Please, allow me to introduce myself. I am Chance Venable, and these are my brothers, Clem Venable, Innocent Venable, and Lemmuel Venable. We are simple traders scraping by as best we can."

"Yeah?" Taara said. "What do you trade in?"

"None o' yer business!" Lemmuel snapped.

Chance quieted him with a wave of his hand. "*Замолчите, сейчас же!*" he said to him. "Pardon my uncouth brother, Private. Out here in the wilds we have seldom occasion to practice our good manners. We trade in sundries— barley, tobacco, spirits when we can, fine finished goods, and scrap metal when we happen upon it. You must pardon our attention. Surely an apparently abandoned ship such as this would be a rare find for the likes of us—*un cadeau rare*. We beg your leave."

Stenstrom thought it over. He remembered Lilly's warning, however these four didn't seem to be any great threat, and, what they said made a bit of sense, they might have indeed thought the *Seeker* to be an abandoned hulk and were hoping to cash in on their good fortune. He couldn't fault them for that. "Well, I'm not one to hold a grudge. We shall overlook this matter. However, do not try my patience any further. You are free to go."

Clem looked around. "Where's yer' security detail, Gov?"

"En route, sir," he responded. "Now, I suggest you turn around and walk out the way you came. I'll not ask again. My first officer has an eager trigger finger and a full fifty caliber mag."

"Yeah?" Clem said, puffing himself up a bit to match Stenstrom's size.

Chance Venable laughed. "A-heheh. Now, now. We have a unique situation here, Lord Belmont. Please attend from our perspective: you fly no flag, you have no apparent crew besides that what stands before us, and no motive power—we scanned you quite thoroughly. There is also no bonded captain of this ship at present as the MFV *Seeker's* current status at Fleet is determined to be: half-scuttled. Given all that, by Fleet rule, this ship is deemed rudderless and we have every right to board her as fair salvage. Additionally, are you, by chance, the same Paymaster Stenstrom of Belmont-South Tyrol who currently has twenty-two minor and four major queries posted for your detainment at Fleet headquarters, hmmm?"

Clem stepped forward. "Sounds like we got us a hardened criminal on our hands, a real scalawag."

Innocent balled his fist and clapped it in his open palm. "Looks clear we'd be doin' the League a favor bringing you in fer' justice. Mebbe' there's a reward."

Lemmuel grinned in anticipation. "An', it looks to me like all the crew you got backin' you up is that twerp standin' over there and this little girl holdin' the big gun."

"This little girl could kick your ass up and down the corridor," Taara replied.

"Ah . . . well then, let's go, Babe!"

Stenstrom drew his NTHs. "Enough! Now, you lot need to turn around and march back to your *Webber* out there, and I'll forget this matter ever happened. If you choose to tarry a moment longer, I shall tan your hides in lead right here and now."

The brothers looked at each other and slowly raised their hands. "*Hay que aguita...* Dear me, looks like you have the drop on us, a-heheh," Chance said. "We wish no troubles here, Paymaster. Come on, boys, let us retire. We are clearly overmatched by this galactic scalawag and his fearsome crew."

They slowly began moving back toward the hatch. Stenstrom moved into an advantageous position where he was close enough to cover the Venables, yet remain far enough away that they couldn't rush him and hope to be successful. Taara skirted to his right, SK at the ready.

"Oh," Chance said stopping and turning around, "Paymaster, before I depart I must know. That coat you wear, are you always in the habit of wearing a garment once used by the Hoban Royal Navy—a Grand Plantain's coat if I'm not mistaken, and a mask to boot? You are quite the cad."

"It's my good luck charm."

Chance tittered. "I see . . ." he said in a sinister voice. "How quaint."

Things unfolded quickly. In a sudden movement, Chance Venable reached out and snatched both NTHs from Stenstrom's grasp. It was a lightning strike, faster than any person should be able to move; it happened so fast Stenstrom didn't really know what to think. *How did he reach him in the first place? There was no possible way!!* It seemed for a split second that Chance Venable's arms expanded to two or three times their normal length, stretching out past the seedy frills and the rotten sleeves, reaching out and seizing his NTHs.

Whatever had happened, the end result was undeniable—Chance Venable was now pointing his NTH's right at him. Stenstrom was flabbergasted.

In a similar blink-of-an-eye move, Clem pulled Taara's SK out of her hand. In a matter of half a second, they were both disarmed and menaced with their own weapons.

"Hmmm," Chance said. *"Meine Schätzchen, es scheint, als habe die Feier begonnen. A-heheheh!!"* Chance looked at the pistols. *"Ich glaube, mein Schwein pfeift!* NTH's if I'm not mistaken, very nice. LosCapricos weapons of House Belmont. Can kill anything, I hear tell, living or dead, real, unreal, man or machine. *C'est juste?"*

"Not sure what you're talking about," Stenstrom said.

"Oh, please, I do have my sources, truth be told. These are NTH's, no doubt about it."

Chance stood there beaming, like a vulture eyeballing a dying bit of prey. "Lemmuel, Innocent, shackle them please."

The two grubby fellows produced three sets of manacles and roughly bound their arms behind their backs. Lemmuel pulled Taara's Monica from her belt, admired it a moment, and tucked it into his sash. They then pushed them into a kneeling position, the four Venables standing triumphant in the flickering light of the corridor.

"A-heheh, a shocking turn of events, indeed. Now then," Chance said casually pointing the NTHs at Stenstrom. "Oh, and by the by, our name is not Venable—I believe that was the name of the most recent family of unfortunate wayfarers we waylaid and killed in space. My name is Chance Drury and we are the Drury Brothers."

"The Drury Brothers are dead!" A-Ram cried.

Chance Drury smiled with glee. "Are we? I don't feel dead. The Venables, now they're dead, I agree. Now, what to do with the three of you?"

Lemmuel approached and gave the kneeling Taara a rough kick in the stomach. "Lemme' have this Marine bitch! I wanna' show her a good time!" He seized her by the sideburns and yanked her head up. Lemmuel was aching to mess Taara up—a sadistic little man.

Clem shook his head and gave a toothy grin. "Nah . . . Let's feed 'em to the Cronyns nice as ya' please; that's what I says."

Taara, looking up the barrel of her own gun, scoffed. "Cronyns? Cronyns don't exist, Shinepole," she said, adding a dirty name from Bazz.

"Ya? Think so? Oh, they'd like ta' chaw down on your little carcass, Missie," Clem said.

Lemmuel took exception. "No! She called you ah 'Shinepole'! I want her, I wanna' hear her scream! I love making jumped-up little whores like her scream!"

"Shaddap an' do as yer' told!" Clem barked. "She's for the Cronyn's an' thas' the end of it, les you want me shoved up yer' works right in front of her so's she can watch!"

Lemmuel stewed and was visibly raging.

Chance stood there with Stenstrom's NTHs and lorded over the situation, enjoying every moment. "No, no. *Der Chorstuhl füllt sich mit Arschgesichtern!* I hear tell there's a ship coming to rescue this bunch. Not a Warbird, but a scout-ship under full sail. The *Demophalon John*—only a short distance away too. Да имаш да вземаш! That is a *Tekel*-class ship, I'd say minimum compliment of eighty-eight souls aboard. We shall give the scout ship and her miserable crew to the Cronyns, and then, when they're done, we'll salvage the hulk. By the Belt, this haul is made to order!"

Creation, Stenstrom thought, *how does he know this stuff?*

"Eighty-eight souls," Innocent said. "That'll keep `em happy for a spell, won't it?"

"My very thought, though I always detest taking Fleet vessels—somebody is sure to come looking for them, *oh bien,*" Chance said. "Still, we'll guide them in nice as you please, then ride out the aftermath, as we always do, nice and sweet."

"They'll not fall for such a thing, whatever it is you're planning," Stenstrom said.

"Oh?" Chance replied. He paused a moment, then: "*Seeker* to *Demophalon John,*" he said, his voice taking on an echoing, broadband-type sound to it. Chance Drury was speaking in Stenstrom's voice—a perfect match.

After a moment, Stenstrom heard a response. "Go ahead, Bel, did you get your Com fixed? You sound a lot better than before, though we don't have a picture. What in Creation happened to you? We've been worried sick." It was Captain Gwendolyn's voice.

"We managed to cobble something together, Captain, and our ship is a mess. It looks like we've reached our wits end with this old beater; everything's shot. We'll send you our coordinates. Can you come and get us with all speed?"

There was a delay, then: "Well, I must say I'm a bit surprised after the fuss you made, but sure, I'm glad you've come to your senses, Bel. We have your coordinates and are only about a half hour from your position. Sit tight and we'll be right there."

Stenstrom couldn't let this continue. He had to warn her. "Gwen!" he yelled from his kneeling position. Chance cocked the NTH and pointed it at A -Ram's head, furrowing the muzzle into his hair.

"Yes, Bel?" she replied.

Stenstrom winced and lowered his head.

"Nothing, Captain—sorry," Chance said in his voice. "I'm just eager to get off of this wreck. We shall stay on station and await your arrival."

"And Bel?" Gwen said.

"Yes?" Chance responded.

"When we get back to Fleet, don't forget we're having lunch. Whatever you're having, ale, beer, spirits, it's on me, okay, and while we eat, I'll teach you a card game or two. There's a game I love called canasta. You'll be a natural."

"I'll hold you to it, Captain," Chance replied rolling his eyes.

"Call me Gwen, all right? How many times do I have to tell you?"

"Of course, Gwen. *Seeker* out."

Chance giggled. "A-heheh. *Je suis impressionné.* Canasta, how droll. She sounds like a Zenon—too bad for her she won't be making that lovely lunch date at Fleet, and nor shall you. There," he said, his voice back to normal, "that wasn't hard, now was it? Little does your friend know what's in store for her. I almost feel sorry for the lady—what the Cronyns are going to do to her and her crew—really is quite a mess. Now, where was I— *no me puedo recordar.* Ah yes, what to do with you three?"

"Kill 'em, Chance, and be done with it," Clem said looking around. "I'm thinking this Warbird will do us up nice. We can use her to get those golden braggarts in the Tank off our backs once an' for all."

"Nah," Lemmuel said. "She's stripped. Got no engines, jus' like this little girl here." He kicked Taara again. She whuffed.

"Kick me again ... and I'm going to ghost you, Shinepole!" she replied in a surprisingly icy voice.

"Not if I ghost you first, darlin'!" He kicked her a third time and she wheezed in pain.

Chance looked around. "Lemmuel please—Для любви к Богу. I realize you enjoy showing the ladies a capital time; however, there's really no need to knock her about. These three are a pack of cretins and rogues just like we are, so let's show a modicum of respect to our peers, shall we? And, yes, I agree with you, Clem, this ship, with a bit of touching up, shall do us nicely. I am invigorated—*revigoré.*"

He stared down at A-Ram. "You, sir, you shall have the distinction of going first, a-heheh." He pointed the smooth-bore, iron barrel of the NTH at his skull and smiled, exposing his picket-fence of yellowy teeth. "Then let's get on with it. This is nothing personal, and, at least we're not giving you over to the Cronyns like we are that Zenon woman—be thankful for that. *Auf Wiedersehen.*"

Stenstrom looked up. "You might want to forget about him and worry instead about me."

Chance glanced at him. "And why is that?"

Stenstrom rose up, free of the manacles, the lock picked clean. He waved his hands. In a flash, he had six MARZABLE daggers nested between his fingers. He swept out with his left hand, and the daggers buried themselves in Chance's arm and hand. Chance, greatly surprised, dropped the NTH.

"Heilige Scheiße!"

Stenstrom cast the three daggers from his right hand and hit Clem in the neck and face. He cringed and bent over. "You huntin' dog!" Clem yelled.

Chance recovered from his shock of getting stabbed and fired at Taara. Still shackled, she nimbly rolled out of the way, the flashing green globe just missing to her right, clipping her coattails. With a roar of delight, Lemmuel dove onto Taara. "Now we's gonna' dance, bitch!" and they rolled about on the floor.

Clem, daggers protruding, kicked A-Ram over and pointed Taara's huge SK at his head. He pulled the trigger.

Nothing happened. Puzzled, he examined the gun. "Oh, jeep-doggy, she's palm-spranded it!"

Stenstrom thanked Creation for A-Ram's good luck and shook his hands again. Six lime green Holystones appeared between his fingers. He quickly threw them at Chance and Clem, where they exploded into a stout tangle of spider webs. Chance had completely disappeared in the mass, Clem too. Innocent was partially captured, as was the struggling A-Ram.

Stenstrom dragged A-Ram free of the webbing.

"Zavallı köpek! Think you're smart, do you?" came Chance's muffled voice from within the webbing. "Innocent, get me out of this!" He tore at the webbing.

A few feet away, Lemmuel and the shackled Taara tumbled about, she using her legs fairly effectively while he toyed with her—apparently enjoying attacking a lady. He glanced up and saw Stenstrom quickly undoing A-Ram's shackles. He lined A-Ram up and threw Taara's Monica. The large knife spiraled through the air and got A-Ram in the brim of his hat, pinning it to the wall. Taara, taking advantage of the moment, reared back and head-butted him in the jaw.

"Ow!" she cried, nearly knocking herself out.

From within the mass of webbing, Stenstrom heard a familiar clicking sound. He dove for A-Ram and pushed him out of the way as a lit-up, green mass came shooting out of the webs.

"NTH—shot!" Stenstrom yelled.

Growling, Taara peppered Lemmuel with bites and kicks as Stenstrom created several more daggers and pumped them into his scrawny chest. He was seemingly unfazed. He easily pulled the hissing Taara off him by her shackles and seized Stenstrom by his HRN coat. He then conked them together once or twice and threw Taara down the hallway, right into A-Ram, sending him sprawling.

Stenstrom recovered and, hauling back, socked Lemmuel square in the jaw.

It was like hitting a block of iron. Lemmuel spat and gave him a ruinous head-butt in return.

Everything spun. He picked Stenstrom up by the collar of his HRN and threw him into the airlock, where he landed upside down with a thud.

"Now I'm gonna' git ya, Missie!" Stenstrom heard him yell. "Come here!"

The hatch shut and sealed with a hermetic "hiss!"

Inside the airlock, Stenstrom recovered, stood, and banged on the hatch, but he couldn't open it—it was locked from the other side. Through the narrow window he could see hints of movement in the dark corridor beyond, covered up mostly by the sticky tangle of spider webs created by his Holystone throw. He thought he saw a flash of green light traveling down the hall—another NTH shot.

Someone ran by—was that Taara? No, it was A-Ram, Lemmuel hot on his heels.

Another green flash.

Creation! His friends could be dying on the other side of the hatch.

12

—THE SISTERS' FIST—

He thought to pick the lock and open the hatch, but there was nothing to pick, no exposed locking mechanism to get his hands on.

He continued desperately pounding on the hatch in fear of what was happening to his friends on the other side, and for Captain Gwendolyn was sailing into a trap of some sort.

The Cronyns? What are those? Didn't sound good, whatever they are.

There was a shot and a strobe-flash of green light through the window.

Stenstrom struggled with the hatch.

A voice entered his head, a chiding, laughing voice.

You are our Fist. Camalopardus is out. We lend you our power.

He felt something filling him up.

He looked at his hands. For a moment they no longer looked like flesh and blood; they looked metallic and machined, like the hands of a thoughtfully crafted robot made of silver and gold.

He pushed on the hatch door and, surprisingly, it opened this time.

No, it didn't open—it was twisted and wrecked. He had pushed through it, past the stout metal and hermetic seals, and bent the armored hatch like it was made of spun sugar.

No time to consider what he'd just done. He ran into the hallway to save his friends.

Down the corridor, A-Ram and Taara were hunkered down in a service nook. Lemmuel was fiddling around with Taara's SK, trying to get the palm sprander off (apparently Clem, partially stuck in the web, had tossed it to him). Chance had escaped the web and was pressing with green shots from the NTH pistols. Clem was still stuck in the web and was swearing to beat the band. Innocent was tearing at the web, trying to free him.

Although Chance appeared to know quite a lot of things, he didn't seem to know that the NTH shots could pass through obstructions, such as walls. That was the Rumalore working—false information about the capabilities of the NTH. That flaw in his knowledge was saving Taara and A-Ram at the moment, for he kept trying to shoot around the wall.

Stenstrom fell on Innocent and Clem from behind.

"What the—!" Innocent choked as Stenstrom hauled back and cuffed him in the face, knocking him into the wall some distance away.

Chance turned to shoot Stenstrom with his own pistols and was shocked.

"*Mein Gott!* What are you?" he asked, staring at him. "You're like us? You're like us!" He leveled the NTHs at him.

Stenstrom quickly seized the barrels of the pistols and got them out of

Chance's hands before he could fire.

No, he didn't pull them out of Chance's grasp—*he pulled his NTHs away with Chance's hands still clinging to them*—they hung there like two grim decorations, trailing streamers of flesh and gore. Chance, handless, roared and drew away. Clem freed himself from the remains of the web and attacked.

Stenstrom turned the pistols, cocked and fired, getting Clem in the chest. He groaned and fell over, clunking hard to the floor.

Chance started to say something, but Stenstrom was on him. He picked him up and roughly head butted him.

"*Z kurwy syn!*" Chance piped, and Stenstrom head butted him again with bone-crushing force.

A strange sound filled the corridor at that moment—a rapid, hitching guttural sound, like a machine gasping in its death throes: "EEEE..uuuuu . . . GGGGHHHHHHH . . . EEEEE!!" The noise seemed to be coming from Clem. Taara gritted her teeth and A-Ram covered his ears. Stenstrom blocked out the noise and threw Chance, head over heels through the smashed air lock into the hold.

"你產生泡沫!" came from beyond the hatch.

Picking up the fallen Clem, Stenstrom also threw him into the air lock.

He then turned to attend to Lemmuel. Taara and A-Ram had exited their hiding place and were engaging him, though they didn't appear to be having much luck. Lemmuel spun and threw Taara aside. He aimed the SK at her and pulled the trigger, but it didn't go off—again it was palm spranded. A-Ram worked his way behind him, while Taara engaged afresh from the front, charging him with her lowered shoulder—a spitting little ball of fur she was, even shackled. A-Ram fell to his knees and, with Taara pressing him backwards, Lemmuel tripped over him, shoulders back, filthy shoes in the air.

The SK flew out of his grip as he fell.

A-Ram sprang and grabbed it. He struggled with the heavy weapon, aimed and pulled—again nothing happened—the palm sprander defeated him too.

"I'm gonna poke ya, Missie!" Lemmuel roared, trying to stand. Taara hauled back and kicked him square across the face with her hard, Marine Brussard boot. His face seemed to fall apart and go shapeless for a moment, like a sack full of broken glass.

Stenstrom picked Lemmuel's scrawny body up with one arm and tossed him into the air lock along with Chance and Clem. There was a commotion of bodies colliding within.

"Get these damn things off me!" Taara hissed, leaning over and presenting her shackled hands. Stenstrom quickly removed them from her wrists. "Gimme' this!" she yelled, snatching her SK from A-Ram and clearing the palm sprand. She saw Chance peeking out of the air lock door and laid a roaring burst on it—he backed away into the interior as the blast riddled and blackened the hatchway.

With another wave of his hand, Stenstrom produced three red Holystones and three more lime green ones. He cast two reds into the smashed hatchway and they burst into hot flames—Chance screamed from within. He then cast the greens and thoroughly covered up the smashed inner hatch of the docking ring air lock with webbing, preventing them from exiting.

A-Ram ran to the controls and hit the purge. The outer doors opened and Chance, Clem, and Lemmuel Drury were swept out into the vacuum of space, Stenstrom's webbing sucking in with the change in pressure, but holding. The venting pushed on the *Heade-on-the-Hearth*, and she lightly bounced into the neck of the *Seeker*, still grappled on by her metal tentacles.

Taara's eyes grew wide. "Hey!" she managed to say. She pointed.

Behind A-Ram, Innocent Drury rose up.

Stenstrom let fly with three more MARZABLE daggers, getting him in the face and chest. With his other hand, he threw a red Holystone which he had saved—Innocent burst into green and red flames.

Taara got a bead on him and loosed a burst. There was a throaty blast of gunfire and a spray of blood. Innocent fell forward, riddled to the chest by fifty caliber fire from Taara's SK, the corridor filling with the smell of cooking flesh and gun smoke.

"Good Creation!" Taara exclaimed, running her hands through her hair, her SK smoking. "What in the name of Hell was that? It's a damn good thing I never removed my palm sprander from my gun, or it would have been curtains!"

"Are you two all right?" Stenstrom cried.

A-Ram nodded and looked at the webbed up hatch of the air lock as he shut the outer doors. He noted the twisted wreckage. "You did this, Bel?"

"I suppose so."

"When you first came out of the air lock, you looked a little strange," he said.

"How so?"

"I didn't have time to take it all in, but you looked like a robot. Just for a moment."

Stenstrom shook his head. "Must be the Sisters' doing somehow."

Taara pulled her Monica from the wall and approached the fallen, mangled form of Innocent Drury. She gave him a kick, stirring up tails of dark smoke. "Did you see how fast those guys moved? These are eaten-up looking Shinepoles—they shouldn't be able to move that fast."

"What is a Shinepole, Taara?" Stenstrom asked. "Enlighten me."

"It's not a nice name to call somebody on Bazz."

"How were they doing all that stuff, Bel? How did they know the things they knew?" A-Ram asked, quite shaken. "And how did they contact the *Demophalon John*?"

Stenstrom slid his NTHs back into his sash. "I have no idea. They must have had some sort of Com device or long-range holo-mon hidden on their person. Speaking of which, let's get to the bridge at once and raise Captain Gwendolyn. We've got to tell her she's heading into a trap."

A-Ram pointed at Innocent's dead, smoking body. "What should we do with him?"

"Leave him for the moment; we've not the time. We'll dispose of him later."

They moved down the hall at a run. "Chance Drury mentioned something called the Cronyns. What are those, Taara?" asked Stenstrom.

She cleared the chamber of her SK and cocked it. "Bad dreams, Bel, and I don't need the MOLLY to tell me that," she replied, trotting at his side. "They're supposed to be evil spirits who eat your dreams and lead you astray, trying to cause you harm. On Bazz, in the old days just after the fall equinox, there was a two week period that we called the 'Time of the Cronyn'. During that time, we'd start having bad dreams; then we'd begin hearing things, seeing things. As the stories go, you couldn't trust your eyes or your ears. People sometimes would walk right off a cliff and have no idea they were falling. Sometimes people would gravely wound themselves and have no idea they were hurt—that sort of thing. People stayed home during the Time of the Cronyn and hid, doing as little as possible and hoping to ride it out, but, every year, lots of people got hurt or killed. Your boy, Darius Jones, rose to prominence during the Time of the Cronyn—he didn't seem to be affected by it. That was a long time ago though, and now it's just an excuse to drink and not work. I never believed in them myself."

They climbed the lift shaft and arrived on the bridge. "A-Ram, get us some space from that pirate ship out there, and then, once we've room, we'll pick up some speed, Slap her hard amidships and sink her!"

A-Ram took the helm and Taara flew into her seat at the Missive's Panel. "A-Ram, pull us away and swing up, Z minus 4:45pm, Taara, raise the *Demophalon John* if you can."

A-Ram spun the wheel and the *Seeker* banked away, as usual, moving backwards. "She's grappled on out there, Bel. I can't shake us loose."

"I've got the Captain, Bel," Taara said. "Audio only—the Com's messed up."

Stenstrom was relieved. Static came down from the Com.

"Gwen, is that you?"

"Paymaster, I'm right here," came a reply over the Com. "What is your situation?"

"Gwen, that previous transmission you received from us was bogus. We ran afoul of a group of pirates calling themselves the Drury Brothers. They told us that they were attempting to lead your ship into a trap of some sort—I don't know the exact nature of what they had planned, but it didn't sound good."

"I see," she said. "Sobering news."

"Gwen, I suggest you return at once to Kana and report the situation to the Fleet. Tell them that they should send an armada to sweep this area and keep a weather eye for something called the Cronyns. I don't know what they are, but the Druries were planning on feeding you to them."

"Yes, excellent, Paymaster. I shall make sail for Kana at once and advise them there."

Stenstrom stood and looked up at the ceiling. He sensed something was wrong.

"Gwen, you seem awfully compliant. What about your mission?"

"My mission is important, but secondary at this time. You advised me of danger in this sector and I see the good sense in it."

Stenstrom rubbed his chin. "When we spoke initially, Gwen—what did you say you were going to do to me?"

Her voice came back over the Com a moment later. "As I recall, I invited you to play cards."

Taara looked into the visor. She muted the Com. "Bel—we're not sending out any signal. It's being jammed and we don't have the power to overcome it."

Stenstrom turned to A-Ram. "Are we free from the *Heade- on- the -Hearth*?"

"No."

"Taara, un-mute the Com."

She did. Stenstrom continued. "You didn't mention wanting to play cards, Gwen. As I recall, you mentioned wanting to knock my teeth out. So, to whom am I currently speaking, please?"

There was a crackling pause. Then: "A-heheheh. I fancy your ship, Paymaster," came Gwendolyn's voice. "It's a little weedy, but nothing a few acquired parts won't fix. You're going to die, sir; you know that, don't you?"

"Identify yourself please."

There was another pause. "Come into your office and see for yourself. *Je vous ose à* a-heheheh."

Stenstrom drew his NTHs and headed toward his office door, Taara following.

He took a deep breath and went in.

Outside, through the windows of the office, he could see the girded bulk of the *Heade* still latched onto the neck of the *Seeker*. Two figures floated near the window—bobbing in naked space.

It was Chance and Lemmuel Drury. And, though they had no pressure suits, they both appeared to be very much alive. Lemmuel was, with one hand, clamped onto the outer skin of the ship, and with the other he was holding onto Chance, who had no hands and was badly charred, his hair and clothes mostly burned away.

Eyes glittering, Chance's mouth started moving, and the Com came back on. "You've no idea what you're dealing with here, Paymaster. We inhabit the spaces in between the mundane and the well-traveled. The small stretch between Kana, Onaris, and Bazz isn't so small, and that is where we prey on the unwary, in the heart of the League, yet right under its nose. You and your friends on the scout ship are our prey, our latest victims. You are simply among those unfortunate souls lost at sea and hailed in memoriam. Your empty chair shall be saluted with raised glasses and thumps on the chest."

Taara lost her bearing a little. "What in the Name of Creation are you?"

"*Je suis le diable*. The devil . . . a-heheh . . ."

Stenstrom aimed his NTHs at the window. Chance drew back and gave a hideous grin, his burned face nearly splitting open.

"What are you going to do with that, Paymaster, shoot us? You'll out your window and space yourself. NTH's do quite a lot of damage, I so I'm told. *Le c'est une vraiment grande explosion, eh?*"

"Don't believe everything you hear."

Stenstrom pulled the trigger. The hammer swung and a green ball of energy lanced out, passing harmlessly through the window and out the other side, hitting Lemmuel in the chest. He thrashed in surprise for a moment then was still. Stenstrom cocked the other NTH and fired at Chance. He partially hid behind the bulk of his dead brother and the green shot hit Lemmuel in the shoulder, sending both of them spiraling away toward the aft of the ship.

He watched them flail into the distance. "A-Ram!" he yelled, "I want a 360 degree wing roll on my mark!"

At the helm, A-Ram kicked a lever on the floor. "Ready!" he said.

Stenstrom waited a few seconds more, then: "Now, A-Ram, roll!"

A-Ram spun the wheel and the *Seeker* barrel-rolled fast, the *Heade* moving with it through about ninety degrees of the roll, then it let go, its gangly bulk spiraling away, tentacles flailing like a tick that had been pried loose of its prey.

"Oh, look!" Taara cried with glee. "The *Heade* got one of them, did you see?"

Through the window, Stenstrom could see that the bulk of the *Heade* had plowed into one of the Druries before it let go. The second Drury, and they couldn't make out which one, managed to avoid getting hit by the *Heade*, but instead got clipped by the rolling wing of the *Seeker*—his body rocketing off in a random direction like a ping pong ball smacked by a fast-moving paddle.

"Serves 'em right, the buggers!" Taara said. "Creation, Bel—what are we dealing with here?"

"I truly have no idea. Is the MOLLY telling you anything?"

"Nope. The MOLLY seems to be a whizz with technical stuff, but a little less so with the weird, and those Shinepoles were way weird."

They left the office. "What happened?" A-Ram asked at the helm. "What was that?"

"Our friends were back."

"Those guys? The pirates? Outside?" A-Ram was a bit panicked.

"Yes. Which gives me a bad thought. The one we left in the corridor, Taara, you hit him with an SK burst, right?"

"Yep, got him right in the chest, full auto. Probably put ten fifty-cal slugs into him. No man could survive that."

"And no man could survive naked in space without a pressure suit, yet the two of them didn't appear inconvenienced in the least. I recall hitting Clem Drury previously in the chest with my NTH, and we did not see him out the window just now, so I'm assuming he's dead somewhere." Stenstrom started for the lift.

"Where are you going?" Taara asked.

"Back to the docking ring to make sure our friend is still where we left him, good and dead. And, if so, I'm going to Space him out."

"You're not going alone."

"Yes, I am. You two stay here. A-Ram, get us into position to finish the *Heade*. I want you to create some distance, lay on two, and sink it. Taara, keep trying to raise the *Demophalon John*." He handed A-Ram one of his NTHs and went out into the dark of the lift shaft. "If anything comes through that lift door and it's not me—use it."

Stenstrom made his way down the dark lift shaft and out to the waiting corridor beyond.

MORGAN-JETERIX, LADY OF THOMPSON

13

—Morgan-Jeterix—

H er face was killing her.
Captain Gwendolyn snatched the report out of her crewman's hand.
She looked at it, her green eyes flashing. "Allistar, I told you I wanted this
status report three hours ago!" she yelled, her voice ugly.

Her cut face had been completely sealed, but it hurt like anything. She felt
mad and short. To top things off, she was quite worried about Paymaster
Stenstrom—what had happened, where did he go? Her worry and pain, all
these things mixed together in her soul and let the Grizzly Bear come out in
full force.

"Yes, Captain, I'm sorry." He stood there looking at the floor.

Gwendolyn felt a wave of anger pass over her and was on the verge of
giving him a good lashing, but, for her new friend, the Paymaster, she was
trying to turn a new leaf and better herself. She sighed and took a deep breath,
allowing her anger to diminish. Her face was stinging. "It's all right. Just try
and be a bit more punctual next time," she said lightly touching the wound.

"Aye, ma'am"

She paced the small bridge. Crewmen bustled about. "Sensing," she said
turning to a crewman near the front of the bridge, "do you have anything
yet?"

"No, ma'am, the sector is clear."

"A dead Warbird cannot simply vanish. The *Seeker* has to be here
somewhere. These are the correct coordinates they gave us, yes?"

"Yes, ma'am."

"Very well. Keep looking."

The navigator checked his settings. "Ma'am, I must inform you that we are
currently well out the shipping lanes on the lee side of Druries Belt. I highly
advise we return to the lanes and call for an organized search party."

"Noted. Keep looking. The sooner we find the *Seeker*, the sooner we're
windward of Druries Belt and back in the lanes."

She turned her attention to the Com officer. "Com, send to Fleet—advise
them of our situation, current position and heading."

"Ay, ma'am. Message sent."

"Thank you. Now, raise the boatswain. Tell him as soon as we make
contact with the *Seeker*, I want him to run out a Christmas gun. He shall then
carefully—and I emphasize 'carefully'— shoot out their improvised drive
engine, and we will board. I want to ensure Paymaster Stenstrom doesn't
suffer a change of mind. I want him and his crew brought safely out of there
as soon as possible. No more games—this is getting too dangerous."

"Aye, ma'am."

"Once aboard, he and his crew shall be treated with the utmost respect and courtesy, understood? I expect all present to go out of our way to make them feel welcome, so let's look lively."

The holographic displays moving about the Navigator's head spun. Something blinked. "Ma'am, new contact bearing 7:45AM of 11:16PM."

"Is it the *Seeker*?"

"Looks to be. It is a large metallic object, offering a Mag-reflection that is typical for a *Straylight*-class vessel. It is not flying its standard colors."

"They must be shutdown. Plot intercept solution. Com, send to *Seeker*, please, and raise Paymaster Stenstrom if possible."

The helmsman, pressing buttons at his small chair, banked the ship and soon the dark mass of the *Seeker* jogged into view in the display.

The *Demophalon John* had a small view screen and several large, holo-infused, blue-filtered windows that were lit up with various displays and readouts. Gwendolyn often didn't look at the screen. She looked out a window and saw, far off, a small form holo'ed with a red circle. The ship was still quite a ways off in the distance and Gwendolyn glanced at the screen to see enhanced detail.

It was the *Seeker* sure enough.

The *Seeker* was dark, all running lights off and the roving eye of the main sensor dead. She was flipped over in relationship to their orientation, and was slowly spinning to port.

"Com," Gwendolyn said, "Any luck raising the *Seeker*?"

"No, ma'am."

"They must have blown their engine. Keep trying. Are we detecting any venting?"

"No, ma'am, the *Seeker* reads as whole with a sufficient pressure of breathable gasses within to support life."

The doors to the bridge opened and in walked Morgan-Jeterix, decked out in her black uniform with an array of silver tools peeking out of her pockets and a winged helmet sitting on her head. She was a Hospitaler of Samaritan class. Scout ships normally didn't have Samaritans aboard, but, being favored with Admiral Derlith, he had managed to get one for her regardless.

✳   ✳   ✳   ✳   ✳

Morgan was a lean, but solid, lady with hair that was blonde and braided in many, thin, beaded twists under her silver helmet. Most Hospitalers were Browns, but Morgan was not a Brown—she was a lady of Thompson, an old family from the Hala region of Kana. She became a Hospitaler, Gwendolyn had heard, because she wanted to, because she felt a personal calling. Her smooth skin had that "tanned-hide" look that many Halas had. She wore a large ring on her right hand emblazoned with a proud "E" for the Ephysians, an esoteric order within the Hospitalers that Gwendolyn didn't know too much about.

She and Lt. Gwendolyn did not get along most of the time. Sometimes they did, and sometimes they were just on the cusp of becoming friends, but that was more the exception than the norm—their personalities appeared to be too similar in certain regards and, therefore, they clashed at inconvenient but predictable moments. The two often fought openly and were occasionally not on speaking terms, but Morgan was a good Hospitaler and was a handy asset to have around. Morgan had engaged in several brief but very public and rather messy affairs with some of Gwendolyn's crew (both male and female), which she did not approve of at all. She'd also heard whispers that Morgan had a thing for her as well, though she tried to not think about it much.

Morgan also was a registered empath and supposedly bore a tattoo that only the Sisters could detect branding her as such. Being empathic, she involuntarily knew the feelings and surface thoughts of another without overtly being telepathic. She had the annoying habit of saying out loud what Gwendolyn was thinking. It was not only frustrating for Gwendolyn, but embarrassing as well, to have a running tap from the well-spring of her mind to the open, wagging mouth of Morgan. It was mortifying—anything coming out of Morgan's mouth could be hot, right off her brain.

✳   ✳   ✳   ✳   ✳

Morgan adjusted her helmet, as it always seemed to sit askew on her head on top of all those tightly run braids, and she walked up to Gwendolyn.

"I recommended that you sit a spell," she said in her Hala-inspired, Thompson twang. "You actually lost a fair amount of blood from that cut before I could get it stopped."

"I've work to attend to," Gwendolyn replied curtly. "Do you need something?"

"Yeah, I'm worried about him out there too. Tough to be all prim and proper when you're worried, isn't it? I could give you a sedative."

There she goes again. "I really don't know what you're talking about, Morgan."

"I've heard he's really handsome."

"Who is?"

"Paymaster Stenstrom."

Gwendolyn flushed up. "What do you want, Morgan? I'm really rather busy."

"Reeling in the Paymaster, I know. I wanted to share my findings with you. That cut, I know how it was made."

"All right, let's hear it."

Morgan looked around, seeing the crew moving about the bridge. "In private, Captain."

"I've no time for dramatics, Morgan. Helm, match PM base with *Seeker*, and lock." She gave Morgan a hard look. "Out with it."

Morgan huffed. "Fine then. Your cut was made with Shadow tech, no doubt about it. A micro-point beam to be precise. The presence of Shadow tech prevented your blood from clotting—you would have bled out in short order, had I not sealed it."

Gwendolyn stopped what she was doing. "How in the name of Creation did I get cut with Shadow tech?"

"You tell me, and, I might add, that wasn't just any old cut with Shadow tech; whoever did it to you is a master."

Morgan suddenly looked around. "What's that noise?"

"What noise?"

"That!" she said impatiently. "That loud beeping sound. It sounds like an alarm of some sort to me."

The crew looked at Morgan, clearly thinking her mad. "I don't hear an alarm, Morgan," Gwen said, impatient.

She spun around. "You're telling me you cannot hear that? Creation, my eardrums are going to burst. Beep! Beep! Beep!"

She turned to the Com officer and pointed at him. "You! What are you doing?"

The Com was confused. "Pardon, ma'am?" he said.

"You're standing there with your arms held out in mid air, touching nothing."

He looked down. "I'm manning my position at the Com."

Morgan pointed to his left. "The Com's over there—you're standing over nothing right now." Morgan glanced at the windows. "And what, may I ask, is that?" she said pointing at the window.

By this point, the crew stopped what they were doing and became a bit apprehensive. Hospitalers often did strange things—but this display was too much.

"We are currently involved in a rescue and recovery operation, Morgan. Thank you for the update. Please allow us to continue—I believe you are upsetting my crew."

Morgan pushed her helmet back. "What are we rescuing?"

"Paymaster Stenstrom and his crew off the Warbird *Seeker*. Is that not obvious?"

"What's that outside?" Morgan pointed to the windows again. "Oh, dear Creation! We nearly got de-paneled by an asteroid just now!"

Gwendolyn turned to the screen. There she saw the approaching form of the *Seeker* floating alone in a clear field.

"An asteroid? As I said, there's nothing out there but the *Seeker*, which we are endeavoring to rescue. Have you gone blind?"

Morgan marched up to one of the windows. "Doesn't look like any Warbird I've ever seen. It looks to me that we are heading straight for a small cluster of planetoids."

Gwendolyn turned back to the screen. There was the *Seeker*, slowly approaching, its orientation now in synch with theirs after the helm corrected for it. "Morgan, I think you need to take one of your potions and rest up a tad." She thought back to Paymaster Stenstrom, and one of the insults he used on her. "Perhaps your braids are a bit too tight and your skull and brain require circulation!" There—that was a good one. See, he was already having a positive influence on her.

Morgan didn't appreciate the joke. "Captain, you know as well as I that my House can see through Cloaked illusions."

"So you enjoy saying."

"I think we're flying right into one!"

Morgan's eye grew wide. "Grab onto something! Everybody! Brace for impact!"

And before Gwendolyn could say anything in reply, the ship was rocked by a massive collision.

Everything went dark on the *Demophalon John.*

LADY ALESTA OF DARE

14

—A Falling Star—

Lady Alesta prayed by the great tree, hoping for a bit of inspiration. It was odd—she usually found divine guidance coming to her at the strangest of times; while sleeping, eating dinner, doing her chores—just not when she was praying like she was supposed to do. It was getting cold and she wanted her bed. She had stoked the fire in her small room before coming out so that the room would be snug and toasty for her upon returning. A large bell mounted on a post near the tree was showing signs of frosting over.

She was wearing the standard clothing of her order: a white woolen smock that went down to her knees, lined with home-spun frills, a belt of red and green shells stitched together and tasseled with gold thread that she had loomed herself, several beaded necklaces made of smooth, painted wood beads and the same red and green shells as her belt, and a long, open green brocade robe lined with embroidered gold fabric.

Most everything she wore she had made herself, and her belt and her necklaces were infused with the love of her Star—they protected her mind and shielded her from sight.

Her thick black hair was held up with several wooden sticks stuck in near the nape of her neck, creating a large bun. Without the sticks, her hair would have gone down to her ankles. She hadn't cut it in years, She sometimes wondered if she had a "special someone", a person to whom she'd given her heart, what he would think of her wooly appearance; the clothes, her hair, her unshod feet. The road she had chosen for herself was indeed a lonely one.

Her feet were getting cold—she wished she was allowed to wear shoes when praying, but they were forbidden. Cold, tired of kneeling, she stood up and brushed off her clothes. No inspiration was coming to her. She rubbed her hands and blew on them, her breath steaming through her fingers. She turned to make her way across the green back to her room.

She looked up at the close sky one last time.

She could see the star shining there, the star that only she and her brothers and sisters could see.

The Star of Merian, lighting up the sky in a yellow veil.

$$* \quad * \quad * \quad * \quad *$$

She had been a Pilgrim of Merian since she was very young. Growing up with her family in Dare, she had always been able to see a star that nobody else could. She was a lady of the Dare line, 10th order—there were a lot of Dares in Dare, and her order was placed somewhere in the middle. They weren't the richest; nor were they the outlanders either.

The star she saw was a bright, yellowish globe, easily the biggest star in the sky. On clear nights, and sometimes during the day, she even thought she could see a red cloud moving around the star in a slow spiral.

She asked her father what the star was called—it was so pretty.

"What star?" her father asked.

"That one, just there."

"Where?"

It became clear to her in time that she, of all her brothers and sisters and friends, was the only one who could see that star with the red cloud. Sometimes that made her happy as she had something so beautiful all to herself, but other times it made her sad. Such a pretty thing should be shared, should be available for all to see.

When she was twenty-three, she went into Dare market with her parents to gather items for the Fall Feast. The Fall Feast was a big event in the Barrow region, celebrated proudly in the cities of Dare, Saga, Rhoda and Tuk, and there was much planning to be done.

When they got to market, there was quite a commotion going on beyond the usual comings and goings of the shoppers and traders. Many were gathered around the square and were hooting and hollering at a small group of people wearing green robes and white smocks. The people were laughing at them.

Alesta went to her mother. "Mother, who are those people? And why are they being laughed at?"

Her mother tried not to look in their direction. "Those people are Pilgrims of Merian—just a cult of harmless zealots."

"Why are they being laughed at?"

"Because they have silly ideas. Just ignore them."

Alesta was curious. She pulled away from her family and approached the crowd gathered around the Pilgrims. There were five of them standing in the town square, trying to pass out literature, which nobody seemed to want to take, and they had a collection basket, which had a fair amount of money in it. "Here—for real clothes and breath mints! Brush your teeth next time, Pilgrim!" people derided as they tossed in money. Nobody was harming the Pilgrims or roughing them about, but those in the crowd were sharp and vulgar with their jabs and quips.

Through the heckling, she listened to what they said.

"It is our sworn mission to bring you good news," they said, shouting above the noise. "We bring you news of the Elders. They are not gone. They are with us still."

"I don't see them!"

"Where are they?"

"Hiding in the clouds surely, full of tuck and play!"

"Hahahahaha!"

The Pilgrims took the ribbing with serene patience. "The Elders are there for you to see; all one need do is look."

"All I see is you with your muddy feet and outrageous skirt, quite out of line and well off the hook!"

"Hahahahahaha!"

"Put some pants on, Pilgrim—your legs are a fright."

"With wickets like those, the ladies surely take flight!'

"Haaaaaaaaaaahahahahaha!"

The Pilgrims took it in stride. "The Star of Merian is plain. Lift you your eyes and revel in its light."

"Again, your legs are blinding all else from sight!" a jokester mused.

"I see nothing but pale skin and patches of hair."

"He's either a very ugly troll, or possibly a half-shaven bear!"

"Hahahahahaha!"

Alesta spoke up. "I see it," she said in a tiny voice.

Everybody quieted down and turned to her. The Pilgrims were shocked. "You? My dear, you see the star?"

"Yes."

The Pilgrims made their way through the crowd and approached her. The people in the crowd rubbed their chins. "What star? Where is it?"

"It's over there," she said pointing to the west.

The Pilgrims were open-mouthed. "You can see it! You can see the star!"

"It's a big yellow star that's always out, and it has a funny red cloud floating around it."

✳   ✳   ✳   ✳   ✳

Before a year had passed, Lady Alesta herself stood with the Pilgrims of Merian wearing homemade clothes and green robes. She held literature and got laughed at in the town squares of Kana and beyond. She had given up everything she had to join them, her fine gowns of Dare and lovely shoes cast aside. Her mother had gone into mourning over her decision, grieving for her daughter as if she were dead.

"Don't cry, mother," she had said. "I hear a voice that will not yield."

"No lord or goodly man will have you. You will be alone forever wearing rags," her mother said.

"I believe this is my calling. This is what I am here to do."

The Star called to her and she became a Pilgrim of Merian.

In the modest dens of the Merians, she learned to speak their secret language. There they spoke of the Star. She discovered that it watched over them, and that most could not see it—not even the Sisters. They told her that the Elders were there, orbiting the star, waiting for them to be rejoined with their children.

And, there was much work to do. The Star demanded it.

They sent Alesta out into the night when they thought she was ready to pray, to seek enlightenment. The Star's judgment for her would dictate the rest of her life, no matter what.

On her knees in the snow, she prayed for hours, her skin freezing, her feet numb, her fingers close to frostbite.

None of it mattered.

Her efforts were rewarded. In delirium she heard the star speak to her.

It said: *Save all those who fall astray.*

Such was her command, and she would follow it without fear or question. She walked the Merian's Road with her brethren, and was taken into the stars with her brothers and sisters, to a secret place where she could pray and do as she was commanded.

Her road was to be the most dangerous; the Star commanded it.

As she readied to return to her room and modest bed, she saw a star fall. It traced a gentle line across the sky and disappeared behind the nearby planetoid.

Edam, the Star called it.

Hell.

Alesta often saw stars falling into Edam, and she knew what it meant.

She watched the star fall, and a tear came to her eye.

"Lost souls! Lost souls!"

Her prayers had been answered, though not quite in the way she had expected. Gathering her robes, she ran to the nearby bell and began ringing it, the small shards of frost vibrating off it as it rang. Beyond, lights in her small village came on in response to her ringing of the bell. She could see outlines of people moving about in their rooms through their frosty windows, getting dressed.

The Pilgrims of Merian, impoverished, laughed at, disregarded, never failed to answer the call of the bell no matter what the hour.

Save all those who fall astray.

In Edam there shall be many who need saving.

15

—The Druries—

NTH at the ready, Stenstrom made his way toward the docking ring. Though the corridor was now quiet of the preternatural groans and shrieks that had earlier plagued it, the silence that now pervaded was ominous and nearly as bad. The dim lighting, routed via the generators by Taara on the bridge, flickered a little bit.

He reached a crossroad. He was now familiar enough with the layout of the ship to know that around the corner to his left was the docking ring. If everything was as it should be, then the dead body of Innocent Drury, stabbed, burned, and riddled with fifty caliber slugs, should be right there where he'd fallen.

But, and this was a big "but"—seeing Innocent's two brothers floating about in space alive and well made all bets void. Stenstrom was certain he'd leap around the corner and Innocent Drury would be gone, lurking loose somewhere on the ship, creating all manner of chaos.

That's how things seemed to go on this ship—the improbable would probably happen.

Stenstrom stood there, propped up against the wall, grappling with his courage. He could smell the burnt flesh and explosive shells of Taara's gun lingering in the corridor from the battle that took place earlier. He cocked the NTH's hammer, checked the cinnabar wedge to make sure it was in good and tight and wasn't cracked, took a deep breath, and jumped out, barrel leveled.

Lying in a pool of drying blood was the body of Innocent Drury, face down, his arms tucked up beneath him like he was praying. His body still smoked a little.

Stenstrom breathed a sigh of relief and swallowed. "Com," he said.

Taara's voice, a shower of worry, came down in reply. "That you, Bel? What's your status?"

"I've arrived at the docking ring—Innocent's still here, right where you shot him down."

Taara's voice over the Com sounded relieved. "See—he took a full SK burst to the gut—that's tough to spring back from."

Stenstrom aimed his NTH. "Yes, well, I'm going to put one into his dead body just to be sure—the NTH never fails."

The hammer swung in its fussy manner and he fired a green globe of energy that pierced Innocent right above his shoulder. His body didn't move as the globe struck it, just lay there—nothing unusual with an NTH shot, as its globes of energy normally did little visible damage. Knowing the infallible killing nature of an NTH shot and feeling much better, Stenstrom slid the pistol back into its sash.

"A-Ram, what's the status of the *Heade-on-the-Hearth*?" he asked.

"We're just swinging into position now," came his reply over the Com. "Another few minutes and we'll ram her into bits."

"Good. Just say when, and I'll give the order."

As Stenstrom stood there, he thought he heard a distant clank. The lights overhead surged, and then went out, wrapping him in darkness.

"Taara, what's happening?"

The Com sputtered and quickly faded. "Bel, we've lost the *Westminster*, this very moment."

The Com buzzed. "Taara?"

"Bel—we . . ." And the Com went out.

Struggling in the dark, Stenstrom produced a Holystone and shook it, creating a soft glow. He suspected deviltry. Taara's handiwork so far had proven reliable, and the *Westminster* didn't just now go quiet by itself. Holding the Holystone up, he strode over to the fallen body of Innocent Drury, the wounds and ripples of his body thrown into grotesque relief, and gave him a kick, flipping him over.

He looked down.

Laying there was a pile of clothes with a ruddy skin inside that looked like a fallen, scorched cocoon. The skin was slit open and hollow—no innards, no skeleton, just a shot-out, burned husk.

"Taara!" Stenstrom yelled. "A-Ram!!"

Nothing.

The lights in the corridor surged back to life for a hopeful moment, and then went out—for good this time, it seemed.

He flushed up against one of the walls and drew his NTH again.

For a moment, he had no idea what to do.

Come on, Dav. Dunks, give me an order! Father, tell me what I'm supposed to do!

Mother—Mother, what am I supposed to do?

Lilly, tell me what to do . . .

Stenstrom sat there and struggled, trying to regain his composure.

He had to square up with the fact there was no Captain Davage or his father or mother, or Lilly, or even Lt. Dunkster around to prop him up. He was the captain. This mess was his to solve. Taara and A-Ram: those were his people to keep safe.

This is what he wanted, dreaming as a boy by the fountain, in his rusty office aboard the *Sandwich*, and on the red velvet crush of the Admiralty floor—now here it was.

Enjoy.

He took a minute or two and sat there in the dark, allowing himself to be weak. Then he stood and set to it.

First thing's first: *The Westminster.*

So, where was the *Westminster*? If Innocent Drury was out to cause mischief, then that's where it would be easiest to do so. Of course, Innocent Drury wouldn't know that the *Westminster* was their sole source of locomotion, nor would he know where it was berthed.

Yet, Innocent's horrid brother Chance appeared to have command of a vast cache of up-to-date information, and he couldn't rule out the possibility that Innocent had access to it too.

He had to head to the *Westminster*, secure it, and get it going again. Then he could deal with whatever sort of grotesque creature Innocent Drury was under his stinking hide.

So where was it? If his memory served him, the *Westminster* was bolted down in the big Ripcar bay, number 5.

NTH in hand, hammer cocked, he made his way through the dark, his Holystone lighting the way. He could feel the slightly sickening tug of the ship banking hard to the starboard. A-Ram must be lining up the *Heade* for a ramming shot.

Or, maybe, the pirate ship out there is attacking. Maybe A-Ram was maneuvering for their lives up there.

He had to hurry.

After a bit of blundering about, he felt his eyes getting used to the dark. What at first looked to him like pitch black, even with the lit-up Holystone, was now half-way passable. He could see the floor, as well as the ceiling and the girders and panels lining the walls. He waved his hand in front of his face and could see it just fine; he could even see the silver embroidery on his coat sleeve. He let the Holystone drop and continued on without it.

Good. He got to the lift shaft. He'd have to go down two levels and bear down the neck of the ship toward the rear section, and then go up three levels into the tower; with the *Seeker* there was always a lot of walking, unlike the *New Faith*, where one could take a lift to just about anywhere. He knew the tower layout pretty well, and shouldn't have too much trouble finding his way around once he got there. He opened the door to the lift and waved his NTH around, half expecting Innocent Drury to pop out of any convenient shadow at any moment.

He had just begun to make his way down when he noticed something. Squinting, he could see hints of something fibrous and stringy stretched out across the opening of the lift shaft. He could see it was a sort of rugose wire strung from the port side of the shaft to the starboard. It appeared taut, but irregular, like a thick gauge wire that had been pulled tight but wasn't quite straight. At intervals, he could see things jutting up from the wire—barbs or pointed razors that stuck up in a predatory manner.

And, he could now see that that one strand wasn't the only one stretched across the shaft—there were many. The shaft was clogged with them, like a messy spider web of barbed wire.

Innocent Drury has been busy, left him quite a grisly present, he thought. Such a spectacle only made the whole mystery of the Druries all the more delectable. He had to admit his curiosity was peaking at what he would encounter when he met Innocent Drury again. Were they demons? Were they creatures like Lilly?

Stenstrom was about to head back out of the shaft and find an alternate route, when the ship was rocked with a massive, pounding blow dead astern.

BOOM!

Caught unaware, Stenstrom was rocked from his perch out into open space—into the lift shaft and the carpet of waiting razor-wire below.

LT. GWENDOLYN, LADY OF PRENTISS

16

—The Dream Begins—

When Captain Gwendolyn, Lady of Prentiss, opened her eyes, she saw her ship in great disarray. Most of the bridge crew were down, some badly wounded. Crewman Allistar, the fellow she'd just yelled at for giving her a late report, was near the navigator's position, face-down on the floor. She struggled to get to him, but her FEDULA, a rapier-like weapon of her House, was tangled up in her coat. Could have been worse—it could have been tangled up in her flesh. Carefully, she freed it and stood.

Pain, great pain in her leg. She disregarded it and got to Allistar, rolled him over, and saw his face covered in blood from a deep wound. His blood made a large red stain on the floor.

There were groaning sounds and signs of distress all around her. The bridge was a charnel house. The Navigator, Lt. Merce, was out, though he showed no outward signs of injury. The Helmsman, Crewman Protherow, appeared to be dead. The Com officer, Lt. Sai, was sitting up against the wall, groggy, holding his head. Gwendolyn made her way to the helm. Unlike Warbirds, with their elaborate wheeled set-ups, the helm on the *Demophalon John* was nothing more than a small panel with a number of levers and gauges that controlled the movement of the ship. Not nearly as precise and maneuverable as a *Straylight*, it, nevertheless, sufficed on a small scouting ship. The levers all appeared to be floating, out of joint. She tried to re-adjust them as best she could, but helmsmanship really wasn't her area. She guessed at the positions. She then checked the helmsman—as she thought, he was dead.

Ahead, crumpled up near the rail, was Morgan-Jeterix. Her silver helmet lay some distance away, upside down. Some of her Hospitaler tools had emptied out of her pockets and lay on the floor all around her.

"Morgan!" Gwen managed to say as she stumbled toward her. "Morgan, wake up. We're sure to have wounded all over."

Morgan appeared to be out. Gwendolyn shook her. "Morgan, wake up!"

She groaned and slowly her eyes opened. "Oh, Creation, it's you . . . What happened?"

"I don't know. We appear to have crashed."

Morgan closed her eyes again. "Did I not tell you we were about to crash?"

"We can discuss that further later, Morgan, for now we've wounded needing tending, casualties to sort out, and . . ."

"Yes, casualties. This is all your fault. Never listen to me, do you? You arrogant cow . . ."

Gwendolyn roughly pulled her up by the scruff of her black Hospitaler uniform. "Morgan! Yes, yes, you're right—I'm an arrogant cow! This is my fault! You can call me all the names you want, as you start tending to my crew! There's Allistar—help him!"

Morgan shook her head, trying to clear it, and unsteadily went to Crewman Allistar. As Morgan worked on him, Gwendolyn went to the main Sensing station and peered into it.

The sensor was ruined, full of static, and random streaks of color that bled across the screen. No good—no readable data.

She could hear the ship "gassing" all over—trying to equalize pressure. Clearly, the hull was breeched somewhere. At least some of the automated systems of the ship were functioning.

Gwendolyn spun around, not quite sure what to do. This was a calamity—situation unknown, location unknown, personnel still on duty unknown. They needed rescuing in a bad way. "Com," she said after a moment to Lt. Sai, "Com, get me Engineering. Right away, please."

Sai blinked at her in a vacant manner and slowly began to stand.

Nothing, silence from the Com. "Com functional but unanswered, Captain," he said, still groggy. "We have internal, we can ... receive, but our outgoing range is very limited. I think . . . we lost our mast."

"Keep trying. See if you can raise anyone, yes?"

She turned to a dazed crewman who was just now picking herself up. "Crewman, I need you to find the boatswain. Tell him I want an accurate injury report, and then I want all wounded organized into a large area—the mess, Cargos one and two—anyplace that can hold them. Morgan and I will then be down to begin treating them. Go now!" The crewman left the bridge.

Gwendolyn returned to Morgan. She was closing the wound on Allistar's forehead. "How is he?"

"He has a compound depressed fracture of the skull," she said continuing her work. "I suppose he's lucky to be alive."

Gwendolyn stood and went to a window. Outside was a solid, inky black. "Where are we?" she said, almost to herself.

"I told you, Captain, we were heading straight for a cluster of planetoids. We're probably crash-landed on one."

"And, Morgan, you were aware of this how?"

Morgan threw down her instruments and got into Gwendolyn's face. "I have told you that my family can see through illusions! You have never properly appreciated my candor and clarity of vision! We just flew into a minefield of illusion. If I were not such a lady, I think I would ..."

"You'd what—hit me? I don't see anything stopping you! Go ahead, let's get this out of the way, so that we can—"

Morgan was gawking wide-eyed at the windows.

Gwendolyn turned.

Outside, in the darkness, a round pair of red, unblinking eyes stared in through the windows.

"You see that?" Morgan cried.

Gwendolyn was transfixed. She just stood there and stared at the eyes.

Then, after a long stretch of time, the red eyes turned and vanished.

"Did you see that?" Morgan said again, walking to Gwendolyn's side.

"Yes, yes, I saw it."

"What was it?"

"An animal of some sort; I'm not a zoologist."

Feeling disoriented, suspecting she was heavily concussed, Gwendolyn assisted Morgan as she tended to the remaining bridge crew.

She looked back to where Allistar had been lying in a pool of his own blood.

The blood was gone.

"I feel it coming," Morgan said.

"What?" Gwendolyn asked.

"Illusion, forming all around us."

Gwendolyn vaguely felt herself falling into a strange dream. She must be delirious.

The Com beeped—an incoming message. "What's that message Com?" she asked, hopeful.

Lt. Sai was not there.

She made her way to the Com to answer it herself.

"What are you doing? There's no message," Morgan said as she worked on another crew member, her voice unsteady.

Gwendolyn hit the button. "Yes this is Fleet scouting ship *Demophalon John*. We are in immediate need of—"

"Gwendolyn!" came a sharp, unpleasant voice over the Com followed by a lurid pause.

"Hello?" Gwendolyn asked. "Is anybody there? We require assistance."

"Who are you talking to?" Morgan asked.

"Gwendolyn!" came a hideous shriek. "This is your aunt! What a silly, weak little girl you are! He's out there close by, and I want you to kill him, do you understand?" Her voice became a demonic howl. "I want you to kill him, Gwendolyn! Kill! KILL HIM!"

She put her hands to her face and backed away. She felt herself plummeting into a dream.

A Self-Portrait of Josephus,

Lord of A-Ram

17

—Lord A-Ram—

"We should never have let him go alone," Taara said, holding the NTH. She cocked it and fired—nothing happened.

Girls couldn't fire an NTH, Bel had said. Guess he was right.

Everything had been working wonderfully. Using the remaining charge on the Missive's Panel, Taara had managed to get a few shipboard systems hammered out. The ship was moving reasonably well under power from the *Westminster*. A-Ram had gotten a fair amount of distance between themselves and the pirate ship. He was going to line it up, build up some speed, and Slap it into bits. That grungy *Webber* out there would never stand against an armored behemoth like the *Seeker*.

Stenstrom called up from the docking ring—the body was still there, which was good news.

And then, the *Westminster* vanished off the grid—pop!—like it had never been there at all. It was like somebody pulled the plug, and the ship went dark again.

The bridge was still lit up—the stolen generators providing power.

A-Ram stood behind the helm—it barely turned. Taara fiddled around with the Com, trying to get it started again. All of the sensing and scanning equipment was dead.

A-Ram cursed. "Taara, I need you to go into Bel's office and shout out the position of the *Heade-on-the-Hearth*. I have no idea where it is. My screen is dead here."

Taara ran into the office. "I don't see it!"

It's got to be out there—it can't have gone far. I had it all lined up."

"I think it might be to our left. Go that way."

A-Ram pulled on the wheel and the *Seeker* banked steeply to the left.

"Hey—there it is—to our 10pm. It's turning. A-Ram, it's firing!"

A series of hard shocks rocked the *Seeker*.

A-Ram hung onto the helm. "What in Creation was that?"

"It was an energy beam of some sort—looks like a hot cassagrain."

"On a *Webber*?"

"They've got a moveable long-barrel cannon mounted under the ship's nose, and that's what they're hitting us with!" Taara's voice was panicked. "A-Ram, they're coming around again for another pass!"

"Where?"

"7:30pm!"

A-Ram tugged on the helm with all his might, feeling the ship protest. "Do we have any weapons at all?"

"Take a guess, A-Ram!"

The *Seeker* was rocked again. "A-Ram, the dorsal quarter, rear section, is starting to glow!"

Her voice became a shriek. "Watch the tentacles! Watch the tentacles—it's trying to grab us!"

"Taara, all we've got is partial maneuvering thrusters. What am I supposed to do?"

He pulled on the helm and tried to present the other side of the ship to the *Heade*, to give the heated-up quarter of the hull time to cool and to create some space. The helm fought him. He pulled harder. Of all the great men who had once turned this wheel, in its time of greatest need, a tiny man from Calvert would turn its pegs. He would not be meek, he would not be denied, A-Ram bent the helm to his will. Taara watched the *Heade's* movements. "A-Ram, I think he's going for the *Westminster*. He's heading for a shot in that direction. High noon!"

A-Ram cursed, kicked the bars, and pulled on the wheel with all his might, forcing it to turn, forcing the ship to respond. He spun the nose around trying to get the *Westminster* as far away from the *Heade* as possible.

Another rumble from outside. Hit again. "Where'd he get us, Taara?" A-Ram shouted.

"Rear-quarter ventral!"

Good, A-Ram thought—armor's thickest there.

The *Seeker* shuddered.

"They're hitting us long, A-Ram!" Taara cried. "They're pouring it on!"

"Fine—let them! Taara, do we have any locomotion at all?"

She thought a moment. "No! Without the *Westminster*, no!"

A-Ram spun the helm as the *Heade* came about and blasted them again, its cassagrain lighting up cherry red.

"A-Ram, watch out! A-Ram!!"

. . . *A-Ram!!*

✳   ✳   ✳   ✳   ✳

Adjutant Lt. Josephus, Lord of A-Ram, lived in the flower-potted, balconied Fleet apartments south of the main complex yard just a block or two from the weedy growth of the Great Armenelos Forest. The forest surrounded the city and was constantly threatening to engulf it. His apartment was small, but well-appointed and decorated in a sunny fashion—he'd done it himself, Lord A-Ram having a love of bright color and texture. He had tried his hand at various artistic pursuits: painting, sculpting, and so forth, but his skill was limited. Some of the paintings he had finished were colorful enough, but all were rather formless and abstract in nature.

He came from a House Minor in Calvert. His father was Lord Joshuah, and his mother, Lady Rihan. He was the youngest and the smallest of all his brothers and sisters. Coming from a Calvert House, the A-Rams didn't live in a huge manor or stately villa; instead, they lived in a serviceable townhouse in the heart of St. Edmunds a few blocks from the docks on St. James Road. A-

Ram had no complaints—he had had a good life.

His father was a fisherman, owning a few boats berthed in the St. Edmunds dock that normally brought in enough money to keep the family living fairly well. The House of A-Ram was originally a House from the eastern city of Dee hailing from the old House of Aramtwillinger, but when the Sisters announced that they were going to destroy the city of Dee for decadence and vice, the House broke apart—the Houses of Twill and Atlinger moving north to the new city of Dee, while the House of A-Ram went south-west and re-settled in St. Edmunds. The A-Rams thought it best to get back into the Sisters' good graces, and avoiding Dee altogether would be wise. They took the name "Aram," but when they submitted their patent to the Sisters at Valenhelm, they miscopied it, coming up with the legal name "A-Ram," which the Sisters refused to correct afterwards.

Such would be their usual treatment from the Sisters: miscopied, mishandled, and unsatisfied.

The A-Rams would have an occasional and rather sordid history with the Sisters through the years, with each event lessening them ever more in esteemed sect's eyes. All Houses wanted the Sisters to approve of them, and the A-Rams were no different. Clovis of A-Ram had become a noted chef at the Empire Hotel in St. Edmunds, however, when a Sister came to sample his latest dish, a bad piece of halibut made her dreadfully sick, bending her over to full-blown food poisoning complete with carpet kneeling and projectile vomiting right there in the hotel dining room. That incident, however, paled in comparison to the Brandtball Affair years later, where Lord Arlie of A-Ram, the Charger of Beasley Canning Brandtball team, put a Sister from Saga Convent into the wall, and, subsequently, into traction while attempting to make a rough play.

Such things the Sisters tend not to forget, and so the House of A-Ram fell off the Sisters' Programmability schedule entirely and became "untouchable". When one poisons a Sister, when one injures her playing Brandtball, one can bet they won't want to have Programmability anytime soon.

Untouchable. Venti Nomi.

A-Ram.

Everybody helped out with the family trade—his mother and his siblings included. His brothers went out with father every day to harvest the catch. His mother and sisters waited to help unload and process the fish when they returned. When Josephus grew old enough to accompany his father out to sea, he was miserable. Not only was his eyesight appalling, he was a grand klutz as well, making messes on the boat, tangling nets, and losing catches. He was also chronically sea sick, and that was something he never got over. Eventually, father, shaking his head, relegated him back to the shore where he helped out with the women—his older brother Ephelrood tormented him relentlessly on the matter. Helping mother was no small chore—she kept everything regimented and precise—possibly that's where he learned to keep a clear, uncluttered head and work in a logical manner, from his mother's teachings.

As he grew, he learned that salt-sprayed and sunny Calvert was considered a lowly place, the least of places on Kana, unlike the stately lands to the north and the west, and the mountainous regions far to the north where he heard the god-like people with blue hair lived.

What was wrong with Calvert? The weather was warm and the people were good; not overly rich or fashionable, but cheery and neighborly none the less. People helped each other in Calvert, would go out of their way for each other. Calvert was a good place.

Then, there came word of strange doings—of murders, people turning up dead. The wharves and sea-sides began buzzing of a "Fiend" who was committing the murders—the Fiend of Calvert. People began looking at each other twice, strangers became untrusting—the Fiend not only killed men in the streets, he killed a little bit of the spirit of Calvert too.

Josephus was terrified of the Fiend; who was doing this? Who could do such a thing? His brother loved to torment him. "It's me, Joe, you little fish monger . . . I'm the Fiend . . . and you're next."

In an attempt to protect him and his school-age brothers and sisters, A-Ram was sent off to day school in Dee, where the Fiend so far hadn't showed, coming home only on the weekends.

Josephus was a fine student and was generally at or near the top of his classes on a consistent basis. The top students of the school were often invited to have lunch with a faction of important ladies known as the Sisterhood of Light—it was an honor, he was told—the Sisters were wise and influential and currying their favor was the key to success in the League. Sitting at the large table, he was in awe of these tall, skinny ladies dressed all in white, each with a huge, cranked headdress, shaped like the wing of an airship. The Sisters never spoke, but their presence spoke volumes, and their gaze could stop you in your tracks. Many of the students sitting at lunch were selected to read essays and poems they had written to the Sisters. Josephus wanted to read something to them, and he was determined to sharpen his writing skills so that he too might one day have the honor.

He wrote a short poem about summer that delighted his teachers, and, he got his wish. He was selected to stand, approach, and read to the Sisters at lunch. He stood with his paper and stepped forward, his ugly black glasses trembling on his face. The Sisters' presence was piercing. They sat with perfect posture, their arms wrapped up in thin strips of white cloth like bandages beneath their loose robes, their delicate hands holding their soup spoons. They sat there looking at him with inscrutable eyes, the wings of their headdresses bobbing slightly.

Josephus choked up; he couldn't summon the courage to read his poem. After a while, humiliated before his snickering classmates, he returned to his seat, devastated.

When school let out for the summer, he returned home. The Fiend was still on the prowl and his parents kept a close eye on their son. He told his mother of his shame before the Sisters. And she told him it was probably just as well; the Sisters didn't favor Calverts much—they preferred the Remnaths and the Zenons, and their favorites, the Vith, with their god-like abilities and their blue hair. She also mentioned something about the Sisters' Program— and that they rarely considered the House of A-Ram worthy. His brother, Ephelrood, liked to tell his friends he'd had Programmability with a Sister, and that she'd fallen in love with him in the process. He received occasional notices from the Sisters, he said it was correspondence from his "Sister Admirer". A-Ram managed to get a quick glimpse of one of the notices once. It was a warning from the Sisters and a fine for lying to the people regarding Programmability. Josephus didn't understand what his mother meant, about the Sisters' Program and all, and his brother often told lies, so that wasn't a surprise; he simply knew that he'd lost something special when he couldn't read his poem to the Sisters. How he wished he had had the courage to read it to them. Maybe they would have liked it.

That summer, he found himself bored, waiting there on the docks for his father's boats to return. One day, while poking about the shed his family owned, he found something hidden under a tarp. Pulling the tarp aside, he discovered a small, open-aired vehicle of some kind, barely big enough to seat four people. It reminded him of a mechanical dolphin. It was a faded blue, with seats and a dash full of control mechanisms. He ran out onto the dock, found his mother, and demanded to know what it was.

She told him it was an old Sub-Orbital—an airship that hadn't worked in years. Apparently his older brother had messed it up somehow and nobody ever bothered fixing it. The A-Rams weren't air people; they were sea people.

But, A-Ram was fascinated. He spent the rest of the summer working with it every day before the boats came in. He studied up—discovered the ship was a Merc22 Sub-Orbital built by a now defunct manufacturer in Zenon. In the greater scheme of Sub-Orbital classification, the Merc22 was a Class 4, just a toy, small and under-powered. It was a starter vehicle not rated to go very high or fast.

Taking apart much of the rusty internals, he soon had a pile of parts lying about the shed and no idea where he'd gotten them from or how to put them back into place. His brother Ephelrood made a big deal about it, saying he had been planning to fix the craft "next week," but now Josephus had ruined it beyond hope of repair.

"Great going . . . dweeb!"

For his sixteenth birthday, his parents gave A-Ram a powerful gift: the MOLLY, the LosCapricos weapon of his family, delivered in a plain box complete with a certificate from the Sisterhood of Light. They told him that the MOLLY could do wondrous things. It could allow one to do things one might not ordinarily be able to do, and know things one shouldn't know. His father apparently used the MOLLY to help him steer his boats to where the fish were, and his mother admitted she used it to know exactly what sorts of fish he had caught and how best to prepare for his return. His brother swore the fabled powers of the MOLLY was nothing but a hoax, for he'd tried to use it for all sorts of grand things and never got anywhere with it.

Josephus didn't listen to his brother, as he was in awe—here it was, the MOLLY—it looked like a golden charm in the shape of a fish and, apparently, despite his brother's protests, it could work minor miracles. The MOLLY was rumored to have come from a captured chest of cursed Xaphan treasure won from a sunken ship during the Battle of Sorrander-Quo. The Sisters took the chest, determined the pieces possessed arcane properties, and, not certain what to make of it, smelted the pieces into various trinkets and distributed them to a number of House Minors of low repute for "Testing Purposes", the A-Rams being one of them. His parents, though, were full of warnings. They said the MOLLY came with a cost—you couldn't use it without first registering with the Sisters, and its overuse could imperil his soul.

Being a remarkably empirical boy, Josephus decided to test the MOLLY, to see what it could do. There was an eating contest that was held every year in Calvert Square, a messy affair with blueberry pies. He decided to enter it and use the MOLLY, to see what might happen. There was a pre-generated form his parents had for using the MOLLY. He filled it out and sent it along to the Sisters, wondering what their response would be and how long it would take.

He didn't have long to wait. He got back a quick response. The Sisters weren't kind in their assessment. In every column they responded with the words NEGLIGABLE and INSIGNIFICANT and OF NO CONSEQUENCE. Their final assessment: APPROVED: LEAST CONCERN.

Though Josephus was just a little boy—he began to understand full well that the Sisters, those ladies in headdresses he so wanted to impress with his poem about the wonders of summer, didn't think much about him and his family. He'd heard of his uncle the cook and his other uncle the Brandtball player and their embarrassing misadventures with the Sisters, but those stories meant little to him. Here, in his response from the Sisters, was proof of his family's lowly situation with them, and that was galling for him.

He went out, MOLLYed up, and won the eating contest—all the big-bellied older kids scratching their heads, wondering how such a small, skinny lad could have put so much pie away. The MOLLY really did appear to work if used properly. With it, he could probably have the Merc22 fixed in no time. But, as the Lords of the Contest pinned his ribbon on his chest in the sunshine of Calvert Square, the Sisters' comments rang through in his mind:

NEGLIGABLE ...

INSIGNIFICANT ...

LEAST CONCERN ...

He made a momentous decision at that point, especially for a child. He decided he was going to fix the Merc22 all on his own, and, what's more, once he fixed it, he was going to teach himself how to fly it; again, all by himself. If he could do such a thing, perhaps the Sisters would approve.

Working all summer, he gathered as much information as he could from the Holo-net, from the libraries, and from the handymen down the lane—even though the Fiend had everybody worked up, there still remained a good measure of neighborly decency floating around Calvert. The handymen got used to seeing him every day, always with fresh questions. Soon, he had a basic understanding of the simple systems making up the Merc22: there were the Collective systems and the Cyclic systems, the superchargers and the gyroscopes governing it all, Unified thrust and harmony of control. Pouring over his materials, reverse-engineering the craft, he discovered what had happened to put the vehicle out of commission: his brother had damaged the mechanical linkages controlling the canards and flight surfaces, and the two bottle motors mounted in the rear were blown out—apparently from improper use. Ephelrood had, as the handymen put it, flown the Merc22 "out of the envelope" and the result was a dogged-out ship.

He figured all this out on his own—no help from the MOLLY.

Josephus saved his money and scoured the nearby junkyards, looking for the correct replacement parts. As a birthday gift, his parents bought him the two replacement bottle motors. Finally, with everything re-installed and fitted, the Merc22 was ready to go.

A complication occurred when his brother appeared.

He discovered all the work Josephus had been doing and laughed at him— no way, no way could that old wreck be fixed, for he had tried himself and couldn't do it. When he found out that the Merc22 had in fact been fixed, he was elated and Commed his friends that he had fixed the old Merc and was coming to take them out for a spin over the rooftops. A-Ram was terrified; his brother had been the one who wrecked it in the first place, and would probably do it again.

All that work was about to be shot to the moons.

He ran to the shed just as an unsightly gaggle noisily stepped onto the dock. It was his brother, one of his meathead friends and a bouncing pair of painted trollops from the cemeteries arriving fueled by smoking menthols and clinking bottles of cheap spirits.

"Oi, Joe! Get away from my ship, you little bug! You'll mess up all my hard work!" his brother cried.

"Let's get him!" his friend yelled with glee. "Let's pull his pants down and throw him in the water!"

Straining with all his might, A-Ram pushed the Merc out onto the dock and jumped into the cockpit. He could hear his brother and his friends running up fast across the planks of the dock.

bump . . . bump . . . bump . . . bump . . .

"Joe, I'm going to pull your little wings out, you fly! You worthless bug!" his brother called on the run, throwing an empty bottle of wine at him.

He set the controls and took off down the dock just as his brother and his crew got there, dodging a hail of thrown bottles and shoes as he climbed into the air.

"I'm going to get you, Joe!" his brother yelled.

Flailing about in mid-air, he struggled with it, like an unruly bronco. He knew from his reading how the controls worked—that pulling back on the yoke made it go up, and pushing forward caused it to descend. He knew the side stick controlled the collective attitude of the vehicle and the foot pedals made it yaw, or slide. After a few minutes and a few close calls, he'd almost hit the roof of the Empire Hotel and caused a group of strollers in Calvert Square to scatter, he got the hang of it. After an hour of playing in the clouds, he had mastery of it, soaring over the colorful seaside of Calvert, waving at the people below.

Thus began his love of flying and the sky, moving in the direction of the sun far away from roving Fiends, from the ocean that made him sick, from brothers who mocked him, and the Sisters who disregarded him.

✳   ✳   ✳   ✳   ✳

When he was twenty-nine, A-Ram made an appointment to see Lord Catherbaum, the local House Major lord in St. Edmunds. Though he was a Great Lord, Catherbaum was a man about the neighborhood, often seen strolling the docks with his bags of purchases or sitting in the lobby of the Empire Hotel laughing out loud and smoking with the comers and goers. He was on a first name basis with Josephus' mother and father, and he often bought his father's catches. A-Ram's goal was to join the Stellar Fleet. He wanted to become a helmsman; he wanted to fly a great ship and, for that, he needed a Letter of Recommendation. He had high hopes—he could fly, he could soar. All he needed was the chance to prove it.

In reviewing Lord A-Ram's petition, Lord Catherbaum didn't have good news. He sat there behind his desk, hands folded, and quietly laid it out for him. "Josephus, you know I think you a fine young lad, and I would happily draft you a Letter of Recommendation, but let's be reasonable. You wish to be a Fleet helmsman—your eyesight is so poor, and, not only that—it's uncorrectable via surgery. You have your opticals there, but I know the Lords of the Fleet—they would not look kindly upon that. Even the Marines, I . . ." He cleared his throat. "Additionally, and I don't know if you're aware of this, but the Sisterhood of Light has long placed a *Venta-Nomi,* upon your House's patent. They think your House is flawed, imperfect, not worth their Program. You are, in their eyes, untouchable and the Lords of the Fleet would see that, and disqualify you because of it. A lot of nonsense really, but the Fleet values the Sisters' assessments."

Josephus sat there and felt ashamed. "I'm sorry," Catherbaum said.

Venta-Nomi. Flawed, imperfect?

Untouchable. Unwanted.

He was devastated. He looked at his hands through his glasses, quietly stood and left the office.

"Josephus, wait!" Lord Catherbaum said catching up to him. He put his hands on A-Ram's tiny shoulders. "Wait. Please attend, for I do not wish you to walk out of here thinking that this is any of your fault. I've seen you flying that little ship around, and I'll wager your skill against anybody's. The Sisters and their damned *Venta-Nomi!* Who are they to place summary judgment on you . . . on us? They've never given the people of Calvert our due—never! We are good people, thought low by the rest of Kana. Even when there's a mad killer in our midst, slaying us at his whim, we can get no help—just another dead man in Calvert—who's to bother? Who's to care? Well, I care, and I'm bringing in someone of my own, some fellow from the north who wears a mask, paid out of my own coin. I've heard he gets results. And, tomorrow, I march with our people to Calvert Square, and we shall demand justice, and there will be justice for you as well, Josephus. There is a contest that I know of in the spring—oh, it's just nonsense, but if you win, you shall have an honorary admittance to the Fleet. It's not much, but, if you win, you shall be in the Fleet, and once there you can make your own way, and make them see you for who you are."

Having no idea what to make of that, Josephus left Lord Catherbaum's office and went home.

✳   ✳   ✳   ✳   ✳

Josephus lay in his bed. In the morning he would go to Dee and participate in an essay-writing contest that Lord Catherbaum had signed him up for. To the winner went a low-level administrative position in the Stellar Fleet. It wasn't much, but, assuming he could win the contest, it might lead to better things.

It might . . .

He was excited.

As he tried to settle his thoughts and get some rest, he thought he heard some sort of commotion outside. His room was on the top level of the family townhouse and sounds carried up there. It sounded like a struggle, a distant crashing getting steadily nearer, then he heard a loud toppling sound coming from the roof overhead, followed by: *bump, bump, bump, bump* . . .

Footsteps, somebody running across his rooftop, and then the sounds were gone. He would come to know that the footsteps were the Fiend of Calvert, running for his life from the Mad Lord of Walther.

That was the last time the Fiend was heard of in Calvert.

That was also the last night of Josephus' old life at home. A new day was soon to dawn, and a new life as well.

18

—An Unusual Errand—

There was a rather thick envelope sitting on his desk as he came into the office that morning, the envelope simply reading: JOSEPHUS.

A-Ram had been at work in Admiral Derlith's office for ten years. He had worked his way up over the years after winning his essay-writing contest in Dee, starting in the Fleet's cavernous mailroom. He was liked well enough, and often praised for his uncluttered mind and his admirable work ethic, but, his glasses and his ever-present "Sister Problem" kept him from advancing—quite unfair. Most of the people who started in the mailroom at the same time he did were promoted years ago, or kicked out for not passing muster.

Eventually, he received a great promotion, by default. Admiral Derlith of the 3rd Fleet, Lord of Cone, was in need of a new adjutant, for his old one had quit in a froth. The post of assisting an Admiral was normally a highly sought after job, but this was the dreaded Admiral Derlith and the paucity of applicants to join his office was notable. Admiral Derlith was a known crab-head, a hard and often humiliating man to work for. And not only was he a yeller and a screamer, there was something strange about him, something haunting and unsettling hanging over him that was palpable enough to be noticed by all. In any event, Josephus was game, and for lack of anyone else seeking the job, he was posted to the Admiral's office.

Admiral Derlith, gray-haired, big-toothed, was indeed a difficult man to serve—short-tempered, critically inclined and fickle in his caprices, he often called him out and reproached Josephus in public in a brusque, loud manner. But, Josephus endured, patiently, serving the Admiral in a competent manner. Despite his unflattering treatment of him, the Admiral was a kind benefactor, paying him rather well and personally seeing to his needs. His biggest problem was his glasses, as the Admiral refused to allow him to wear them when guests were present in the office. Too ugly.

JOSEPHUS, the envelope read.

It was just a touch after four bells, and the office was quiet and dark. He set his armful of things down and opened it. Inside was a rather thick letter from the Admiral.

It read:

Josephus

As you might well be aware, today is Tuesday. It is possible you might also be aware that on Tuesdays you are normally expected to retrieve my uniforms from the bags, shine up the office tea set, and type my usual correspondence.

Today, however, I have a novel set of errands for you to accomplish that supersedes all else. As follows shall be a detailed set of instructions. You are to follow the instructions TO THE LETTER; there will be no need for you to deviate from the instructions, question or embellish them in any way. Follow your instructions to a point, complete your task, and tomorrow we shall resume our routine as usual.

OVERVIEW—You shall retrieve five small parcels currently located in places listed hereafter. The parcels are small, each not weighing more than five pounds. You have been provided with a compartmented carrying satchel (please see below).

CARRYING CONTRIVANCE: You have been provided with a custom carrying satchel that you will need to complete this errand. The satchel is located in the bottom drawer of my credenza. You will note the interior of the satchel is compartmented into five sections. Each section of the satchel currently contains a key—you shall need these keys to complete your errand (see below). The parcels you collect shall be placed into each compartmented section. I would appreciate you placing the parcels in order of acquisition in the satchel from left to right.

KEYS: As stated above, there are five keys contained in the satchel. The keys, from left to right, shall be situated in order of their required use (i.e., the first key on the left shall be the first key you will require; the key immediately to the right of that shall be the next one required, and so on).

PARCELS: As above, the parcels you shall collect are fairly small, will weigh no more than five pounds each, and will be packaged in a standard paper delivery wrapping. The contents of the parcels are rather delicate, and I will advise you not to handle them any more than is necessary to secure and place them into your carrying satchel. Once placed within the satchel, do not remove them from their compartment. WARNING—Do not mingle the parcels; again, keep them in their separate compartments. And, for Creation's Sake, do not open them—that goes without saying.

CARRYING WEIGHT: Again, I do not anticipate your carrying weight to exceed twenty pounds. If you feel this weight is excessive, you may, under my authority, requisition a pull float from billeting for your use. Authorization code: A11B946621

MEAL ALLOWANCE: As this errand shall consume the better part of your morning and afternoon, I have set aside a money bag containing fifty Fleet solaris for your use to be spent for breakfast and lunch at your discretion. Given the current rate of exchange, the money should be sufficient to purchase you a respectable breakfast and lunch. You may use all of the money left to you; however, if your costs exceed the sum in the money bag, you will have to pay the difference from your personal funds. I pray you use the money wisely. You shall find the moneybag inside your custom carrying satchel.

DETAILED ITINERARY:

6 Bells: A Fleet coach shall be waiting for you at the Billson Avenue dock—he will await you under the name: Lord A-Ram. You will have until 6 bells and one quarter to board the coach. Do not be late.

Instructions to Driver: You shall inform the driver to take you at speed to the Grayson Memorial Land, Air and Stellar Port at 1 West Munson Street, King's Way, Armenelos.

7 Bells: You shall arrive at the Port. Instruct the driver to wait and enter the West Portico. Once inside, proceed to the locker yard and locate locker A1501. Using the first key in your satchel, open the locker, secure the parcel within and place it in the open compartment. You will no longer need the first key and will discard it.

Proceed now to the East Portico of the port and locate locker W884. As before, using the next key in your satchel, open the locker, secure the parcel, and place it in its compartment. Discard the key at that time.

9 Bells: *You shall then re-board your coach and head west to the incorporated hamlet of Mystery.*

Instructions to Driver: *You shall inform the driver to take you without delay to the Mystery Land and Air Port located at 5234 Borgelund Way, Pitcairn, Mystery.*

11 Bells: *You shall arrive at the Port. Again instruct the driver to wait. Inside, proceed to the locker yard and locate locker 155673. Using the third key from the left, open the locker, retrieve the parcel within and place the parcel in its compartmented section. Discard the key.*

Once you have secured the parcel, your task is done at the Mystery port. Your next destination shall be a great distance from Mystery. I recommend you take the time to have breakfast; however, I advise you not tarry past 12 bells.

12 Bells: *You shall then re-board your coach and head east to the city of Conwell.*

Instructions to Driver: *You shall inform the driver to transport you at speed to the Gates of Esther Land, Air and Stellar Port located at 77 Withelwell Road, Monforton, Conwell.*

16 Bells: *You shall arrive at the port. Instruct the driver to wait. Inside, proceed to the locker yard and locate locker Blue 888 and use the key located in the compartment second from the right. Use the key, secure the parcel, place it in its compartment, and discard the key.*

Once you have secured the parcel, your task is done at the Gates of Esther Land Port.

17 Bells: *You shall then re-board your coach and head south-east to the city of Dee.*

Instructions to Driver: *You shall inform the driver to take you to the City of Dee Land, Air and Sea Port located at 1622 Monmouth, Seaquay, Dee. Once arrived, you will instruct the driver to carry on and return to the Fleet. You shall receive additional instructions at the Port as to your return arrangements back to the Fleet Complex.*

19 Bells: *You shall arrive at the port. Inside, proceed to the private locker area and locate locker BN77789A. Use the final key, secure the parcel and place it in the compartment. Once secured, you will have successfully retrieved all required parcels.*

FINAL INSTRUCTIONS*: You shall receive a final set of instructions at the port. These instructions shall contain the address where you are to deliver the satchel and the details for your return arrangements to the Fleet.*

I cannot accurately describe to you what you shall encounter in Dee; however, I pray you use your best judgment in the matter.

I will thank you to accurately, and safely, follow these instructions and be returned to Fleet no later than 25 Bells. I shall have no further need of your services for the remainder of the day, but will expect you to be at your desk promptly at 5 bells the following morning for work as usual.

Signed
Derlith, Lord of Cone, Admiral of the 3rd Fleet.

The letter was a typical Admiral Derlith creation—full of detail, leaving nothing to chance. He went into the Admiral's office, dark and quiet in the early morning, and pulled open the drawer to the credenza.

Sitting inside was a black carrying case, rather on the largish size with an ugly but functional set of handles. He pulled it out and set it on the Admiral's desk. It was a clamshell-style case, opening from the top like a carpetbag. Inside, as promised in the letter, were five neatly laid out compartments running the length of the bag labeled "1" to "5", each section about four inches wide. Lying within each compartment was a key. The keys were of a simple style—clearly keys that would fit into a lowly, disused locker at a public port. Also sitting inside was the money bag the Admiral had promised.

The lining of the case was an odd, flexible latex covered with a gritty and unevenly sprayed-on layer of gray paint that had a very metallic quality to it.

He closed the case, got his hat and proceeded to leave the office. First, though, he watered the Admiral's plants and readied the coffee set—all the Admiral would have to do when he got in is turn it on and he would have his coffee. He then locked up and headed in the direction of the Bilson Avenue dock to await the coach. He expected a long day ahead of him.

✳ ✳ ✳ ✳ ✳

The hover coach sped across the Kana Avenue toward Conwell—a broad green highway cutting through the Great Armenelos forest. There was no roadway or macadam or concrete making up the highway, only a winding passage of compacted earth that hindered the growth of trees, where only tough short grasses could take hold. Lining the avenue were grand estates and fine Zenon manors mixed into the dense, vine-filled tangle of the forest.

Josephus had already collected three of the parcels—the whole exercise had gone just as the Admiral had laid it out. He arrived at the ports and asked the driver to wait. He then walked in, found the lockers (which was probably the most difficult part of the procedure), opened them and got the parcel out. The parcels, again as advertised, were small, square packages of a soft nature. He thought he could hear sand or some other gritty material hissing about within the carefully wrapped paper. He slid them into their compartments.

It could be said that Josephus, always a bright, big-headed fellow with a flighty imagination, often embellished his daily doings, transforming the mundane into the suspenseful and the extraordinary—imagining, as he watered the Admiral's plants, that he was tending to some infirm alien species, or that, when he fetched the Admiral's mail, he was retrieving some piece of covert intelligence crucial to the safety of the League.

All sorts of rubbish like that.

But today, he couldn't help but feel his fanciful embellishments were hitting a little too close to home.

He was certain he was being followed.

The feeling began rather early on, as he was searching for the lockers in Armenelos Port. He had the quick notion that his footsteps were being retraced and his actions scrutinized from afar.

He'd look back, checking over his shoulder, and, as usual, there were people there, moving randomly, going about their business, betraying nothing that would prompt him into believing that somebody was actively following him.

He tried to shrug the feeling off. When he got to the port in Mystery, the feeling returned, if anything a bit more forceful this time. He decided to sit down to some breakfast, as there was a lovely café nearby that he was partial to. As he ate, he caught glimpses of something behind the usual traffic of people—just a hint of somber cloth, a brief silhouette that added up to nothing concrete. He hurried, finished his breakfast, and left, getting on the coach and moving off eastward into the heart of the forest.

As the lovely green highway floated past at a comforting speed, he began to relax, settle back, the partially full satchel sitting in the seat next to him. He thought to shut his eyes for a bit.

As his eyelids closed, he saw something.

He sat up and stared out the window.

Standing at the side of the avenue was a tall figure wearing a gray cloak and a broad gray hat. The figure stood before a stand of dense growth holding its hands out in front of it in a rather threatening manner. The cloak and hat that the figure was wearing obscured most of its body and made trying to determine its features or its gender pointless.

It looked to him like he imagined the Fiend of Calvert might appear. There were no clear descriptions of the Fiend, and even scholars and tradesmen seeking to profit from the Fiend-lore varied widely in their personal interpretations of how the Fiend should look. Some envisioned him as a scruffy, tattooed sailor, coming ashore for murder and mayhem, and then slipping safely back to sea. Others saw the Fiend as a proper gentleman, dressed for a night on the town wearing a gasmask, as the Fiend left no Genetics behind for the Evidencers to collect.

A-Ram had always imagined the Fiend as a tall figure clad in gray, thin and agile, his clothes covering up most of his body, except for his grinning mouth and teeth.

. . . and that was, for the most part, what he was seeing standing by the road.

As the coach passed by, the figure stood there, motionless. A-Ram put his face to the window glass and gawked at it—it was simply a person standing by the road-side, but its intent seemed odd. Its presence felt malicious.

As he passed, it glanced up, ever so slightly. Its hat covered the upper portion of its face, he could see hints of a chin, and a mouth pulled back into a mirthless grin.

The figure fell into the distance in just a moment as the coach continued on its rapid way. Straining to see, he thought he saw the figure step out onto the avenue green and watch as the coach moved east.

He was relieved when he got to Conwell. He'd been fretting a bit about this gray figure standing on the side of the road. He bounced down out of the coach with his satchel, trying to convince himself he'd dreamed the whole thing.

As he made his way into the port, he again had the feeling he was being followed. Turning as he had before in Armenelos and Mystery, he looked back, expecting to see nothing. Across the street, standing in the sunshine, was a tall figure in gray—the same one he'd seen standing on the Kana Avenue, the bustling people moving around it as if it were invisible.

But, that's not possible. How could a person standing on the side of the road travel so fast and get here ahead of him?

He dismissed the idea as hogwash, chided himself for being foolish and hurried inside.

After he secured the parcel, feeling oddly invigorated, he decided to have lunch. He took his time and enjoyed his meal, sitting in a nice café in the center of Conwell. He was impressed by this lovely city and thought it truly a place he should return and explore in greater detail. With his nearly full satchel sitting next to him, he relaxed and even thought to order a spot of dessert.

As he looked over the menu, his heart leapt into his throat. Sitting at the far end of the café was the now familiar figure in gray—closer this time. Much closer.

A-Ram left the money bag on the table, grabbed his satchel, and fled back to the waiting coach.

✶　✶　✶　✶　✶

So far, with the exception of his phantom pursuer, the day had gone according to the Admiral's plan. He arrived in Dee—a city he was much more familiar with and got out of the coach. As instructed in his letter, he dismissed the coach and watched as it floated down the lane, joining the flow of traffic.

Holding his satchel, which was getting a little heavy (he wished he'd opted to get the float lift), he marched up the steps toward the grand entrance to the port. A helmeted guildsman in blue wearing a cloak and holding a Masan pulse rifle stopped him.

"Afternoon, citizen," the guildsman said.

"Good afternoon, sir," Josephus replied.

"Do you have business in the port today?"

"I do."

"I'm afraid I cannot allow you entrance to the port."

"Why not?"

"Your bag is reading as slightly radioactive. It's not harmful; please have no fear, but our regulations are clear—your bag will have to be inspected and properly shielded."

A-Ram looked at his satchel. Radioactive?

"I'm not embarking on a trip. I simply need to go in and retrieve a bit of property that is stored there for me."

"That's fine. Please, attend across the street." The guildsman pointed to a small building. "If you have temporary business in the Port, you may, at no cost, check your bag there and retrieve it once your business is concluded. A momentary inconvenience I assure you; however, it must be done. Otherwise, I cannot allow you to enter."

A-Ram thought a moment. "I'm from Calvert—I recall no such regulations."

"It's new—there was an incident where a group of scalawags from Onaris attempted to blow up City Dock. The Magistrate of Dee has enacted a standing order to visually inspect all bags prior to entering the port until further notice. A bit of paranoia perhaps, but there it is."

He considered his options and looked across the street. His instructions were clear—handle the parcels as briefly as possible. He opened his satchel and pulled out the final key. "You say my bag is radioactive, sir?" he asked.

"Yes—not much, but it triggers my goggles here. You might be surprised how many mildly radioactive items are rolling around out there—I'm seeing things everywhere. Again, it's nothing harmful and just a formality until things blow over around here."

He considered his situation. He assumed that the checking of his bag would add no more than a few minutes to his process. It shouldn't be a problem. He took the final key from his satchel, marched across the street, waited in queue for a few minutes and checked his bag. He received a baggage ticket.

Armed with his key and his letter and his ticket, he entered the port and waded into the locker area. After a bit of fruitless searching, for these lockers were not setup nearly as orderly as they were in the other ports—again Calvert lagged a little behind everybody else, doing things not quite as well as is done elsewhere. Eventually he came to the correct one and opened it.

Inside was the usual square parcel wrapped in brown paper and an envelope.

He opened it:

To: Josephus, Lord of A-Ram

You are to be congratulated. You have done well in executing this important assignment, and you shall be justly rewarded.

Bring your satchel to: 1144 Dunwoodwell West, Fehklar, Dee and go to apartment 212. There you will deposit the satchel and you shall receive your reward and your ticket for your return journey to Armenelos.

Signed: Unsigned.

He read the letter. It was vague and a little unsettling, clearly written in a hand other than the Admiral's. This was very irregular—to deliver a satchel to a civilian address when, for the whole time, he'd been operating under the notion that he was performing Fleet business.

And why was the letter unsigned.

And why were the contents he had picked up radioactive, albeit slightly so?

He bent down and picked up the parcel. Unlike the other parcels, this one didn't rattle; instead, it had a clay-like, moldable quality. If he squeezed with his fingers, he could feel the contents changing shape slightly.

He recalled the Admiral's warning to not handle the parcels too much. He tucked the parcel under his arm and headed back out toward the street. It was best to finish up and get back home. He'd ask the Admiral in the morning what this was all about.

As he neared the street to get his satchel, he heard someone clearing their throat.

Standing a few feet away was a Sister, on the smallish side in her white robes and headdress. She was looking over her shoulder at him. She stood there for a while.

"Great Sister, is there something I can do for you?" he finally asked.

She glanced down. There was a small puddle on the street in front of where she wanted to cross.

He was a little dumbfounded. A Sister—a woman who could probably boil away the puddle with TK or wish it away, or do any of a number miraculous things to make it vanish, was content to wait for Josephus to do the chivalrous thing and lay his coat down for her.

Venta-Nomi

Flawed . . .

Imperfect . . .

He set the parcel aside, and took his Fleet coat off. He laid it out over the small puddle and the Sister lightly stepped over it. His coat barely got wet, the puddle was so small.

She then looked back at him, lifted her arm and touched his face. The white wrappings of her thin arm went up past the loose folds of her robes.

Her small hand was so warm. She smiled at him, curtsied and went on her way.

Josephus took his coat and thought about what had just happened.

Did that Sister know he was *Venta-Nomi?* Would she have cared?

Holding his coat, he sat down by the curb and picked his parcel back up. He was filled with a sudden longing. He forgot about his task.

Venta-Nomi

Flawed.

Imperfect.

Unwanted.

Those words kept flashing through his mind.

Her smile.

Her warm hand on his face.

Those thoughts flashed too.

Without realizing it, he was crying, holding the parcel to his chest. He didn't want to be *Venta-Nomi*. He wanted the Sisters to like him, to accept him—everybody wanted that, and perhaps he wanted it a little bit more. He wanted to do great things and be a great man, so that the Sisters might look at him and be impressed, to look past the bad halibut and bad Brandtball of the past and see him for who he was.

He was filled with ambition and desire, and as he sat there lost in thought holding the parcel, he noticed it became strangely warm and also became much more freely bendable than it had been.

Creation! How long had he been sitting there, weeping like a school boy?

Don't handle the parcels any more than is necessary . . .

Thoughts of radioactivity entered his head. He got up and found a Guildsman and had him scan the parcel for radiation. The Guildsman looked at it and reported he saw nothing—no radiation, which was a big relief.

He retrieved his satchel from across the street with his ticket and placed the warm parcel into its slot. His task was done and he wanted to go home.

✳   ✳   ✳   ✳   ✳

1144 Dunwoodwell West. The fairly happy streets of Dee gave away a bit to a more fallen down area. Hidden by the façade of a respectable street-front, the interior was crowded with crooked buildings and unpainted, termite-infested wood. Even being a Calvert man, A-Ram found himself a bit appalled. This area was a dreadful slum at its worst.

Eventually he found the correct address. The building was a tenement, an uneven three stories in height, the shape of an elongated 'L', and tiled half-heartedly in lime and white with a fair amount of the tiles fallen and piled up around the base of the building. The whole structure of the building appeared rotten and ready to come down; even the yard it sat in was barren of grass and strewn with unhealthy rocks and discarded refuse.

He stood there for a moment and wondered if he really wanted to go in. His instructions were clear, but it didn't seem safe, structurally or socially—who knows what sorts were waiting inside.

Desperate to get this over with, he opened the creaking door and went in. Inside was a seedy corridor lined with sullen doors of old, mirthless wood. The place reeked, not smell-wise or anything tangible like that; rather, it had a terrible feel to it. He felt overwhelmed, felt something pressing down, waiting to get at him.

At the end of the corridor was a creaky stair leading up. Carefully, he made his way up, the steps groaning and teetering a little with each step.

At the end of the corridor was his destination: 212. The oppressive feeling he had struggled with on the first floor was doubled here on the second.

212.

It seemed an unhealthy, unholy place—why, he didn't know. He felt certain that whatever was waiting for him on the other side of the door was the end of his life, the last thing he would ever see.

His death was on the other side of that door.

He was no match for his fear—he turned and fled, moving back down the steps in a clumsy racket, out the door and into the street, shuffling as fast as he could go until he spilled back out into the more reputable sections of Dee.

He purchased a ticket back to Armenelos out of his own money and took a rumbling, slow pub-trans across the forest. He didn't arrive back at the Fleet until 28 bells—he was exhausted after a long day. He brought the satchel and placed it in the Admiral's office. He'd apologize to him when he came in and say, in his judgment, he didn't believe the final drop-off point was safe.

He decided to head back to his apartment to grab an hour or two of shut-eye.

Moving slowly, he made his way down the sparsely populated complex.

He wasn't overly surprised when the figure in gray came upon him; he expected it, rather. It seemed inevitable. He was certain the figure in gray had been waiting for him behind door 212 in Dee. It hadn't been able to settle with him in the slum of Fehklar, so it would do so now. It made perfect sense to him.

It reached out and seized him by the arm. A-Ram was too bewildered to put up much of a fight. He was filled with a complacent, rather peaceful sort of utter terror. He wouldn't be inconvenienced long; it would all be over soon. The figure dragged him into a nearby, out-of-the way place—a bathroom and pulled him in.

Inside, a small Marine was sitting cross-legged on the vanity top, tossing back a flask of something, boots removed and set aside, streaks of dirt running down the sides of her face.

The Marine, a tiny black-haired girl, looked at them and blushed. "Oh, you guys want to be alone or something?"

The figure in gray appeared startled and released him. He quickly stumbled away, reaching for the bathroom door that seemed an eternity from his grasp. He bolted out, followed shortly by the Marine girl. She also seemed quite scared. She hadn't even collected her boots.

He went to security and reported the matter. They searched the complex, but found no mysterious figure in gray. He saw the Marine from the bathroom, a little intoxicated and on-duty as well, bootless, getting berated by her superiors. A-Ram watched with a bit of discomfort as she was taken away to be disciplined.

That little Marine probably saved his life.

Later, he sat down and explained what had happened to the Admiral. He thought the Admiral might be angry at him for not fulfilling his instructions to the letter; and he was angry—he was furious in fact, but not at him.

Speaking in his kindest voice, the Admiral thanked him again for fetching the parcels, and for his vigilance, and told him he would be compensated for his pub-trans fare back to Armenelos. He also bade him to not worry about the figure in gray.

The Admiral said he would take care of the situation, and that he was sorry he'd been inconvenienced.

True to his word, A-Ram never saw the figure in gray at the Fleet again and what became of the satchel and the parcels he'd collected was out of his concern.

19

—Innocent Drury—

S tenstrom climbed up out of the lift shaft. He had been badly tangled in the razor-wire gift that Innocent had left for him. He should have been hopelessly impaled.

But, as he was quickly discovering, the Sisters weren't kidding. He bounced off the bedding of wire and found himself barely inconvenienced. Once he got over the shock of his situation and acknowledged the fact that he wasn't hurt, he casually pulled the wire away, the odd strands easily breaking and being tossed aside. Somehow, even his HRN coat wasn't torn or ripped—apparently the Sisters wanted his carefully crafted "costume" to not be destroyed and imparted their protection on it as well.

He emerged into the dark of Deck Five and quickly made his way down the hall. The hallway was plunged in pitch blackness, but he could see just fine.

For just a moment, you looked like a robot, A-Ram had said.

The It Man, the Sisters said.

We will lend you our power . . .

He pondered that as he continued down the corridor. A robot. He recalled seeing the Mad Lord of Walther up close as a boy at Rustam, and he clearly recalled thinking he looked like a silver and gold robot. He too was the Sisters' Fist—whatever that was.

He pulled the final bit of razor wire off his clothes and looked at it. It was odd and sinuous, a little slimy, almost organic in composition. The barbs looked hard and sharp, of a bony sort of composition.

The ship gave another shudder, long and protracted this time.

He needed to hurry.

He moved out of the "neck" region of the ship and into the winged rear section. Now, all he had to do was go up three levels, put on a pressure suit, go into Ripcar Bay 5, as its doors were open to naked space, and somehow fix the *Westminster*.

That's all.

Ahead was a lift shaft that he could climb up. Situated in front of the shaft was a tangle of more razor-wire. Clearly, Innocent had been here.

He pulled the wire down, not being hurt by it, but still mindful. He hacked his way to the lift shaft and entered, finding the interior of the shaft also clogged with strands of razor-wire. He climbed up as quickly as he could, clearing the stuff away with swipes of his hand.

Several minutes later he emerged on the correct deck. The corridor was clear, and he saw the various boxes of items they had stolen from Dry Dock 275. He recalled Taara chirping happily as they sorted through their assortment of stolen booty.

He heard something, a sort of quizzical, machine-like groan.

He looked around, NTH at the ready. He didn't see anybody.

Quickly, he put on one of the pressure suits, steamed it up, the helmet lighting in colorful displays and readouts, and entered the sub-lock to Ripcar Bay 5 with a momentary rush of air, as the bay was currently open to space.

The bay was completely clogged with razor wire. It was stretched out everywhere running this way and that, making the whole bay look like a badly cobwebbed barn. In the middle of all this confusion was the *Westminster*. Its condition was impossible to discern—he had to get closer.

Clunking ahead, he pulled aside the strands, making a slow path. He arrived at the ship and looked it over. It was off and darkened. The bullet-shaped, white hull didn't appear to be damaged at all—the plates (what he could see) were intact, the front glass was fine, and he could see the quiet crew seats within.

The Lady in Gray had once sat in one of those seats . . .

So, what was wrong with it?

He moved back along the length of the ship, clearing the razor wire as he went. There was the open panel that Taara had set up. She had strung a cable and connected it to the *Seeker's* mainframe—she did a great job, her MOLLYed-up smarts proving to be quite effective.

The cable was missing. Looks like Innocent simply popped it out. It didn't look like he ripped it out or damaged it in any way—as, apparently, he wanted to still make good use of the *Westminster* later once A-Ram, Taara, and he were eliminated. So, all Stenstrom had to do was find the cable, hook it back up, and re-fire the *Westminster*.

The ship gave a long, protracted shudder. Looking back through the open doors of the bay, he thought he could see movement and flashes of reddish light.

He made his way in that direction, clearing himself a path as he went. When he got to the bay opening, he could see that the *Seeker* was in a slow, rolling battle with the *Heade-on-the-Hearth*.

The *Heade*, although in the general shape of an old *Webber*, was clearly not simply a derelict spacecraft decades old—it was articulated like a gigantic insect, studded with robotic armatures and other odd technologies, and crawling with small guns. It was reaching out for the *Seeker* with tentacles tipped with claws, surveying it with clusters of robotic eyes, and firing with a cassagrain-style main weapon mounted on a long armature that reminded Stenstrom of the proboscis of an assassin bug.

The stars slowly churned about as A-Ram, far away on the bridge, struggled to match turns with the *Heade,* using nothing but maneuvering thrusters—a nearby thruster every so often spat out a torrent of compressed propellant as A-Ram moved the wheel.

The *Heade* moved rather nimbly. It darted in, reaching out with its tentacles, trying to snare the *Seeker*. The thruster again roared as A-Ram matched its maneuver, and the *Heade* fired a long, burning arc of cassagrain weaponry from its main gun, hitting the *Seeker* somewhere in the tower section above.

The *Heade* came about, and A-Ram banked the ship, forcing Stenstrom to hold on, and then the enemy fired again, hitting the *Seeker* in the rear quarter this time. Though he had no propulsion, no hermetics, and no weapons, A-Ram was doing a masterful job of giving the *Heade* different angles to hit. The *Seeker* was heavily armored with dura-plate, and the only way to really damage her was to keep hitting the same section with cassagrains over and over again, heating the armor up to the point of failure. A-Ram wasn't letting them do that; he was forcing them to strike different areas of the ship, thus prolonging this one-sided struggle. And, he was clearly successful in keeping the *Heade* from latching on with its tentacles—that was key.

The thrusters blasted a torrent again and the *Seeker* did a slow roll. The *Heade* came in again. Seeing it up-close, Stenstrom could clearly see the different sorts of techs strapped to the ship that didn't belong there.

He could see that their cassagrain main weapon was mounted on flexible, robotic pods and could articulate about, giving them a vast field of fire.

He wondered. His NTH was fully able to kill robots and robotic machines. Maybe he could hit the robotic pod and put the cassagrain main gun out of commission. It might just work.

He waited a moment or two for the ship to swoop in, which it did, tentacles waving, casually displaying its underbelly, knowing full well that the *Seeker* couldn't shoot back.

A-Ram rolled away and matched the turn, the *Heade* appearing to momentarily come to a stop as he did so.

There was the robotic pod, moving the cassagrain about in a smooth arc. He lined up a shot.

Something approached through the tangle of wire behind Stenstrom, something that rattled the floor with pounding steps.

Stenstrom turned.

There, emerging through the tangle, was Innocent Drury.

He didn't look at all like he remembered Innocent Drury looking, but it had to be him. He was nine feet tall—obviously quite a bit larger and bulkier then he had appeared previously when he looked like just a thin, scabrous man.

He was some sort of mechanical construct; a bizarre robot. His metal body was man-shaped (he had arms, legs, and something that passed for a head) but he was bulky and mechanical, his body only vaguely man-like. His hands were big and blocky, nipper-shaped, with at least twenty variously sized fingers on each hand. His feet were squared-off and robotic.

He appeared to have a rigid central framework at his center, like a metal skeleton of some kind. On top of the framework was an abundance of movement. His "body" was composed of a multitude of metal squares, each about half the size of a fist and all colored a deep hunter green—similar to Stenstrom's coat. The squares were adorned with blinking lights, and they were made on some sides with recessed tracks, while other sides had obtuse rail-like ridges sticking out—Stenstrom was reminded of a tongue-and-groove system of joining pieces of wood together. These green squares moved, travelling about on top of each other, the ridges jutting out of the square's sides fitting into the grooves of other squares seamlessly—like the pieces of a gigantic, interlocking puzzle. The green, blinking squares on Innocent's body were constantly travelling about, changing his shape in a bee-like cloud of movement—it was as if he were composed of many tiny robots piled up on top of each other to create a single huge, blocky one.

Such technology. He'd seen robots before on Planet Fall and Bustoke, where they were most common, but he'd not seen any quite like this.

On the area of Innocent's body where a stomach might be placed, the green squares had joined together to form a spinning bin or pan. Organic, flesh-like tendrils of stuff kept dripping out of the rotating pan and slopping to the floor. It reminded him of a grotesque sno-cone machine, spinning, spewing molten flesh instead of flavored, shaved ice.

That must be where the fleshy razor-wire came from.

At his shoulders was an array of variously sized antennae, some rather short, while others were long and flexible. He was broadcasting and receiving data through the antennae—Stenstrom could feel the strength of the incoming and outgoing signals vibrating his teeth.

Innocent didn't have a head, per se; instead, he had a large, hinged monitor screen that could fold up and descend into the cavity of his chest. A straight line of light that oscillated in the center was all that was displayed on his head-screen.

Although Stenstrom couldn't hear it in the vacuum, he could imagine Innocent making a skittering sort of sound, like a torrent of data being broadcast.

They stood there, regarding each other for a moment.

Stenstrom quickly raised his NTH, cocked the hammer, and fired. The blast hit Innocent in the chest—about a dozen little green squares either fell off and clattered to the floor of the bay, or went dead and lost all lights and movement.

Apparently, in this blocky, robotic form, Innocent was too decentralized to kill with a single shot—he was like a colony of little robots working together, each one alive all by itself.

Innocent raised his fist. In a surge, the green squares migrated en masse to his fist, where it got huge, like a massive hammer.

Stenstrom tried to fade into the shadows, but he couldn't—there was too much razor wire about—he had no space to move.

Innocent swung, flattening Stenstrom into the bulkhead wall, where the metal deformed around his body, making a sort of form-fitting imprint with him in the center.

As he got punched, Stenstrom dropped his NTH, and it spiraled away from his hand and was caught up on several strands of razor wire.

Innocent turned to it and, spewing fleshy material from his chest, covered the weapon in a thick, tumor-like ball wreathed in razor wire blossoms.

A moment later Stenstrom's partially flattened helmet cracked and depressurized in a cloud of rapid condensation.

He felt all the air rush out of his lungs.

This was it!

Stenstrom sat there, buried in the bulkhead, his pressure suit no longer holding pressure. He considered his situation—he should be dead, squashed flat, helmet cracked and sputtering. His pressure suit was making air, but it got pulled out of the crack in his helmet just as fast as it did so.

He should be dead—flattened, suffocated in his pressure suit, his blood boiling in the vacuum.

But, as far as he could tell, he was fine.

He felt fine.

He considered what he had done up to this point. He had smashed his way through the docking ring, passing through the hatch effortlessly. He pulled Chance Drury's hands off without a thought—and certainly, Chance had to be a robotic creature similar to Innocent. He was able to see clearly in the pitch black corridor

A-Ram said, that, just for a moment, he looked like a robot.

The Mad Lord had looked to him like a robot as well.

And, apparently, he was a man just like the Mad Lord . . .

Innocent Drury didn't pay Stenstrom, stuck in the wall, venting gasses, any mind—clearly assuming he was dead.

He gave his cracked helmet a slight pat with his nipper-like hands—rushing air vapor answered in response.

With that, his head screen folded up and disappeared within his body cavity as did the cluster of antennae on his shoulders.

The multitude of green squares traveling about his body began rearranging themselves in a flurry, locking into place, compacting down smaller and smaller. A collection of squares twisted about, creating a perfectly formed head.

Soon, the huge, blocky robot that had punched Stenstrom into the wall, appeared like a smallish, green man made of metal; he even had a toothy, weather-beaten head and a phallus of locked-in green squares. A funnel of flesh-material came twisting out of his stomach and coated him completely. After a moment, Innocent Drury stood there, naked, but otherwise perfectly man-like. He pulled cancerous-looking stalks of mal-formed flesh away from his body and cast them aside. He teased the flesh at his scalp, creating an unruly nest of frizzy hair.

He seemed to be arguing with someone unseen—probably with his brother over on the *Heade.* Silently cursing, he turned and marched toward Stenstrom and began pulling what he thought was his dead, flattened body out of the indentation in the wall.

Stenstrom's fist shot out and clobbered Innocent in the face, knocking him back into the tangle of razor-wire. He then pulled himself fully free of the wall.

His brand new flesh lacerated, Innocent clambered out of the tangle and stared at Stenstrom, clearly astonished.

His mouth moved, but was silent in the vacuum. The Com housed in Stenstrom's pressure suit came to life—Innocent's voice filtered in, partially masked in whine.

"What in Creation are ya'?" he said.

Stenstrom responded in kind. "What are you and your folk?"

"We's eternal, we are. We serves our masters and they's given us eternal life for our trouble."

Outside, the *Heade* screamed by. Guns mounted to her broadsides sparkled and the bay was carpeted in contained explosive shells. Stenstrom was hit at least a dozen times, his pressure suit shredded.

Innocent raised his scrawny arms and charged. Stenstrom, unharmed by the strafing run, stood his ground, hauled back, and landed a hard shot to

Innocent's rib area, doubling him over. He balled his fists up and swung, getting him in the jaw. Arms and legs flailing, Innocent rocketed into the far wall of the bay. He bounced into the bulkhead. Just at that moment, A-Ram hauled the ship around in a sudden movement, and Innocent went out through the open doors of the bay into space, his naked body looking like a huge mandrake root as he spiraled out.

Certain he'd not seen the last of Innocent, Stenstrom turned to his NTH, which was balled up in an ugly, fleshy cocoon. He tore at the cocoon with his fingers—the fleshy material being remarkably resilient and durable. Finally, it gave way and Stenstrom pulled his pistol free,

He ran to the edge of the Bay.

Outside, there was Innocent moving about. He wasn't flailing or out of control; he was moving with precision. The flesh-spewing hole in his stomach was now protruding and directed down toward his legs, like a nozzle. Streamers of flesh were squirting out in a rapid dash, dash, dash succession and he was apparently using it like a jet.

He hovered in front of the bay, about a hundred yards distant. He fumbled with something in his hands, hiding what he was doing from view. As he worked, the long shaft of a green lance or missile appeared, getting longer by the moment—apparently, Innocent was shedding some of his green squares and using them to create a weapon of some sort.

Stenstrom wasn't going to give Innocent a chance to finish whatever he was doing. He cocked and fired, aiming for his head.

He moved his nozzle and darted away from Stenstrom's shot, where it missed over his shoulder.

Stenstrom cocked the hammer to fire again, but Innocent had finished his work.

He had created a ten-foot long, missile-like lance that was lit up with blinking lights. He hauled back and threw it like a javelin heading directly for Stenstrom.

Stenstrom aimed and fired, hitting the lance in the nose. Its blinking lights went out and it careened off target. But it was too late.

The dead lance hit Stenstrom across the chest, knocking him backward into the tangle of razor wire with incredible force.

And then there was Innocent flying in on his jet stream of flesh like a ghoul.

He flew into Stenstrom, pounding the base of his neck with devastating blows. His left hand changed shape and expanded into a hideous claw, stretching and tearing his artificial flesh. Before Innocent could use the claw, Stenstrom punched at it with a back fist. The claw lost its shape and fell apart with the force of the blow, many green squares breaking through the layer of flesh and scattering about.

Innocent reached up, trying to rip Stenstrom's helmet off. He seized Innocent's arm and wrenched it out of the socket, the arm quickly changing shape and roiling with movement, like a dead bird full of bugs. He tossed it aside.

"Ye' can't beats us. We's eternal," Innocent said over Stenstrom's crackling Com.

"That right?"

Stenstrom picked him up by the chin. "Where is Captain Gwendolyn?"

"In a place ye can't get to her. She's going to be eaten by th' Cronyns, she is."

"Where? Where are these Cronyns you keep talking about?"

Innocent didn't answer him. Stenstrom squeezed and his chin collapsed.

"I'll be rememberin' this score, les' ye' forgets," Innocent said. "Now, this is personal betwixt us."

He rolled his eyes back and opened his mouth. A moment later, Stenstrom could hear a boiling, frenetic cacophony of noise being broadcast by Innocent through his helmet.

Stenstrom reached down and ripped his head off, where his body went limp.

He went to the open bay and searched for the *Heade*— there it was, coming in fast and angry, its cassagrain cannon swinging around ready to apply a blast to the Ripcar bay, frying everything in it.

The thrusters ticked, A-Ram steered into the *Heade*, forcing it to veer away or collide, an encounter the sturdy *Seeker* would surely win.

There was its belly. There was the cannon's armature. Stenstrom lined up his shot and fired. His green blast travelled across space, and hit the pod. Without any great fanfare the cassagrain stopped moving and froze in place.

The *Heade* twisted away, apparently alerted that something bad had happened and moved out of his field of view.

Given respite, Stenstrom checked the *Westminster*, certain shells from the *Heade* had riddled her into wreckage. To his surprise, the *Westminster* seemed sound. The shells had bounced off. He smiled as he looked her over. She was armored plated. Apparently that's what she had been doing in Dry Dock 275, having a brand new carapace of armor plating installed for Admiral Pax, turning her into a bullet-proof chariot. Why the Admiral needed such a thing Stenstrom had no idea.

He found the power cable and hooked it back up to the *Westminster*. All by itself the ship powered on and fired its engine.

20

—THE SEARCH FOR

THE *DEMOPHALON JOHN*—

"Bel!" Taara cried.

Stenstrom climbed up to the bridge and threw Innocent's body to the floor where it fell with a surprisingly heavy thud. He tossed in his severed head and his arm as well.

"A-Ram flew like an old pro, Bel. You should have seen him."

"I did see. Well done, A-Ram."

"What happened with Innocent Drury?"

"I got him, he's here. He's a robot," Stenstrom said brushing himself off. "I guess all of his brothers are robots as well."

Taara knelt down and looked at him. "Pretty complex. Never seen one like this before."

A-Ram had a thought. "They're Flesh Replicas. I remember now, the old stories of the Druries. According to mariner legends, they were a bunch of worthless pirates from Onaris a few centuries back—problem was nobody could get rid of them. Sink them, kill them, and they came right back to rob and pillage again. Druries Belt right outside the window there was named after them. Annoying lot. Always preying on the weak and helpless, always appearing when things were most favorable to them. They operated out of a place called The Swarm."

Stenstrom pulled Innocent's flesh apart, revealing the tightly packed, green metallic innards. He reached in and pried several of the green squares away from the core—they were dug in surprisingly snug.

"He's mostly made up of these things—like a bunch of little robots working together to form a large robot. They sort of move about in a chaotic fashion, one riding atop the other—I was reminded of a bee hive, an organized cluster of many individuals working together under a collective mind."

Taara took several of the green robots and gazed at them. "This would actually be a Mecon, a 'Mechanical Construct', a bunch of little robots working together to create a large one. This is an elegant little design."

Stenstrom pulled the covering of flesh away, revealing his circular stomach cavity.

Taara covered her nose. "Wow, that stinks! Oh, it's like smelling a bucket full of guts."

Holding her nose, she took a few more squares out and examined them. Two squares in her hand suddenly formed together and started moving on their own. Perplexed, she watched the squares struggle, adding on two more squares until the mass undulated like a tiny worm.

Tara pulled the squares apart and they went dead. "That was weird," she said. "These squares suddenly linked up and appeared to form a rudimentary colonial consciousness. Kind of cool."

A-Ram was concerned. "If we refer again to the legend of the Druries, then, we can expect to have not seen the last of any of them. The Druries always came back—that was the hallmark of their infamy."

"He did mention that he was eternal before he signed off. I also recall he made a furtive sound before he died—as if he were broadcasting a blizzard of data."

"I'll wager he was off-loading all of his up-to-date thoughts and memories and transporting them to a remote location where a new body shall await him, and be fully briefed on all his prior activities once made whole," A-Ram said.

Taara shuddered. "At least that explains how his brothers were floating around out there in space, right as rain. I have to tell you that really gave me the creeps, flat out."

Stenstrom stood and paced around. "So, what about Captain Gwendolyn have we been able to reach her?"

Taara shook her head. "No, Bel, we haven't. And she's not on the scopes either."

"She said she was only half an hour from our position. Even in our diminished sensing state, we should be reading her plain as you please. She should be right on top of us."

"Unless the Cronyns got her," Taara said, fiddling around with one of the green robotic squares from Innocent's body.

Stenstrom plunged back into his chair. "A-Ram, make sail. I want the captain and her ship found immediately. Forget our previous mission to Bazz—our new mission is locate the *Demophalon John* and ensure the safe rescue of all souls aboard."

A-Ram took the helm. "Shall we head back to Kana and inform them there of our findings?"

"No, it's taken us days to get this far, and just as long to get back to Kana or be in Com range. I don't know if the Captain and her crew have that time—we have to assume they are in dire peril and in need of immediate rescue."

"Heading?"

"A-Ram, you said the Druries operated out of a place called 'The Swarm', what is that?"

"Not certain. Asteroid field I suppose."

"Remember when Taara caught that brief glimpse of a large body on the sensors? I'll bet that's The Swarm lit up in the lantern's beam. Let's navigate there now."

Taara began the calculations.

He turned to Taara. "So, these Cronyns, tell me about them Taara."

"There's not much to say, Bel. They are some sort of beings that used to terrorize my people with illusions for two weeks every couple of years. Evil spirits that could make you hear and see things."

Stenstrom thought a moment. "As the Druries referenced them by name, we must assume they are real entities and somewhere in the near vicinity. It's also reasonable to assume that we could, even now, be under the sway of their illusions, yes?"

"I guess so. Yeah, I guess so." Taara looked around.

"That body we scoped in the lantern light has got to be it: this Swarm, this Cronyn World and even though we can't see it we know it's there," A-Ram said.

"Agreed. Chance Drury said something about toying with Captain Gwendolyn and her crew before eating them. Perhaps these creatures somehow derive sustenance from the fear and confusion their illusions create. They may, even now, be feeding on Captain Gwendolyn and her crew by locking them into some sort of squalid diorama and allowing it to play out. Though it might sound morbid, such a situation may buy us a bit of time to sort this out and perform a rescue."

Taara was ready with her calculations. "A-Ram, go nine pegs hard a larboard, Z plus 22. That'll send us right where I saw the contact. You know if I think on it, there's an old story about Darius Jones—you know, the Sisters 'It Guy' from Bazz. According to the story, he took a long journey following a guiding star to a place of shallow seas and many moons. There, as the story goes, he fought the Cronyns and that was that. Haven't heard much from them since. It's: Jones 1, Cronyns 0."

"Many moons, that could be A-Ram's Swarm?"

"But, we don't have the lantern anymore," Taara said. "How are we going to detect it?"

Stenstrom sat there and had a thought. "Innocent Drury and his brothers seemed to be in cahoots with the Cronyns, that they feed them, provide them with prey."

"Ok . . ."

"So, as these characters are robots—highly advanced, but robots just the same—they must have some sort of technological method of detecting them, of seeing through their illusions."

Stenstrom went to Innocent's body and began pulling him part, his body crumbling into a huge amount of green squares. "He was packing all sorts of antennae and sensory equipment."

Taara joined Stenstrom, and before long, with little green squares littering the bridge, he pulled his sundry antennae and his head screen out of his body cavity. "What do you make of this, Taara?"

She examined the hardware. "Give me a little bit," she said, flopping down onto the floor and crossing her legs.

With Taara sitting amid the scattered wreckage of Innocent's body, Stenstrom went into his office. There, standing in the darkened room, he gazed out the windows, seeing the stationary stars and the curtain of Druries Belt.

Out there somewhere was Captain Gwendolyn and her missing ship.

Part 2

The Woman

in Gray

LADY VENDRA OF CONE

1

—THE TWILIGHT OF CARINA—

Her life ended that night at the grand Nether Day ball, looking around on the floor for the man whom she given her heart to and not finding him. Where did he go?

Where indeed.

Stolen—she stole him from me!!

Lady Vendra of Cone had longed to meet Lord Stenstrom, the eighth son of the Zenon House of Belmont, in person for months. They had shared a steady correspondence, his letters being full of excitement and grand adventure as he sailed the stars on his Fleet ship, the *Amazing*. His letters to her were things she came to cherish, and she waited anxiously each day to see if one might arrive. Thinking him something special, she followed the old Remnath tradition of no vids or live coms—if he wanted to see her, it must be in person; if he wanted to speak to her, it must be longhand with pen and paper. How happy she was when she convinced him to come to the grand Nether Day ball in Falz. Oh, how it would be a gala affair, and she promised a night they would both remember for the whole of their lives.

It certainly was that, as she stood there alone on the floor looking for her man whom the silver-haired strumpet, Lady Jubilee of Tyrol, had just stolen off the floor.

She lived in a mental cloud of her own making for years after that. She went to the Sisters, enraged.

"I declare Wirguild! I want revenge!"

The Sisters reviewed her petition. Their Marines: "We see you have set Wirguild upon the entire House of Belmont South-Tyrol. We cannot allow that. You may have Wirguild upon Lady Jubilee of Belmont South-Tyrol, and that is all."

"I want to kill them all!"

"You may not."

And she left Valenhelm, her tail between her legs. She was frightened of the Sisters. She could not go against the Sisters.

✳   ✳   ✳   ✳   ✳

She tensed up in her rainbow colored gown, pulling the long hairpins from her head—glistening in her hands. Her heart pounded.

Her enemy, Lady Jubilee, stood there a few feet away. She shook her hands and conjured from nowhere six silver daggers between her fingers like claws.

They circled. Vendra had longed for this moment, to come to grips with

Lady Jubilee—to kill her. She reared back and struck out, ready to plunge the hairpins into the bitch's hated chest.

Lady Jubilee disappeared and her strike missed.

"Ha! What a sight," came her smug voice. "I could kill you anytime I wish."

Vendra turned, where was she? "Fight me fairly!" she cried, brandishing her hairpins.

"Fair, there is nothing fair about this, is there?" She felt a foot roughly kick her in the rear, and she fell, dropping her hairpins.

"This is ridiculous," Jubilee said, again from the shadows. "This isn't a fight; this isn't Wirguild—this is murder. I suggest you pick yourself up, move on, and find a man in some other pasture; otherwise, the next time we meet, I will kill you."

Her hands, skinned after the fall, stung. She slowly stood.

Jubilee's voice was taunting and chiding. "To think that you could hurt me with your little Wirguild and your hair pins. How pathetic."

How pathetic . . .

$$* \quad * \quad * \quad * \quad *$$

The open letter sat on the bed. She'd read it many times.

He had written this letter, had touched it.

Stenstrom . . .

She wanted to hate him, like she hated Lady Jubilee. But she couldn't. She savored the words on the paper, touched them with the pads of her fingers. She tried to find hidden meaning in the words, some encrypted message, but there appeared to be none.

In the letter, he apologized for what happened at the ball, that it was all his fault. He said he was sorry, that he wished her feel no pain, no harm, but that his heart was lost to Lady Jubilee. He said it was quite beyond his control.

It's not your fault, my love . . . she did it. She put a spell on you.

Lady Vendra stood gazing at herself in the mirror, nude, her closetful of colorful Cone gowns all thrown aside.

She looked at her thin body, at her unskilled hands. There was her gaunt face, unable to smile.

How pathetic . . . came Jubilee's voice time and time again.

She turned to her clothing and threw the beautiful gowns out the window. She saved one garment—an ugly gray dress that she'd never worn before, put it on, and then threw herself out the window too, falling several stories to the grounds below, her gowns spread out like colorful, fluttering tissue paper all around her.

$$* \quad * \quad * \quad * \quad *$$

Lady Vendra survived her suicide attempt, the Hospitalers mending her broken bones and lacerated tissues. In examining her, they declared her insane.

"She is mad. Her soul is lost," they said.

"She fell in love with a man and lost her mind," her mother said in the darkness.

"Such things happen," the Hospitalers said.

Not knowing what to do, her House of Cone sent her off to Carina 7 to live out her days in a convent of stone for troubled women—the madness festering within her was a scandal and needed to be kept quiet. A remote, seldom travelled world was an ideal place to keep her.

Carina 7 was far off and rather disassociated with League society. It was perfect. There, she could spend her days in quiet, undiscussed comfort in a convent surrounded by other troubled women.

She arrived at the convent and was given a small room. The pale Grand Dames of the convent assured Lady Vendra's family that she would be well taken care of, and that they had brought her to the right place.

The Cones were worried as they took in the dark skies and mirthless environs, listening to the perpetual thunder rumbling. Her mother, Countess Jessathiela, had a change of heart. She could not leave her daughter in such a maudlin place.

The Grand Dames assured her mother Carina 7 was just the place for her daughter. The climate was ideal for Lady Vendra's care, the expertise without peer. Why, with a bit of luck, they might even see her make a full recovery; such miracles happened often on Carina.

Comforted and hopeful, the Cones boarded their transport and left, confident that she would receive the kind of care that she needed in a discreet setting.

No sooner did they break orbit, then the Dames of the convent convened in Vendra's small room, she sitting there, mouth open and flaccid, only mildly aware of what was going on around her.

"Yes," they said slamming the door shut behind them. "Your House has done you a great service. We have seen your like many times. You are neither mad nor insane—you are downtrodden—you are beaten. You are lost to your rage."

Lady Vendra mumbled something.

"What's that?" The Grand Dames asked. "Speak up!"

" The . . . sorrow, the regret . . ."

"Oh," they sneered. "Such things have no proper place. You shall see. We have schools here where we can teach you to harness your madness—your scorn. We can teach you things here that are unheard of. We can teach you the art of hatred and revenge and your quaint feelings of sorrow and regret will be naught but distant memories. Simply stand, and be one with us."

Drooling, Lady Vendra sighed and stood.

Though a chartered League world, Carina 7, or simply Carina as the locals called it, was an odd, poorly understood place. Far from its parent star, its brightest days were nothing more than a dim twilight, the surface of the planet warmed mostly by prolific geo-thermal energy that radiated out from the planet's core with great efficiency. Laced with giant calderas and supervolcanoes, much of the surface was pocked with bare, scalded rock and towering geysers. In the north was a fair amount of habitable land, grown green with imported low-light plants and studded with gothic, fortress-like castles. The original inhabitants of Carina were members of a vast harem serving the mysterious Emperor-King of Ming Moorland, a non-League world several clicks away past the great nebula. Forgotten on the dark world of geysers and imported plants, the harem grew and was left lonely. When they were called upon by the Emperor-King, he abused them, sometimes torturing and killing them in droves, making them fight to the death. He also used Carina as a place of reward for warriors in his service who pleased him. The warriors could go to Carina and do there anything they wanted . . . anything.

The women of Carina, abused, tormented, kept pale in the dark, raped and murdered, developed a powerful hatred of men—of all men. They kept their numbers replenished via ovarian fusion.

When the lords of the League came, they found themselves terminally unimpressed with the gaudy men in their odd clothing—at least the Emperor-King was a man who knew what he wanted, whereas these League types were powdered fools. Standing side-by-side with the League men were the Sisterhood of Light, a powerful matriarchal organization whom they found themselves greatly admiring. As they listened to the lords and envied the Sisters, they found the League had a fair amount to offer, and they craved the protection and technology the League promised. They became a chartered League world in 000271EX, though the odd climate, dark days, and frosty nature of the female inhabitants discouraged most who thought to migrate there. They participated very little in general League doings and were, most often, left alone.

✻ ✻ ✻ ✻ ✻

Over the next few years, Lady Vendra learned many things. In dark classrooms of stone and perpetual twilight, she learned the arts of seduction and deception. She was taught how to fight, using methods designed to hurt and maim men. She learned that men could easily be manipulated by scent of body and tone of voice. Occasionally, bands of snatched rogues and other scoundrels, unlikely to be missed, were brought to her, and Vendra was free to practice her newly learned skills upon these doomed men.

She felt something of a grim rush of pleasure as the men easily died before her.

She learned that men could just as easily be enslaved. She was taught the esoteric doctrines of *gynology*—the science of controlling and killing men through sex, scent and substance. Through *gynology*, she learned that the female pheromone was a very versatile tool, and she mastered the art of increasing her pheromones as needed. She was also taught that the male psyche, when stimulated into the heights of ecstasy, could be permanently and drastically altered by way of chemical and hormonal means introduced through the tip of the phallus. She was introduced to "The Barb," a studded, diaphragm-like device that was inserted into the womb. The Barb was smeared in chemical substances, and would repeatedly prick the phallus of a male sexual partner while at the height of bliss. Once pricked, the man could be paralyzed, made blind, killed, or, best of all, made a hopeless slave of her scent.

She was warned: "The Barb is illegal—Sisters will kill you should you be discovered in its use, though the Sisters themselves make practice of it," her school masters told her.

That was a recurring theme she came to learn—the Sisters publically decrying a thing while secretly making use of it.

The Sisters were a long point of study. Though greatly admiring their undeniable power, the Dames of Carina found the Sisterhood of Light a significant threat. The Sisters were too enamored with the men of the League, were too ready to give ear to them, to placate them. The Sisters should put the men to heel, to subjugate them and kill them if need be—and as they were unwilling to do so, they were, therefore, a threat. Vendra spent several months learning to best the Sisters, to evade their vigilance. The Sisters could read minds even from a great distance, and thus trained, her true thoughts were quite hidden from the Sisters, giving them only a sham core of simple thoughts to read.

Her training continued, and the men brought to her to practice upon continued. She was a model student, a master *Gynologist* in the making.

2

—THE TENETS OF REVENGE—

The last thing she learned was possibly the most important. She learned how to hate and how to wage revenge.

In the stone classrooms of Carina, she learned the Six Carinan Tenets of Revenge:

1: A Master revenge is decades in the making.

2: Revenge should strike at the Heart many times and at the Flesh only once.

3: Failure to Act when the time is ripe is the poison one drinks.

4: Patience is the key attribute in conducting Revenge.

5: Uncertainty is Revenge's deadliest weapon.

6: There are no Innocent Bystanders in Revenge.

Revenge on Carina was an all or nothing proposition, utterly vicious and invariably fatal one way or the other.

Armed with this new education, Lady Vendra's family was summoned. They were told that, under their care, she was restored to sanity. Elated, the House of Cone came for Lady Vendra and the Woman in Gray went home.

★　★　★　★　★

She took her time as she settled back into her manor, her family glad she was well and returned to them, seemingly recovered. Externally, she appeared fine, and she said all the things they expected her to say. Her father bought her a whole wardrobe full of new Cone gowns of vibrant colors—how she used to love them.

Little did her family suspect that she never once wore any of those lovely gowns. She never wore anything but gray again and a pair of button-up boots in the Carina style; however, to her family's eyes, to her friends' eyes, they saw her wearing Cone gowns. Her skills with deception and disguise were near perfect.

At a leisurely pace, she put her plans for revenge against Lady Jubilee into motion. She followed the tenets; she took her time. She resumed her place in Remnath Society. She attended social functions and drank tea with her circle of friends, returned to them whole and much wiser.

She began her work.

She told her friends that she had been on sabbatical on Carina 7. She spoke about how harrowing the trip there and back had been, how space travel was not nearly as safe as the public had been told. She knew Lord

Stenstrom of Belmont was in the Fleet and was soon to be made captain of a ship. She also knew that the lurid stories she told of mutiny, mishaps, sodomy, and botulism would take wing and travel all the way to Esther and the ears of Lady Jubilee. Whispered secrets in League Society moved fast.

Uncertainty was indeed a powerful tool. Lady Jubilee, fearless for herself, was no doubt hand-wringing in fear for her handsome husband doing such a dangerous job. The seeds were planted.

Next, she needed a network of slaves to do her bidding without question. She went to Calvert, a place no one would ever expect a fine Lady of Cone to go and stayed in an exclusive room at the Empire Hotel. There, in the dark twisting streets, she preyed upon the dirty urchins and filthy men that were there in quantity.

Pretending to be an innocent, bewildered woman, she had no trouble luring the men in, ending up flat on her back in seedy rooms and crooked inns, playing service to drunken, stinking men who, with every thrust, made themselves more her slave, for waiting deep within her womb was The Barb, doing its job with terrible effectiveness. Sometimes she didn't enslave them; sometimes, behind closed doors and stark naked, she fought and killed them, just for the fun of it, their screams and dying pleas soothing her. There were no shortage of victims in Calvert, and no shortage of suspects to take the blame for the killings that had cropped up in earnest. She carried with her chemicals from Carina that removed all trace of her passing, leaving no material for Evidencers to find. Eventually, as years passed by, she developed a thirst to kill more and more men—sometimes she would go to Calvert not to collect slaves, but simply to kill. "The Fiend of Calvert" as the mysterious killer was soon to be called, was loosed upon the region. She loved seeing articles about "him" in the posts and the pictures of the Fiend as a man in a gas mask made her laugh, none suspecting a skinny woman in gray was responsible for it all. From her room at the Empire, she collected slaves and made dead bodies, snickering into her tea and acting shocked as she sat in the hotel dining room and lobby, watching the Evidencers and Gifted Inspectors sift through non-existent genetic evidence and Stare for the guilty, not knowing her Carina-trained mind was unpierceable.

Soon, she had a whole gallery of filthy men who would do anything she asked, and a pile of dead men that she had made, killed by her hand. There was an old, underground vault near the ruins of Woodward where she kept her men, within easy reach whenever she needed them, and they roamed the ruins alive, but in a daze, a hopeless trance. Far away in Calvert, the dirty men and drunken louts were burning with fear.

One of the first things she did was order one of her slaves who had access to an old Xaphan *Merci* freighter to load it full of shaddout and encounter the Fleet Vessel *Amazing*—where Lord Stenstrom served as the Com officer.

"Encounter the *Amazing*, and then detonate the shaddout," she told the man, and he did it without question, killing himself in the process.

Returning to Remnath and lying low, she listened to the winds of gossip. Her slow-burn efforts were working—Lady Jubilee in distant Tyrol was said to be beside herself with fear, desperate for her husband to quit the Fleet.

Splendid. Additionally, she learned that Lady Jubilee had told her husband that he would have no sons until he met her wishes.

And Lady Jubilee was true to her word, punching out one daughter after another with regularity every two or three years.

The obvious thing to do was strike at her children. The frustrating thing was Lady Jubilee was a tight-fisted, controlling mother and getting to her children was difficult. She sent her remaining Calvert Men-Slaves out to scout the Belmont South-Tyrol manor and grounds. They reported the grounds encompassed five square miles of old Merian lands south of the city of Tyrol. There were no obvious technological protections about, yet *something* appeared to be protecting the grounds, for several men who got too close disappeared without trace and were not seen again.

Her army of slaves was utterly disposable, and she continued, sending them off on one-way missions. She succeeded in poisoning one daughter with tainted candy placed on the grounds, but nothing happened except that her hair turned blonde instead of the usual black or that odd silver color.

These Belmonts were damnably tough.

So, Lady Vendra sat back and waited. Something would present itself. She needed to be patient.

$$\star \quad \star \quad \star \quad \star \quad \star$$

Lady Jubilee was up to her fifteenth daughter, over forty years had passed, and even Vendra's remarkable patience was beginning to wear thin. She decided to change her tactics a bit and went after Lord Stenstrom directly. She had generally avoided attacking him—perhaps it was because she still loved him, even the dark school mistresses of Carina couldn't beat that out of her. Her love for him was a tiny ember in the dark she labored to keep alive and warm. In any event, it was time to make something happen. She began making herself available at Fleet—her brother, Derlith, was a newly minted Admiral and with his connections, she had the run of the place. She had dinner with Captain Stenstrom many times, her appearance disguised—yet another skill she'd learned on Carina. However, unlike the Calvert men whom she easily had her way with, Captain Stenstrom showed no interest in her beyond what the demands of social civility called for. The other men at the table were near fainting with the amount of pheromones she was pouring out, but Captain Stenstrom did not react—apparently he was protected by a natural addiction to his wife's scent.

She sighed, she collected new slaves, but could never enslave the one man she truly wanted.

So, her attempts to "get" Lord Stenstrom failed—however, the effort was not a complete loss. At one of the dinners she attended, she overhead Captain Stenstrom talking to another captain about inheritances. Evidently, the captain that Lord Stenstrom was talking to was going through a nasty rite of succession with his two sons, as they both claimed to be the next lord of his House—it was quite a scandal. Lord Stenstrom admitted that he himself had no sons, and the captain he was talking to laughed. "Well, I thought I had problems," he piped.

Lady Vendra listened, and the wheels started turning. The House of Belmont South-Tyrol had no sons, no succession of line, as spelled out in the rigid rules of Kanan society.

That's how her revenge would proceed.

3

—A Love Potion—

Lady Vendra sat in her Remnath manor and considered the situation. Fifteen daughters. Lady Jubilee had to be doing something to prevent the creation of a boy-child. Lady Vendra knew from her Carina training that it was possible to pre-select the sex of one's child without using external methods, such as the Hospitalers used. The Black Hats could do it with Shadow tech, Carina adepts could do it with concentration, and there were any number of herbal methods that would work as well. That must be how Jubilee was doing it—via herbal methods.

Vendra began a fresh attack. She circulated information that the House of Belmont South-Tyrol could not have males—that Lord Stenstrom was not virile in that manner. As with everything, the attack took time to put into place and grow. The years rolled by, daughter after daughter were added to the Belmont household, and Lady Vendra continued the pressure. She began venturing into the Zenon region and frequented areas where she knew the distant relatives of the Belmont South-Tyrol House would be. And she filled their ears full of tales of the South-Tyrol's soon to be lost House, and all their wealthy holdings and lands redistributed to the lords of the city of Tyrol. She even added the tidbit that the lords of the city had already drawn up plans reapportioning the South-Tyrol manor grounds.

That really got the people talking. Weeks later, she began hearing how the cousins and distant relatives of the Belmont South-Tyrols were actually going there in person to present themselves and make their various cases for the favorable distributing of lands and properties after the passing of the lord and lady.

The very real problem of succession began to tell on Lord Belmont, and Lady Vendra caught wind of him making his concerns known to Lady Jubilee. By this point, they had twenty-nine daughters, and Lord Belmont knew that they would be left with nothing should there be no male heir.

Lady Vendra's revenge had been in progress for over eighty years. Now, it was time to really apply the screws to the House of Belmont South-Tyrol.

Unfortunately, she had run square into a series of troubling setbacks. Her stockpile of slaves in the Woodward vault was raided and decimated by a paid vigilant from the north known as the Mad Lord of Walther. One man, by himself, got through all her defenses and killed most of her Calvert men, rendering the stronghold useless.

She tried returning to Calvert and snaring more men, but again, the Mad Lord presented himself.

Piecing together information taken from the Woodward vault, he discovered the Fiend of Calvert connection—and personally investigated her doings in the region. Showing remarkable skill, he tracked her down, rousted her out of her Calvert lair, killed many of her remaining slaves, and engaged her across the rooftops as she tried to flee from an adversary whom she, even with her Carina-taught skills, was no match against. She had become jaded and careless, giving the Mad Lord no regard; nevertheless, she quickly found he was no ordinary man—he was strong beyond compare, impervious to harm, and seemingly immune to the female tricks she threw at him as they battled.

She was lucky to escape. Licking her wounds, she added the Mad Lord's name to her list of people to hate.

Rightly fearing the Mad Lord and his continued investigations, she decided to go off-world for a time and recover from her ordeal, which, as it happened, served her needs nicely.

Bazz was a fine world to get lost in, as there she could bide her time and hide in plain sight. While Carina was most certainly a female-oriented world, Bazz was a more male-dominated place. The men there were arrogant and sweaty. Their heroes were all men. The women of Bazz were noisy and pugnacious but clearly subservient. They even wore their hair in a certain way (those long strands of hair they called "Mollocks") to announce their marital status to the grotesque men. She considered going on a murder spree, but thought better of it.

As she sweated it out in the tawdry villages, she became aware of a virility potion the Bazzers called the "God Sperm" tincture, a chemical extract that ensured the creation of a boy-child, and not just any boy-child, an exceptional boy child—Lord Sixtus of Grenville was said to be a product of the God Sperm tincture. This tincture was some sort of Bazz tradition, once again heralding the men over the women.

Finding the heat and humidity intolerable, she allowed herself the luxury of renting an Atmospheric to create her a pocket of dry, cool air. Settling in, she found a reputable pharmacy that sold the tincture in the city of Dyson-Clampton by the banks of the Dan River. It didn't take her long to enslave both her Atmospheric, creating the pocket of cool air around her, and the apothecary himself, the two of them making sweaty love on the balcony under the hot, Bazz summer sky as the Atmospheric stood nearby. Her new slave told her that he had, in addition to the God Sperm tincture, a foolproof love potion that worked on pheromones. He would simply take some of her scent, create the love potion, and any who drank it would be lost to her.

He advised, though, against mixing the two—random and unexpected things might happen.

Excellent—this appeared to be working out better than she had hoped for. Sitting at a café, she quickly penned an unsigned letter to Lord Belmont, informing him of the existence of the "God Sperm" tincture and hoped to put a powerful seed into his head.

4

—The Ganaada's Curse—

The plan was working. Several weeks later, sitting in a Bazz café with her Atmospheric slave, doing her best to avoid the terribly hot local cuisine, she caught wind that Lord Stenstrom was on his way to Bazz personally to fetch the God Sperm potion, which she was going to make certain that he did not receive. Instead, he would get the Bazz Love Potion, and that would be that. All she had to do was wait until he arrived and monitor the transaction to ensure he took the potion she wanted him to take. She sat at a nearby cafe and watched. Trying to blend in, she dismissed her Atmospheric, and fanned herself at her table without much success.

And, it couldn't happen fast enough. She'd had her fill of Bazz and Bazzers in general and was ready to return to civilized Kana as soon as possible. The locals, a pesky, sweaty people leaching spices from their pores and growing hair in places where hair ought not to grow, she couldn't walk down the street or take a meal without street vendors and self-styled mystics harassing her the entire way. She had come to Bazz to blend in and hide; however, her fair complexion and her use of an Atmospheric fingered her as a Kanan lady of means and the Bazzers gave her no peace. The worst of the lot were these strange, loud women prowling the cafes and wharfs wearing gypsy garments. They called themselves "Ganaadas" and claimed to possess mystical powers. With no shame and little tact, the Ganaadas would approach and demand she secure their services, waving their depleted Cred Sticks in her face.

"You got a bad flow around you," the Ganaada would say. "I can fix, just cost you 1500 creds."

Though Lady Vendra tried to be respectful of women and promote their success as she was taught on Carina, these Bazz females were intolerable. They were noisy, hairy, stinky, and they seemed to gravitate to her, peering through crystals and other totems and babbling about the "bad flow" around her.

A lot of Bazz nonsense. And, as the Ganaadas were female, she had nothing in her bag of tricks to combat or control them as she could with males. She simply had to sit there and endure them.

✳   ✳   ✳   ✳   ✳

She watched Lord Stenstrom, sweating in his Fleet uniform; he had arrived in the square a bit early. She hadn't been expecting him until the morrow, and the pharmacy was closed. He made his way to a small inn on the other side of the square and stood at the counter, hoping to rent an air-conditioned room and pass the time. This was the moment to strike. There he was, alone, unsuspecting and vulnerable, and she was running out of patience. In her jaded observations of Bazz, she learned that Bazzers assaulting each other and having minor scuffles in the street were common and paid no attention to. If she were to walk over there and assault him in plain sight, nobody would pay it any mind or come to his aid.

She pushed out her chair and made her way across the square. Time to take Lord Belmont one way or the other. Why wait? Why linger on this barbaric hellhole any longer than necessary? By sundown, she would be returning to blessed Kana, arm-in-arm with Lord Stenstrom at last.

As she neared the center of the square, a heated scuffle broke out in front of her. A grotesque Ganaada and some little, black-haired girl urchin were going at it, clawing at each other, ripping clothing and throwing each other about, their two heads of black hair and tassels bobbing around and whirling in concentric circles. Unseemly fights were always breaking out on the streets here on Bazz she noted, but this particular fight was inconvenient. The two were going at it hard and literally ripping each other's clothing off. Shoes flew. Somebody started waving a Cred Stick around hoping to take wagers on the fight. Interest quickly piqued. A circle of people formed to bet money and watch as the girl and the Ganaada rolled around with unskilled fury. People cheered as blows were landed and as one combatant got the upper hand only to lose it moments later. Vendra had to push her way through the crush of noisy people, and it was slow going.

When she got through to the inn, Lord Stenstrom was gone, her opportunity lost. She felt hot and tired and returned to her seat at the cafe and ordered a drink. Frustrated, she would wait for her scheme to unfold as planned.

$$* \quad * \quad * \quad * \quad *$$

The next day she was back in her seat at the cafe as she waited for Lord Stenstrom to arrive at the pharmacy. Soon, a Ganaada came up to her table and became particularly forceful and rude, demanding money. She noted the Ganaada's face was marked up and bruised and she recognized her hideous clothing; this was the Ganaada whose ill-timed fight had foiled her attempt to get at Lord Stenstrom the day before. She wanted her to hurt, to feel pain. She stood up and dragged the foul woman out of the cafe and into the alley where she proceeded to beat her. Vendra hamstrung her in both legs, making her into a cripple sobbing in agony. Leaving her in a pile of rubbish, she brushed herself off and headed back to the cafe.

The Ganaada stirred. "I curse you," she mumbled from behind, half insensate in the trash. "I curse you to the Circle!"

Fine. Whatever. Savage from Bazz, lay there in the trash and lick your wounds, and be thankful you're not dead.

She returned to her seat at the cafe and ordered a refreshment. As she waited for it to arrive, she felt a sly hand slide into her pocket. Whirling around, she caught a small, black-haired girl, whom she recognized as one of the apothecary's worthless nieces, trying to steal her purse. She was in a filthy state, torn clothes with a black eye. She was always rumpled up and unsightly. Vendra thought at first to break her arm and send her off crying, such was the state of her mood, but instead, she smiled and opened her purse, giving her a few coins. She patted her on the head. "Off you go," she said and the girl with her ridiculous "Mollocks" scurried away.

Hopeless urchin, she thought—what good would she ever be?

$$\ast \quad \ast \quad \ast \quad \ast \quad \ast$$

It should be any time now. The afternoon seemed odd, the frequent Ganaadas roaming the street gave her a wide berth; they must have heard how she gave a beating to one of their own and wanted nothing further to do with her, giving her only sideways glances. One of them made an odd sort of gesture toward her, joining her thumb and forefinger together forming a crude circle, and then she scampered away.

At last her patience finally bore fruit.

There was Lord Stenstrom emerging from the inn, no doubt miserable in his hot Fleet coat. She watched as he crossed the square, approached the pharmacy, and entered.

Stenstrom . . . All of this is for you . . .

Inside, she had marked a bottle of tincture the apothecary was to sell to Lord Stenstrom, one that was full of love potion laced with her pheromones. She wasn't going to take a chance. Lord Stenstrom thought he was purchasing the God Sperm tincture—instead he would be getting nothing but the love potion laced with her scent. Smiling, Lord Stenstrom left with his purchase.

$$\ast \quad \ast \quad \ast \quad \ast \quad \ast$$

Whatever happened to the love potion after that, she did not know, for Lord Stenstrom never came calling for her, as the apothecary promised he would. Months rolled by with no results. Something happened—somehow Lord Stenstrom didn't get the love potion, or it got mixed into the God Sperm tincture by mistake. How could this be? She'd labored for this opportunity. She stormed into the pharmacy and grilled the apothecary for information. He told her the day Lord Stenstrom came to buy the tincture one of his nieces had tried to steal something from the store before he arrived, and, in catching her, they made a mess, spilling and knocking over bottles all over the place.

That must have been what happened—the bottles were fouled, and, therefore, who knows what Lord Stenstrom took.

Good Creation—these Bazz savages—if only she could kill them all! In frustration, she murdered him in a slow, humiliating session, making him suffer for hours, and then burned his apothecary to the ground.

She then murdered her Atmospheric slave and departed Bazz on a discrete Fleet transport ship called the *Westminster*, arranged by her brother's office, vowing that if she ever returned, it would be to face the devil himself.

$$\ast \quad \ast \quad \ast \quad \ast \quad \ast$$

Two years later, Lord Stenstrom the Younger of Belmont was born, after a difficult pregnancy that was nearly the end of his mother.

Though the love potion had been a failure, the tincture he took had been a raging success—as shown by the end result. Finally, after eighty-plus years, she had her prime target. Her revenge would take full flight against Lady Jubilee's son.

She decided to thoroughly terrify Lady Jubilee with several harassing attempts on his life. Using an array of hastily acquired and disposable slaves, she sent them out to the Belmont South-Tyrol grounds, and many times they never returned.

She did the obvious things, placing a deadly wasp into his nursery, attempting a few intentionally ham-fisted abductions, just to make Jubilee sweat. On a lark, she tried a ploy where she had her slaves place a steel animal trap from Bazz in his play area, which, apparently, failed miserably.

5

—Imprisoned—

Lady Vendra became rather curious about this baby boy born to the House of Belmont. He began to dominate her thoughts.

She wanted to see him, to look him in the eye, though she wasn't sure why. Disguising herself, she went to Tyrol and waited, biding her time as always.

There was Lady Jubilee one day, pushing a stroller with two of her daughters. One of the daughters, a slightly chubby one, wanted something from a stand, and Lady Jubilee turned for a moment to get it for her.

Lady Vendra struck. Within that moment, she had the boy and was off. Quickly she took him to the waterfront, thinking to drop him into the sea—after all, there were no innocent bystanders in revenge.

It would be perfect—perfect. Lady Jubilee could have no more children, so she had heard. Not only would she be killing the boy and breaking Jubilee's heart, she would be putting an end to the Belmont-South Tyrol line as well.

She had only to drop him in—her revenge was finally at hand. Now was the time.

The decades of waiting . . .

She looked at him.

That perfect little face, bright eyes, a tiny baby's smile.

How he looked like Lord Stenstrom . . .

She forgot all about the last century of revenge. She forgot about Lady Jubilee, and Carina and the sordid entanglements of revenge. She forgot about her rage, and all the souls who had died at her hands. She forgot about the Third Tenet: Failure to Act. She knew that not doing what needed to be done at this perfect moment, after so much time and planning, could be the death of her.

For a fleeting moment, she sat by the water with the infant, just like a new mother would with her son, and she held him, humming slightly.

Just for a few minutes, she discovered what it was like to live the life of a simple mother, to feel the joy that went along with it.

What happened after that was a blur, a clouded rupture of movement. Something came at her and hit her full in the face.

Everything went black and she had no idea what was happening.

✳   ✳   ✳   ✳   ✳

There was a storm raging all around.

She heard voices around her, could feel eyes staring. Then it became clear. The Sisters. They had her.

The vise around her was tormenting—unendurable. She fell back into her

Carina training—pretend to submit in the face of an insurmountable enemy, feign weakness and show fear. Let them think you are beaten. Let them think they are in control.

"Please, please, stop! I die! What do you want?" she cried.

You attempted to kill the son of Belmont South-Tyrol and are in violation of your long-standing Wirguild. Thus, you are our prisoner and out of the League's eye. We have questions for you . . .

"I'll answer anything—anything!"

You recently attempted to poison your enemy, Lady Jubilee of Belmont South-Tyrol. We want to know what additive you used in the poisoning. We demand it.

Lady Jubilee?? Poison??

She hadn't tried to poison Lady Jubilee. There was the fiasco with the God Sperm tincture and the love potion on Bazz, but that was all.

Why were the Sisters so interested in that?

The vice tightened. She felt her life and her sanity ripping apart.

Simply tell us what you used, and all this can end. You shall be sent home, free and goodly. We shall even kill Lady Jubilee of Belmont South-Tyrol for you, if you wish. We shall take care of everything. Simply tell us what you used.

Kill Lady Jubilee? No . . . NO! This is between me and her!

She is mine! Mine!!

She babbled in torment. "I don't want her dead—I want her on her knees, wailing for death. I want her kneeling at the gravesite of her son!"

You are in a position to demand nothing! Tell us what we want to know!

Somewhere deep within, her resolve formed again, bubbled up, and built a wall around her. Despite her training, she was defiant. She would not be meek. "Lady Jubilee is mine! I will tell you nothing."

Tell us!!

And her torment began, for years, her hatred sustaining her through the ordeal.

$$\ast \quad \ast \quad \ast \quad \ast \quad \ast$$

After an unknown length of time, her tormentors became unsure, their arrogance faltering

Has she revealed her secret?

—She has not.

Time is of the essence. We cannot hold her forever. She must be returned unmarked and whole.

—She will not reveal unto us her secret. We must know what she used.

The Ex-Commons has heard the arguments of her kin, and desire her release.

—Let them be damned!

We cannot go against the ruling of the Ex-Commons. We will extract her secret, and then release her, whole and unmarked!

And they came at her again, doling out pain, shouting threats. She, however, rode out the torrent. Let them prod and scratch. Let them wail.

She laughed.

✳   ✳   ✳   ✳   ✳

She clutched her cloak about her now frail body as she rode in the coach, her family all around her, concerned, supportive. The hills rolled by. It had been years since she'd seen these hills, but she knew every one of them. Soon, the manor appeared in the distance.

She was home. Her health was shattered, and her body somewhat bent. Yet, she had won.

✳   ✳   ✳   ✳   ✳

Pampered and caressed in riches, she recovered from her ordeal quickly in the familiar confines of her home.

The Sisters.

She hated the Sisters, for their cruel embrace, for stripping her bare, for hollowing her mind into a cesspool of vapor, and applying agony to her flesh.

She was now going to return them the favor. She was going to apply the brand to their flesh, as they had done to hers. There was room in her soul for all the things she hated—there was room aplenty.

She had learned much during her pained captivity. Her tormentors, aloof in their arrogance, allowed their thoughts to be heard.

A name kept popping up: the *"It Man"*. The *It Man* had returned. And he was everything to them.

The It Man? What is that? Who is that?

Everybody, it seemed, had a hero; everybody had someone whom they looked up to, and to the Sisters, the It Man was that somebody.

It took her a while to piece it together, but, eventually, a picture formed. There was not one, but two It Men running around—one was mature and in service for the Sisterhood, the second was new, a work in progress—a happy surprise that almost slipped through their fingers.

She wasn't clear on who the second It Man was; his identity was a secret the Sisters kept well. The first It Man, however, she discovered fairly quickly—Terrance, the Mad Lord of Walther.

The Mad Lord of Walther? The man who destroyed her lair under Woodward? The man who nearly "got" her in Calvert? Coming from her social circles, she knew the Sisters publically disdained Lord Terrance of Walther, for his bravado, his vigilance. They mocked and belittled his exploits.

But look, behind the scenes it was quite a different story. Terrance, Terrance, their beloved Terrance. How they secretly worshipped him, drew strength from him. Again, as with the Barb and with other things, the Sisters had a tendency to disdain a thing in public and embrace it in private.

Yes, of course, of course! Outwardly mocking him, yet, secretly controlling his actions, it was a classic ploy. So, the Mad Lord is their beloved It Man, is he? It made perfect sense to her—if she could inflict great pain on the It Man, then she would inflict great pain on the Sisterhood, and, even better, she could have revenge for being bested by him in Calvert.

Yes, yes . . .

Therefore, the It Man, the Mad Lord of Walther, was doomed.

But, how to go about it? As she knew firsthand, the Mad Lord demonstrated great strength, speed, endurance and resistance to damage, and he easily defeated her even when she was at her fighting best in Calvert. Looking at her now, she was a wrecked, frail woman huddled up under a blanket in the warm Remnath climate, a distant shadow of what she once was.

Nevertheless, he was doomed.

6

—THE TAKING OF SEDGWICK OF KOLD—

S he had indeed learned much as the Sisters captive. She had discovered ways to spy on the Sisters, to hear their hidden ethereal conversations from far away; the League, as she learned, was rife with their infernal chatter. Safe in her Remnath home, she could sit out on the manor terrace with her blanket and a cup of tea and tune right in on them, hearing everything.

The covert spying sessions revealed much to her. Near the vernal equinox, she listened to a solemn gathering of the Sisters taking place somewhere far to the north, as they summoned someone to their presence whom she thought was the It Man.

Terrance of Walther did not appear.

Instead it was Lord Sedgwick of Kold, the Pirate of Remnath, a scalawag and arch enemy of the Mad Lord of Walther. Was he in their service too? He had to be.

Yes, of course—how deceptively simple. The Sisters commanded Kold, making him go here and go there, and where he went, the Mad Lord would follow. It was through Kold that the Sisters commanded Walther, using their alleged public animosity toward each other as a cover.

Kold was always an enigma. He was a known criminal, yet he and his men had never killed anyone, only rarely resorting to "roughing people up." He and his band stole things, of course, but their thefts were never anything big—and the Mad Lord was always there to foil them and return the booty. And their battles were always a cavalcade of swashbuckling swordplay, fisticuffs, and daring do—very romantic, and, now that she understood the truth, clearly staged. She fancied Kold and the Mad Lord were actually friends, simply fulfilling their roles for their masters: the Sisters.

Hmmmm . . . very interesting.

She knew that Lord Kold and his band of pirates made berth on the shores southwest of the city of Champion. She went there alone, attired in her usual, a simple gray dress with button-up boots and her hat. She didn't even bother to disguise herself.

The pirates were remarkably easy to find. They laughed and cajoled the frail woman and she was dragged into his presence. Lord Kold sat in his gaudy chair, a fat, round man with an unhealthy-looking beard. He was loud and threatening, but she knew it was mostly an act.

She went to the offensive. She insulted him, challenged his manhood and boasted that she, a frail woman, could service not only he, but all of his men as well, and be ready for more once it was over.

Kold and his men took the bait. He ravished her joyously, laughing and chiding, his men encouraging him on. He flopped her onto the table as his men feasted around them and demonstrated his prowess. He pricked himself over and over again on the poisoned barb hidden deep within her womb, and then passed her off to the next man down the table, and on and on as if she were a basket full of hot rolls being shared by all. She took control of them by the shores of the sea one by one, though the strain of bedding so many men and the splintery surface of the wooden table nearly killed her. Before the night was over, Lord Sedgwick of Kold, the garish man, the fop, was hopelessly poisoned and addicted to her scent. He and his lot now belonged wholly to Lady Vendra of Cone.

She then started slowly so as not to alert the Sisters, neither they nor the Lord of Kold having any idea she had her hooks in him. She joined him on his paltry raids and was amazed by some of the exotic devices he possessed. One especially intrigued her—a Xaphan pendant he called a "Planar Bridge" that he used to rob the outlying Xaphan worlds, and with it she walked the Astral Plane, moving great distances in mere moments. She was pleased with it, and incorporated it into her plans.

Under her control, Kold and his men became actual villains, stealing, killing, and creating small bits of chaos.

She then set out to take the Mad Lord, her old enemy.

Oh, the Mad Lord—the Mad Lord! He was very difficult to snare. He was a known hedonist with an eye for great pulchritude and found the frail Lady Vendra not to his liking. She could not trick him into bed and give him The Barb as easily as she had Lord Kold. None of her Carina-taught charms or disguises worked and she was wholly frustrated. And, she couldn't challenge him directly with a physical confrontation, as she was no match for him …

Or was she? She tormented Lord Sedgwick of Kold for information—the Mad Lord, he had to have a weakness. What was it? What was it?

Kold didn't know of any. She pushed him—find out! The Sisters will certainly know. Find out!

As she awaited some news, it was time to turn her attention to Young Stenstrom of Belmont South-Tyrol again—and this time, there would be no weakness, no mercy.

Hearing that the Belmont children had a predilection to run away from home, she set several men to watch the roads near their manor in case the Lord Stenstrom the Younger happened to come walking down one of them.

Again, her patience was rewarded, for one evening she received a report that the little boy was indeed walking up the road toward Tyrol, carrying a sack of possessions—apparently running away from home. Moving swiftly, using the Planar Bridge to travel quickly between Remnath and Tyrol, she waited for him in a small fox park along with a number of Kold's men—the effects of the bridge causing the area surrounding the park to fade into the Astral Plane for a time.

There he was, wandering into the park—he was growing so fast. As she stood to put a dagger into his heart, he backed away into a tree; there was no place for him to go. He did something unexpected and ran to her, putting his tiny arms around her waist.

Clever boy.

She had another moment of weakness again as she briefly held him, but this time she cast it aside.

As she reared back to plunge in the knife, he was somehow whisked away, right through her grasp. Something black and veiled had appeared and taken him. Additionally, in retrospect, that was the first time she saw the Nargal—a creature she would one day become quite familiar with. It appeared as a small tornado of sand and grit, roaring into the park shortly after Lord Stenstrom vanished, causing her and her men to flee back into the Planar Bridge.

After the fox park incident, she ramped up her efforts to take and slay the boy. Using Lord Kold and his band of louts, she tried to abduct Lord Belmont from a family gathering in Rustam, hoping to cause a stir. The plot was foiled when the Mad Lord interceded, and quite a few henchmen were lost in the process.

* * * * *

The Mad Lord was proving to be a frustrating bore. She had to either get him out of the way or utterly enslave him and take him from the Sisters.

She plied Kold for information. She began to gather interesting tidbits from Kold as he ravished her bony body—about how the Sisters were obsessed with the second It Man. She'd heard of that man before while incarcerated, but could never glean his identity. If she could get to him and deal with the Mad Lord, the Sisters would be utterly devastated.

Finally, Kold had a breakthrough. He learned that the Mad Lord somehow received his power directly from the Sisters . . . that it came from a certain, far-reaching type of starlight. It was possible that, if she could lure the Mad Lord deep underground, he might be deprived of that power and she could take him.

She decided to entice the Mad Lord into battle. She resumed her guise as the Fiend of Calvert. She penned several sinister open letters in which she promised to continue terrorizing the Calvert wharfs if he didn't agree to meet her. She called him out in the letters, calling him "coward" and "fraud," insults certain to bring him out in the open.

Sure enough, the Mad Lord came, and, in a carefully prepared venue, she lured him into a deep mine shaft. There, deep underground, the Mad Lord lost most, if not all, of his power, and Lady Vendra's henchmen were able to subdue him.

There, tied down, she got on top of him, took him into herself and barbed him over and over again.

The Mad Lord now belonged to her just as Sedgwick of Kold did.

7

—The Mad Lord on his Knees—

Taking the Mad Lord paid instant dividends. As her slave, he told her what he knew about the mysterious second It Man. He said he knew who the second It Man was—that he saw him with his own eyes.

The second It Man whom the Sisters had discovered was none other than Lord Stenstrom the Younger of Belmont-South Tyrol, the little boy of Lady Jubilee whom she had repeatedly tried to kill.

That explained much. Was that how the little nipper survived the kill-trap placed in his play pit—with his latent It Man abilities?

Could that also be why the Sisters were so keen on discovering what additive she had put into the God Sperm potion that Lord Stenstrom bought on Bazz? They must be convinced whatever she had spiked the potion with helped artificially create the It Man and they wanted the secret, desperately. To be able to artificially create an "It" Man as needed was invaluable knowledge for them.

So . . . young Lord Belmont was the Sisters' "It" Man, was he? Oh, how things relate—how the circle closes—the Vendetta Circle that she heard of while on Bazz but didn't believe in. Maybe there was something to it after all.

She would make him submit before her, just like the Mad Lord had.

Something completely unexpected happened at that time. When she released the Mad Lord back into the light of day, he appeared to go utterly mad as the Sisters' power jostled about with the poisons she had introduced into his system—now truly living up to his name. He became a raving lunatic.

The Mad Lord went wandering across the face of Kana, babbling the Sisters' secrets, and babbling her secrets too.

Fearing her activities would be discovered, she set Lord Kold against him in open battle.

And it was truly terrible, a much more brutal battle then she would have anticipated. They fought in Rustam, doing a significant amount of damage to the city where, eventually, the Mad Lord prevailed. Torn and ragged, he continued his wandering and babbling.

She couldn't have him spouting her secrets, but there wasn't much she could do to him out in the starlight.

Fortunately, the Sisters took care of him for her. In a public display of outrage, they burned his holdings, stripped him bare, and bore him away, killing him behind their walls, silencing him once and for all.

She savored their thoughts after his killing—wailing, in grief, bemoaning their lost Mad Lord whom they secretly cherished and had to slay like a rabid pet.

It was perfect and well worth the wait. Every tear the Sisters shed was a drop of gold. And the Sisters shed many tears; their grief was succulent.

Sitting back and allowing herself to relax, she monitored the Sisters' thoughts. In a panic, they then rallied toward the second It Man, Lord Stenstrom of Belmont, though he was still only a child.

Now, she could fully turn her attention to him.

8

—THE NARGAL—

O ver the next few years, she and Lady Jubilee played a puerile game of ruse and deception. Lady Jubilee was sending *things* after her—veiled creatures, invisible to all but the most rational of mindsets, sniffing the air and seeking her out. Apparently there was something to Tyrol Sorcery after all. The first few were rather troubling; however, she quickly discovered their weaknesses and was able to divert them reliably by using her slaves, rubbed with her scent.

In the meantime, she learned that the Sisters, ever hiding behind layers of ruse and deception, were planning on controlling Lord Belmont's development from child to young man via external means. They had created some sort of creature they infrequently referred to as a "Nargal." They called it his "Tutor" and "Protector." As he aged, another word entered their vocabulary: "Lover." The Sisters had painstakingly created this "Nargal," this "Tutor" and "Lover" using rare elements gathered from far-reaching places. She also knew that this creature was kept in a pen in a Vith ruin near their stronghold of Westron.

She went to places of great learning in Ferenz and Arden, researching more about Nargals and what they were.

The texts she read were fanciful and unclear. A Nargal was some sort of elemental creature given partial life—a "monster" out of a fairytale and that their summoning was illegal in League space. Again, as before, the Sisters freely went against their own establishment when it suited them to do so.

Seeing great potential to cause mayhem, she researched further, and she listened, ever the fly on the wall, to the Sisters' chatter. Some of the details became clear. The Sisters had created a Nargal of Sand, a useful servant of supposedly limited intellect, easy to program, easy to control. She realized that she had seen this Nargal with her own eyes, at fox park south of Tyrol, years before, when it was new and small. It had looked like a pint-sized tornado of sand.

Ah, but look here. She found old texts in Arden that discussed the perils of Nargals—that, should the proper precautions not be taken, and should certain forbidden ingredients be introduced, a Nargal of Sand could be infused with Elder-like feelings and "think" it was alive.

Sand Nargals, easy to create, easy to control, were also confoundedly easy to taint. Such a tainted Nargal could become unpredictable. Such a tainted Nargal could easily turn on its masters.

More research, more reading. Not much to go on—the Sisters apparently kept a tight lid on such arcane learning. A trip to Onaris, however, was illuminating.

She discovered in a filthy library run by The Hertogs what was needed to taint a Sand Nargal. There were five major components:

BLACK SAND

1: Zerterite: a certain type of mildly radioactive volcanic sand containing copious amounts of obsidian, feldspar, magnetite, and a touch of garnet.

2: Morningwell, a type of flowering plant native to Casiarchus, an obscure world located in the Great Xaphan Nebula.

3: Podantium, an alkaloid (that ingredient was fairly easy to obtain).

4: Magdalyte, a "purple" salt compound illegal in League space for its ability to simulate life in dead bodies (and addle the minds of the living at the same time).

5: Rumbob, a Shadow tech "tar" that was highly emotive—that is, one could infuse it with one's feelings and desires—again, highly illegal.

Such a mixture of "Black Sand" would certainly wake the Sisters' little sandy beast up a little.

Who knows what might happen then.

In her reading, she discovered that it was critical to be careful with the Black Sand components—once combined, the "sand" took on the aura of the person near it—it became "like" that person, infused with that person's feelings, thus adding that element to the Sand Nargal. She was going to put a powerful hatred of Stenstrom, Lord of Belmont into that creature, and a hatred of all he loved. Additionally, and best of all, she was going to add a blind obedience toward her into the sand, making the Nargal her slave instead of the Sisters' slave—perhaps she could use it as a tool or a foil. It might prove useful.

She went to her sisters on Carina and had little success gathering the required ingredients there. Vendra then went to her brother, Admiral Derlith, and mentioned what she needed. He replied that such ingredients were deemed contraband by the Sisterhood of Light and therefore illegal—particularly the Magdalyte, the Rumbob, and the sand itself.

She was unfazed. She pushed him, insulted him, and cajoled him; she even considered putting him, her own brother, to the barb, but reconsidered. She, however, continued to pressure him, until, to her great relief, he gave in.

"All right, enough!" Derlith said, exasperated. Putting his career and his freedom on the line, Derlith procured a quantity of the five components through illegal, back channel means. They arrived shortly thereafter in five separate parcels delivered to anonymous lockers in the cities of Dee (the Rumbob), Conwell (the Magdalyte), Armenelos (the Morningwell and the Podantium), and Mystery (the Zerterite)—it was important to keep the ingredients in the parcels separated, and it was important to deliver them discreetly to different cities, as the importation of many of these ingredients was an offense punishable by imprisonment, or—put together—execution.

Also, great care had to be taken in the transportation of these ingredients, as, once combined, the assimilation process would begin and there would be no turning back. The process would have to be started all over again should that happen—and that would be unacceptable given the difficulty of acquiring the components in the first place.

She required a "mule" to gather the items and deliver them to her personally in Dee, for she had a hideout there that she once used during her heady Slave-collection days. There, she would accept the parcels and kill the mule. She had a thought as she exited the Admiral's office—she saw his worthless secretary, that silly little man with the blonde hair, sitting at his desk researching the Fiend of Calvert. She wondered how many shades of white he would turn if he knew that she, standing by his desk listening to him go on and on about murders, was the murderer herself?

She was eager to find out.

She would be waiting for him in Dee, and when he came into the room, she would reveal herself as the murderer, the Fiend he was so afraid of, and watch him swoon in fear. She might offer him a sporting chance, provide him a weapon, or perhaps a head start to run. Though she was nothing of the fighter she once was, this puny little man would be no match for her. She looked forward to killing him.

$$* \quad * \quad * \quad * \quad *$$

The gathering of the items was going well—the little man in his outrageous hat, hideous optical glasses, and buckle shoes, was following the precise instructions left to him rather well. She followed from afar, using the Astral Plane to shadow his movements. He started the last day of his life in the Grand Port of Armenelos, pushing his way through the crowds, gathering the two items hidden there in two separate lockers. He then moved on via Fleet coach to Mystery where he secured the parcel of Black Sand itself from the station and enjoyed a small breakfast after he'd collected them. She watched, making sure he correctly handled the parcels—should he become careless, should he even come close to mixing them together, then she would strike and kill him.

So far, his careful attention to detail was prolonging his life.

He then took the Fleet coach northeast to Conwell, the trip taking an hour or two. The collection of the components was going well, and she felt a little playful. She gave him tantalizing little glimpses of her, using her Planar Bridge to keep ahead of his coach. She allowed herself to appear tall, in gray, covered in her billowy cloak, her hands kept at mid-riff in a threatening manner. She laughed—she saw his bug-eyed, open-mouthed little face in the window as the coach passed by, the large brim of his hat pushed up against the glass, clearly startled by what he was seeing.

What must be going through his mind?

Arriving at Conwell, she saw him come out of the coach slowly, looking around to see if anybody was out there. He was tarrying about too much for her liking, so she gave him another peek to get him moving—his leggings and buckle shoes churning in flight when he saw her. He went to the station and secured the Magdalyte. Well done. One more to go, then his life would come to an end in her dreary room straight from a nightmare.

He boarded the coach again, and headed southeast to Dee, perhaps the nicest of the Calvert cities. He sat down to lunch by the seaside, eating alone, looking at the people passing by. She allowed him to have his lunch, but when he called for dessert, she had enough and again, gave him a glimpse of her to once again get him moving.

Again, he left his table and hurried on, hoping the crowds of people might offer him safety. He mounted the steps to Dee's small station to gather the last of the items, the Rumbob.

Now, she went to her room on the second floor of a crooked tenement to prepare and await his arrival. As she once did in Calvert, she undressed and sat back. When he opened the door, she would allow him to savor the horror of the moment seeing her nude body seated in a charnel room of tortured dead, then, using nothing but her two hands, crack every bone in his body. She imagined taking him by the hands and whirling about with him as if they were doing a grim waltz, and him dying a little bit more with every turn.

Should be any minute now.

Time passed. Something was wrong. The little man never arrived.

What had happened?

She dressed and went out looking for him. He was gone—she had lost his trail. For some reason, he hadn't followed the last of his instructions and diverted from the plan. Perhaps the seedy nature of the tenement had put him off. Perhaps he sensed danger.

Very perceptive. Surprising.

She figured that he would go to the Fleet and leave the bag full of parcels in the Admiral's office. Using the Astral Plane, she went as far as she could— Fleet Headquarters was sealed against Astral Plane incursions by the Sisters. She went the rest of the way in a fast coach she flagged down and hired. When she got to the Fleet, it was dark and mostly empty. Going into her brother's office, she found the bag there by his desk. All five parcels were present in their compartmented packaging, just as instructed. She had her components, and they appeared whole. Still, the little man was going to die. She went out after him, determined to wring his neck.

She quickly caught up to him—he must have just left the office. She followed him through the vast complex, and, when the time was right, struck, clouding his senses with pheromones. She seized him by the wrist and pulled him into a nearby bathroom where she could murder him in peace.

Unfortunately, the bathroom was not empty. There was some pathetic Marine girl sitting in there on the vanity drinking from a flask. She was temporarily taken aback; that Marine girl—she seemed oddly familiar, though she couldn't quite place her. She wore her hair with those annoying little dangling sickles of hair like they did on Bazz. She must be from Bazz; perhaps she'd seen her there.

While she was pondering that, the little man recovered, pulled away from her grip and fled from the bathroom. She thought to first kill the Bazz girl and take off after the mule, but she had a Marine communicator chattering somewhere in her coat. One cry for help and the complex would be put on alert. She might have to flee; there might be a spectacle. She decided not to chance it.

No matter, she would settle with Lord A-Ram later.

* * * * *

Her brother, Admiral Derlith, was surprisingly angry and forceful the next day. He surmised from A-Ram's account of the day's events that she had planned to do something sinister with him.

She told the Admiral to mind his own business, least he know what was good for him.

Surprising. He shot back that he suspected her of committing all sort of crimes, and that only the memory of her, as she was long ago, before the Nether Day Ball and the convent, prevented him from going to the authorities. He also told her that he had a dossier stashed somewhere containing what he thought was evidence pertaining to her supposed activities. He said that, should he go missing or become addled, the dossier would circulate and she would become a wanted fugitive.

She was impressed—he had never shown her any backbone before. Among his many conditions for keeping quiet was her to promise to leave Lord A-Ram alone. He was an innocent man, and knew nothing.

Fine—what difference did he make?

✳ ✳ ✳ ✳ ✳

Installing the "hated up" package into the Nargal was quite troubling—almost as difficult as gathering the components. The first few slaves she sent to Westron were never heard from again. The next were transformed into mindless idiots by some sort of trap the Sisters had set up protecting the compound. She decided to try using Lord Kold's Planar Bridge, which was a risky gamble as the Sisters might be ready for such a thing. And, indeed, the Planar landscape surrounding Westron was studded with deadly traps.

She travelled north using conventional means as the Sisters' holdings were all blocked from Astral incursions using the Planar Bridge. She skulked about the hills and pine forests of mid Vithland, looking for a way to pierce the Sisters' defenses.

As it happened, the creature came to her.

She saw it as a massive tornado of wind and sand, just as it looked in fox park years before; only now it had gotten much bigger. It reached up high into the sky, nearly touching the clouds.

And then it changed, collapsing down and disappearing into the pine trees. Moments later the small, unassuming form of a blonde-headed girl wandered out of the woods. She seated herself by the bank of the river, bathing her feet in the water. She absent-mindedly toyed with the mud lining the bank with a stick.

Vendra approached, startling her.

"You frightened me," the Nargal said.

Vendra smiled. "I'm sorry, and no need to be frightened of me. I am merely a lady enjoying the afternoon."

"I've never seen anybody out here in the woods, except my mothers."

Vendra looked around, taking in the wooded scenery. "Then people in this area don't realize what they're missing. So lovely. What is your name?"

"Lilly."

"Ah, very pretty name."

The Nargal had been apparently scratching something into the mud with a stick.

"What are you doing?" Vendra asked.

The Nargal flushed up a bit. "Nothing."

Vendra leaned over. The Nargal had been writing the word "Bel" in the mud with her stick.

"What is 'Bel'?" Vendra asked.

"'Bel is my love. I love Bel."

"Bel is a fortunate fellow. Does he live near here?"

"No, he lives far away. I'm only allowed to see him every so often, though I miss him so."

"Who prevents you from seeing him?"

"My mothers. They only allow me to see him infrequently."

Vendra was sly and full of cunning. "One should not be kept from one's love. Can you draw me a picture of him so that I may see what he looks like?"

The Nargal puzzled over it. It moved the stick about in an uncertain fashion. "I . . . he's . . . rather like . . ." The Nargal put the stick down, flustered. "I can't draw."

"Can't draw?"

The Nargal was concerned. "Is that bad?"

"Proper ladies are expected to paint pictures of their men; it's the custom."

"And, if the lady can't paint?"

Vendra smiled. "Then, unfortunately, she stays alone. How sad."

The Nargal sat there, confused, in a growing panic. She processed this troubling information in her Nargal brain. Her blonde hair puffed up and she seemed to grow in size a bit as if she were about to transform into her whirling tornado form. "What can I do? What will Bel think of me?" Her voice had the edge of desperation in it. "Can you help me?"

Vendra reached into the folds of her dress and produced the package full of tainted sand. "Of course I can. Take this," she said. "It will help you. It will lead you to your love. With this, you can be with him whenever you want. With this, you can be whatever you want to be."

She looked at the package. "What is it?"

"Magic sand. Here. Take it."

The Nargal thought about it, and then happily took the package full of "magic sand" that she thought would lead her to her love. Sand hissed within the paper wrapping.

"This will help me learn to paint?" the Nargal asked hopefully.

"Most certainly," Vendra replied.

The Nargal smiled and thanked her. She walked away with the package tucked under her arm.

Vendra watched her depart, her eyes narrowing.

Magic sand that will lead one to one's love . . . If only such a thing existed.

Weeks passed, leading into months. Vendra was burning to know what the results of her tainting the Nargal were. Surely now, befouled with her black sand, it was filled with utter hatred of Lord Stenstrom. She tried calling out to it, as she did for the men in her thrall, but it didn't respond.

Risking much, Vendra again ventured out to the wooded hills of Vithland, hoping to encounter the Nargal she now owned. She had to have information.

She reached the shallow river where she'd seen the creature before, and there it was, once again sitting by the water. Its hair seemed longer and even more golden than last time. It seemed to be carrying itself in a more mature, regal fashion. The Nargal had out a small palette of watercolors, some cloth, and a selection of fine two and three-haired brushes. It was sitting by the stream painting into a tiny golden locket, very fine and meticulous work requiring a sharp eye and steady hand. With regularity, the Nargal stopped what it was doing, peered into the stream, beheld its own reflection, and set back to work in the locket.

"Hello again!" Vendra said, approaching.

The Nargal looked up and smiled. "I knew you were there."

"Ah, I pride myself on my stealthy passage. How is it you knew I was there?"

"I sensed you. It is good that you have returned, I was hoping to see you again."

"Oh?"

"I wanted to thank you. The Gift you gave me was truly wondrous."

Vendra was elated and cautious at the same time. If the Nargal now hated Lord Belmont, she showed no outward signs of it. "I'm glad it helped."

Confound it, what had come of the Black Sand??

You, Nargal, belong to me! Bow before your master!

Vendra glanced at her palette and brushes. "What are you doing?" she asked.

"I'm painting. I'm making a gift to present to my love."

"A self-portrait?"

"Yes."

"Ah, such a warm and heartfelt gift, may I see?"

"Of course." The Nargal put her brushes down and held up the locket. Inside was a tiny, partially completed portrait of herself, blonde-haired and blue-eyed, done dot by dot in watercolors. Even only partially finished, Vendra could see that the painting was exquisite and full of skill.

"And this is for your love? That 'Bel' fellow from afar?"

"Yes, it's for no other."

"And you still love this man?"

"Oh, yes, more than ever. I've worked so hard on this painting. I want it to be perfect."

Vendra was stumped. What happened to the tainted sand? Clearly it had had an effect. The Nargal now could paint with rare talent whereas before it had none, but what about the hatred and malice she poured into it? If anything, the Nargal was even now more enthralled with the Sisters' It Man.

Oh, this was a dismal failure.

The Nargal put her things away and stood. "You need to go back home, or wherever you're from, it won't be safe here in a few minutes and I bid you fair warning."

"It won't. Why not?"

"Because I'm going to go see Bel. He needs me."

"Have your mothers authorized your seeing Bel?"

The Nargal paused. "I don't really care what my mothers want. I'm going regardless. So please, I bid you safe passage and good afternoon."

Vendra's ears pricked up. Ah, the taint is having an effect after all. Rebellion is forming within the Nargal. Independence as well.

Good, very good. That was something she could work with, manipulate.

Vendra took her leave, but, instead of departing, she waited behind a tree. She wanted to watch what was going to transpire. After several minutes waiting, however, she wished she'd taken the advice and fled.

The Nargal transformed into a savage tornado, churning the earth and ripping through the trees, climbing into the sky, parting the clouds, terrifying to behold. Vendra had to hang onto the tree for dear life in the tempest.

The Sisters' thoughts in the next few weeks were telling.

—The creature is exhibiting unusual traits.

The creature was not in its enclosure yesterday . . . it escaped.

—Was it found? Was it found?

Yes, in Esther

—We detect a taint in it—it has been poisoned.

How?

—Its task is nigh complete. When it is of no more use . . . kill it. Be done with it.

9

—An Invitation to Dinner—

A year passed and nothing significant happened. The Sisters thoughts gave away nothing too much out of the ordinary. The taint she had applied to the Nargal had not immediately taken great hold or manifested itself to any extent. She'd hope it would rip him limb from limb, but so far it hadn't. Curious and needing information, she set out to test Lord Belmont directly, to see what he was made of. He was an It Man like the Mad Lord, so he must have similar power, which was daunting—however, he was young and inexperienced, and, possibly, unaware of his status. She thought to test him, to prod him, to see what sort of a man he was. If he was a weakling, she might just barb and take him right there and then.

She heard that he was newly attending school at the University of Bern—and for a young man whom she knew to have been isolated and sheltered his whole life by his bitch mother, a bustling environment like a university must certainly have him on edge. He might be confused and lonely . . . and extra vulnerable.

Disguising herself as a charming student, she travelled to the school via Planar Bridge and couldn't find him about the grounds mingling with the other students—apparently he wasn't coming out much, which, she supposed was to be expected. She stationed a few of her remaining men about the campus, with orders to keep an eye out for him.

Eventually, they spied him, walking alone on the green in his Tyrol clothes. She Bridged in and quickly found him wandering amongst the buildings.

He looked so much like his father. He had grown into such a handsome young man . . . again, as when he was a child, that creeping weakness came up. When face to face with him, she had a hard time doing what needed done.

She stammered, losing her cool, and invited him to share dinner with her. And, she truly did want to simply sit with him and share a meal. Maybe she, over a hundred years his elder, could somehow inspire his heart—no barbs, no tricks. If she couldn't have Lord Stenstrom the Older, perhaps the Younger—the It Man—would do.

Perhaps that might be the ultimate revenge after all.

Lord Belmont, however, resisted and refused her invitation. Spurned again, she left his presence and thought of another plan. She decided to give it to him full bore. She stoked up her scent to maximum levels and went after him. She would take him by force, barb him by guile, and have him in turn.

But he was gone. Surely he couldn't have quit the area so soon? She looked around and couldn't find him. Just like his mother had done decades earlier, he had simply vanished into the shadows. She was determined to follow him and pounce while he was weak. She pulled a bottle full of Man detector from Carina out of her bag, rubbed it on a steel ball and placed it on the ground. The ball rolled into the nearby greenery.

He was there; he had to be, hiding somehow. Just like his mother had once faded into the shadows, so too could he. She reached into her bag and slipped on a pair of barbed knuckles. If he was there, she was going to physically overcome him, pull him away and take him.

The sirens went off; bad weather was wafting up. A funnel cloud formed over the school; people all around were scrambling for cover. She saw it in the sky.

It wasn't a funnel cloud—it was the Nargal, she could recognize it by its brownish color. It was huge, even bigger than the last time she'd seen it. What was it doing? What incredible timing. Or was it merely bad timing? It must be protecting him, watching over him.

Gods!!

Completely frustrated, she opened her bridge and went back to Jacarta, determining once and for all that coming into Belmont's presence personally was not a good idea. She couldn't control herself, and his pet Nargal was a deadly nuisance.

She had to regroup.

The Nargal gambit finally appeared to be paying off.

The Sisters' thoughts grew frantic two years later:

—It killed a Sister yesterday. It is out of control.

Enough, be done with it. Our It Man needs it to guide him no longer. He has gone where we wanted him to go. We have shown it to him—he now knows what it is. Its purpose is done.

—No, no, it has fled.

Where could it have gone?

—Find it! Kill it!

Where indeed . . . Where indeed . . .

So, there she sat in her familiar terrace, looking out on her familiar hills.

What had ninety years of hate and revenge bought her?

Lady Jubilee was dead at last, though of natural causes. The Sisters It Man was dead. And now the second It Man, Lord Stenstrom of Belmont, was at roam in a stripped-bare ship. She had persuaded Admiral Derlith to place several beacons aboard the ship so that she could hone in on it with her Planar Bridge and torment him with her men. When she discovered that the Admiral's adjutant had joined in with Lord Belmont, she sent a few of her slaves to leave him several calling cards, knowing Lord A-Ram's fear and preoccupation with the Fiend of Calvert.

Something killed her men and destroyed her beacons. Possibly the Sisters had done it, more probably, it was the Nargal, protecting her "Bel" to the last.

Small matter. Lord Belmont was soon to be humiliated and knocked off his chair, and possibly killed by her niece, whom Admiral Derlith had sent after him.

While her personal control was certainly questionable in Lord Belmont's presence, surely Lady Gwendolyn, an undeniably cold woman worthy of Carina itself, would not be so swayed. Vendra had made a minor project out of her, hoping to fill her with all the rage she had felt over the years.

The closed Vendetta Circle, the Ganaada on Bazz had said everybody's in it with her.

She sighed.

Ninety years of revenge and hatred. Lots of dust and an empty bed.

Empty soul.

Her sisters on Carina had taught her much: patience, skill and resolve. The only thing they hadn't taught her was how to live with an empty life full of old bones and cold shadows.

What of the sorrow, my sisters, what of that? You promised to rid me of it, yet it remains. What am I to do?

Years ago, when she sat there by the sea holding the tiny Lord Stenstrom—the man she was even now scheming to humiliate, then kill—that was the only time in the past ninety years she'd been truly happy. How wondrous it had been to hold a child in her arms and be a mother if only for a few moments. Her sisters on Carina had taught her nothing of that.

Circles on a page. A landscape full of curses and voices from the past.

With Lady Jubilee passed away, the dark, murderous person she'd become on Carina was dying as well, becoming less and less with each passing day, joining Jubilee in the grave at long last. The Dames of Carina taught her that Revenge, Scheming, Getting Even with those who wronged you was all that mattered.

"Look at me in your final moments, you bastard, and know who bested you!"

What were paltry things like hope and love compared to the majestic finality of Revenge, they would argue.

What indeed? She wondered as she looked at herself in the mirror, no longer a dark frightful presence, just a bent mirthless form life had passed by: Can this be me?

She'd watched life evolve at the Belmont Household despite her efforts to derail it. She watched the comings and goings, the little triumphs and the tearful tragedies, all part of daily life, and there she was, still angry, still stuck in the past alone on that ballroom floor. She watched Jubilee's son, the "It" Man, survive all the murder attempts and roadblocks she could hurl at him, overcome an overbearing mother, a tainted Nargal and a dead ship, and keep trying, keep plowing ahead no matter what, giving chase to his dreams. She remembered his eyes as she raised the knife to kill him, so full of dreams. Perhaps there was much to be learned from that. Hope and perseverance were things the Dames of Carina never put much stock in, and perhaps they were wrong. Could it be that revenge was nothing more than a fitful cry for attention from a desperate, empty person?

Look at me!!

She did something ninety years overdue, something she'd wanted to do for a long time but hadn't the courage. She got out a piece of paper, not gray, but soft pink. She steadied her hand and picked up a marker. The old curse was closing in on her. Anymore, when she tried to write, her hand did of its own will and drew an endless number of scrawled names inside an ugly circle. The names of faceless dead men and her name mixed in there as well, a murdered victim just like the rest. Damn Bazzers and their magic, they'd gotten to her after all.

Paper after wasted paper came and went: scrawl, circles and names shouting out from the grave. She concentrated, forced her hand to obey. She wrote, with all the strength she still possessed:

"To my Dearest Stenstrom the Older, Lord of Belmont-South Tyrol. I have been seeking the words to write this letter for far too long . . ."

Ninety years of hatred and scheming, fading into nostalgia and regret. Revenge was fleeting, it was deceiving. What was strong? What endured; the tiny ember of love she'd managed to nurture and keep glowing all that time. As she wrote, she prayed for his son, the man she'd tried to kill, prayed he might somehow endure just a bit more, complete his mission and get to Bazz. If he could do that, then perhaps there was absolution to be had for them both.

"Look at me, sir," she fantasized herself saying to him, "I have done these terrible things, and I beg you to forgive me."

She finished the letter, sealed it, and called for an attendant to send it on its way. It sat there on the silver plate, ninety years in the writing, the long-awaited triumph of hope and love over anger and revenge.

Part 3

The Pilgrims

of Merian

THE PILGRIMS OF MERIAN

1

—Nightmare—

Beep . . . Beep . . . boop, boop, boop . . .
Captain Gwendolyn kept hearing that noise as she stood on the bridge. It was a vaguely familiar sound, and she was sure she knew it from somewhere, but couldn't quite place it.

It was just out of reach. It was troubling, maddening. It was a sound she knew she should know. She tried to put it out of her mind.

Even on a tiny scouting ship, the bridge was a bustling nerve center of activity. The navigator sat there surrounded by holos and grids, the red and blue faces of the AM/PM wheels slowly rotating and readjusting as the helmsman, sitting nearby, occasionally corrected the ship's course.

On the other side of the bridge, the Com stood behind his panel, monitoring all inbound and outbound communication traffic. The vast majority of the messages were automated, one of the ship's myriad of systems trying to talk to others and needing command approval to do so. It was a rather stodgy system, but it effectively kept the ship from being taken over by outside or hostile forces.

Through the windows, Gwendolyn saw the stars moving by in a tide of white, yellow and bluish dots of bigger or lesser size.

Their current mission had come down from the Admiralty: transport a visiting dignitary to an important meeting. She had to shake her head—scouting ships, always taking this person here and that person there, each one a priority. Basically, they were an overly large taxi.

The lift doors opened. Someone came through.

It was the dignitary. There he was wearing his usual long black coat and hat.

"Evening, sir," Gwendolyn said. "It is evening back home you know. Rather late, actually."

Beep . . . Beep . . . boop, boop, boop . . .

There's that noise again. Gwendolyn looked around.

"Captain," the dignitary said, "she is at it again. Your crew is beginning to panic. I think you need to take action."

She nodded. "Yes, you're right. I'm sorry you have been made a party to such a thing."

"It's all right. Please, shall we?"

Gwendolyn stood and straightened her coat. "Thank you. You needn't come. This is ship's business. You should return to your cabin and rest."

She excused herself and walked into the lift. The dignitary joined her.

Nervously, she selected her floor.

Beep ... Beep ... boop, boop, boop ...

"Pardon me," she said as the lift began moving, "do you hear those sounds?"

"What sounds?" the dignitary asked. "I hear many sounds. Can you be more specific."

"Never mind."

Several moments later, the lift arrived at the proper deck. Captain Gwendolyn and the dignitary stepped out.

Beep ... Beep ... boop, boop, boop ...

"That noise is driving me crazy. I'm sorry, sir, I should be more mindful."

"Again, I hear nothing out of the ordinary."

They walked down the hall, passing the occasional crewman as they went. Gwendolyn looked up at the dignitary. He was so tall. "If I may, sir, you promised you'd tell me why you wear that mask. You haven't forgotten your promise, have you?"

The dignitary's gem-like blue eyes sparkled through the holes of his lace mask, the HRN at his collar glinting in cursive gold lettering. "No, I haven't. Please, let us attend to this sorry matter, then I'll keep my promise."

Gwendolyn walked at his side, struggling to keep up; the man had such long legs.

"Then what, then what are you going to do?" she asked.

He smiled. "Then we'll to your quarters, we'll have at a game of cards, and then who knows—just you and me. That's what you want, isn't it?"

Gwendolyn, shy, fumbled with her FEDULA for a moment. "I ..."

"Isn't it?"

Beep ... Beep ... boop, boop, boop ...

That noise was driving her mad. "Yes ... yes ..."

They rounded a shallow bend and arrived at a door.

"Here we are," the dignitary said.

Gwendolyn stood there, her thoughts still wrapped around what was to come like a giddy school girl awaiting a promised treat.

The dignitary knocked on the door. "Morgan . . ." he said. "Morgan, darling, we're here . . ."

There was a troubled bumping about from within the door.

"Go away!" came a panicked reply. *"All of you, go away! Leave me alone! I'll kill anybody who comes too close! I've already killed all the ones you set against me. I can! I'm a Hospitaler, a trained killer! I can fight! I will fight again if I must!"*

The dignitary laughed. "Come now, Morgan, you don't want to hurt anybody, do you? You're just making this harder than it must. It needn't be so . . ."

The dignitary opened the door. It was dark on the other side. He motioned for Gwendolyn to go in. "Go on, Captain, through there."

She hesitated. He approached, his hands finding places decency demanded they did not.

"Remember what awaits," he whispered into her ear.

Gwendolyn felt her body react. She drew her MiMs. "All right . . ." She stepped through the doorway. "All right . . ." she repeated.

On the other side of the door was a nightmare version of the bridge: dark, in disarray, huddled bodies pushed in the corners, pools of drying blood on the floor, the place tinged with howls and gibbering shrieks.

Through the windows a skittering, wavy sort of light funneled in, illuminating the place in a kaleidoscope of shimmering lighter and darker spots. It was like being at the bottom of a deep aquarium, standing by the glass, watching the fish swim—just like the ones in Fazo that her uncle used to take her to see.

"Morgan?" she said.

Somebody rustled in the distance. *"I said keep away!"* The voice she heard was ragged and flecked with panic.

Gwendolyn stepped further into the bridge. "Morgan, I'm not going to hurt you." Feeling her MiMs in her palm, she tightened her grip on the handle. *I'm just going to shoot you in the head, and then I can have him . . .*

Beep . . . beep . . . boop, boop, boop . . .

That noise—it was deafening.

Just then, Gwendolyn saw Morgan-Jeterix, Lady of Thompson. She was standing there near the wall holding her Jet staff out.

"Come to kill me, Captain? Is that what they sent you here to do?"

"Nobody sent me here to do anything, Morgan. I just want to have a talk. Your behavior is frightening my crew." Her knuckles went white as she squeezed the MiMs in her palm.

I'm just going to aim at your head, pull the trigger, and that's that. Then you can have peace, and I . . . .

Such thoughts as these she indulged in.

Morgan shifted positions and set her Jet Staff to the ready. Gwendolyn would need to be careful—Hospitalers were nothing to trifle with.

"I've been watching you, Captain, wandering aimlessly around the bridge, lost in your little dream, acting it out in mid-air, talking to nobody. They've got you! It's just an illusion!"

Gwendolyn stood in front of her. She readied to raise her MiMs and shoot. She wanted to look her in the eye when she pulled the trigger. If Morgan managed to survive the MiMs shot, then she'd draw her FEDULA and they'd fight to the death. Gwendolyn was as deadly with it as Morgan was with her Jet Staff.

Morgan's image vanished. Gwendolyn spun around, trying to see in the dark. "Where are you, Morgan?"

"Illusions are a funny thing, aren't they, Captain. I can Cloak and Paint illusions; I inherited this skill from my grandmother . . . she was a Vith, had blue hair and everything. And I can Cloak too, but nothing like what They can do."

Gwendolyn stood her ground and looked about. "I'm trying to help you."

Morgan's voice came again. *"My grandmother . . . you know what happened to her? Have I ever told you? My grandfather was killed in a battle with the Xaphans. Halas had no business going to the stars, she said, and look what happened to him. Dead. She . . .*

couldn't bear the thought of going on without him. She recreated him, in illusion, and she spent the rest of her life interacting with a person that only she could see. She grew gaunt and famished; she stopped eating, washing, and she completely withdrew into her own mind."

Gwendolyn looked down at her gun. "What's the point of this, Morgan?"

"Illusions, Gwendolyn! My mother used to make me go up and feed her—she roamed around on the fourth floor of our manor. It was so hard to get her to sit still, to open her mouth and eat. Usually she said nothing—just stared off into space. One time, though, one time I got her talking and she sounded almost like a sane person. She said that everything, beyond the limits of her head, was a nightmare. The real world was a place of uncertainty, and sadness, and dead husbands and lost memories. She said she'd rather stay where she was and be happy. And that was that . . . I never heard her speak again. She just continued on, soiled and starving, walking hand-in-hand with the illusion of my grandfather until she died in the fire that consumed our manor years later."

The door to the bridge opened, admitting a shaft of gold light from beyond. He was standing in the doorway.

"We're waiting for you, Captain," he said. "She's over there." He pointed.

Something appeared in the dark. There was Morgan-Jeterix. She was lying supine on the floor at the base of the Com panel, her expanded Jet Staff resting at her side. She was reaching up, trying to get at the Com panel's control board.

Around her, six crewman lay dead, twisted up, staved to death. A variety of improvised weapons were scattered about.

"Captain Gwendolyn," she said. *"So, here I am. I'm dying . . . they want me dead because I can see. I can see everything. I'm hurt, been attacked. They set the crew against me. I had to kill them. I didn't want to but I had to. One of them hurt me before they died—it wasn't their fault. They didn't know what they were doing. Can't reach my wounds, in my back. I'm bleeding out . . . can't stop it. Going into shock. Gwendolyn, help me . . . please! Fight it! See what there is to see. The windows! Look to the windows and see!"*

Gwendolyn glanced at the windows. Just that same watery darkness.

Wait.

Something big moved past the windows and then was gone.

"Morgan," Gwendolyn said, "I'm going to help you."

"You are? What are you going to do with that gun you're holding?"

"I'm going to help you, Morgan," she said, cocking the MiMs. "And then he and I . . ."

Morgan struggled a little and tried to pick up her jet staff. *"You mean Lord Belmont? That's not him, Gwendolyn . . . and you know it."*

Beep . . . beep . . . boop, boop, boop . . .

Morgan weakly pointed at the Com. *"Hear that? That's him, Gwendolyn! He's out there, looking for us. He's trying to help us. For Creation's sake, answer the Com, and save us all!"*

She slumped to the floor.

Gwendolyn smiled and shook her head. "No, Morgan. He's right outside, and he's promised me things. I'm going to do this, quick and painless, and then you'll have peace, and I'll have peace. I've wanted this for a long time."

"You've . . . only just become acquainted with him."

Again, Gwendolyn shook her head. "No . . . no, I used to hear my aunt talking about him all the time in the parlor with my mother when I was a girl. I would hide and they didn't know I was nearby listening. My aunt would talk about Lord Belmont, and how she hated him and his mother. And my mother, she would speak up and say how my aunt was trapped in a closed circle that could have no good end. My aunt didn't care—she was caught up . . . Now, he's just outside the door, waiting for me. I want to go to him, Morgan."

"But, you first have to kill me, is that right?"

"Yes."

"There is nothing but an illusion on the other side of that door. You and I—we're both ladies of Great Houses. We could have been such friends—we should have been. We wasted the opportunity that we had. We're both too similar in many regards, and we are both at fault. I understand how you feel . . . and They understand that too. They've given you what they think is the perfect illusion. The man standing outside that door is everything you want him to be. He'll say everything you want him to say, do everything you want him to do . . ."

BEEP . . . BEEP . . . BOOP, BOOP, BOOP . . .

So loud! Gwendolyn bent over and covered her ears.

"That is him, Gwendolyn, the real thing, the man you say you want. I'm too weak to fight you, I haven't much time left. You need to make a choice. Kill me and go to the illusion and have everything you want for as long as it lasts, or . . ."

BEEP . . . BEEP . . . BOOP, BOOP, BOOP . . .

". . . answer the Com and face the uncertainty of the real, imperfect person; venture out into the nightmare that is the real world. On the other end of that Com is the man that you really want, whose heart you could truly stir, whose love you could genuinely earn . . ."

Gwendolyn stood over Morgan-Jeterix. She laid there, blood slowly throbbing out of a deep wound in her back where she couldn't reach. Her tightly braided blonde hair was scattered about her head as if pre-arranged. Her Hospitaler helmet was missing. Absentmindedly, Gwendolyn looked around for it.

She swallowed. *"So, what's it going to be, Gwen?"* She closed her eyes and didn't say anything else.

Gwendolyn pulled the hammer back on her MiMs. She thought about Lord Belmont standing on the other side of the door in his black coat.

Wait, was his coat black, or green? She didn't know. She thought it was black, but maybe it's supposed to be green—HRN coats were always green in her courses at the Fleet.

Was Morgan right? Was the man standing out there just an illusion provided to her by *them*, the things moving around in the dark, sucking her dry, feasting on her turmoil?

BEEP . . . BEEP . . . BOOP, BOOP, BOOP . . .

Was she to become a lost soul, like Morgan's grandmother?

She safed the hammer, holstered her MiMs, and went to the Com panel, stepping around Morgan to do so.

"Gwen . . . what are you doing?" came a voice.

She pressed a few buttons on the Com. "I'm saying hello."

A form stood there by the door. *"Why? I've promised you . . ."*

She looked at him. "I know you have. And I really wish you would."

The Com snapped open. "Gwen? Gwen, is that you?" came a worried male voice behind a load of static.

"Bel?"

"Yes, it's me. We've been worried sick about you and your crew. What's your status?"

"I don't . . . I don't know . . . My Hospitaler is in bad shape. I think she's dying."

"Do you have any knowledge in the medical arts?"

"No . . ."

A spry female voice came on. "What's wrong with your Hospitaler?"

Gwendolyn squinted in the dark. "I think she's been stabbed in the back. She's . . . bleeding, in shock I think."

"Oh, that's easy. Tell us what you've got, and we'll talk you through patching her up. Do you have any medical instruments?"

She looked around. "Morgan ... she has all her tools in her pockets I think."

"Fine, lovely, we'll use those."

By the door of the nightmare bridge, she could see the shape of Lord Belmont standing there.

"Bel, are you out there?"

"I'm right here, Gwen . . ."

"I'm right here, Gwen. Taara and I are going to talk you through patching up your Hospitaler, and then we're going to get you out of there."

She smiled a little. Once and for all, she chose the voice on the Com over the image in the black coat. "Don't forget, Bel, you promised . . ."

There was a pause. "Oh, oh yes . . . I certainly did promise. You're absolutely right," he said in a quizzical voice. "But first, you've got to help us get your Hospitaler on her feet. Agreed?"

"Ok, what do I do?"

✳   ✳   ✳   ✳   ✳

Sometime later, Gwendolyn finished sealing the large wound on Morgan's back. She had a number of Morgan's instruments scattered out in front of her. Her hands were red with blood.

Several times during the procedure, she saw things: her hands weren't where they were supposed to be, and she thought she had one of Morgan's knives when she was really carrying nothing at all. One time she saw Morgan as a corpse, withered and dry.

She concentrated on Stenstrom's voice over the Com, clinging to it like a drowning person holding onto a piece of wood. She made them repeat their instructions over and over, and they patiently did so. In a sea of illusions, she treaded water, just barely, at the surface.

"That should do it," Taara said over the Com. "Great job, Captain. How is she?"

Gwendolyn knelt down. She could hear Morgan breathing. She felt her neck. There was a steady pulse. "Ok. I think she's ok."

Stenstrom spoke. "Smart work, Gwen. Now, can you give us your position?"

She looked around at the darkened bridge. "I . . . I don't know where we are . . ."

"It's all right, Gwen. Find a safe spot, and stay there, try not to move around too much. These creatures are supposed to be able to make you hear and see anything they want. If you stay stationary they'll have a harder time of it. Meanwhile, we're searching for you. You can't be far. We're going to get you out of there, Gwen."

He paused a moment. "We're going to lose signal in a moment here. Sit tight and try not to move around too much, promise?"

"All right . . ."

The com went to static. Gwendolyn straightened her coat and sat down next to Morgan, who was out cold.

As the darkness closed in laced with hidden bumps and cries, she took Morgan's limp hand and held it. "Sorry I was going to shoot you."

Without his comforting voice, she was led away, falling off a cliff of sanity and feeling herself plummet.

She fell and fell . . .

2

—THE MERIAN'S ROAD—

The Merians assembled in their simple hall and shared a meager breakfast of bread and savory sauce. Lady Alesta sat on one of the benches, quietly eating, her thick black hair held up with her combs.

A man stood in his robes and addressed the group. "Brothers, sisters . . . friends, Again, souls have gone astray into the mouth of Edam. Again, we hear the Star's call, and again, we shall not fear. We shall walk our Road and perform the duty for which we have been commanded. I look among you, see your pure faces, and am proud to call myself a Merian. Who, besides we, is brave enough to walk our road? Who has sacrificed as much as we have? Eat well, friends, for this meal, as always, may be our last. Trust in our Star to deliver us from evil."

Alesta finished her breakfast and was lead out with the others onto the green. It was a chilly morning and she held her green robe to her. Her shoeless feet were freezing. She looked around the huddle of modest buildings, the sparse line of trees, and the outlying cluster of fields where they grew their food. After that, there was nothing—bare, lifeless rock.

The Star gave them this little place, on a tiny ball of wayward rock that had no business supporting life. Here is where the Star needed them. Here, it maintained them, for nearby was Edam, the world of terror, the world of evil they were tasked to keep watch over. She looked up and it filled the sky, a gray, oblong world, outwardly, a peaceful-looking place. Here, they watched the skies, waiting for the lost souls to arrive on Edam—which happened with remarkable frequency.

These simple, defenseless people stood as sentinels at the gates of Hell hoping to lead the unwary away to safer pastures. That was their mission.

In the center of the green ahead was a large, flat-bottomed boat, pointed at both ends, made of stout timbers and bearing a Merian sail. The boat was tarred black and generously decorated with red and green symbols. The boat sat solidly on the green—an odd sight as there was no appreciable water anywhere near. Weeds grew up around it. Stairs were placed at the boat's center on either side. Alesta really didn't like the boat; its tarred surface always got her clothes dirty.

Noisily, the Merians clambered up the steps and into the boat's large, open deck. Lady Alesta shivered as she awaited her turn to board.

Finally, a man took her hand and helped her aboard. She found a spot on one of the benches toward the rear of the boat and sat. She reveled in the warmth as others piled in tightly next to her. The larger men all sat toward the rails and unhitched the long oars that were positioned there, lowering the decorated paddles down to rest on the frosty grass.

As always, the boat appeared just big enough to accommodate the people who were piling into it. It was always just big enough, no matter how many or how few people climbed aboard. Such were the Merians, awash in poverty and simple things that weren't so simple. The boat that got bigger and smaller as needed was the Star's boat. And that wasn't all. There was the simple belt at her waist made of red and green shells, a modest, home-made item. Yet, that simple belt shielded her from evil sight; time and time again it worked. All she had to do was have faith in the Star, and she would be protected. And there were the thin beaded necklaces she and her people wore to allow them to see through the nightmare creature's illusions. Again, the key was faith.

The Tools of the Merians, which they took to battle, were simple, homemade and quite effective. The only tradeoff—they had to be primitive— no modern contrivances, no power. In the presence of power, most of their Tools failed, and so, to accomplish their mission, they allowed themselves to exist in apparent squalor.

The boat on the green filled, Lady Alesta waited. There was an eerie quiet as everybody settled in.

One of the brothers mounted the platform at the back of the boat and took the tiller.

"The Road comes. Be ready!"

She looked around. The faces of some sitting nearby were lowered toward the floor boards of the boat, their mouths moving in prayer, and others were blankly looking up, resigned to what was to come—they acknowledged her with a slow nod.

She contemplated her fate as the familiar wall of fog drifted in and formed around the boat. Here she was, a Lady of Dare of the 10th Order, wearing home-made clothing and home-made items of mystical properties, shoeless in the freezing cold, once again plunging into the heart of darkness, ready to give her life for those who were often hardly grateful.

Still, this was her calling, to face the denizens of Hell unarmed with her adopted brothers and sisters. She would change nothing. The Star's words to her were a comfort and re-affirmation: *Save all those who fall astray.*

All around the boat was a tunnel of fog and an unearthly stillness. Ahead was the yellow beacon—the Star, the same one that demanded much of them, demanded that they have nothing, and allow themselves to be laughed at and scorned. It was the same Star that also demanded that they offer their lives time after time before a merciless enemy.

"Ready . . ." the brother at the tiller said. The men at the oars readied and braced themselves.

CRACK!!

And then came Edam the raging sea and the gray sky over a pelting rain. The boat plummeted, was rocked in the sudden surf and was battered at its sides. Alesta held on as the men fought the waves.

"Brothers, we must row!" yelled the man at the tiller.

Their longboat was suddenly in the middle of a storm-tossed sea, the prow rising and falling in the steep waves. Lightning stroked overhead. Rain and sea-spray soaked them.

Alesta closed her eyes and huddled up against the driving rain.

Up and down, the prow of the boat rose and fell, Alesta's stomach being jammed up into her throat as the boat went to near vertical in the waves.

"*Hay-Two, row!*" the man grappling with the tiller cried, trying to synch the rowing. "*Hay-Two, row!*"

This storm on the water was worse than normal, more savage, more pounding. She glanced out at the angry sea and saw a frighteningly tall wave quickly coming in to her right.

The brother at the tiller saw it too, and he pulled with all his might to turn the prow into the killer wave.

They would be swamped!

The boat rode up the side of the wave, nearly going past vertical as it crested the top.

After the passing of the mammoth wave, the Merian's boat found calmer waters, and it picked up speed as the men's rowing became more effective.

"*Hay-Two, row!*" the man at the tiller continued to count.

There was a loud whine overhead.

Alesta looked up.

A gangly vessel appeared through the belching clouds and soared away to the north, making a noisy fuss as it went. Lady Alesta had seen that ugly vessel many times, flying over the water, scanning with rain-flecked searchlights and other means. It flew low enough that she could read the name plate on the boat's blackened nose, though she knew it by heart: *Heade-on-the-Hearth.*

Lights rained down, panning over the rolling water as it passed overhead.

The lights caught the Merian's boat square, lighting it up for a good second or more in white light.

The ship paid them no mind and continued north. Alesta knew they were cradled in the Star's grace. She knew the vessel overhead could not see them. The Star, though hard and demanding, did not leave them completely defenseless. The Star could not be seen by most; nor could they in their primitive boat.

They were invisible; all they had to have was faith.

The vessel flew ahead several more miles and became interested in something in the water. It hovered and shined its sundry beams of light down.

Something stuck up out of the water.

Suddenly, the tillerman! "A-lo!" he cried, and wrenched the prow to the west, the stable boat coming close to tipping as a result of the violent maneuver.

As the boat bore west, Alesta caught a glimpse of something breaking the water for a moment, something long and black, something swimming with a large heaviness, making a bulging wake as it passed.

When the tillerman thought it safe, he steered the boat again in the direction of the distant mass sticking up out of the water.

Alesta looked at it—a collection of large metal tubes arranged around a central disk, once painted white, now a patchy, scorched black, lit up in the round circles of the *Heade's* spotlights.

The drowning vessel had a name: *Demophalon John,*

"Make ready!" he cried.

The *Heade* quit its lights after a minute or two and veered away to the north where it disappeared on the horizon.

With every oar-stroke, the Merians in their tiny boat got closer to the lost souls their Star had sent them to save.

3

—LOST IN THE BRIARS—

"That was bang up work with Gwendolyn," Stenstrom said as Taara, her sleeves rolled up, blushed. She enjoyed receiving compliments.

"It's nice being able to do this without having to worry about getting attacked by a bunch of demons," she replied. "Now I can really work."

The *Seeker's* bridge was literally knee-deep in little green squares that once made up the body of Innocent Drury, some piled up in neat stacks, others scattered about.

After a good bit of tinkering, Taara had figured them out enough to be able to string them together into a long chain ending in the antennae they'd mounted atop the Missive's Panel.

"These are all individual units, each self-contained and fully functional— sort of like cells in your body. The only thing is they don't appear to have a brain, so, without a central consciousness to control them, they go limp, though there's nothing wrong with them individually, per se," she said.

They had mounted several antennae from Innocent's innards to the Missive's station and, behind it, strung together over a hundred green squares to both power and interpret information picked up by the antennae. Finally, the last piece she added was Innocent's head screen.

The screen didn't display any images at first, just sounds and disembodied voices that were rather terrifying to listen to over rigged up speakers:

"They's feedin' aplenty from that ghost ship . . ."

"As soon as they's dead, we'll put the ship in the hopper. We's gettin' low a' metal."

"We needs the Seeker, they're gettin' impatient to go home, they is. They're startin' to make noise about takin' the Heade unless we can offer up something suitable."

"I's ready to rejoin you, and I've a score to settle . . . That man in the coat is mine . . ."

"Do yer' job and tends to the House. You can have's yer' revenge later. They's not goin' nowhere . . ."

"I wants his body trussed up on the front of the ship!"

"Shaddap!"

A-Ram swallowed hard. "I take it our friends are out there afresh."

Stenstrom agreed. "Seems to be. They've obviously got a plant here somewhere with new robotic bodies standing by ready to go. All they have to do is download their current memories and the new ones won't miss a beat."

"And," A-Ram added, "I'll wager they need a steady supply of shipping to provide them with the raw materials to continue producing these flesh replicas."

Working hard, Taara eventually refined the jury-rigged setup to the point that they were able to lock onto the weak signal of the *Demophalon John* and contact a ragged-sounding Captain Gwendolyn.

And then, they helped save the life of Gwendolyn's Hospitaler, Morgan-Jeterix.

As they talked Gwendolyn through the procedure, Taara took several of the other antennae pulled from Innocent Drury's body and slowly panned them around, trying to get a fix on their position.

As Stenstrom spoke to her, Gwendolyn seemed to fade into madness. She gave strange orders, responding to people who weren't there. She reverted in time, speaking like a child.

Taara cut the sound. "She's losing it, Bel. The Cronyns must be hitting her hard."

"What about her position?"

"I don't have it."

"We need them out of there, Taara."

"I'm trying!"

As Taara moved the antennae around, a picture formed on Innocent's head screen. In it, Stenstrom could see the battered interior of the *Demophalon John*, patched into the bridge's Tele-corder. The bridge was smashed, debris was everywhere. There, sitting next to the Com, was Gwendolyn, in a ball, holding the hand of a fallen Hospitaler. Must be Morgan-Jeterix.

"That's them! See if you can get a readout on that position. Gwen! Gwen, can you hear me?"

She slowly looked up. "Bel?"

Stenstrom could see the flickering image of Gwendolyn on the screen, rolling, grainy. Her face resembled the mirage of her from the lantern: face sunken, eyes darting.

"Gwen, I can see you on my screen. I think we're getting close."

She looked around, wide-eyed. "You can? I can't . . . I can't see you." She smiled. "Oh, there you are . . ."

"Just relax and try not to move too much. Tell me what your status is, Gwen."

She strained to concentrate. Stenstrom could hear the occasional wailing and guttural cries of people going mad on her ship. The sounds reminded him of the howling carnival sounds the *Seeker* was making not long ago, but this was worse.

"I think . . . I think we're submerged—the instrumentation is unreliable, but I'm pretty sure. I look through the windows, and I see water, bits of debris and a little light high above. I don't know how deep we are. We . . . seem to be at an acute, nose down angle . . . but our ship-board gravity is still working, for now . . ."

She clutched at her forehead. "Something's out there. I see them . . . moving past the windows." She mumbled, trembling: "My crew, my crew . . ."

"Gwen, your duty to your crew is to stay strong and be a leader. Remember, just a few days ago you were wanting to beat my brains in? Remember that?"

She gave a short laugh and ran her hands through her hair. "Seems like a long time ago."

"Sure does. You need to be that strong lady again. You need to stand tall. Do it for your crew."

Gwendolyn looked as if she were on the verge of tears or delirium. She seemed to be fading away.

"Talk to her, Bel," Taara warned.

"Gwen, how's your Hospitaler?"

She looked around, her eyes blank. "No . . . no, I don't want any more . . ."

"Gwen," Stenstrom repeated.

"I can hear you, Bel . . . Is that you over there?"

"Gwen, how is your Hospitaler?"

Gwendolyn looked down. "All right. I think she's all right."

"What's her name again?"

"M-Morgan-Jeterix, Lady of Thompson."

"Jeterix? What's that—part of her first name or something?"

"I don't know; I've never asked her."

"Well, when she wakes up, be sure to . . ."

There was a clanking in the background. Gwendolyn's eyes grew large with fright. "What was that?" she said, her gaze lost in delirium. "I heard a noise."

"I heard it too, Gwen. It was just the ship."

Gwendolyn was frantic. "No—no it wasn't. There's somebody outside, trying to get in. It's them they're coming for us!"

"Gwen, don't panic!"

She tried to stand. She drew her FEDULA. "Stay back, Stay back, I'm warning you!"

"Gwen!"

Something passed in front of the Com—something indistinct. Gwen gave a cry and started swinging wildly.

Weakly she was taken down, out of sight.

"Taara, what's going on? Do you have them?"

She was working the antennae. "Wait, one more moment!"

A-Ram spoke up from behind the helm. "I'm reading a lock, Bel!"

As Stenstrom stared into the screen, he thought he saw a pair of blue eyes look up at him for a moment, and then was gone.

The screen went dead.

"Got 'em, Bel. I have a lock on their position!" Taara cried.

"Where?"

"7:47AM mark 6:58PM."

Stenstrom turned. "A-Ram, make sail, 7:47AM mark 6:58PM, best possible speed! Let's get the *Westminster* fired up and ready to burn!" He thought about it for a moment. "I have no idea what we're going to face or how we're going to fight when we get there—it's just the three of us and this wounded, toothless bird. But, we're getting them out one way or another. You two, A-Ram and Taara—I've got one hell of a crew around me."

A-Ram held out his hand. "I'm with you, Bel. I've dreamed of this my whole life. To stand at your side in this great Warbird, whatever the outcome, I'm a happy man."

Stenstrom took it. Taara's small hand joined theirs. "Don't forget me. Whatever awaits, let them be damned! After this is over, they'll know where I came from, that I wasn't such a little freak after all!"

4

—THE ROAD FORSAKEN—

Gwendolyn could barely understand what was happening. In her clouded mind, she saw grappling hands reaching for her throat. She tried fighting back with her family FEDULA, but it didn't do any good. She fell back, waiting for it all to end.

Sometime later, she felt soft hands pulling her up. She felt herself walking, an arm around her shoulder.

Boneless, she moved, meekly stumbling toward whatever awaited. She felt herself stepping out into space, the maudlin dark of the ship replaced by sudden gray light. Distantly, she heard her boots thumping unsteadily on hollow wood.

A few moments later, she felt herself being seated on a hard, flat bench. She noticed, with eyes heavy-lidded with delirium, that a beaded red and green necklace had been placed around her neck.

Slowly, things came into focus. She concentrated on the necklace, on the small, polished beads—the red ones appeared to be tumbled stones of some kind while the green seemed to be dyed wood; she could see the grain of the wood through the dye. Standing over her was a small, smiling face, like that of a porcelain doll. A tiny lady looked down on her. She was wearing loose robes, a larger green and gold one over a white one that went down to her knees, tied together at her waist with a green and red belt. She appeared to have thick, dark brown or black hair that was pulled back out of her face, long tendrils of hair hanging down to her shoulders. Around her neck were a number of necklaces similar to the one around her own.

She had remarkable blue eyes and rosy cheeks. Behind her smiling face was a turbid gray sky.

"Who are you?" Gwendolyn asked, shivering.

"A friend," she replied. "My name is Lady Alesta, and we are a humble band of Pilgrims of Merian. We're here to take you home. You needn't fear; everything will be all right."

The girl leaned down and kissed Gwendolyn on the cheek.

"What . . . are you doing here?" Gwen asked.

"We are here to save all lost souls gone astray. It is our life's work."

As she slowly regained her senses, she could see she was sitting in a long, wooden boat with sloped sides and a fairly flat bottom. All around her were similarly dressed people in robes, each one attending a member of her crew. They were Merians, the people she often saw in the square of Prentiss spouting their odd religion—people she never looked twice at.

All of her crew appeared out of their heads. Each wore a red and green necklace.

In a bumpy fuss, people were disembarking the *Demophalon John* via one of the forward docking rings, which was open. Gwendolyn could see that a good part of the aft section of the ship was sticking out of the water at a shallow angle. Conning cylinder Number 1 looked to be fairly intact., Number 2 looked badly damaged.

Nearby, she could see a huddled up Morgan-Jeterix under a blanket, again wearing a Merian necklace.

"Morgan?" she said quietly.

She responded. "Yeah?"

"Is this another illusion?"

"No . . ."

More and more people filtered out of the ship—certainly this wooden boat couldn't carry everybody—however, it seemed just big enough to seat everyone, no matter how many streamed out of the ship.

Soon, the last of the crew came out and the robed men picked up oars and rowed away from the wreck of the *Demophalon John* as it bobbed in the water.

Mouth open, drooling slightly, Gwendolyn took a count of her crew.

Fifty-eight.

Wait, she had over eighty crew under her command. "My people, still on the ship . . . There's more, many more."

Lady Alesta was sad. "We cannot take the dead, my lady. We prayed for their souls and bid them peace."

Gwendolyn's addled mind pondered that. She'd lost nearly half her crew.

As the boat slowly picked up speed, Gwendolyn thought she heard the roaring of rocketry coming from somewhere behind them.

Lady Alesta was sitting next to her and didn't appear concerned by the noise.

"Where, where are we going?" Gwendolyn asked.

"Someplace safe. We shall have a large, wholesome meal waiting for you. Are you hungry?"

"Yes . . . I'm starving . . ."

A tunnel of fog slowly formed from nowhere around the boat obscuring the sea and the sky. There was an unnatural quiet.

"The Road comes. Soon, you shall be safe."

Something happened. The fog abruptly vanished from sight. Lady Alesta, who, up to this point, had appeared quite calm, suddenly stood up in apparent surprise. She looked around.

"The Road?" the Merians said. "What has happened to The Road?"

A small black vehicle, just barely large enough to house a single person, appeared from nowhere at the prow of the Merian boat. A slender figure wearing red and black robes was seated within. The vessel's power plant thrummed.

It looked like a Black Hat to Gwen.

The robed Pilgrims of Merian, who had helped her crew onto the boat, reacted with surprise. They chattered in confusion.

"What's going on?" she asked.

Lady Alesta shook her head and seemed genuinely frightened. "I—I don't know. Our Road has been fouled by a power field. We cannot be carried to safety in the presence of power."

The person seated in the vessel looked at the Merians and the distressed Fleet crew. Morgan lifted her head and locked eyes with the person seated in the vessel. She started speaking.

"Knife, Knife, Knife . . . I am Knife . . ."

"Morgan?" Gwen asked. She'd seen this from Morgan before, her empathic tendencies were at work.

Morgan continued. "This is . . . so much more difficult than I anticipated. The Kestrals have been at work here and the It Man must come to cleanse it. Behold all these people . . . all about to die. Where I go, the It Man will follow. He will come. He must come . . . I'm sorry. I'm sorry you are about to die."

The Black vessel, quickly as it had come, lifted away and vanished. The Merians' boat sat there in the water.

A light shined in the distance, illuminating the boat. Alesta appeared relieved.

"Ah, see, there is the light. Any moment now, and we shall be safe. All is well, all is well."

The light got brighter, and then there was a loud whine.

Something was wrong, and Alesta appeared to know it.

A gangly vessel overflew the boat at about a thousand feet, making a terrible racket as it did so. Gwendolyn strained to get a look at it.

Strange—it looked like part of an old *Webber*-class ship to her. She could read its name plate: the *Heade-on-the-Hearth*.

The name sounded familiar to her.

Spotlights rained down and panned about the water and the aft of the *Demophalon John*.

The Merians murmured in fear.

"No, no," the tillerman said. "Brothers, sisters, have faith!"

"Forsaken, we are forsaken!" someone shouted.

"We must have faith! Our faith is our shield!"

The *Heade* spun about, and its searchlights found their boat and settled on it, lighting it up in cones of white.

There were three splashes into the water. Several moments later, three scrawny men hauled themselves into the boat, their seedy clothes dripping with water. They looked at the huddled Merians and *Demophalon John* crew with a wicked gleam. "Well now," one of them said in a thick voice. "What have we here?"

One of the Merian men stood to protect his folk. A scrawny man, with apparent strength beyond measure seized the Merian by the neck. "Aww, what's the matter, Gov? We're not gonna' hurt ya."

He threw the man down to the deck. One of the other men quickly picked the Merian up by his ankle and dangled him over the side, dunking his head and shoulders into the sea.

The man waved his arms and struggled. "Seems you lot's the ones what been stealin' our pet's prey. Caused us a lot 'o aggravation, ya' have."

The drowning Merian man screamed underwater. His robes fell up over his waist, revealing his britches.

With a laugh, the man lifted him up. "What ya' say?" he said and dunked him again, this time holding him down until the man thrashed no more. Laughing, the scrawny man let him go and his body slipped into the water.

The vessel overhead came down and settled into the waves and approached the prow. A hatch opened. "All right, git aboard. We's goin' to take you someplace nice . . ."

They then herded the Merians and the dazed Fleet crew into the ship. Lady Alesta was terrified.

A Fleet crewman, dazed, in shock, fell to the deck. One of the three evil men came to his side and savagely kicked him. "Get up, ya' Momma's lad!" He kicked him again. "Get up!"

A Merian female knelt down and tried to help the poor man.

"Oh looks, she wants ta' help the miserable wank, does she?" The scrawny man hauled her up and tied them together using a length of rope. The Merian woman wailed at the tightness of her bonds.

The evil man struck her across the face. "Shaddap!" From their ship, the evil men fetched some ballast and tied the loose end of the rope to it. They then kicked the ballast over the side, the rope rapidly uncoiling. A few seconds later, the Merian and the Fleet crewman were yanked over the side and down under the waves, never to be seen again. The Merians collectively moaned in misery.

The evil men selected twenty of the strongest-looking Merians and crew and made them stay aboard as the others were roughly shuffled into the ship. They stood there on the boat, huddled in a mass. One of the Merians dumbly picked up an oar, as if to row away. Gwendolyn saw her boatswain standing there among the men, and Lt. Sai from the Com.

She tried to pull away. She tried to stand with her men. One of the fellows grabbed her by the shoulder and squeezed with crushing strength. "Quit yer' fussin', missy, an' git on the ship!" He then picked her up and tossed her bodily through the hatch.

The port door closed, and the *Heade-on-the-Hearth* soared away. Inside, the foul men lined the Merians and crew up and forced them to look out the windows.

"Look!" they said. "See how we treats 'em."

Gwendolyn's face was shoved into the window, as was Lady Alesta's, her eyes filling with tears.

Down below, Gwendolyn could see the long, flat shape of the Merian boat with the peppering of men standing on the deck.

"Waits for it!" one of the men said.

Lady Alesta couldn't look. She tried to turn away.

One of the men seized her roughly by the chin. "Look out there, Missy! See every bit of it!" He made her watch.

Beneath the boat, something black rocketed out of the water, splintering it into planks and launching its pieces high into the air. Gwendolyn could see the green specks of the Merian men's robes and the white specks of the Fleet crew's uniforms being thrown up into the air and splashing back down.

The screaming, the struggling for life.

The vessel orbited around, lowering a bit. Gwendolyn could see shapes struggling in the water, men thrashing. More black shapes shot out of the water, long, black, worm-like—taking the men whole in a wide open, tooth-filled maw and then plunging back down in a spray of white water.

"Oh yeah, lookee at that! Look at `em go!" the man said.

Again and again, the black shapes launched out of the water, taking the men, eating them whole.

It reminded Gwendolyn of feeding the catfish in the pond near her manor home—she throwing the food in and watching as the fish leapt out of the water to get at it. For the first time in her life, she felt utterly helpless as she watched her men and the Merians, who had tried to save them, die.

I am the captain. I should be down there, defending my men . . .

Nearby, Lady Alesta wept uncontrollably. "My brothers . . . my brothers . . . what has become of us?"

But wait—look. Gwendolyn saw a pocket of three Merians and two Fleet crewmen swimming away from the killing fields, the Merians helping the still dazed crewmen as best they could. They made their way to a large bit of wreckage from the boat and seemed to be unnoticed as the creatures continued devouring some distance away. They got on the wreckage and tried to paddle with their hands and bits of flotsam.

Maybe they could get away and be saved—please, let them be saved.

The man holding her chin laughed. "Ah, would ya' look at that? Some of our ducks trying to swim away." He let go of Gwendolyn. "Jus' a moment."

The ship banked a little.

Please, she prayed. *Please . . .*

The *Heade* banked and a wall of gunfire opened up. She saw the men convulse in the hail of shot, dropping their makeshift paddles. Their raft splintered into twigs. Geysers of white water shot into the air. They fell into the water and floated, facedown, the fabric of their robes spreading out in the water.

"A-har, har, har!" the man bellowed. "Potted `em like a bunch o' bunny rabbits. Did ya' see that, Clem?"

Gwendolyn could take no more.

Her men, and those brave Merians . . . dead. She huddled to the floor, holding her stomach, and wept bitterly.

A soft hand touched her on the back. It was Morgan-Jeterix, bleary-eyed, but coming around. She embraced her.

"My fault, all my fault," Gwendolyn said.

"It's not your fault, Gwen. None of this is your fault."

One of the men leaned down. "Awww, feel rotten for yer' boys down there, do ya?" he said. His eyes lit up in an evil gleam. "Feel bad for yourselves, missie—at least they gots' it quick. No such luck for you . . ."

As the people wept, the *Heade* bore away from the terrible scene below and disappeared into the waters.

5

—THE SWARM—

A-Ram navigated the ship deep into the wild lands, the poorly charted, supposedly empty space between Kana and Onaris.

According to the charts, there was not much out here—just a brief mention of methane ice chunks left over from some primordial comet and a few pockets of noble gasses and the long, charged line of Druries Belt.

A-Ram's helm sensors concurred—there was little if anything interesting out here.

The head screen of Innocent Drury, however, begged to differ.

With Taara carefully aiming the antennae mounted on the Missive's Panel and fine tuning the connection, they could see a massive asteroid field developing all around them. "Looks like the remains of a primordial planet or large moon," she said squinting into the screen. "I guess this is the Swarm A-Ram was talking about."

"Planets clear out the debris in their vicinity," Stenstrom said, "I'll wager that this was some unfortunate planetoid that got pulled apart by the competing gravity of Kana's sun and Onaris' sun."

They continued on, the *Seeker*, wading by the stern through the unfolding fields of smaller and larger rock

"Taara, where is the lock on *Demophalon John?*"

"Right in the middle of all this stuff, Bell," she replied.

With minor course corrections, A-Ram brought the *Seeker* through the rocky field. Ahead was the apparent core.

"Bel, we've got several larger masses on dead approach. I'm reading the *Demophalon John's* signal on the largest one. It's an irregular dwarf planet, reading approximately four-thousand miles in diameter. It appears to be made of ferrous rock and covered with a surprisingly thick atmosphere for such a small body that reads as breathable, and I'm also detecting a warm, liquid sea covering the surface and it's crawling with life indications."

"How is that possible? Any water on such a distant body should be frozen solid," A-Ram said.

"I'm reading a great deal of heat being generated internally. I'm also reading signs of life on a small moon orbiting the dwarf planet. There's no heat being generated internally and no appreciable atmosphere, so I have no idea what's supporting that life—but it's there. It's reading fairly clear."

Taara stared at the watery dwarf planet coming closer and closer. "Is that Cronyn World, Bel?"

"Looks to be."

She did some quick calculations. "It does appear to be moving in a highly irregular orbit—I calculate it coming close to Bazz again in another three hundred, seventy years."

Stenstrom wondered as he looked at the grayish world. "How are we going to do this? What are our possibilities?"

Taara returned to the screen. "Let's see, again, I'm reading a breathable atmosphere, good gravity, and a brackish, shallow sea covering the planet. I read it as no deeper than two hundred feet at any point. Captain Gwendolyn's ship is probably bobbing on the surface. Scout ships float pretty well."

"A-Ram, can we fly in?"

"We can't, Bel—no power to the gas-compression engines."

"All right, we'll need to be creative, then. I'd say we should tuck into one of these outlying bodies and take the *Westminster* down."

"We're not going to be able to land on the water with the *Westminster*. Tach scout ships are not designed for water operations. They don't hover in-atmosphere particularly well, and, additionally, you said the *Westminster* has been armor-plated, we'll sink like a rock if we try to put down on the surface."

Stenstrom stood. "We're going to have to risk it, we cannot just sit here while the Captain and her crew die."

He suddenly felt an overwhelming fatigue. "A-Ram, just get us into position somewhere close, and we'll figure it out from there."

"The *Heade* can fly rings around the *Westminster*. We'll be in a shooting gallery."

His head pounded. All he wanted to do was sleep. He couldn't fight it off.

"Bel, you all right?" Taara asked.

"My head, I need a moment."

He tried to stand, but the bridge spun around him. What was wrong? Was he dying? He fell to the floor. Taara ran to his side, but he passed into darkness before she got there.

6

—THE STAR WEEPS—

S tenstrom dreamed.
He dreamt of his home by the sea south of Tyrol, of Belmont Manor in the fall, the meadow burning with rustic reds and yellows.

Off in the near distance was one of the many Merian ruins that dotted the manor grounds, the old, bumpy stone coated with moss and a windy covering of fallen leaves. The ruin was awash in a yellowish glow. A twisting column of red smoke drifted upward.

He took a step or two nearer and the light faded.

Someone was sitting there in the ruins.

It was his sister Virginia, her face covered by her hands, her Half-Pewterlock hair, a marbling of black and silver, messy as normal.

She was weeping.

"Sis? Sis, why are you crying?" he asked, his heart going out to her.

"My children," she said in a voice that didn't belong to Virginia. "I couldn't help them. I couldn't shield them. I couldn't bear them away."

"Sis," he replied, "you don't have any children."

She stood and paced about, moving in a manner alien to Virginia. "I am not your sister, but she knows me. So many dead. Died ... for me, doing what I've asked them to do."

"Sis, what are you talking about? You don't have any children."

She turned to him, desperate. She grew to giant size, her head splitting the clouds. *"You'll help them, won't you? You're a good man, Lord Belmont. The Sisters have given you their power—you don't need it. You're a good man. I will send you my Road and I beg you take it."*

Virginia faded away, fog quickly filling the ruin. Stenstrom blundered about.

"Sis?" he said.

Ahead he thought he saw a hazy yellowish globe wreathed in a twisting, red cloud.

"You're a good man ... Power down your ship ... My Road comes ... Save my children ..."

✳ ✳ ✳ ✳ ✳

Stenstrom opened his eyes and sat up.

Taara was leaning over him. "Bel?" she asked. "What happened?"

"What's our status?"

A-Ram spoke up. "You ok?"

"Yes, yes. Status?"

"We're on station near a large asteroid. Cronyn World isn't far to our 1:00AM. It's the best I could think of."

Something beeped on the Missive's Panel. Taara turned to the screen. "Contact—incoming object at 1:00am, coming fast straight out of Cronyn World! Guess who it is?"

He thought a moment. He remembered his dream. "A-Ram, Taara, let's get everything powered off."

"What?" Taara cried. "You gone punchy, Bel? What about the contact? It's the Druries coming to get us."

"You heard me—power off everything—the porta-gens, the *Westminster*, even the rigged up screen here. Everything."

"You know how long it took me to get this rig tuned?" Taara protested, her Bazz accent sputtering out.

"Trust me," Stenstrom said.

She wanted to argue, then, began turning everything off.

"Let me lock the wheel real fast," A-Ram said, as he began readying the helm.

Soon, the lights went out and they were in total darkness. "So, we're standing here in the dark with the Druries coming in fast," Taara said. "Are we waiting for something, Bel?"

He looked around. "I'm not really certain. Come on, let's gather around."

The three gathered in the center of the bridge and waited in the dark.

"It's really peaceful," Taara said.

"What's that?" A-Ram said, pointing.

Ahead, a corridor of fog formed, quickly enveloping them. Stenstrom drew his NTH's. "Everybody, back-to-back! Taara, skin your piece!"

They backed into each other, Taara drawing her SK. She handed her Monica to A-Ram.

"What is happening?" A-Ram cried, as they stood in the thick fog. He held the Monica with both hands.

There was a light in the distance

"It's the Road," Stenstrom said. "The Merian's Road. It actually exists."

They could feel the humidity of it, the change in temperature.

"Where's it taking us?" Taara asked.

"Someplace we need to be."

The fog closed in on them.

LADY ALESTA

7

—LADY ALESTA—

I n an instant, they emerged from the fog.

They were no longer on the *Seeker*. They were standing in a small, irregularly-shaped corridor of sweaty black metal with barely enough room for the three of them and almost no light.

A fierce wind blew past them—Stenstrom and A-Ram had to hold onto their hats. Taara's sideburns took flight. They looked around—they appeared to be alone, so they put their weapons away.

"Where are we?" Taara said, having to shout to be heard above the roaring wind.

"Looks to be an air shaft of some sort," A-Ram replied.

"What?"

"An air duct!"

Stenstrom produced three yellow Holystones and passed them out and the corridor lit up in soft light.

"How'd we get here!" A-Ram yelled.

"The Merian's Road—don't ask me how because I don't know! When I passed out on the ship, I had a vision and I was told the Road would come for us," Stenstrom replied.

"How are we going to get back?"

"The same way we got in, I suppose."

Getting their bearings, they found themselves in a long shaft that went on for as far as they could determine. Above them was a cut-stone ceiling. Below was a metal grating that led down to darkness. Taara and Stenstrom made their way down the shaft, trying to find a way out, A-Ram concentrated on the grating, waving his Holystone over it, trying to see within.

"I think these grates service the chambers below us with fresh air!"

"Doesn't smell all that fresh to me!" Taara called out, noting the slightly briny smell to the rushing air.

A-Ram knelt down low and inspected the grates, holding his light close.

He stopped. "Hey, hey—I think I hear something coming from this one!"

Stenstrom and Taara made their way back to his side. They leaned down and strained to hear—sure enough, there was the faint sound of many people rustling about, barely audible over the fast-moving air.

Stenstrom and Taara tried to create a wind brake with their bodies as A-Ram struggled to listen.

"What do you hear?" Taara demanded.

"Shhh!"

He put his ear against the grating. "I hear many people—they sound frightened. It must be Captain Gwendolyn and her crew." He tapped on the grate with Taara's Monica, making a sharp "tick, tick, tick."

"Hello? Hello?"

A-Ram took his hat off and leaned down against the grate as far as he could. "Hello?" he said again. "Is anyone down there?"

There was movement from below. A pale face emerged through a grate at the end of a short shaft. It was a small woman, the hole just big enough for her head and one shoulder. There were hints of hands behind her neck and shoulder, as if she were being hoisted up.

"Who's there?" she whispered.

"Are you a part of Captain Gwendolyn's crew?"

The woman squinted to see. "No, but I think she is here ... there are so many."

"What is your name, my lady?" A-Ram asked.

"Alesta. My name is Alesta."

A-Ram reached through the grate and stretched, taking her warm hand. "My name is Josephus, Lord of A-Ram. Call me A-Ram."

"Can you help us, A-Ram? Can you please help us?"

"We're trying."

The woman squirmed into the vent. A-Ram got a better look at her: pale skin, thick black hair, blue eyes, hints of a green robe.

A-Ram gasped. "You! It's you!" he cried.

She looked up at him "Pardon?"

"I've seen you, standing on our ship through the lantern," A-Ram said with excitement.

"Pardon?" she said again. "I don't understand."

Stenstrom and Taara moved down the shaft looking for a larger opening.

"I've been looking for you," A-Ram said. "Alesta, Alesta, what a beautiful name. I've longed to know it."

Despite the situation, Alesta smiled. "Well, sir, here I am."

There was a clank from below. "A-right, you scum, come here!" came a surly voice through the grate.

Alesta appeared panicked. "A-Ram, A-Ram they're here! They're here!"

She was pulled back down through the hole. She tried to hold on to A-Ram's hand but lost her grip and vanished.

"Bel!" A-Ram cried. "Did you see? It's her, from the lantern. She's here! She needs us, immediately!"

They checked the grate—it was too small for them to go through.

"There must be another way down!" Stenstrom said. "Keep looking."

Taara wandered down the corridor a little. She knelt down and became interested in a small chute. "I think we can go this way."

A-Ram handed her Monica back and she used it to pry open the grate. Before anyone could stop her, Taara climbed in and quickly disappeared. A-Ram hauled himself into the chute and followed. Stenstrom trailed.

It was a three foot by three foot tube that led off at a sharp downward angle and then bent away out of sight. Stenstrom slid down and struggled into the bend. Ahead, he could see two pools of light from Taara's and A-Ram's Holystones.

Stenstrom caught up. They were huddled around a small grate—a brindle light came up strongly from it.

"I think we should go down there," Taara said. "Looks like a long drop, though."

They pried the grate up and out of the way and Stenstrom stuck his head down to get a better look.

Upside down, Stenstrom saw empty, glasslike coffins lined up against the stony wall, stretching off for as far as he could see, like a line of transparent teeth.

"Is there anybody out there?" Taara asked.

"Not that I see."

"How far down is it?"

"About fifteen feet."

Stenstrom lowered himself out of the grate and dropped down. He landed on his heels and the fall hurt him a lot more than he would have figured. He stood there, smarting. Odd, Innocent Drury could punch him into a metal wall and he didn't feel a thing, but, take a fifteen foot fall and he nearly broke his ankle and fell on his duff.

Everything stung.

"Come down, you two. I'll catch you," he said a little unsteady.

A-Ram carefully lowered himself out, his small legs and buckle shoes flailing. He let go and Stenstrom caught him without too much trouble.

Taara then launched herself out of the grate and slammed into Stenstrom, knocking him down.

"That was cool," she said picking herself up.

"Yep," he replied, feeling his aching ribs.

Taara was flush with excitement. She punched him in the arm, getting him in the nerve cluster between the muscles. "Oww!" Stenstrom cried.

She was perplexed. "What's wrong with you? Why did that hurt?"

"I don't know—I don't seem to have it right now. I'm just flesh and blood at the moment."

"The Sisters' power?"

"It's gone."

"Fine timing."

A-Ram looked around. "What, in the Name of Creation, is this?"

"This is, according to League conjecture, where the Kestrals created *Killanjo*. I recall Captain Davage and Countess Sygillis describing it in detail. Looks just like how they described it. They called it a 'Tank'."

Taara shuddered. "Those creepy people with no skin I heard about?"

"Yes. They're placed into these glass containers and soaked in some sort of corrosive fluid until they go mad."

A-Ram was anxious. "Then, we've no time to lose. We must locate the crew at once. And Lady Alesta, she's out here somewhere. Did you see her, Bel? It's her!" he repeated with excitement.

They moved down the corridor, passing coffin after coffin. "Taara, do you have any impressions?"

She thought a moment. "I want to say we need to go in that direction," she said pointing to her right. "We need to wait, though."

"We've no time, Taara!" A-Ram protested. "Alesta."

"No, no, we need to wait. If we don't, we'll have a lot of trouble. I feel it. If we're assuming the Druries are stuffing the crew into these coffins down there somewhere, then we need to let them finish and retire—the very size of this place will work against them. We're going to have a lot of scared and hurt people on our hands, and we need to remain undetected for as long as possible. I don't see the Druries moving around in this area much. Then, once they're gone, we'll have time to free the crew and come up with a plan. How in the Name of Creation are we going to get out of here, anyway?"

"We'll figure that out when we get to it, I suppose," Stenstrom replied.

They moved to the side of the corridor near the coffins and hid themselves as best they could. They seemed to wait for a long time.

"How much longer?" A-Ram cried, impatient.

Taara looked around, "Ok, let's go. That way. Make sure we stay quiet."

Silently, they moved down the corridor, all three of them amazed how long the corridor was. Eventually, they heard something in the distance. They heard a muffled moaning.

A-Ram shot forward, Stenstrom and Taara following.

Ahead, the line of coffins in this area appeared to be full. Indistinct bodies stood inside, pounding on the glass, muffled cries barely heard.

Stenstrom knew from the recollections of Captain Davage what was going to happen. He could see the coffins were partially full of brown fluid, soaking the occupants.

The pain! Captain Davage described the agony the occupants felt as they were driven mad and turned into monsters.

"We've got to get these people out of there, now!" he said.

Taara and A-Ram selected an occupied coffin and tried to open it. "The door's locked!" Taara cried. She drew her SK, silenced the muzzle, and tried to carefully shoot the lock off.

PHOOT!

Her slug bounced off and ricocheted about, A-Ram having to duck.

Stenstrom strode up to the door and tried to pull it open. He expected it to easily open—he should be able to smash this enclosure to bits.

Nothing happened. The surface of the door wouldn't budge; it didn't even bend.

He tried again—still nothing happened. The lid of the coffin looked like nothing more than frosted glass, but it was diamond-like in its hardness. Still—he'd been able to smash through duraplate like spun sugar and break Innocent Drury's robotic neck like a rotten egg.

He recalled hurting himself jumping out of the grate. He suddenly had a thought. "Taara, how far down are we right now?"

"Over a mile, I'm sure of it. Probably a lot more than that."

Over a mile? Could it be that, entombed in this Kestral Tank, the Sisters' light from *Camalopardus* could not reach?

"Bel, this coffin's starting to fill with something."

The person within began a muffled scream. Small fists pounded on the interior.

Taara backed away. "There's got to be a central control panel or something around here." She turned and ran down the hall, past the coffins, her coattails flying and boots churning.

Stenstrom strained again to pull the lid open—nothing. He was no stronger than he ordinarily would be. So here, deep in the Kestral's horrid Tank, he was no Fist, no "It" Man, no Lone Rider. Here he was just a man with naught available to him but his wits and his skills.

He couldn't help but be disappointed.

"Bel, what are we going to do?" A-Ram asked, frantic.

The person's muffled screams become slightly louder. "A . . . rrrm! A . . . rrram. A-Raaam!!"

A-Ram was horrified. "Alesta? Alesta!!" He pounded on the door.

Stenstrom looked at the sophisticated lock for a moment. "I think it's a composite lock of some kind." He shook his hand and produced a Grimtooth pick. With a skittery click, he began working the lock.

"Bel, Hurry!" A-Ram looked down the corridor. "Taara, get back here!"

"I'm trying to figure out how to open these things!" she shouted back. "Hello? What's this?" She shuttled into an alcove.

Stenstrom drowned all the noise out. He put his mind elsewhere, back into the hidden culvert with his mother and two sisters years ago. He recalled the years of hard training, his mother's harsh evaluations and critical eye always present.

He could hear her words in his head. *"No lock shall hold you or keep you out . . ."*

Then, he could feel it.

He didn't hear anything, as this lock had a magnetic mechanism, but he imagined the sound in his head: *click!*

The lid came free and they pulled it open. Lady Alesta fell out, her feet and the front of her clothes covered in a noisome brown fluid.

Stenstrom noted her garb, white and green robes, beads, shoeless. Lots of hair. A-Ram was correct; she was the same Pilgrim of Merian they'd seen on the ship. The apparition was now real. Here she was.

"Get her cleaned off, A-Ram—that's important; that fluid is highly caustic! I'm moving on to the next one!"

A-Ram produced a number of small handkerchiefs from his inner coat pocket, Stenstrom took several.

As Stenstrom ran to the next coffin, he caught glimpse of A-Ram holding the crying Alesta to him out of the corner of his eye, whispering into her ear.

Not a good time for that, A-Ram, he thought. Not a good time at all.

He worked the lock of the coffin, becoming familiar with its complex mechanisms. He had another open, and then another, and a Merian female and a male crewman from the *Demophalon John* came spilling out. He put his curiosity out of his mind—what are Pilgrims of Merian doing here in a bloody Kestral Tank? As he moved to the next coffin, he was about to yell at A-Ram to get to the fallen and start cleaning them off, but he was already doing so, and so was Alesta, apparently recovered somewhat, helping as best she could.

"Hey!" Taara's voice echoed from down the hall, "I think I've got it knocked!"

Before another moment had passed, all the coffins down the line opened, spilling out their living and caustic contents. As quickly as he could, Stenstrom pulled the people out—some Merians, others Fleet crewmen, and there were also a few civilians thrown into the mix here and there. Merchants, by the look of them, with horrid, blackened skin.

There were so many to assist.

8

—The Kestral Tank—

Down the line he came across a tanned, sturdy-looking female Hospitaler with long blonde hair sectioned off into dozens of thin, tightly-wound braids.

Very attractive—sort of reminded him of Lilly in a tanned, husky sort of way. Her eyes were open, though she seemed especially incapacitated. "Are you Morgan-Jeterix, of the Grand Order of Hospitalers?"

She weakly nodded, her eyes cloudy.

"I'm very glad to meet you at last," he said cleaning her off as best he could. "Can you tell me, where is Captain Gwendolyn?"

"Down there, I think," Morgan said, indicating down the far end of the hall.

"Thank you. A-Ram and Lady Alesta are coming. We're all getting out of here."

Several coffins away, he saw a tall woman in a lieutenant's uniform slowly trying to stand, her long brown hair in a tangle. A rapier hung at her side. Apparently the Druries stuffed them in kit, weapons and all, having no fear they would manage to escape.

Despite himself, Stenstrom smiled as he pulled yet another Merian free of a coffin. "Are you Captain Gwendolyn?" he asked as he cleaned the Merian off.

She seemed startled at the sound of her own name. She stood tall, with excellent posture. She appeared to be out on her feet, her mind locked in a loop.

"Captain?" he asked.

She gave a start. She turned. "Lieutenant Gwendolyn, commanding officer, Fleet scouting ship *Demophalon John*." She looked at him without seeing. "What's our status?"

"Status is: getting better."

Gwendolyn shook her head. "That is not a proper response, crewman," Her green eyes were glassy and far away.

The mirage. Stenstrom remembered the mirage, her crazed face. Here it was in person.

"I'm not a proper fellow," he said moving on to the next coffin.

Gwendolyn stared at Stenstrom hard and didn't appear to have any recollection of him—she was confused, lost, on the precipice of utter raving madness. "Who are you? What sort of uniform is that? I shall have to demerit you for being out of dress," she said.

"I'm a friend, remember?" He noted she was wearing a Merian beaded necklace—all of the Fleet crew were.

She blinked as things sorted themselves out in her muddled mind. She exhaled. "Are . . . are you Paymaster Stenstrom?"

He smiled at her. "In the flesh, at last. You are a tall thing after all, aren't you?"

She strode up to him, her boots pounding on the shiny floor, wet with the fluid from the coffin. She stood there in a proud, formal way. "Then I would like to properly introduce myself. I am Lt. Gwendolyn, Lady of Prentiss, commander of the Fleet scouting ship *Demophalon John*, 3rd Wing. I, as of this moment, formally relieve you of your unbounded command now that I have boarded. Please, do not take that as an indictment. I wish to entertain you aboard my ship as a welcome visiting dignitary."

She went silent, apparently expecting Stenstrom to offer a formal greeting in kind.

She obviously had no idea where she was, had blanked the last day or two out of her head. He looked up at her as he cleaned off a Merian's face.. "Hi," he said in return. She was covered in the brown fluid from the coffin, as were her boots, her coat, and her hands, which were turning an irritated shade of red.

Stenstrom stood. "Captain, you are covered in Kestral fluid. It is very bad for you."

As if awaking from a day-time dream, she looked at her hands, pulled a handkerchief from her coat pocket and began dabbing her fingers. "Oh . . . oh. I am sorry for being a bit out-of-sorts." Her whole body was trembling. "Your pardon."

Her handkerchief was equally soaked in fluid. He gently took it from her and tossed it aside, cleaning her hands with his cloth.

She stared at her hands as he worked, as if afraid to meet his gaze. "I am sorry I have had to cost you your chair today. I wish to make it up to you."

Taara linked up with them. "I think that's all of them, Bel," she said, a little out-of-breath.

"What's the count, Taara?"

"Looks like we got thirty-four Pilgrims of Merian, forty-two Fleet personnel, and ten civilians—from Mallets, if their dress is any indication. The civilians appear to be in the worse shape. Who knows how long they've been trapped in these coffins."

Gwendolyn reacted a little. "No, no," she said. "There are eighty-two souls under my command. They are still on my ship at their posts. I was not aware you had civilians aboard your vessel, Paymaster. Private, I wish a complete accounting of these civilians—their names, points of origin, and business aboard a Fleet ship. Report back to me on the hour. Understood? I'll expect a more accurate count next time."

Taara looked at Gwendolyn, puzzled for a moment. "Oh, are you Captain Gwendolyn? She reached up and felt Gwendolyn's bicep through her coat. "Oh, yeah, Bel, I really think she would have beaten the daylights out of you," she said, trying to lighten things up.

"That's really not appropriate, private," Gwendolyn said.

Stenstrom interceded. "Taara, get everybody rounded up—I think there's a sizable alcove down that way," he said pointing behind him. "It's defensible and I think we can use it to recover a bit and get things sorted out. Move them along as best you can—get A-Ram to help."

"Ok, Bel." She trotted away and started pulling people to their feet.

"Captain," Stenstrom said. "May I have a word with you?"

"I don't think now is a convenient time. There's much to do and . . ."

"I sincerely think we need to have a momentary word alone."

She appeared hesitant. "Well, I . . . all right. For a moment only."

They walked down the corridor a bit and found another alcove. Moving deep into it, they stopped. "Yes, Paymaster, what can I do for you? As you can see, I've . . ."

"It's all right, Gwen," he said, interrupting her.

"Pardon?"

"It's all right. It's just you and me here. No crew watching, nobody to see."

"I . . . I don't understand."

"We are not on the *Seeker*—I have no real idea as to where we are, but it's not the ship."

Gwendolyn looked around, trying to sort things out. A long straight scar on her right cheek stood out cherry red.

"Where is your ship, Gwen?"

She became frantic. She gulped in fitful grabs of air. "My ship? It . . . it's crashed—end of mission. No . . . No, that can't be. Where's my ship?"

She righted herself, eyes darting, hysteria moving over her, cross-legged.

"My ship! The water! I must . . . I must . . ."

"Gwen, I know you've been through a lot, and I know you must be in pain. We have a few moments to ourselves, so take it. Sort it out—ride it out. We're friends, remember? Let me help you."

She looked down and put a reddened hand to her hair, then her face collapsed into utter anguish.

She fell into his arms and wept in wracking stages. "My . . . crew . . . dead. Ship . . . lost. They were in my head, sifting my mind. I couldn't get them out."

"Who was? Who was in your mind, Gwen?"

"I don't know—the things in the water. Couldn't think, couldn't see reason . . . Morgan, I think I almost killed Morgan. And then—and then those people, they killed my men on that boat . . . And then they . . . they strafed the survivors, all those bodies in the water . . . I couldn't save my men . . ."

"The Merians, Gwen; where did the Merians come from?"

"I don't know where they came from. They . . . they were trying to help us. They got us off the ship . . ."

Stenstrom let her get it out for a minute more. She dried her tears and gazed at him, a fair amount of the confusion melted away.

"Thanks, Bel," she said, her previous formal bearing gone. "I think I was just a shove away from falling into utter madness. I really needed that. I feel much better—thank you. I've been looking forward to meeting you for some time—just, not under these circumstances."

"How are the cobwebs?"

"Clearing. Thank you. I wish I could be more presentable."

"You're most presentable, Gwen. How's your skin feel?"

Gwendolyn held her reddened hands out and wiggled her fingers. "It hurts. I'll be fine. I'll be fine."

Stenstrom checked her hands. Her skin was red and inflamed, but the Kestral fluid was gone. It was fortunate that she had spent so little time in the coffin.

He checked her clothes—they were damp, but appeared to be quickly drying—at least that was something.

"Where are we, Bel? I think we were taken underwater. How did you get here?"

"I'm not for certain. I think I got here the same way the Merians got here. I'm just not sure how we're going to get back out."

Drying the last of her tears, they made their way back to the group, moving past the open coffins and spilt fluid.

Gwendolyn was highly conflicted as they walked. "I really don't feel up to fighting with you over who's in command, Bel—you or me. I truly don't want it. I don't feel up to it right now, but, for my crew, I have to . . ."

"I wish to conscript you, Gwen."

"What?"

"Your vessel is End-of-Mission, her bell lost. I wish to temporarily conscript you to the crew of the *Seeker*, assignment: Ship's Engineer. I recall you mentioning that you had training in engineering. I think that will . . ."

"Done," she said quickly, approving of his suggestion, the idea apparently taking flight in her head. "I accept. I submit to the conscription and am honored. Good thinking, Bel."

"Gwen, I don't want you to feel that I'm usurping your authority."

"Not at all. In fact, I would argue that going from the captain's chair of a scouting ship to the engineer of a Main Fleet Warbird is quite a promotion. I'm honored."

"It's just temporary."

"Absolutely." She brightened a little, having settled the command issue which, apparently, had been troubling her.

They continued down the corridor. Taara had moved the group a good distance from where they had been confined, which was a good thought. She had gotten them all into a large alcove, where they were all huddled up tightly. Tucked inside, most of the Merians and crew were scattered about on the floor, asleep. Taara was sitting near the mouth keeping guard, humming a song from Bazz, her SK laid out on her lap. She looked dreadfully tired. Morgan-Jeterix was next to Taara, either asleep or unconscious, her Marine coat draped over her. A-Ram was asleep nearby. Lady Alesta was tucked up next to him, also quietly asleep, her head resting on his chest. She had shared her green robe with him, the both of them bundled up within it.

The whole alcove was full of the sounds of people sleeping—a rather peaceful sound.

He looked down either end of the corridor, seeing nothing but coffins and tubes stretching off into infinity. No Druries in sight. He listened—he heard the steady pounding throb of machinery. Seemed safe for the moment.

He carefully stepped into the interior. The Fleet crew was suffering from overwhelming fatigue. Those who were still awake seemed as addled as Gwendolyn had been, their mental state delicate at best. Stenstrom knelt and introduced himself, the crew listening with mouths lolled open. As with Gwendolyn, after a little talking, they began to sort themselves out and make sense of what had happened to them. Elsewhere, he saw the Merians soothing other crewmen, holding them, singing in their ears. They acknowledged him with a simple nod as he passed.

The Merians showed a remarkable toughness that greatly impressed him. Without wanting to wish this situation upon anyone, he was glad they were here, nevertheless.

He returned to the mouth of the alcove. "See anything, Taara?" he asked quietly.

"Nope. Just a whole lot of nothing."

"I suppose it's a good thing—these people are exhausted."

"I'm not doing too well myself. A situation like this just makes you tired. I'd almost rather the Druries show and get it over with."

Gwendolyn looked wearily down the corridor. "Any thoughts on who those men might be? They're monsters."

She shrugged and closed her eyes. "They're called the Drury Brothers."

Gwendolyn seated herself. "The Drury Brothers? Aren't those pirates from antiquity?" she said. "I recall my uncle telling stories about them when I was a child. Silly tales, like the Boogie Man; the Druries would fall upon lone travelers when they were at their weakest and take flight the moment help arrived."

"Sounds like them," Stenstrom said.

"But that would make them at least 400 years old."

Taara gave a wry smile and flared her tired eyes. "Boogie Man never dies; that's what we say on Bazz."

Gwendolyn's state of mind appeared fragile. Though she tried to mask it, her eyes betrayed her—she was utterly terrified.

"Taara, let's not ascribe any supernatural powers to these cretins, for they don't deserve it," Stenstrom said. "The Druries are robots, Gwen, nothing more."

"Robots?"

"Actually, they're mechanical constructs; Mecons," Taara corrected.

"Regardless, they're well-crafted and highly complex. I took one down myself on the *Seeker* and discovered the truth."

Gwendolyn wasn't convinced. "They didn't act like any Mecon I've ever seen."

"Ghosts in the machine," Taara said. "Their spirits override their circuitry and haunt the logic." She craned her neck and looked down the corridor. "I get the creeping feeling there's a lot more than just four of them running around here somewhere, and the sad thing is they could hit us any moment and we're just sitting ducks."

A-Ram awoke and shifted his position, Lady Alesta moving with him. "Looks like you've made a friend," Stenstrom said quietly.

"She's quite the thing, isn't she?" He gently adjusted the ends of her thick, black hair.

"Sure is."

Stenstrom saw Morgan asleep under Taara's coat. "How's Morgan-Jeterix?" he asked.

Taara looked at her. "She fine, but she's in no fit state to go on a long hike. She's going to have to be carried out of here, and so are all these civilians we just picked up. I did manage to salvage most of her Hospitaler instruments and scanners—those might come in handy."

"Are you trained in the medical arts?" Gwendolyn asked.

"Nope."

"Well then, how are you to . . ."

"It's a long story, Gwen," Stenstrom replied. "But, if anyone can, it's Taara."

He gazed down the corridor, deserted, except for the long line of clean glass coffins. He kept waiting to hear the sounds of the Druries charging down the corridor—but so far he heard nothing but the steady rumble of machinery.

He turned to all the people huddled in the alcove, both Fleet crew and Merians. "Gwen, how long has it been since you and your crew have eaten or had anything to drink?"

"I can't recall—it's been awhile." She toyed with the Merian necklace around her neck, rubbing the beads back and forth with her fingers.

"And you don't know where these Merians came from?"

"I really don't. As I said, they got us out of the ship. They were trying to help us. They put these necklaces on us, and the dream began to fade," Gwendolyn said.

He shrugged and spoke quietly. "Tell me about it in more detail later, Gwen. We can't stay here for long. Taara, how deep are we?"

"At least three miles. And, I don't think there's an accessible entrance or exit to this place that we can use. I'm pretty sure we're under the sea on Cronyn World."

"There's got to be a way out."

Stenstrom stood. "I'm going to scout around and get a feel for the layout of the place, perhaps there's a more defensible area to hide in, or an obvious way out. We can formulate a plan when I get back." He pulled one of his NTH's and gave it to A-Ram.

Gwendolyn stood and brushed herself off. "I'm coming with you. It's not safe."

"No, you stay here Gwen, and keep everybody quiet. I won't be long."

Taara smiled. "He'll be all right. He's really sneaky—they'll never know he's there."

Gwendolyn was determined. "No, no, he'll need my help." She adjusted the scabbard of her FEDULA and cocked her MiMs.

Stenstrom did his usual fade into the shadows.

"Bel?" Gwendolyn said, looking around, still holding her MiMs. "Bel?"

"See, I told you," Taara said. "I have no idea how he does that—but he promised he'd show me. Isn't it cool?"

"Bel?" Gwen said wandering out into the corridor, trying to keep her voice down.

Stenstrom laughed a bit as he proceeded down the corridor, certain that, of all the skills his mother taught him, the ability to move unseen was the most useful.

Now to it.

As before, he was in a long corridor lined on one side with glass coffins, about seven feet tall and three and a half feet wide. He called them "glass," for he had nothing else to call them—they looked and felt like glass, though, as he now knew, they were much, much stronger than glass. Above him was a metal ceiling thoroughly packed with tubing and wires, marked at intervals by grates admitting air. Below was a clean stone or concrete floor polished to a mirror-like shine.

On the other side of the corridor, to his right, was a maze of machinery and piping—very complex and very well-crafted, eventually giving way to a large alcove exactly like the one his people were hiding in down the way. A simple railing, painted olive green, ran along the length of the piping. Apparently, the alcove was some sort of expanded maintenance area. As he moved, keeping to the shadows, he began to see a pattern to the machinery, piping and alcoves: they repeated every hundred and fifty feet—apparently, they serviced a set number of coffins in brown fluid and oxygen and then began again. Each coffin, he saw upon close examination, was serviced with two thick hoses and a web-work of delicate wiring.

He was struck by how clean and orderly the whole place was, everything from the shiny floor to the painted pipes and railing were squeaky clean and well-maintained—not a speck of dirt or dust to be found.

And, another thing: not another soul for as far as he could see. The place seemed to be quite deserted.

He continued on, wondering how far he'd come. How big could this place possibly be?

After he'd walked a good mile or so, the machinery and piping to his right gave way and opened up into a gigantic space. He went to the railing and looked over the side. He saw a huge artificial chasm. On the other side of the chasm, about a thousand feet away, was a similar corridor to the one he was standing in. Below, he could see more corridors dropping down into the distance until they faded into darkness. The same for above, floor after floor of long corridors strewn with glass coffins.

He leaned over the side and looked up. That certainly must be the way they had to go.

He continued on—part of his thoughts quickly becoming convinced that this place was truly endless. He wondered about the Kestrals. Clearly, they once used this mammoth facility to create *Killanjo* at their leisure—soaking the unfortunate victims in the coffins for an unknown length of time to sufficiently drive them mad and bend them to their will. *Killanjo* were the Kestrals favorite low-level servants and horrid terror weapons, terrifying to behold and utterly disposable. A Tank facility like this could produce them by the legion.

But, the Kestrals were gone.

He had been at the conference with Captain Davage and the Sisters at Armenelos following the Kestral Affair. Though he didn't understand all of what was said, apparently the Kestrals came from very far away, well past the outer reaches of Xaphan space, and had access to Kana and the League at large by means of some sort of temporal device that was determined to be located in the Hala lands of Kana. He'd stood in it himself. This device allowed the Kestrals access to the distant past and allowed them to step out of thin air without the need for star-ships or vehicles of any kind. The Kestrals were not human; they were some sort of shape-shifting species and were immune to the effects of temporal gravity. And, he recalled that the Sisters fell upon the Kestrals temporal device and laid it waste—in theory denying the Kestrals its further use from their fastness in the distant future.

So, if that was the case, and the Sisters' assessment that the Kestrals were no longer able to reach the League at will was correct, then this facility is most likely abandoned, or populated only by those who were present at the time of the temporal device's destruction—the Druries and possibly a few now shipwrecked Kestrals. The Kestrals' horrid facility was marooned in League space.

Escape. Just how were they going to do this? They were, as a group, exhausted from fear and their ordeal, hungry, near-psychotic, and in pain from the coffins and the Cronyns' mental attacks (Gwendolyn had seemed at the brink of insanity not long ago). And, they had to think about the wounded—Morgan-Jeterix and the civilians they'd found—those would have to be carried, a grueling task considering the distances involved. And what about the Merians? He thought about the Merians' Road—the mystical wall of fog that transported him, Taara, and A-Ram here in a flash. He didn't expect such a Road would be available to spirit them back out. It could not be so easy.

No matter—they were all getting out of here. No one was to be left behind.

He continued on, feeling far away from his people and he wanted to return to them. The sheer size of the place and the loneliness began to get to him, and he felt spooked.

After another half mile, the corridor ended in a down turn of pipes, hoses, and cabling. He looked around—there simply had to be a way up, though no apparent way presented itself. The Kestrals' habit of simply teleporting where they wanted to go was proving inconvenient. Assuming nobody in the group had the Vith Gift of Waft, (He didn't have it, and he didn't think Taara, a

Bazzer, or A-Ram, a Calvert, did either; it was possible Gwendolyn could and perhaps some of her crew—the Merians certainly couldn't do it), they needed a physical way to ascend to the surface and climb out. He supposed that they could try climbing up the open face of the chasm to the next level above and so on—he could do it, Gwendolyn no doubt could, as well as Taara—but what about the rest? Could they, even assisted, make the climb, and then to have to do it over and over again? Not possible. They would be terrified, and some might even refuse such a route. There had to be another way.

Investigating the compaction of pipes and tubing overhead, he discovered a fairly wide hole leading up to the next level—apparently some sort of raceway allowing for the connection of piping from floor to floor. He checked the floor of his current level and found the same thing—a large hole about eight feet wide full of tubes. If all floors had a similar hole, then they could climb up and out. He dug into the cables leading up, and they were a tight mess, the hole seemingly packed solid. He produced a MARZABLE and poked around, finding a number of ties that he could cut and discard. After several minutes of work, he found he had cut enough ties that the solid mess of tubes and cable began to give way. Soon, squeezing through the mass, he emerged on the level above. Just to make sure the feat wasn't a fluke, he tried it again, and soon made it to the next level after several minutes. He did two more floors, and found that the ascent, though tight, was perfectly possible and much safer than climbing up the open face of the chasm.

Good—good. So, unless something else presented itself, this was how it had to be.

Moving quickly, he made the long walk back to the others to relate his findings.

*   *   *   *   *

When he got back, he was greeted with a terrible commotion. One of the civilians they'd rescued was on a rampage. He stumped about with blackened skin. His eyes were alight in madness. He drooled and gnashed his teeth.

He was holding Taara's SK, waving it around.

"Now look," she said holding her hands out. "I know you don't want to hurt anybody. Give me my gun, and we'll try to get you relief."

The civilian stood there holding the gun in a shaking grip. "Gotta' get out . . . gotta' get out of this . . . it hurts! Ah . . . ah . . . Creation, it hurts!"

He waved the gun around in his shaking grip. He put the gun to his temple. "It hurts . . ."

He pulled the trigger, but nothing happened—the palm sprander preventing the gun from firing.

Stenstrom got behind him and pulled the SK from his grasp. The two struggled for a moment. He slipped a Pink Holystone into his palm. He put his arms around him and together they slumped to the floor.

"Gotta' . . . get out . . ."

"You're fine," Stenstrom said. "You're fine. Just relax. Hold on tight to the Holystone and relax."

The civilian, though still in pain, calmed and relaxed a little in Stenstrom's grip. Taara fetched her gun. "I was just sitting there when he jumped me—and I wasn't sure if I'd set the palm sprander on my SK—good thing I did, or his brains would be all over the place. The poor fellow's in a lot of pain, Bel. He's out of his head."

Stenstrom picked him up. "The Holystone should keep him quiet until we can get him help." He carried him back into the alcove and gave a pink Holystone to the rest of the civilians—all of them writhing and blackened, the Merians trying to assist them. The pinkies seemed to be helping a little.

They sat back down at the mouth of the alcove and Stenstrom described his findings.

"And you think taking this route is our best option?" a very tired-looking Gwendolyn asked. "And, by the by, I can't Waft, in case you were wondering. A few of my crew can, I think."

"That makes two of us. Climbing through the tubing is the only option I saw. It's a little cramped, and doubtless many shall need assistance, but that shouldn't be an issue. We will assist all those needing it."

Taara was skeptical. "I don't know, Bel—I just don't get the feeling going up is our best bet."

"What are your thoughts?"

"I'm pretty sure if we go all the way to the top, we're going to find nothing but stone once we get there." She paused. "I really think going that way is the way to go." She pointed down and to her right a little.

Gwendolyn rubbed her eyes, heavy with bags. She had a straight, clean scar on her right cheek.

"Gwen, how's your skin?"

She nodded. "It's all right."

"Why don't you get some sleep; we all need to rest up before we get started anyway," Stenstrom said.

Gwendolyn didn't argue. She laid her FEDULA down in its sheath and was about to lay her head on Stenstrom's shoulder, but saw Taara watching and instead tucked up onto the cold floor next to him. Moments later, she was asleep.

"See, told you she likes you," Taara said.

A few moments later, A-Ram, carefully stepping over sleeping people, joined them. "Oh, how I wish we had some coffee," he lamented, stretching.

"Welcome awake, A-Ram. We were just discussing our plan for getting out of here. I thought to lead the group up, but Taara thinks we should bear down and to the east—if that way is east."

"I was thinking about what Lady Alesta was telling me."

"You mean your girlfriend over there?" Taara said, smiling.

A-Ram thought about it. "Yes—why yes, my 'girlfriend'. I rather think so. She was saying that they have been coming to this watery place for years, freeing those lured in by the Cronyns. They call it Edam. Apparently ships crash into this planet with a fair amount of regularity—not Fleet ships normally, but smaller, solitary vessels: merchantmen, yachts and the like.

Alesta and her group watch for the arrival of fallen shipping and come to this place in an effort to save them. They don't use starships to arrive here; they use something Alesta calls 'The Road'."

Stenstrom smiled. "The Merian's Road—It's some sort of arcane portal leading from one place to the next. The wall of fog we saw aboard the *Seeker*—that was the Merian's Road I'm certain."

"Alesta says, in this case, their Road was dispelled, and has led to this situation. A small vessel appeared on their boat just as they were about to make good their escape—the arrival of that vessel fouled the Road and threw off their cloak of invisibility as their faith waivered. She says the vessel with its power field dispelled the Road."

"I suppose these events prove there truly is something to the Star of Merian that they claim exists. When I passed out I saw my sister, Virginia, and she was sitting in one of the Merian ruins scattered about our manor. She was crying—she said her children were dead, and that she couldn't save them My sister Virginia has always claimed that she can see the Star of Merian—that it's plain as day to her. I think that this Star of Merian was talking to me through the image of my sister. The Star was pained by what had happened to the Merians and the Fleet crew. She told me to depower the *Seeker* and a Road would come for us."

"Alesta also says that there was someone in a red and black robe sitting inside the vehicle that foiled their escape," A-Ram said.

"Knife. It sounds like that Knife person we saw in the Sisters' presence. She is supposed to lead me in the direction the Sisters want me to go. Obviously they wanted me here, in this Kestral dungeon, and they want me to destroy it."

"Yes. I thought much the same thing, and, apparently, they don't care who suffers in the meantime." A-Ram looked back at the sleeping Alesta. "Look at all these innocent people."

Gwendolyn awoke and looked at the floor in uncomfortable misery. She took off her coat and wadded it up into a ball to use as a pillow.

"Gwen," Stenstrom said, "it's all right. Come here, please, and sit next to me." Bleary-eyed, she glanced at Taara.

"Don't worry about Taara. Come on, Gwen, make yourself comfortable and get some sleep."

She scooted up to him and laid her head on his chest. Stenstrom draped his HRN coat around her. She took a deep breath and sighed.

"Take your boots off; you'll feel better," Taara said, her boots long since removed. Gwendolyn didn't respond. Instead she closed her eyes and she slept.

Taara smiled. "Stubborn. Ah well, what'd I tell you?"

"So, let's organize out thoughts. Clearly, this facility is a Kestral Tank where they create *Killanjo*. As the Kestrals are now denied access to the League, this facility is now cut adrift and abandoned. Now, what is the Cronyn connection to this puzzle, and, in turn, what is the Drury connection?"

Taara spoke up. "The Cronyns are probably here to protect the facility, to prevent it from being detected by the League. I mean—look where we are—just a crotch-shot away from both Kana and Onaris, the bloody heart of the League, on a dwarf planet that does not appear on any charts. They're using their skills with illusion to cover everything up."

A-Ram agreed with that line of thought. "And, I'll wager the Druries are here, in turn, to feed and maintain the Cronyns and possibly maintain this tank. You say that, at one time the Cronyns actively attacked Bazz—they must have been here on this water-logged rock the whole time, starving, and sought to satiate themselves by feeding on the people of Bazz. Four hundred years ago—that's when the legend of the Druries sprang up on Onaris. I imagine the Kestrals captured them, found them to be of suitable disreputable ilk and imprinted their minds, recreating them as powerful Mecons, here to oversee this facility and stealthily seek out discreet prey to feed to the Cronyns."

Quietly, so as do not disturb Gwendolyn, Stenstrom responded. "That might also account for the Druries' apparent need for metal—recall, Chance Drury mentioned wanting to take the *Seeker*, I assume, for salvage. If that's the case, they probably need to keep themselves stocked in refined metals for the construction of their replacement robotic bodies and the upkeep of their ship. I got a good look at the *Heade* as I battled Innocent Drury, and though it's in the basic configuration of a *Webber*-class vessel, it's packing a host of add-ons. That's the key—the Druries must have a large dock here somewhere—large enough to house a starship or two. And, I'll wager the *Demophalon John* is currently in it—and I'll further wager that the *Seeker* is there too. We did see an incoming blip just as we powered off."

A-Ram was distressed. "Pardon me," he said. He stood and made his way out of the alcove and, choosing a direction, went down the corridor.

A minute later, Alesta quietly appeared. She stepped to the mouth of the alcove and looked around. She held her green robe shut.

"He went to the bathroom," Taara said.

She blushed and sat down, waiting for him to return.

"Lady Alesta," Stenstrom said. "I wanted to thank you for doing what you could for Lt. Gwendolyn and her crew. You and your folk are very brave. I have always admired the Merians, and I do so now more than ever."

She smiled. "Thank you, sir. And thank you, for coming to our aid. We are very blessed."

"I believe your Star came to me and asked us to help you. We arrived here in a wall of fog," Stenstrom said.

"That is our Road," she replied.

"May we expect that 'The Road' will return and spirit us back out?"

She shook her head. "No, my Lord. There is too much power here. In the presence of power, the Road will not form. We may be deposited into a place brimming with power, as this place is; however, we cannot be retrieved unless the power is cut or otherwise dispelled."

"So, unless we turn off the lights, we're stuck here?" Taara said.

"May I ask, Lord A-Ram says he saw me on your ship? Is that true?"

"Yes," Taara answered, "and he hasn't stayed quiet about it since."

Alesta was confused, she turned to Stenstrom. "My Lord?"

"We saw you in the light of an arcane lantern. A-Ram was very taken with you. He has been most anxious to make your acquaintance. "

Alesta smiled and blushed a bit. "He is in your service?" she asked.

"He's my Master Helmsman," Stenstrom replied. "And, I'm proud to say, he's my friend as well."

"Mine too," Taara said. "He's a great guy."

Alesta nodded. "Helmsman, he steers your vessel?"

"Yes, a very important posting."

"Where is your ship? I shall inform you that the people are sick, and hungry, and need tending as soon as possible."

Stenstrom looked back, saw the lumpy huddles of sleeping people jungled up in the alcove. "Our ship is far away. We're on our own down here."

A-Ram returned. Alesta looked up at him and burst into a smile. She opened her green robe and invited A-Ram to sit next to her. He did and she snuggled into his side, closing the robe.

Stenstrom put his arm around Gwendolyn and she settled into him a little further, gripping him tightly. "Taara, A-Ram, I think I'll let Gwen sleep for a bit, then I'm heading out again."

"Where you off to this time?"

"I'm going the way you suggested—east and down a little. I'm going to see if the *Seeker* is nearby. If so, I'm going to board her and get us food and drink, and then we're getting out of here."

Alesta took off several of her beaded necklaces. "Sir, may I offer you and Lady Taara one of my necklaces—it shall protect you from the unreal."

Taara took one and put it on. "Thanks," she said.

Alesta put one around A-Ram's neck and straightened it for him. She gazed at him with big blue eyes. "For you," she said softly. She then offered one to Stenstrom. "Please, good sir."

Stenstrom reached out and took it. "With great thanks," he said.

He started to put it on, and felt a warm hand stop him. It was Gwendolyn, partially awake. "Wear mine, Bel." She took off the necklace she was wearing and put it around Stenstrom's head. "I want you to wear mine."

9

—THE DOCK—

Stenstrom made his way down the corridor, this time in the opposite direction from the way he'd come. Again, the going was long, with the unbroken line of coffins on his right this time, pipes, hoses and wiring on his left. As before, he came to an open space to his left and he stopped to get his bearings.

He was surprised by what he saw. In the near distance was a wall of rough hewn stone. He could see several bulbous spheroids of glass and metal sticking out of the rock face, lit up in effulgent, yellowish light like several transparent zeppelins sticking out of the rock. Housed within the spheroids he could see a black latticework of machinery, gantries and walkways. He saw what looked like a highly advanced dock and hints of calm water.

And he could see the battered nose of the *Demophalon John* looming over the dock, he was sure of it.

There she was, Gwendolyn's ship. There was a tiny, ant-like cloud of mechanized movement all around her, like the corpse of a bird being dismantled in a slow, methodical fashion by a colony of ants.

So, their theory had been correct. The *Demophalon John* was being taken apart, bit by bit.

Looking further, he found he could access the spheroid by way of a gantry several levels down. He quickened his pace.

Shortly, he got to the end of the corridor. It was a relief, to finally reach the end. He guessed he'd gone about a mile and two-thirds. Given the length of the other side of the corridor, he guessed the corridor was nearly four miles long in total.

As on the other side, there was a hole cut in the floor for the plunging descent of wires and tubing. He cut their ties and moved them aside. He squeezed in.

He went down three levels. Ahead, a gantry snaked along the rock-face wall and entered the glass spheroid. Moving in the shadows as only he could, he worked his way across unseen.

From his new vantage point, he could see the *Seeker* floating at the dock next to the *Demophalon John* through the spheroid's glass. The *Seeker* towered over her. It was a stirring sight, and he took heart. The Druries must have intercepted the depowered ship shortly after they departed, found it abandoned, and grappled it down to the planetoid's surface using the advanced tech mounted on the *Heade*.

Moving quickly, he entered the spheroid. At once the atmosphere changed. The lengthy, coffin-lined corridors beyond were clearly deserted and out-of-use; here, however, near the dock, such was not the case.

He instantly heard the sounds of intelligent movement, metal clanking and muffled conversations.

Druries. There was Clem, over just beyond the threshold, and also Innocent. Both were stumping about, fully clothed in their dingy wares, looking like nothing more than two scrawny men who'd seen a hard, unhealthy life.

They shambled into the interior of the spheroid. Stenstrom followed.

He needed information—he needed to know what their capabilities were and were not. It was a terrible gamble, but he had to take it, his people were depending on him.

He made a deliberate noise.

"Whass' that?" Innocent said turning around and walking right past Stenstrom.

"It's nothin'," Clem said. "You been jumpy lately."

Innocent looked around. "Ya? You'd be too—that guy in the coat we fought gives me the creeps—an, we ain't caught him yet—he was nowhere to be found on his ship when we hauled it down."

"The life ring was gone. Mebbe' he an' his lot abandoned ship. Mebbe' the Cronyn's done eaten him by now."

"Mebbe', mebbe'—but I doubts it," Innocent said. "He could be squealin'. He could be bringin' th' Fleet."

Stenstrom moved right past them.

"The Fleet won't find us—the Cronyns'll see to that."

Stenstrom listened to this exchange. They couldn't detect him. It seemed when the Druries were compressed down into their man-like state, their vast sensory abilities were no greater than any ordinary man's would be. All this— their foul, accented language, their distressed clothing—their pretending to be scrawny men when they were in fact huge, vaguely man-shaped Mecons indicated that all of their frailties, fears, and mortal limitations were imprinted into their computerized brains right along with their despicable nature, reducing them in their scope and the manifestation of their power.

They were machines playing at being foul, unrepentant, cowardly men, armed with boundless cruelty and limited intellect. They didn't need to be overly smart to fulfill their role—just had to be mean and unprincipled.

An excellent bit of information, Stenstrom had learned all he needed. He looked around, and there was nobody other than the three of them at the moment. He decided to try and take them out—two less to have to deal with.

He crept up behind Clem, aimed his NTH, and got him square in the back. Instantly, without saying a word, Clem crumpled to his knees, then fell over, face-first.

Innocent looked. "What are ya' doin'?"

Stenstrom got Innocent too. In this compressed form, their robotic bodies were fully subject to being killed by his NTH pistols—when spread out and expanded, their decentralized bodies were much more resistant.

He hoped they didn't figure that out as this situation progressed.

Stenstrom then tried to drag them off into the shadows and stash their wretched bodies. He could hardly move them—they were so heavy. Grunting, straining, he managed to slide them out of the way, but the effort of it was monumental and completely exhausting. His It Man abilities would do well at this moment, but, of course, he was denied them. He had to rest up a bit after his ungainly chore was complete, as he'd had so little sleep and was near exhausted.

He returned to the shadows and continued.

Ahead was a vast chamber cut of solid rock. The *Seeker* and the *Demophalon John* were floating side-by-side in shallow water by a highly mechanized dock—the *Seeker* dwarfing the much smaller scouting ship. There were a number of robotic arms mounted all about the *Demophalon John*, cutting off orderly pieces of hull plating with huge torches, swinging over and dropping them onto a vast conveyor belt, which ferried the hull plates off to a large hopper. The *Demophalon John*, its hull cut away in sections, looked like a skinned and partially dissected animal, the mechanical innards of the ship on gory display.

Above Stenstrom were several levels of walkways connecting offices, mezzanines, and other support structures all made of gangly black metal.

There were a number of robotic arms mounted near the *Seeker* as well, but they weren't at work cutting it up; quite the opposite, they seemed to be at work adding parts to her hull. The arms were busy welding some sort of brace to either side of the rear of the ship. Additionally, two cylindrical tubes, each about a hundred feet long and twenty feet high, were being constructed nearby by other robotic arms, some arms at work welding, others machining complex parts out of solid blocks of metal; other arms delicately adding circuitry to the interior of the tubes.

The tubes looked, to Stenstrom, like Xaphan-style stellar engines.

What were the Druries up to?

More movement caught his eye.

Overseeing the work on the dock was Chance Drury, holding an open chart of some kind. At his side stood two bizarre creatures. One of the creatures looked like a giant-sized circular ball of frizzy black hair, supported by four jointless, prehensile legs, also covered in black hair. The other was some type of prehistoric bird with a sharp beak and long, flapping wings.

The creatures intently watched the progress on the ship as Chance, showing them the chart he was holding, pointed various things out.

These creatures must be shape-shifting Kestrals, possibly stuck here in this facility after the Temple of the Exploding Head was destroyed.

It came to him—he knew what was going on. Marooned here, far from their home and no longer able to simply Blink back using their temporal anchor point, the Kestrals were planning on hijacking the *Seeker* and using her to return home, possibly via an alternate temporal anchor point elsewhere in the cosmos. The Druries probably found the *Seeker* a sturdy, worthy craft capable of making a long voyage through tractless space, simply needing engines—and, hence, the two new engines being constructed for it nearby. Therefore, the *Demophalon John*, damaged beyond easy repair, was to be scrapped, melted down, and turned into parts for the *Seeker*, which would then be sailed a great distance back to their destination, wherever that might be. He could not imagine that the Druries would want to part with their modified *Heade-on-the-Hearth*, so the addition of the *Seeker* was a godsend for them, no doubt.

Good to know. Good to know.

He moved away to his right, toward the hopper—he wanted to see where it went. Along the way, he passed three Clems, two Innocents, and five Lemmuels, all moving about, cursing in their fashion, doing this and that. The Kestrals appeared to have them all quite agitated.

He saw a clear hierarchy forming. Chance, as their leader, was sort of like a queen bee—with only one of him running around at any given time, while the rest were workers and present in quantity. There were a few Clems moving about, a greater number of Innocents, and a whole lot of Lemmuels performing the manual labor and drudgery.

Following the hopper as it led away from the dock, he found it went into a vast adjacent room, thousands of feet in diameter and several stories high. The room was set up like a vast assembly line: automated machinery was bolted to the floor everywhere, moving in well-timed unison. The collected metal was received from the hopper and went into a small, but highly effective furnace, where super-heated slugs of metal were then extruded into various dyes and molds and worked with precision. In the distance, Stenstrom saw four bands of color reaching up into the heights; he saw bands in green, red, blue, and yellow. The bands, stacked neatly into tall, individual chutes, were composed of tiny robotic squares—obviously, the green squares were for Innocent and the other colors for his brothers.

He looked at the whole set-up and took it in. Taara liked to ascribe supernatural attributes to the Druries, saying that they were in fact manifestations of the Boogie Man; but here it was, nothing but a product of automation, technology, organization, and a twisted conception.

Lined up beneath the chutes on hooks were man-shaped robotic frameworks hanging from a silent assembly line that snaked off into another section of the room. The robotic frameworks were preloaded with a number of antennae and a folded up head-screen. The frameworks seemed peaceful as they hung there—asleep almost.

Something was coming at him from his left!

He quickly aimed and fired. The NTH shot hit what looked like a seated person several feet away. Investigating, it was a primitive robot seated in a stuffed chair. It was a "soup can" robot with a cylindrical torso and basic, articulated arms and legs, its feet nothing more than a simple set of casters. It had a pair of cone-shape metal funnels bolted to its chest area, almost like a pair of breasts. It had a primitive servo-motor head and sported a wig of blonde hair and full latex lips. Scrawled across the torso was the word: DUNCE.

Stenstrom could only wonder what this thing was used for.

As he puzzled over it, a long bank of computerized machinery came to life in lights and sounds. Screens printed high-speed readouts and hydraulic pressure built up with a hissy fuss. The line of hanging bodies gave a clank— the bodies nudging into each other, and they began moving in assembly-line fashion.

The first body in the line stopped underneath the chute populated with green squares. Like ice cream being extruded from a tap, the green squares filtered down onto the body. Knocking about in a cloud of movement, the squares covered it from bottom to top—Stenstrom was amazed how many green squares it took to cover the frame—the green chute above was now almost empty.

Covered with squares, the green, blocky body moved on to a finishing station where specialized squares for his head, stomach section, and phallus were added. These squares were not green, but a shiny silver color.

The next body in the line stopped under the red chute and soon was similarly covered.

Two robots, Innocent in green and Clem Drury in red, were newly created—possibly to replace the ones he'd just dispatched.

In front of a flickering screen, a massive amount of information was then downloaded to them—their rotten souls and their demented memories converted to computerized patterns. Their large head screens came out and unfurled. A huge amount of data was printed off on the screens as they received the information.

An automated piston slowly came forward. Behind the piston was a rack of seedy Drury clothing, just waiting to be put on.

The two blocky robots, one red, one green, finished receiving their downloads. They then clunked away in ponderous steps and began changing, their head screens retracting, the squares moving about their bodies in a symphony of coordinated movement, locking into place, shrinking, and becoming dense.

Flesh shot out of their stomachs, and soon there stood a naked Innocent and a naked Clem.

"What in th' name o' Creation jus happened?" Innocent asked as they walked up to the rack and selected clothing.

"I dunno'," Clem replied. "We was standin' in th' anti-chamber when all of a sudden, here we are."

The two began dressing.

"Wha' we gonna' do with our new guests marinadin' in the Tank out there?" Innocent asked, pulling a white shirt on.

"Who cares. Let `em rot. This place is shut down. This is our dung hill now. Once we gets rid `o those two golden Sad-Sackers, we'll need to start thinkin' bout our future. Mebbe' we's can use this facility for our own `selves. Create an army of slaves and have at Kana."

Stenstrom watched. Beneath the rack of clothing was a track carrying refuse back to some unknown point—Innocent and Clem pulled off lumpy bits of mal-formed flesh and tossed them into the refuse track—like a tailor pulling off loose strings from a new coat.

He didn't wait. Stenstrom slotted up behind Innocent and shot him in the back. He instantly fell into the refuse track. Clem shortly followed him, the two of them balled up with the rest of the trash.

That's what happened to you, babes . . . again, Stenstrom thought, taking devilish pleasure in killing the Druries.

He watched their dead, naked bodies, Innocent wearing a partially buttoned shirt, rumbling back to the refuse center, arms and legs akimbo.

Stenstrom had a thought. He went to the rack of hanging robotic bodies. The rack was delicately calibrated, with each body hanging on a hook separated by removable spacers. He pulled several spacers out, dividing the first few bodies. Not spaced out correctly, there should probably be quite a mess when the system starts back up again.

Oops, he thought. *So sorry about that.*

He then had at the various consoles and stations involved in the complex creation of these monstrosities. He fired his NTHs, "killing" the various bits of equipment and circuitry. He felt greatly satisfied by all of this.

He then stole back out of the automated room onto the dock

He encountered a group of Clems walking by. One of them was yelling. "Get that shite a-workin', or I'll have my wank up ya! Now move!"

"Yeah, yeah, shut it!" came a reply. Near the wreck of the *Demophalon John*, he saw a single Lemmuel working on one of the robotic arms cutting up the hull plates high above. He had a panel open and was waist deep into it, performing some sort of maintenance. As Stenstrom previously guessed, in the hierarchy of the Druries, Chance was at the top, Clem and Innocent were somewhere in the middle, and Lemmuel, the most common of all he'd seen, was at the bottom, doing the "crap" work whenever it needed doing.

"Camon', you bitch!" Lemmuel cursed, having issues with whatever it was he was working on. He rose up and threw his tool aside, where it clattered to the dock near the water.

Cursing and lamenting, he reached out to pick it back up and start again, his arm doubling in length.

Stenstrom sprang, shooting him in the neck. Without a word, Lemmuel's body balled up and did a cartwheel into the water with a proud "ker-splunk!" He sank quickly and did not reappear, a few bubbles dancing to the surface marking his sinking.

Stenstrom returned to the shadows and quivered. *Ohhhh, but wasn't that fun . . .*

He resumed his mission and approached the *Seeker*.

Chance and the two Kestral monsters were still standing there, observing the work. Chance then motioned for them to follow him. He walked toward the cylindrical engines being constructed nearby.

"And here, the engines are well under construction, as you can clearly see," Chance said. "With the refined metals derived from the Fleet wreckage, we shall have just enough materials to complete construction in a hundred hours, and all the necessary metallurgy may be assumed as the Fleet uses high-grade materials. *C'est le bon truc.*"

The Kestrals gazed at the engines with interest. The one in the guise of a reptilian bird changed shape, transforming into a tall, toga-clad, golden woman. She stepped into the circular intake and looked close-up at its workings.

Chance responded to some question he was being asked. "Oh, yes, we have salvaged the coils from the scout ship; however, they are far too small for such a heavy vessel—they would not last you long into the deep sea before they burned out—*hou la!* These stellar engines we are constructing shall work nice as you please. I have personally leant to their engineering and vouch for their construction."

CHANCE DRURY

The Kestral woman stepped out of the engine intake and opened her mouth to an impossible diameter, like a snake readying to devour a large prey item. She vomited in a projectile spray on the engines, coating the front ends in glistening fluid. She then closed her mouth and turned to Chance.

He rolled up his chart and clapped. "Ah, well done, my mistress! *Que bonita!* Our endeavor is now properly anointed and blessed!"

More questioning.

"Once the engines are complete, we shall then stock the ship with provisions for a several month-long voyage," Chance said. "We shall set out and abduct a passing ship, a freighter, merchantman, or other lone vessel. We shall then process the crew and ready them as quality foodstuffs for your consumption during the voyage. Fear not, masters, for you shall eat hearty— *avoir un bon dîner,* a-heheheh."

The Kestrals appeared to be pummeling him with questions.

"Oh, yes, yes. This is a *Straylight*—a classic ship, as tough as they come. I am rather envious—I should like to plant my personal flag on such a craft. With this vessel, you may rest assured your trip shall be swift and uneventful."

As the group inspected the engines now dripping with Kestral vomit, Stenstrom saw an opening into the frontal section of the *Seeker*. Quickly, he started to go inside.

"What is that?" Chance said.

Stenstrom froze. Chance took a few steps forward and looked around.

The Kestrals came to his side. "I thought I saw something," he said to them.

He took another step forward—he was just feet away from Stenstrom, who was hiding near a dock baffle.

He clapped the rolled up charts he was holding into his palm several times. "Clem," he said calmly.

"Aye?" came a radio-like response.

"You have stowed the most recent batch of 'Trogs' in the tanks, yes?"

"We have."

"Did you have any issues? Did any try to escape?"

"Nah, they were all zapped out, like usual."

"How are they reading?"

"We're not reading nothing, Chance. None o' the stuff out there's properly functionin' since we got cutoff."

"I see. We shall have to design custom telemetry units of our own to compensate. When time allows, I wish a manual inspection be made of their tanks and an exact head-count delivered. I shall not tolerate this continued inefficiency—*entiendo?*"

"You an' that fancy talkin' you like to do. Ok. It'll be awhile, as we's a deadline to keep. We're tryin' to crack into the bowels o' this scout ship an' get at the good metals there. Fleet ships a' whole lot tougher than the usual rustpots we's snag. The dock cutters are having a hard time with it, and some are goin' down with the effort."

"Please inform Lemmuel that he may work the problem day and night until engine construction for the *Seeker* is complete, or I shall have him reconstituted in the female DUNCE body and compel him to inhabit it for a year or so, understand?"

"Aye."

"I would rather we not dance with the Fleet; however, the situation calls for remarkable action—our masters demand immediate return to their home . . . *ezek vezetői nekem nehéz*. Proceed as best you can. Be advised, we shall shortly have a need to set out and intercept a passing craft. The captured crews shall be prepared as foodstuffs to feed our masters for their long voyage. They must be alive; that is a must—ensure the *Heade* is serviced and ready for launch."

"Why can't we jus' prepare those fools we got in th' tanks now?"

"Because, they are to serve as *Killanjo* deckhands for our master's voyage home—they are to crew the *Seeker*. Inform Innocent he shall accelerate the Trog's soak to speed the process. They must be fully ready in one hundred hours. *Comprenez?*"

"Yeah . . . yeah."

Chance appeared inspired. "Ah—look at what fate brings us. In twenty hours, I am reading that a scheduled flight of school children from the Kanan city of Champion are to be bouncing down the lanes on their way to Onaris for a field outing at a lovely museum in Innari. How sweet. I want the *Heade* made ready, I want their ship lured off the lanes, and I want the children taken and processed. A-heheh, they shall make for tender eating. Inform Lemmuel, I want no breakdowns with the cassagrain weaponry this time, or, again, it's to the DUNCE with him."

"Aye, twenty hours, the *Heade*'ll be ready."

"Fine. *Vamos! Andale!* Chance out!" He looked around one more time and then stumped back to what he was doing.

Stenstrom had a clear shot at the back of his head—no way he could miss. He burned to get this started, to settle with the miscreant, and then go marching into the assembly area and await his re-construction, only to kill him again and again as a kind of recurring purgatory that he so justly deserved, with himself cast as the punishing angel. Perhaps, with the damage he created on the assembly line earlier, Chance might come out mal-created or only half-made as some sort of deformed midget—wouldn't that be grand? Or, better yet, he could make Chance get programmed into the dreaded DUNCE body and dance around in it.

But, such a thing would be selfishness in the extreme. He had his people to think of, and he had to attend to their needs before indulging his own. He could not endanger them by alerting the Druries before he was ready to do so.

He aimed his NTH and pulled the trigger without cocking the hammer.

Another time, Chance Drury, another time . . .

Stenstrom then carefully made his way into the *Seeker*.

The interior of the ship was lit up, the Druries having tapped it into a central power grid. He saw a Lemmuel wandering around with some tools, but that was it—the ship was, at this point, deserted.

He went to the bridge, taking a lift, which was working. This was the first time he'd ridden in a lift since he took command of the *Seeker*—rather ironic, he thought. Once there, he saw that Innocent's remains had been cleared away. At the Missive's Panel, the Druries had installed a computerized node of some sort with a flat, ovular view screen. A sinuous, acid-like line of color traced across the display.

The Druries have been busy getting the *Seeker* ready to take the Kestrals to wherever they needed to go, and they were planning on using the Fleet crew and the Merians as *Killanjo* ship hands in the process.

The good thing was, given the information he'd just received, the Druries couldn't monitor the tanks beyond—this facility must have been at least partially controlled and monitored by the Kestral homeworld, and the far-flung link had been severed—that was something working in his favor. The Druries, therefore, could not know that they had been freed from the tanks.

They were also heavily occupied trying to get the *Seeker* ready for its voyage, the Kestrals understandably impatient, and they had their hands full—that bought Stenstrom and his people additional time.

But, as Chance said, the Druries would soon be setting out, this time to acquire live provisions for the Kestrals' voyage—children, kids on their way to Onaris to visit a museum in just twenty hours. He couldn't allow them to fall victim to the Druries.

Looking around, he saw the box of insta-meals that they stole from Dry Dock 275. He counted—eleven meals for over fifty people. That would have to do for now.

He took the box, and hunted around for the bottled water they'd stolen. It wasn't anywhere he could quickly find, so he settled for a mesh sack full of warm cans of gasol that A-Ram had previously scrounged, and left the bridge.

Outside, Chance and the two Kestrals were gone. Beyond, he could see the *Demophalon John* steadily being taken apart. The Druries had stacked up several of the ship's Stellar Mach coils—the twenty-foot tall rings of tightly wound wire were being assembled to be taken somewhere via a massive treaded craft—probably to the furnace for smelting as the coils were too large to fit on the conveyor belt.

Stenstrom put down the box of insta-meals and the sack of gasol he was carrying.

He was going to misbehave a bit before leaving.

He reached the craft. It was a squat, treaded design, meant to haul large, heavy items. It had a round, robotic node at its front packed with blinking sensory equipment. He gave the craft several shots with his NTH and the node went dead. The weight of the coils, no longer being actively supported by the workings of the craft, began to lean noticeably.

Moving on, he went to several of the robotic arms that were currently busy cutting apart the *Demophalon John*. They were bolted to the dock by means of a large cylindrical base. The base had a door for maintenance. Stenstrom tried the door and found it locked.

After a shake of his hand and a quick action, he had the door open with a magnetic lock pick; all manner of cables and circuit boards fitted inside. He reached in and shot the circuitry several times. Far overhead, the robotic arm went dead, swaying slightly.

Satisfied, he mounted a red Holystone inside, and he tricked the lock of the door as he closed it, knowing it would not reopen without a savage struggle. When a Lemmuel did manage to get the door open, a tongue of fire from the Holystone would belch out.

He then repeated the procedure on several more arms, breaking the locks on each one as he went.

Have fun with those, Lemmuel, old boy.

Felling rather happy with himself, Stenstrom retrieved his box of insta-meals and the sack of drinks and stole off—completely undetected. He returned to his people.

✳ ✳ ✳ ✳ ✳

"Who's there?" Taara said, poking her head out of the alcove. Gwendolyn's head soon followed.

"It's me," Stenstrom said emerging from the shadows. He set down the box of insta-meals and the sack of gasol. "I've been to the *Seeker*."

"It's here?" Taara cried.

"Yep, and I've brought food and drink. I think we've got about ten or eleven insta-meals and about a dozen cans of warm gasol. I couldn't find the bottled water."

"Yeah, I used the bottled water to take a shower," Taara confessed. "Sorry."

He reached into the box and pulled the meals out as people gathered around.

"Lady Alesta," he asked, "can you go through these meals and equally portion them out seeing that everybody gets a share?"

She smiled and took them. "Praise be to you, sir. I will, thank you."

Half an hour later, Alesta and A-Ram gave everybody a third of a helping of insta-meal and a quarter can of gasol. It wasn't much, but the food was a life saver; it had been so long since the crew from the *Demophalon John* had eaten a proper meal.

As before, Stenstrom, Taara, Gwendolyn, and A-Ram sat at the mouth of the alcove eating their food. Between them, they had two cans of red and green gasol, which they shared. Morgan-Jeterix was nearby, eating her meal with lady-like precision. Though still quite weak, she was becoming more alert by the moment. Lady Alesta was in the back helping to feed the civilians, who were in bad shape. Their skin, ravaged by the Kestral tanks, was in severe distress, and they cried out in agony. Helping them as best he could, Stenstrom produced several, fresh pink Holystones and put them in their hands, partially re-sedating them.

As the group ate, Stenstrom saw A-Ram and Alesta exchange frequent glances.

He laughed—*Making love to a Sister one day, winning the pure heart of a Pilgrim of*

Merian the next, you've certainly come a long way for the better, A-Ram. Well done.

"So, here's what I discovered. The *Seeker* and the *Demophalon John* are in a large bay about two miles from here, three levels down," Stenstrom said as he ate. "The *Demophalon John* is partially taken apart and melted down. The Druries have several robotic arms mounted to the wharf, cutting and slicing off squares of the hull and feeding them into a hopper. They also had many of her SM coils stacked up on the dock. For the *Seeker,* they've got other plans. As we speculated, there are two Kestrals marooned in this facility. The Druries are in the process of retro-fitting a pair of alien engines to the *Seeker,* which they plan to give to the Kestrals so that they may voyage far into the deep sea, destination unknown. They probably have another temporal anchor point out there somewhere that they wish to utilize to return to their home world. They are also planning on using the Fleet crew and Merians to man the ship for the voyage as *Killanjo.*"

"Are they currently aware we are no longer imprisoned in the coffins?" Gwen asked, concerned.

"No. I heard Chance and Clem Drury discussing that very topic. It seems a fair portion of the monitoring of this facility was accomplished remotely, so, with the link to Kestral space broken, the Druries currently have no way of monitoring the goings-on out here. And, in that lies a bit of concern. Clem Drury has been ordered to personally inspect the coffins and count up all those present. He, however, has more pressing issues at the moment, as I sabotaged a good number of the robotic arms disassembling the *Demophalon John.* From Chance's tone, readying the *Seeker* for their Kestral masters is their top priority at the moment. And, they are planning on setting out and capturing a ship full of children to use as live food for the Kestrals on their trip back."

"Kids?" Taara cried.

"In twenty hours. Obviously we cannot allow that to happen in any case."

Gwendolyn was finishing her portion—a bit of beef with rice. "What about the Druries themselves?"

"I counted at least a dozen—the four of them being repeated quite often, except for Chance Drury, of whom I only saw one. They seem to be concentrating their activities on the docks near the ships." He turned to Taara. "Taara, what's our capability right now with the *Seeker?*"

"None—she has no coils and, therefore, no way to power her gas-compression engines. She is, for the most part, a dead ship. Did the Druries say how long it would be until they completed the retro-fit?"

"One hundred hours."

"Well shoot, why don't we just wait until they're done with the engines, storm the ship and take it. Creation—they're getting it ready for us," Taara said.

"That's an interesting thought, but you're forgetting about the children, Taara. Also, the bad thing is the Druries are going to come looking for their 'crew' well before then and shall be, no doubt, put off when they find those coffins empty. We can't wait for that to happen—we can't place them on the offensive. I think what we'll need to do is pile up into the *Westminster* and high-tail it out of here—let them have the *Seeker*. Do you think we'll all fit?"

Gwendolyn spoke up. "The problem with that is an old tach-scout ship like the *Westminster* will not be able to fly through water, as we're assuming that the entrance to the docking bay is deep underwater. It just can't do it; its engines aren't designed for such a thing."

"And, she's too heavy to float up to the surface," Taara added.

They sat and thought for a moment. Farther back in the alcove, Lady Alesta was carefully feeding one of the civilians, who was quietly begging for relief.

"I think, Bel, what we should do is occupy the *Seeker*," Gwendolyn said.

"To what end? She's useless."

"I think as far as being a place to easily gain entrance, hide and defend, the *Seeker* is ideal—she's like a fortress. Also, I think there's a way to get her powered up prior to the Kestrals stealing her."

"I'm listening."

"We can take the J400 SM coils from the *Demophalon John* and mount them on the *Seeker*."

Taara disagreed. "J400 coils are too small for a *Straylight* Warbird."

"Yes, that is true, but, they provide up to thirty-five percent power of the *Seeker's* maximum—more than enough to run the gas-compression engines, get us up through the water and into orbit. We can run them at overboost—that'll burn them up in a hurry, but, all we need to do is get to either Kana or Onaris—just a few hours journey at speed, and we'll have power for communications."

"Assuming that the J400 coils haven't hit the Druries shit-can yet," Taara said.

"Yes. Bel, you said the coils from the *Demophalon John* have already been unmounted?"

"Three or four of them, though some appeared to be damaged."

"Well then, the Druries have done the hard part for us. The coils on a scouting ship are very difficult to remove without a proper dry-dock and tooling due to the smaller size and tight internal tolerances of the vessel. All we'd need do then is pop them into the *Seeker*."

"It's that easy?" Stenstrom asked. "Just pop them in?"

"Well," Taara said jumping in, "a *Straylight* is designed to be able to change its coils in a battle-situation, so they're fairly easy to mount."

"Quite correct," Gwendolyn said, licking the sauce off her plate, obviously famished.

Stenstrom offered the rest of his portion of beef and noodles to Gwendolyn. "Here, Gwen, have the rest of mine. No, the hard part will be getting everyone past the Druries. They're everywhere down there, and there's the Kestrals as well. So, here's our task—we shall need a detail of qualified people to get the coils mounted on the *Seeker*. We shall also need someone to lead the rest of the crew and the Merians and civilians to safety aboard the *Seeker*."

Gwendolyn put her plate aside. "I'll lead the coil detail. I'll need crewmen: Allistar, Novak, Sandyman, Flora, and Turkaluu to assist me."

"And I'll come with you," Taara chimed in. "We'll pop the covers and pull the plugs on coils 6 and 13—that should give us the optimum use of the reduced power output."

Gwendolyn marveled at Taara. "And, you say you've no engineering experience?"

"Not a bit."

"I'll be happy to learn how you have access to such detailed and accurate information. I agree with your assessment."

Stenstrom was pleased for Taara, that Gwendolyn offered her a compliment. "So it's done. Gwen, you wrangle the coils from the *Demophalon John*, and, Taara, you get the *Seeker* ready."

"Bel, how are we going to lift the coils? They weigh several tons each."

"The robotic arms. We'll commandeer some."

"Are we going to be able to operate the robotic arms?" Gwendolyn asked.

"I'll do it," Taara said. "I should be able to make something out of them."

"And I'll lead everybody else onto the ship," A-Ram said. "Where should I take them to?"

"Take them to the frontal section, decks four or five, and put them in various quarters. That area of the ship should be easy to defend from attackers and give the people a wealth of places to hide should hiding places be needed," Stenstrom said.

Morgan put her plate down. "If someone could get me to the ship's dispensary, I might be able to create a salve which will help ease the civilian's pain. And, when we get back to the League, we in the Ephysians have learned that the damage to skin elasticity and oil levels caused by prolonged exposure to a Kestral *Killanjo* Tank can be mitigated and reversed with a carefully treated soda bath infused with various salts. I'm confident these poor souls can be fully recovered and made whole provided we get them to the League soon."

Stenstrom nodded. "Good—well, I see no reason to delay. As soon as we finish up our meal, we're leaving. Let's not give the Druries time to mess up our coils. We can expect a minimum two mile walk ahead of us. Additionally, we'll need to descend three levels via the pipe holes I described earlier, cross the gangway into the dock area, and make quick entrance to the *Seeker*. The port frontal gangplank was down. When I was last there, the *Seeker* was empty. With any luck, that's still the case.

Taara finished up her meal. "What are you going to be doing, Bel?"

"I'm going to be diverting the Druries. I am going to create a fiasco and force them to come to me, giving you, with luck, time to move the coils."

"How are we going to recover you?" Gwendolyn asked.

"I'll recover myself. Don't worry about me. Get the ship working and get these people out of here; that's the main thing."

"Bel, don't be stupid!" Taara barked. "We're not saving everybody else just to leave you behind. Think up another plan because that's not acceptable."

"It's all right; the docks must be a little closer to the surface. I got all my stuff back while I was there. I'll be fine."

Taara was skeptical. "I think you're lying, Bel. I think you're just saying what I want to hear."

"What 'stuff' are you referring to, Bel?" Gwendolyn asked.

"Never mind. And, I've no intention on marooning myself here—I'll get back to the ship on my own."

Stenstrom stood. "All right, it's near time. Let's get finished up. We're moving out."

✳   ✳   ✳   ✳   ✳

Stenstrom led the group down the corridor, moving as quickly as they could. The Merians had made rudimentary slings out of their robes and from parts of the insta-meal boxes and were bringing the civilians along, dragging them mostly on the shiny surface of the floor—Stenstrom's pink Holystones keeping them as comfortable and quiet as possible. He was quite pleased by their progress. Taara trailed the group, with A-Ram and Lady Alesta shuttling back and forth making sure everybody stayed together.

Stenstrom carried Morgan-Jeterix. Though weak, rest and her meal seemed to be working wonders. She was smiling and alert.

"I think I rather could get used to this," she said as he carried her. "You're such a strong, handsome man."

Gwendolyn, walking nearby, rolled her eyes.

"How is your wound, ma'am?" Stenstrom asked.

"Please, call me Morgan, and it's fine. It's itching somewhat, which is a good sign. After nearly killing me, Gwendolyn did a good job of patching me back up."

Stenstrom looked back to see how the group was coming along. "If I may, you said your name is Morgan-Jeterix. What is 'Jeterix'? Does that mean something?"

She smiled. "It means 'I'm available' . . . in Thompson." She took one of her braids and waved at him with it. She looked at his collar. "Hmmm, HRN—what does that stand for I wonder—no, no, let me guess. 'H' is certainly for 'handsome', 'R' I'm guessing must be for 'ripped', and 'N' must stand for 'naughty' . . ."

He laughed. She noticed his mask. "What is that mask you're wearing—I'm intrigued." She gently touched it with the tips of her fingers. "Oh, it would be like unwrapping a present. Ladies of Thompson are very forward; therefore, I'll ask you—Paymaster, are you spoken for?"

Gwendolyn interceded. "All right, Morgan, I believe the Paymaster has carried you long enough. He needs his hands free—we might be beset upon. Put her down, please."

"What for?" Morgan cried as Stenstrom put her down.

"I'll carry you, Morgan. As I nearly put one between your eyes, I owe it to you."

Gwendolyn knelt down and picked her up fireman-style, slinging her over her right shoulder, Morgan's rear-end sticking up in the air.

"I don't like this," she said into Gwendolyn's coattail. "I would like the Paymaster to continue carrying me. I'm going to get sick."

"Feel free to vomit, Morgan," Gwendolyn said, moving on at a brisk pace.

Sometime later, they reached the break in the wall to their left. Stenstrom called Gwendolyn, Taara, and A-Ram to look.

"Down there, through that round glass window, that's where the ships are currently berthed.

Gwendolyn peered over the railing. "I see the prow of the *Demophalon John* at dock."

"The *Seeker* is directly to her right. Now, see that gantry way a few levels beneath us?"

They saw it.

"That's how we're getting in. I shall precede the group, enter, and create a diversion. A-Ram, the port gangway is down, so get these people in and scatter them in the frontal area as quickly as you can. Gwen, how long do you think it will take to get the coils transferred?"

"Not long, assuming we can get those robotic arms working in our favor. Just a few minutes to swing them over and install them, and then about thirty minutes to get them calibrated. Not to worry, we can get through the water with the coils out-of-Cal.. As soon as I finish, I'm joining you, Bel."

"No, Gwen—no. I'll be fine. You need to get yourself aboard."

Stenstrom resumed walking. "Come on. We've a bit farther to go."

They made it to the end of the corridor, and, after a great deal of effort, made it down three levels moving through the holes. Finally, the gantry way awaited.

"Here's where I leave you," Stenstrom said. "Remember, I'm depending on you to get these people safe, A-Ram. That's the main thing."

Gwendolyn wanted to say something, then Taara came forward, her little face in tears. "Give 'em a tug for luck, will ya', Bel?" He reached out and gently tugged on her sideburns. She embraced him. "We're not leaving without you, Bel."

Alesta came forward, and he took her small hands. "How blessed we are," she said. "Just when my faith was at its lowest, our Star sends us you three. May the Star walk with you, Lord Belmont."

"And with you, Lady Alesta."

Gwendolyn approached.

"Paymaster Stenstrom, "Morgan-Jeterix said, grabbing his attention. He smiled and knelt down. "A moment, please."

"My Lady," he said.

She reached up, took him by the cheek, and kissed him on the lips. Then she whispered into his ear. "When I see you again, I'll tell you what 'Jeterix' means, deal?"

"It's a deal."

With that, Stenstrom withdrew and allowed the group to pass by and get into position. He watched them as they passed, looking intently at their faces, studying their features. He mused his mother once did the same thing as he and his sisters filed out of the grand dining hall every day, she would stand back and watch them all pass, saying nothing, just watching. He'd always wondered what she was doing.

Now he understood. All these people, strangers only hours ago, were now under his charge, were his to keep safe. He memorized each face, taking personal responsibility for each one. He drew his weapons and faded into the shadows, ready to go forth and defend them with his life.

Gwendolyn spun around, trying to see him in the shadows.

10

—"Hallo, Boys!"—

Stenstrom easily made his way back to the dock area. He climbed up to a high perch with a commanding view and assessed the situation.

Down below, he saw the two vessels. Many of the robotic arms he'd damaged around the *Demophalon John* still appeared to be down—several Lemmuels in attendance at the far end of the dock trying to fix them. Stenstrom noted they were having significant issues opening the maintenance panels—a few had been mangled open. Some were scorched by hot flames.

In front of the *Demophalon John*, the treaded cart carrying the coils had toppled over—they were stacked up four high nearby, and a Lemmuel was lying on his back trying to fix the cart, a surly Clem watching.

Chance Drury and the Kestrals were not in sight, and the *Seeker* appeared to be rather forgotten for the moment.

Well, he thought, no need to delay. He drew his NTHs, cocked the hammers and lined up a shot on Lemmuel.

Stenstrom hit him in the chest. He kicked out with his legs once or twice, dropped his tools, and went still.

Clem appeared to take no notice. He kept right on yelling at the now dead Lemmuel.

Stenstrom cocked again and got Clem in the back. He dropped into a sort of kneeling position and then fell into full prayer before the feet of the dead Lemmuel.

Two Druries down—at this point, the docks were fairly clear. Taara, Gwendolyn, and several of her crew snuck toward the *Demophalon John*. Two people Wafted onto the port wing of the *Seeker*.

Good Creation, an Innocent was walking in their direction! They saw him and tried to take cover near the water's edge. He stopped and turned, having heard them.

Gwendolyn somehow got behind him and, with weapon drawn, sliced his head off with her rapier-like FEDULA—a weapon that appeared to do a lot more damage than a light rapier-like sword should be able to do.

Innocent pranced around headless, his array of antennae sprouting from his neck cavity. Stenstrom lined him up and fired, getting him in the chest where he fell. Gwendolyn and her team then, together, worked to hide his dead, heavy body. They roughly rolled him into the water with a plop.

Looking around, he saw the going clear as Taara began on one of the working robotic arms—good thing he didn't sabotage them all. They had the panel open and Taara was plunged into it, her red Marine coattails and the butt of her SK sticking out of the panel as she worked. The lofty arm overhead swung about in little, jerky stages as she fiddled with it.

The action on the docks so far had been an anticlimax. Stenstrom had expected nothing less than a chaotic melee on the docks. He had been anticipating slaughtering the Druries wholesale, and had readied himself for it. So far, the Druries were completely taken by surprise.

Taara appeared to have success. The arm swung about under full control, extended and descended to the rear hull of the *Seeker*. Working in concert with the crew standing on the wing, the arm opened the Stellar Mach vent coverings. The vents swung open like the cover of a book. It took only a minute or two.

Next, Taara swung the arm down to dock level. Gwendolyn, still holding her FEDULA, approached the stack of coils and inspected them. She turned and said something to Taara.

The huge, towering arm came gently down. Per Gwendolyn's direction, Taara lifted off the coil stacked on top and set it aside. She then picked up the one that had been underneath it and turned it around, showing it to Gwendolyn, who carefully looked it over. Approving, Taara then hoisted it up, swung it over, and carefully placed it into position in Stellar Mach 6. She then gently closed the SM vent.

It was that easy. One down, one to go.

Taara brought the arm back to the dock. Gwendolyn dismissed the next coil, settling on the bottom one. Taara lifted it, showed it to her, and then hoisted it up.

"Whas' goin' on?" came a loud voice from below.

There was Innocent Drury on fast approach—Creation, Stenstrom had become mesmerized with watching the loading of the coils.

"Who're you?" he cried as Gwendolyn faced him with her FEDULA.

Stenstrom aimed and fired.

Missed.

Three Lemmuels appeared from their work and proceeded to that area of the dock at a run.

Stenstrom cocked and fired, getting one, and then another. They fell hard, one tumbling into the water with a rough splash.

Taara, using the robotic arm, swung it over and, still holding the coil, squashed the third Lemmuel roughly to the dock, little blue squares skittering away from his flattened body.

Gwendolyn and Innocent were in close quarters, and Stenstrom couldn't fire without possibly hitting her. She dropped her FEDULA and got behind him, using wrestling holds and grappling techniques to neutralize his considerable strength advantage.

They fell to the floor. Such a mismatch couldn't last, and Innocent managed to pry her off him. He got her down and raised his arm to hit her. Such a blow would be her death.

He was knocked back a few steps—Taara unloaded a silenced burst from her SK into his chest and he toppled away from Gwendolyn. Clear, Stenstrom fired and got him in the back, dropping him. Some of the crew came out of their hiding places and helped Gwendolyn while Taara quickly swung the coil over to the *Seeker*, dropped it into SM position 13, and closed the vent.

That done, Taara brought the arm back down to the dock and positioned its massive fingers into a loose fist, where the crew climbed in and secured themselves. Gwendolyn and Taara joined them. Taara looked up and motioned for Stenstrom to come down and join them as well.

They froze.

Chance Drury appeared, followed by five Clems and an Innocent. They saw the group huddled in the fingers of the robotic arm.

Stenstrom acted. "Hallo', boys!" he shouted loudly. "Did you miss me?"

All heads turned to him. Chance smiled a bit. "I assume I am speaking to Paymaster Stenstrom of the *Seeker*. *Je suis correct?*" Chance said in a clear voice.

"Aye!"

Chance considered his response. "What are you hoping to accomplish here, good sir? You must know you are in a desperate situation. For you and your people here, this docking bay is the pit of hell. *Usted quemará en ello.*"

"Is it? You were good enough to pay me a visit, so I thought I'd respond in kind."

Out of the corner of his eye, Stenstrom thought he could see a line of people moving toward the *Seeker*. They were difficult to see—invisible almost. The Merians' belt—they must be able to move invisibly when they wish.

Stenstrom had to keep the Druries occupied—this was the critical moment.

"You feel like dying today, Chance? You know I am going to kill you, right?"

He laughed. "You do not seem to understand. We are eternal. We cannot be put to ground. Our hearts cannot be stopped, our voices cannot be silenced. *Besser als Sie haben versucht.*"

"But, you already are put to ground, dust-eater. You are dead, long dead, tainting the earth with your foulness somewhere—and I'll wager all the worms that had the misfortune to feed upon your carcass probably died of a stomachache. You and your three uncouth brothers died four hundred years ago, and, even when you were alive, you weren't really men, were you—you were cowering jackals, feasting on the weak and the helpless while tucking tail and running full flight from anyone who showed an ounce of strength. Now, look at you—nothing more than a bit of bad data, imprinted and downloaded. You are four tin cans playing at being men, dreaming of foul things, and I am going to see you to an end once and for all!"

Chance had a good chuckle. "A-heheh. *C'est un fait?* That bipedal, flesh-and-blood lung sack you're wearing is overrated in my mind. And, let's be honest, you are just as much a robot as I am." He glanced at the people in the robotic arm. "Are these your fellows here, your devotees—they must be. I am going to order them abused, *viole*, and then order them slain . . . right now, while you watch. Clem, fetch that lot!"

The robotic arm suddenly began moving by itself—Taara apparently prepared a pre-recorded sequence for the arm to follow. The arm lifted them high into the air and swung them over the *Seeker*.

Chance, quick as could be, worked his hands and created a long lance of yellow squares. Before Stenstrom could react, he hurled the lance at the arm, its tail fire lighting in midair. The people cradled into the arm's fist jumped out and fell onto the *Seeker's* wing just as the lance struck the arm and exploded like a missile, rocking the arm on its long mount.

Stenstrom lined his guns up and fired.

Missed, Chance ducked away. He fired again, going for Chance as the Clems and the Innocent moved about in confusion. Chance was a slippery customer, and appeared to guard his existence carefully. He ducked, moved away, and ducked again, allowing Clem to take one in the chest for him.

Ah!—Chance was cornered by a pier—his head swiveling in fright. Stenstrom cocked, aimed and fired.

The hammer fell. Nothing happened!

Damn! The cinnabar striker cracked. He aimed with the other pistol and fired, getting Innocent. Chance made a break for it. He ripped out of his clothes, assuming his blocky robotic form, his cluster of yellow squares buzzing about in an agitated state on his robotic frame.

Stenstrom replaced his striker with a fresh cinnabar from his coat and resumed firing. He hit Chance in the arm, and again in the shoulder—yellow squares fell away. Again, in this decentralized form, the NTH couldn't kill him at a shot.

Chance stopped, and formed two long lances of yellow squares. He then hurled them in Stenstrom's direction. He hauled himself over the side and plummeted as the lances exploded above him.

"He's there, he's there!" Chance yelled in a robotic voice. Clems, Innocents, and a horde of Lemmuels poured onto the dock from all quarters.

Stenstrom returned to the shadows. He gunned down one Drury after the next, the dock becoming quickly littered with their fallen bodies. Colorful squares of red, green and blue, like children's blocks, mingled.

"Where'd he go?" Clem cried.

"Use your antennas, you ponderous slugs!" Chance roared in his robotic voice. "Find him! Kill him!" Of all the Druries, Chance seemed the most at peace with being a machine, while the others appeared to prefer to stay man-shaped, as if to convince themselves that they really were men, not machines.

Several Innocents expanded into pulsating green masses, their head screens unfurling and antennas popping out.

"Thar' he is!" Innocent screamed, his cluster of antennae turning in Stenstrom's direction.

Stenstrom fired at his head screen, where it immediately went dead. Innocent staggered about and fell, his green squares abandoning his body frame like rats from a sinking ship.

Behind them, Stenstrom saw, just for a moment, the main sensor on the *Seeker* light up and then snap back off.

Come on, Gwendolyn, get that ship working!

He continued his barrage. Druries were falling like lead weights.

There was an angry clamor from behind him.

Druries were now pouring out of the assembly area; some were clothed, others nude, and some were in their robotic shape. Additionally, the tiny squares fleeing the Druries whom he'd blinded were coming together in a colonial fashion, forming rudimentary, inchworm-like constructs of red, blue, and green squares. Stenstrom saw several of the inchworms forming on the dock.

"*Hay, chingado!* Do not allow the rogue cells to form together; they might create an Intelledrone!" Chance cried.

Some of the Druries ceased their attack and began stepping on the inchworms or pulling them apart. A Clem picked up a particularly large one, its tail wrapping around his neck.

Stenstrom fired, killing Clem, where he and the colorful, wormlike Mecon fell into the water.

The caustic scene Stenstrom had envisioned had finally arrived. Druries were everywhere, and they were all spoiling for his hide, the dock filling with the sounds of cursing, splashing, slapping metallic feet, and booming explosions.

But, as he had hoped, all eyes were on him—the *Seeker* was clear, and his people were aboard.

Chance and ten Clems appeared to be directing the action from the rear. The Clems were creating a steady stream of red, lance-like missiles and were firing them off in quick style. Explosions blossomed.

Stenstrom could not stay where he was. He gunned down two naked Clems and made his way toward the *Demophalon John*.

He climbed the side and got on top of it, raining shots down on them. Fired lances came up at him in answer, where they exploded against the side of the *Demophalon John*, the sturdy ship able to ward off the brunt of the explosion. Lemmuels climbed up after him—he gunned them back down. They stubbornly clung to their man-shape, which he could kill with a shot. Several robotic Clems came up, all blocky and red, and he shot their head screens, blinding them, their squares scattering off and falling into the water.

Stenstrom was cornered; Druries everywhere, a steady barrage of missiles incoming. There wasn't much left for him to do but plunge into the water and start swimming.

He jumped, seeing a long fall in front of him.

Something seized him by the coat. He was hauled back, spun overhead, and slammed to the hull.

Things spun around. He thought he could see a Lemmuel standing over him, the hem of his coat in his hand.

Stenstrom raised and fired, hitting Lemmuel in the gut where he dropped. A Clem fell on him. His raised his fist and rocked Stenstrom in the right shoulder blade. He dimly felt and heard a number of bones break with the hit. He wretched blood.

Innocent stood over him. "Oh, whas' the matter, Gov? Thought you was strong?"

He reared up and brought his foot down on the back of Stenstrom's leg. His knee collapsed and his thigh bone splintered.

"Bring him to me!" Chance squealed from below. "Bring him here! Bring him here now!"

Clem picked the shattered Stenstrom up and threw him down to the dock, where he fell into the water.

Two Lemmuels roughly fished him out. Dripping, he was thrown down on the dock.

Chance approached, a buzzing collection of yellow squares. Now that Stenstrom appeared to be hopelessly quelled, Chance compressed back into man-form. His head screen rolled up and descended into his chest. The myriad of yellow squares flipped around, sliding compactly into place. Flesh oozed. Soon, a scrawny, naked Chance stood there. A Clem came to his side and draped a coat over him, which he held shut with his right hand.

Overhead, two golden crow-like creatures flapped down and landed on his shoulder. The Kestrals.

"Good Paymaster," Chance said in a soft, almost tender voice, "well met, again." He took a deep breath. "Oh, dear, you made a good showing of it, I'll say." He looked around at the piles of fallen Druries. He moved his hands and created a long barb from yellow squares.

"Better watch him, Chance," Innocent said. "He was real strong on his ship."

"Yes, I recall that, a-heheh. He tore my hands clean off, didn't he? You say we're machines, robots, Mecons, whatever you wish to call us—you looked rather robotic yourself as we battled. I clearly recall another fellow who once did the same thing. You may have heard of him; his name was Darius Jones. I can remember his face, plain as day, and you say I'm a machine, for I have my memories just like you have yours. The thing of it is, as I recall, on the surface Darius Jones could do a number of remarkable things—however, way down here, under the sea, under the stone, he couldn't really do much of anything, except cook, for which he had a delicate touch, ah-hehehe. Something about the stars gave him power. I'm assuming it's much the same with you. No starlight down here, ah-hehehe. Too bad."

He glanced back at the *Seeker*. "Clem, take a group to the *Seeker*. Board her, scour her, and kill any you find. I've a suspicion our friend here has freed our Trogs."

"What about the crew for the *Seeker*?"

"We'll hook-in others. No, no, this current lot dies. *Entiendo?*"

"Aye!" Clem turned to Stenstrom and drove his arm down on his shattered shoulder. "I'll save ya' a leg or two, Gov! Camon', boys!"

A group trundled off in a laughing gaggle, spitting on Stenstrom as they passed.

Chance smiled. "So then, Paymaster, I must consider this carefully. What can I do to cause you the maximum distress? *Les choix.*"

He took several steps forward, using his yellow barb as a walking stick. He poked Stenstrom once or twice with it. "What say you? Any thoughts?"

He hauled back and chopped Stenstrom's right hand off at the wrist. "There, a hand for a hand seems only fair, wouldn't you say?"

Stenstrom reacted very little. He just lay there, spewing blood. His fingers twitched.

Chance continued. "I suppose the gratuitous spectacle of letting you watch your fellows aboard the *Seeker* die holds sway—has the maximum shock value. Then, I think I could do with putting you in the tank and turning you into my own personal *Killanjo* slave. That has great appeal, I must admit—though you shall be of limited use with only one hand."

Chance's eyes lit up. "Ohhhh, *je l'ai!* I know. We'll set up a little ring here on the dock, and force your fellows to fight each other to the death—that always makes for great sport. You'd be surprised how life-long friends turn on each other when confronted by such a quaint topic as death. It is really quite a thing to see."

Chance turned to several Lemmuels. "Clear a space for these people. We're going to have a show. Clem!" he barked.

"Aye!" came a response.

"On, second thought, bring any you find to me!"

"We're not findin' anybody!"

"They're there. Keep looking. *Chcę ich przy życiu!*"

As several Lemmuels began clearing a squared-off space on the dock, the Kestrals took flight.

They transformed into two, toga-clad females. They strode up to Stenstrom. One of them picked up his trembling body and closely examined him.

The Kestrals spoke in gibberish.

"I detect he has a destroyed collarbone and shoulder, along with a shattered right knee and femur-bone, and he's missing a hand. He is no longer a threat," Chance answered.

The Kestrals mumbled something else.

"Yes, Elders are rather fragile," Chance replied. "Very poor construction."

The Kestral picked up his severed hand and ate it whole, crunching it up and then swallowing. She then began digging about in Stenstrom's broken shoulder. He squirmed slightly, in muted agony.

The Kestral found a large piece of shattered bone, and tried to pull it out of the wound.

He stifled a pain-clogged shriek.

From the tower of the *Seeker,* a bullet-shaped ship came blasting out. It circled, overhead. A Clem fell headless from the ship and splashed into the water.

The *Westminster!* Stenstrom could see A-Ram's large hat through the front glass.

"*Pour l'amour do Dieu!* Destroy that vessel!" Chance cried, ducking for cover.

Lances of red, green, and blue went up; the tiny ship rose and fell to avoid them.

The hatch opened, and a figure came leaping down. Steel flashed and the Kestral fell, quickly dissolving into amber goo.

It was Gwendolyn and her FEDULA.

She came to Stenstrom's side and tried to pull him up.

The other Kestral reacted badly. She raised her hand and a red cone of light shot out, bathing Gwendolyn in it.

She dropped her FEDULA and screamed.

Chance watched with glee. "Burn her, burn her up! Ah-hehehe!!"

Gwendolyn dropped to her knees.

Then three silver daggers entered the Kestral's arm and chest.

Three MARZABLES from Stenstrom. He let three more fly, getting her in the trunk.

The Kestral stood there looking at the daggers sticking out of her.

He shook his good hand and three more MAZARBLES appeared. He threw them, piercing the Kestral three times in the forehead.

She appeared a bit puzzled, then fell apart into an amber mess.

He crawled to Gwendolyn's side. She was slightly smoking.

And there was Chance. He reached down and picked them both up by the scruff of the neck. "I really didn't like them anyway," he said shaking their bodies. "You have done me a nice favor, actually. Now, with that lot gone, we can truly lay some terror on the League. We'll raise an army of skinless demons and sail out in ghost ships. We'll hit Kana hard and split the League in two, fading back to the shadows whenever we like."

The *Westminster* came around and dropped height, skimming the docks and plowing into a host of Druries, flattening some, knocking others into the water. Chance raised up Stenstrom and Gwendolyn and presented them. "I have your people, here! I'll kill them nice as you please!"

The *Westminster* banked away, and was struck by a red lance. It smoked, was hit again and crashed into the water.

11

—The Star's Revenge—

Chance gave a cry of victory. Stenstrom was thrown to the floor, surrounded by a gallery of Druries who whooped and laughed. Innocent stepped forward and gave him a hard kick to the midsection sending him flying.

"Yeah, mate . . . this is gonna' be just grand. I've got lots a' plans for you. We're gonna' be real chums 'fore long."

He kicked him again.

"Leave him alone!" Gwendolyn screamed, reaching out for him. Several Lemmuels held her down, and one kicked her smoking FEDULA away.

They laughed. "Oh, I hear a lady cryin' out for a little attention! You feelin' hungry, Paymaster?" Lemmuel asked.

"He looks real hungry," Clem said.

Lemmuel brandished a small knife. "Well then, let's feed 'im!"

Gwendolyn struggled, but they held her down. Lemmuel pulled her coat and shirt away revealing skin. He began cutting, Gwendolyn screamed.

As the army of Druries closed in, something caught their attention high above.

"What in the name of Green Grass is that?" Chance said, leaning back, mouth open.

High above, something floated. It was some sort of round globe, yellowish, wreathed in an undulating column of hissing red smoke.

Stenstrom glanced at it—it looked, from his sister's frequent description, like the Star of Merian.

"For my children . . ." an ethereal voice said. "whom you so cruelly murdered . . ."

The dock filled with a twisting funnel of fog. The Druries were making a terrible racket, yet the whole place fell into an unnatural calm as the fog took hold.

It's the road, the Merian's Road, Stenstrom thought.

High above, through the fog, four gleaming points of bluish light appeared.

Four stars in a rectangular constellation shone down bathing in dock in starry light.

Camalopardus.

Stenstrom was filled with starlight, and his smashed body became whole once again with the Sisters' Power. His bones were mended, his hand regrown. He threw off the Druries and knocked them away from Gwendolyn. He took Innocent to the ground and utterly destroyed him. Alone, he flew into their ranks, toppling them blow after blow.

He tore at them, pulling them apart, smashing them to bits.

He ripped the manufactured flesh from their bodies and hung them with it.

Robotic arms and legs, sculpted heads, and colored squares piled high on the dock in a mountain of metal and wire viscera.

The Druries had never known such terror.

Chance went running. He headed down the dock moving as fast as he could. "Kill the woman! Kill the woman!" he shrieked.

The Druries came at Gwendolyn, trying to get to her. Stenstrom stood over her, smashing, destroying.

A Clem created a lance, reared back and threw it. It sped toward Gwendolyn.

Stenstrom caught it in flight, spun it around and threw it back toward the Clem. It exploded.

There was a rumbling from the water. A towering creature made of a patchwork of red, green, and blue squares burst into the air. Metal tentacles reached upward, grasping the remains of the *Demophalon John* and the pole-mounted robotic arms mounted on the dock.

"Good Creation! Intelledrone!" a Clem yelled. "It's a big one! Get it, kill it—It'll be the end of us all!"

The Druries turned their attention to the robotic beast and made to engage it in battle. Tentacles came down; screaming Druries were lifted and pulled into the water.

Two crewmen Wafted onto the dock near Stenstrom in a cloud. He picked Gwendolyn up and handed her to them. "She's wounded. Get the lieutenant and any in the *Westminster* back into the *Seeker!* Get the ship out of here by any means you can!" he shouted, and they bore her away.

The battle at the water's edge was desperate and near hopeless. The raging robotic monster in the water was rapidly getting bigger. It reached up and snapped the poles mounting the robotic arms like twigs. It then consumed the arms, adding them to itself, the huge fingers of the arms opening and closing, infused with a new colonial consciousness.

The Druries assailed it with exploding lances, blowing large pieces of it off, only to have those pieces replaced almost instantly.

It seized the bullet-shaped hull of the Westminster and set to work on it. Stenstrom thought he saw the expansion of a Waft cloud in the cockpit as the robotic monster incorporated the ship into itself, the hull being plopped on like a rudimentary head.

The giant Intelledrone reached out with its metal tentacles and seized the flailing, screaming Chance Drury. Stenstrom stood and watched with pleasure as it commenced to beat his body roughly against the hull of the *Westminster*. It reminded him of Lt. Kilos from his *New Faith* days, and how she had a bad habit of cracking walnuts with her forehead in the mess.

Bang, bang, bang. Chance Drury's robot body fell apart into a host of yellow squares instantly absorbed by the Intelledrone.

Explosion after explosion rocked its growing body. With flailing metal tentacles, it seized one Drury after another and pulled them apart, taking the tiny robots making up their bodies and adding them onto itself.

Through the chaotic din of shouting and monstrous bellowing, another sound came to the front, a great whistling roar from nowhere growing louder and more throaty with every passing moment threatening to deafen all on the dock. There was only one thing that made such a terrible, glorious sound.

It was the *Seeker*, its engines spinning up, its dormant systems coming live and proud. Its main sensor came to a dim but steady glow lighting up the dock. It strained against the shackles the Druries had thrown across it, throwing them aside, freeing itself. The *Seeker* had been mute and silent since the Admiralty had scuttled her, now she would roar.

Stenstrom listened and watched the ship break free. Now, whatever happened to him on the dock didn't matter. He had done his job, his people were safe.

Stenstrom found his lost NTHs and put them back into his sash. Let these monstrosities consume each other. Good riddance in any case, and he could only hope the Druries suffered mightily in the process.

He saw something come running back out of the assembly room. It was a boxy, funnel-breasted robot with the word DUNCE painted on its torso. It was running fast on spindly legs, sort of high-stepping, knee-kicking as it ran.

It was Chance Drury, back again, wearing the DUNCE body; it had to be him, for it carried itself like Chance did. Apparently no other bodies were left for him to wear.

"To the *Heade*! Get to the *Heade*!" several Clems screamed.

"No!" Chance yelled in a panic from the DUNCE's latex mouth. "You stand here and fight this beast! I shall go to the *Heade*!"

He was carrying four metal tablets, each one stained red, blue, green, and yellow, which he clutched to his soup-can breast as though they were precious. He headed for the levels above at a high-stepping run.

Those tablets must be the source code information for reconstituting the Druries.

"Chance!" Stenstrom roared, following at a run. Climbing a ladder, Stenstrom saw him standing at a large control panel. Pressing buttons, he opened a set of doors somewhere high above and a wall of water at high pressure came rushing into the docks, ready to wash away any standing in its path. He then turned and ran into a long corridor.

Stenstrom was hot on his heels. He entered the corridor just in time to see a door closing at the far end. He charged, covering the distance quickly, and crashed through it. Through the door was a small control-room with a chair and numerous monitors. There was a hinged, yellow device sitting on the floor. As Stenstrom entered, it came to life and sprang shut, like a loaded mousetrap and then exploded, devastating the room. When the smoke cleared, the room was destroyed, the door had been blown off its frame, the control desk melted to slag and was on fire; however, Stenstrom appeared fine and unfazed—even his clothes seemed untouched.

He could hear the powerful rushing of water behind him. The place was rapidly flooding.

There was a burning staircase at the far side of the room. Stenstrom ran up them. Atop the stairs was a short hallway paneled in silvery metal.

He topped the stairs and ran down the hallway. The hallway opened up into a dock, similar to the one below, only it was much smaller.

There, mounted on a robotic sling, was the *Heade-on-the-Hearth*. He saw DUNCE-Chance clattering up the closing gangway, arms and legs flailing as he ran, carrying his tablets. His blonde wig fell off and floated on the water.

Quickly, the strange ship coiled and came to life, like a warhorse confined in a tiny stall.

A bank of guns mounted on the *Heade's* port side rotated in his direction. He dove out of the way as a hail of explosive fire splintered the doorway.

Behind him, a surge of water came rushing in as the dock quickly began to flood. He thrashed through the water. He reached out and found the girders of the *Heade*. He locked on and gripped hard as a set of doors opened ahead. With a clank, the ship surged out of the flooded dock and soared down a tight, twisting tunnel. The tunnel suddenly headed upward as Stenstrom held on for dear life. He became vaguely aware that the *Heade* was consistently smashing against the side of the tunnel in an obvious attempt to scrape him off. He could feel the pressure of the ship against his body and the roughness of the tunnel wall.

Ahead, a pressure hatch opened with a dark stain of water suspended high above via containment. At speed, his coat flapping like a flag in a stiff breeze, the *Heade* surged through the containment into the pitch black of the water.

The lights went out, and Stenstrom felt the crushing squeeze of hundreds of feet of water on top of him. He could see the occasional flash of strobe lights mounted on the *Heade* and the bluish glow from the engines. The water felt rather warm as he surged up through the depths. Warm blackness turned a greenish-blue, to an eruption out of the water into the stormy sky.

The *Heade* quickly gained altitude as Stenstrom hung on. Having no issue maintaining his purchase on the ship, he began hand-over-handing to make his way to the crew capsule about seventy feet ahead.

He could hear the rush of wind and the roar from the engines as the ship rocketed skyward. He pulled off several large pieces of girder and tossed it down into the intake of the nearest engine.

The engine sputtered and flashed. He tore off more metal and tossed it in.

The engine exploded.

The vessel leveled off at several thousand feet and descended a bit. Stenstrom pulled more pieces off the ship and threw them aside as he climbed forward, ripping off a thruster and other assorted bits.

The *Heade* lowered to about a hundred feet above the water and slowed to a near stop, the damaged engine smoking in an inky manner.

Something in the water below caught his attention.

A huge, dark mass formed in the water. Something leapt out, spanning high into the air. It was coal black, streaming with water. It was long and tubular like a massive earthworm about ten feet wide and an unknown length long. It had a round, flattened head with a circular, tooth-ringed mouth like a hagfish, and its serrated, ivory-white teeth stood out from its dead-black body. It had an unbroken ring of red, beady eyes placed in a line just behind its mouth.

That's a Cronyn, Stenstrom thought as the nightmare creature approached, mouth open. *I'm about to be eaten by a Cronyn!*

The Cronyn came up quick, gurgling, and it took Stenstrom and a fair portion of the *Heade* in a single bite.

12

—Words with the Cronyns—

He felt a commotion of deforming metal and sucking innards as he slid into the deep belly of the Cronyn.

He saw an image of his father and his sister, Lyra, sitting in his study.

The NTHs can slay anything . . . no matter how huge and powerful . . . his father had said.

In the slimy mess, he reached down and found his NTHs. He pulled them, cocked and fired. Surely such a vast beast would not be harmed by his tiny pistols, LosCapricos or not.

After a minute or two, he decided to try and crawl out. He moved past the bitten-off girders of the *Heade* and moved into what looked like a tooth-lined gullet. He saw gray light and a row of impressive-looking triangular teeth ahead. He was able to stand and he splashed through the ankle-deep water.

He emerged at the Cronyn's mouth. The thing was dead—it had to be. It floated at the water's surface like a long balloon, its black body, hundreds of feet long, was still.

He climbed up and stood atop the creature. He was all alone, the sky threatening to storm overhead. He looked around. The *Heade* was nowhere to be seen.

He checked himself out. He seemed fine—his destroyed shoulder and knee were completely repaired. His hand, regrown, looked just like his hand should. Even his HRN coat, having been blown-up, smashed and scraped against the tunnel wall, appeared unharmed.

Off in the distance, he thought he could see something sticking out of the water, something wing-like and metallic.

Wait . . . was that, was that the wing of the *Seeker*??

Yes, yes, it was the *Seeker*, and by the angle it was protruding from the water, she was rolled over to her starboard side, mostly flooded and submerged.

He looked down at the water; there was debris everywhere, flotsam from the now flooded Kestral tank far below.

And, there were bits of the *Seeker* too, pieces of metal . . . and bodies.

There were bodies everywhere.

No, no . . . what had happened?

He saw a Pilgrim of Merian floating face down, and some crewmen. There was a blue coat mixed in and a dead face. Was it . . . Gwendolyn?

He dropped down into the water. He pulled her up, her face white and puffy, her eyes sullen in the rectus of death.

"Oh, Gwen," he said stroking her drenched hair, "what happened? I saw the ship--- you had her ready to go. I saw it light up."

He embraced her dead body, as water slopped out of her lolled mouth. Her drenched hair was a mess. She wouldn't like that—she'd want to be presentable. He smoothed her hair with his hand and straightened her lieutenant's collar. He arraigned the beaded Merian necklace hanging at her throat.

Her necklace.

Wait . . .

He looked down. He was still wearing the necklace she had given to him. Alesta was going to give him a Merian necklace to put on, but Gwen wanted him to wear hers.

Wear mine, Bel, she had said, offering it to him as a gift.

Here it was around his neck.

And there it was around hers as well. She hadn't gotten another one yet—she didn't have one as they departed.

Thunder and lightning . . .

Alesta said the Merian's necklace can protect one from the unreal.

Pelting rain . . .

"This is a trick; it isn't real." He held Gwendolyn to him. "This isn't real!"

Illusions . . .

Bobbing on the water.

He reached up and took the necklace into his hand. "Get out of my mind, Cronyns . . ."

He gripped the necklace hard. "Get out!"

CRACK!

He was standing on the dead body of a Cronyn that was rapidly sinking into the storm-tossed sea. Thunder crashed and long strokes of lightning lit up the sky at frequent intervals. Huge waves pounded into its black body. Its mouth, open in death, was filling with each passing wave.

Stenstrom was hanging onto one of the dead Cronyn's teeth. Around him, black masses moved through the water.

One approached. It broke the water and reared up, towering overhead—the black, wormlike segments, the open mouth. The teeth. The eyes.

Stenstrom aimed and fired both his NTHs. The shots hit the gigantic Cronyn. It immediately gave a deflating sort of groan and fell back into the water with slap, creating a huge wave that nearly pitched him into the torrent.

Another Cronyn came out of the water, this time showing only the crest of its back.

Stenstrom killed it just the same.

The storm raged, causing the dead Cronyn bodies to nudge against each other in the whitewash.

Suddenly, he was no longer floating on the wind-whipped water. He was back in the middle of his old dream—back in the sand pit behind the Belmont Manor with Lady Vendra's spring-loaded trap.

His sisters, Lyra and Virginia, were there, staring at him.

"What is this?" he said in a boy's voice, hardened a bit with maturity.

Lyra looked at him and spoke. *"We wish to talk . . ."* Her mouth was full of row after row of serrated teeth.

Cronyn teeth.

"Why have you brought me here? Why this dream?"

"Because you have never really left this place. You remain here to this day. You should have died in this sand pit."

"Yet, I did not. Are you trying to frighten me?"

"We simply wish to talk," Virginia said. The image looked like her, but it didn't act like her in any way. And, there were her teeth, off-color, serrated, rowed.

"There is nothing to talk about! I am going to slay every one of you, as you see I can easily do!"

"Why do you wish to kill us?"

"Why? Because you are evil. Look what you have done? You just tried to kill me three times."

"You were attacked, you defended yourself. We bear you no malice for that. We are not evil, nor are we unreasonable. We live here in this place; we raise our children in the depths. We love our children. We simply wish to survive. We must eat too—our children must eat. Do you deny any living creature the right to exist, to fairly hunt for food?" Virginia said.

"Is this the lament you gave to Darius Jones centuries ago, when he came to kill you as well?"

"It is not a lament; it is simply the truth—it was true then and it is true now. Darius Jones understood. Here we exist as sentient beings, with bellies that need filling, just as your belly needs filling. We have harmed no one in centuries, save for what was brought to us as fair game." Lyra said.

"You invaded our minds, tortured us with vivid dioramas."

"That is an aspect of our feeding, true enough. We give to those we feed upon what they want most to sustain them."

"What about the people on Bazz whom your illusions killed? What about the crew of the *Demophalon John*—I could hear them screaming."

"We cannot know how beings shall react when confronted with their greatest wants. We attempt to be kind; however, we do not overly concern ourselves with it. Are you not humane to your cattle as well? We shall offer you fair trade . . ." Virginia said.

"Trade, what do you have to trade? I have you by the hip, and I'll chase you into the depths if I have to."

"Your ship, and the lives nurtured within—we have it 'by the hip', as you say. We will give you your ship, and you may take it and go. And then we will vanish, and you shall not find us again."

"My ship?"

"Yes, even now it is struggling to the surface. We could easily sink her, a mis-pressed button here, an opened airlock there—the odd necklaces they wear will not protect them from all of us in concert," Lyra said.

They stood there looking at him standing in the sand.

"What say you, 'Man like Darius Jones'?" Lyra asked. *"Our lives for their lives, an even trade."*

Stenstrom thought about it. He looked behind him, to the soft sand where he knew hiding just beneath the surface was a deadly trap. "Shall I walk away, knowing there is death lurking beneath the sand just waiting for the unwary to spring it? Will I have blood on my hands if I let you go?"

He thought some more. "I do hear validity in what you say, and I do not actively try to be a hypocrite. You do have the right to live."

He took a step back into the pit.

SNAP!! The trap lurched out of the sand. He held the trap open with his tiny hands, slowly mangling the metal. "And we have the right to resist being hunted, and to know of the dangers that exist. I shall alert my people what lurks here, and I cannot predict their response."

"Do what you will—that is your right. Then it is agreed. Take your ship and be away. Be at your guard, however, for we shall continue to hunt and you shall not find us here again."

Virginia smiled, and it was hideous. *"Perhaps one day we shall play again, 'Man like Darius Jones', and perhaps it shall be you making the bargains next time, and not we."*

The dream ended. Stenstrom was back in the stormy water, but not much of the Cronyn remained above surface. He leapt to one of the nearby dead ones and stood on top.

The black masses moving through the water came up for a moment in dripping, towering lines, and then dove deep.

Stenstrom stood there for a few minutes as the dead Cronyn steadily became waterlogged.

In the far distance, he became aware of a small but growing pool of light on the storm-battered surface of the water. A circle of dim, green light appeared, strengthening to gray and then white as the *Seeker* crashed, nose first, from the water about a thousand yards away, its brightly lit main sensor making a long, rain-clogged spotlight in front of it. The nose splashed back down in a cascade of white water as the wings surfaced and settled. Lights glittered on the tower section and the running beacons strobed on the wings. The engines screeched as they came up to compression. The nose of the ship came about and caught Stenstrom and the bobbing bodies of the Cronyns in its powerful beam.

The *Seeker* approached, plowing through the water, getting bigger by the moment. Stenstrom then launched himself from the Cronyn's body and soared into the air. He landed on the soaked hull, found a hatch and banged on it.

The hatch opened a few minutes later and there was Taara, Gwendolyn and a few crewmen.

"Elder's Balls!" Taara cried. "Bel!"

She came forward trying to grab him. "I'm all wet, Taara," he said, dripping as he climbed down.

"I don't give a shit!" she cried, throwing her arms around him with a splat. "Holy God, it's good to see you!"

Gwendolyn too came forward. "We thought you lost! Oh, we thought you lost!" she said hugging him around the neck. "Welcome home, Bel."

"You were wounded, Gwen, on the dock. Are you all right?"

"I'm fine now, Bel. I'm fine."

They made their way to the bridge. It was utterly strange for Stenstrom, seeing lights and crewmen walking about the corridors after the lightless, silent journey they'd had so far.

"Taara and I have tried to assign the crew to places where they might serve best. They're not overly familiar with a *Straylight* vessel, but they should do fine. I'm assuming you'll be wanting to conscript them aboard at once."

"Sure will. What's the status of the ship?"

"We were able to gen up some power while at dock, enough to run the gas compression engines and escape the depths; however, we still need to properly calibrate the coils—we'll not make orbit without the coils in calibration," Gwendolyn said.

"How long before we can make sail?"

"About half an hour. I've several crew working on it even as we speak."

"Sounds good. Go ahead and take whomever you need to help you. I'm to the bridge."

Gwendolyn looked like she wanted him to follow her for a moment, and then ran off, grabbing a few crewmen along the way.

Stenstrom continued to the bridge, Taara following.

"How did you get out of the docks?" he asked.

"It was rough, Bel—that big monster down there was ripping things up hard. It ate just about all of the Druries and then started working on the remains of the *Demophalon John*, pulling it down and eating it too. Then, the big bastard turned to us."

"What happened?"

"A-Ram drove the ship backwards out of the docking bay, smashing through a few a retaining barriers along the way. The monster started chasing us through the water but got smashed up as the place began to collapse. That was a Bazz-sized monster. He's probably still down there making a mess."

They got to the lift and Stenstrom went to pry the door open.

"What are you doing, silly?" Taara asked as she pressed the button and the door opened."

"Sorry, old habits die hard."

They arrived at the bridge and the doors slid open. On the bridge was a soft layer of chatter. A-Ram was standing at the helm, and several crewmen were manning the various sensing positions. There were even a few Merians there lending a hand. The odd screens Lemmuel had installed were still there on the Missive's Panel, only now they were lighting up with data—several crew were leaning over the panels trying to figure out what was being displayed. Someone stood at the Com, trying to get familiar with it. Lady Alesta was sitting in the captain's chair, looking back at A-Ram.

Just like Countess Sygillis used to do . . .

Taara walked out of the lift. "Captain on the bridge!" she said proudly.

All eyes turned to Stenstrom.

"Creation, it's good to see you, Bel!" A-Ram said.

Stenstrom clapped him on the shoulder. "And you. Well done getting the ship out of there in one piece, A-Ram."

"It was touch and go for a bit, but here we are. This is one tough old bird."

Stenstrom turned to the crew and addressed them. "Well, I don't know your names, as of yet, but you all are most certainly welcome here. If you don't know who I am, my name is Paymaster Stenstrom, Lord of Belmont-South Tyrol. I am the captain of this ship. I have conscripted Lt. Gwendolyn to the position of ship's engineer, and she's working at this moment to get the ship operational. I would like to duly conscript all of you as well—if any have issue with the conscription, you may disembark once we get back to the League, but I would like to make it clear that I could use every one of you, and if you wish to be conscripted, then your service shall be most appreciated."

"I wish to serve, sir," one of the crew said.

"That goes for me too," someone else said.

"And me as well!"

Stenstrom quieted them down. "I know you have all been through a great deal, as have we all. We've wounded and our clear task is to return to the League as quickly as possible to get them the immediate medical aid they so desperately need. If I had my druthers, I'd rather hunt down Chance Drury, sink him and be done with his wretched hide. However, that task is for the Fleet—we have to look to our own here first."

Stenstrom looked around. "So, let's set to it!"

The crew shouted in unison.

"Right! As soon as Lt. Gwendolyn gives us the go ahead, we're making sail."

The crew resumed what they were doing. A-Ram leaned forward and whispered to Alesta. "*You're sitting in his chair . . .*"

She was startled. "Oh! Oh, I didn't mean to—"

Stenstrom put his hands on her shoulders. "You're fine where you are, my lady. Sit. Be comfortable."

She smiled up at him. "I'm not surprised you are returned to us. I knew the Star would keep you safe—I told Rammy; he was frantic for your safety. I told him."

Stenstrom made his way around the bridge, meeting each of the crew, shaking their hands. He got to the Com. "So, who do we have here?" Stenstrom asked.

"Crewman Clement, sir," the brown-headed man said, shaking his hand. "This is a great pleasure, Captain. We all have heard so much about you, and, I must admit, I felt relieved being with you in the tank. I was certain you would successfully lead us out. I am a gentleman of Mystery. I was the junior Com aboard the *Demophalon John*, but the Com on a *Straylight* is much different. I'm doing my best to get up to speed."

"I'm positive you'll do just fine. Do we have any communications at present?"

"Aye, sir, that we do."

Stenstrom was taken aback—still used to nothing working. "Wow, well then, please send to all Pledged ships at sea: Flash, MFV *Seeker* advises *Heade-on-the-Hearth*, a heavily modified *Webber*-class vessel is at roam in the wildlands between Kana and Onaris, and has been terrorizing this region for some time. It is imperative the *Heade* not escape the area as she is crewed by Kestral-based robotic personages of the Drury Brothers. The *Heade* has been damaged, though the extent of the damage is not known. Advise *Seeker* is unarmed and bearing wounded and shall require immediate assistance to sink or take her a-prize with all speed. That is all."

"Aye, sir, sending message."

He shook his head. "Just that easy, eh?"

"Sir?"

"Never mind."

He turned to Taara. "Taara, where is Morgan-Jeterix?"

"She's down in the dispensary trying to help the civilians."

"We have coils, a crew, communications, and a Hospitaler to boot. I don't know what to do with myself."

13

—Bay 15—

"Would you just look at that piece of man! Come here, you!" Morgan-Jeterix said as she leaned over the patient on the table. She was getting around by using her Jet Staff as a crutch. Stenstrom and Taara were standing in the doorway to the dispensary.

She threw the staff aside and hobbled up to Stenstrom where she put her arms around him and held him tight. "Creation, I missed you!"

Stenstrom laughed. "That's a fine sentiment, Morgan, but you only just met me a few hours ago."

"So? I feel I've known you forever. And just look how handsome, I'm going to have that mask off you before long."

He took a good hard look at her—Morgan was certainly a beautiful woman. And, something else, she transformed before his eyes her skin turning a distinct shade of blue, her smooth skin painted in fanciful strokes from an invisible brush. On her left check and brow was a golden crest depicting a burning globe—the crest of the Sisterhood of Light and, orbiting her head was a single word: *Vida*.

"What is 'Vida'?" he asked.

Morgan was astonished. "You see that?"

"I see the word 'Vida' circling your head. I also see your skin has been painted blue and the official Crest of the Sisterhood of Light is tattooed on your right check."

"The word 'Vida' is Vith for: 'Empath'. My House is branded Certified Empaths by the Sisters and they mark us in a 4-D tattoo so they may easily recognize us, the blue skin, the crest, the word, but only the Sisters should be able to see it."

"I see it now just fine."

Morgan smiled in a seductive fashion and pulled him in close. "Do you like it?" she whispered. "It covers my body. I can show you more . . ."

Stenstrom was finding his thoughts addled, the furnace of his passions just beginning to stoke. This 4-D tattoo covering Morgan's body was the most seductive thing he'd ever seen.

He quickly pulled away and changed the topic. Morgan and a few Merians had the civilians laid out on the tables, and some were on the floor. Several Merians were leaning over them, applying a thick, brackish-looking ointment to their blackened skin. "How are these people doing?" he asked.

"They need the League sure enough," Morgan said, "but they're doing as well as can be expected. I found the stores here in the dispensary nearly empty except for a few sacks of dry soda. The Merians, though, found a quantity of lard in the galley, some salts, and a case of grape brandy which they mixed into a simple but effective salve. With it, their skin is moistened and somewhat refreshed. They should rest easy until we return to the League."

A case of brandy? The brandy he was supposed to deliver to Bazz or else??

Taara spoke up. "That brandy? Did they use all of it?"

One of the Merians looked up, the green sleeves of her robe pushed up to her elbows, her hands covered in salve. "We did, as there were only a few bottles and there are so many here to treat. Were we wrong in using it?"

So, his appointment was cost at last. Not by ruse and stratagem, not by a dead ship, Drury, Kestral, or Cronyn, but by a kind-hearted Merian seeking to help those in need.

"Is it helping?" he asked.

"Oh yes, they seem much better, and many have at last fallen to sleep and are resting easy. They were so desperate for sleep."

"They've got a fighting chance now," Morgan said.

"Are they out of danger?"

"For now, yes."

"If it has helped them, then it was well used. We should be underway soon, and then we'll get them all the help they need in a matter of hours."

Morgan smiled at Stenstrom. "So, you wanted me to tell you what 'Jeterix' means?" she said, approaching him. Her eyes were like pristine lamps glowing bright on a field of tattooed blue.

"I did."

She hobbled into his personal space. Though he had just met this secretly painted woman, he could feel a distinct tension forming for her—a maddening, distracting tension. He wanted to touch her, to savor the feel and, as she was a certified empath, she probably knew all that too. "Well, let me tell you . . ."

"It means 'I'm a blithering, unwashed idiot' in Thompson," came Gwendolyn's voice from behind.

Stenstrom turned. Gwendolyn was standing into the doorway, her arms crossed. "Gwen, how are the coils doing?"

"They're small and under-powered, but they're coming along. Should be ready to make sail in another few minutes."

Stenstrom was amazed. "Excellent work."

"Would you care to inspect them?"

The Com buzzed in. "Captain Stenstrom," came Crewmen Clement's voice.

"Aye?" Stenstrom replied, still not used to hearing such a thing.

"Sir, we have a fix on the *Heade-on-the-Hearth*. A vessel matching her description is besetting a passenger-liner just off the shipping lanes. We're receiving an uncoded distress signal begging for help."

"What is a passenger liner doing off the shipping lanes?" Gwendolyn asked.

"Apparently she's full of Xaphan refugees. They were fleeing to the League," the Com replied.

"Inform the Fleet. Gwen, we need to make sail, immediately."

"Are we going to engage the Druries?"

"We are."

"We have no weapons—we can't fight!"

"No, but we can divert the *Heade* from the liner and hold her here until the

Fleet arrives."

Stenstrom and Taara returned to the bridge.

"What is our status, please?"

"We are reading minimum power reserves required to launch and make orbit," Crewman Allistar said, looking at screens on the Missive's Panel.

Stenstrom turned to A-Ram. "Are we ready?"

"Bel, that we are. The helm is available and ready for travel."

He looked up. "Com, Engineering—Lt. Gwendolyn, we're making sail."

"Aye," her voice came back. "Watch the redlines and don't expect a record dash out of the gates."

"All right, A-Ram. Take us up and get us into orbit."

Stenstrom stood there, with Lady Alesta still sitting in his seat. She was turned around, watching A-Ram work. In his heart, Stenstrom was sure nothing was going to happen. The *Seeker* would sit there stranded on the turbid waves of Cronyn World.

He heard a slight rise in noise.

"Thousand feet," A-Ram said.

"We're at a thousand feet already, A-Ram?"

"No sir, now we're at two thousand. Pitching up and picking up standard parking speed."

"How's it feel?" Stenstrom asked, not feeling the motion at all.

A-Ram looked at him. "Like a dream."

"Sensing, are we still reading the *Heade*?"

"Aye, sir."

"How far?"

"She's at 3:45am, mark 7:17PM, 800 thousand miles. She seems to have stopped."

Stenstrom addressed the bridge. "We've a slight change in plans. The *Heade* has attacked a civilian liner full of innocent souls. We have called the Fleet; however, they are still yet to arrive. We don't have anything to fight with, but, with luck, we can hold them long enough to protect the liner and await the Fleet."

"Creation, Bel, we can hold those fools all the damn lived-long day!" Taara said.

The bridge agreed—after all they'd been through at the hands of the Druries, they were spoiling for a fight.

"So be it. When we arrive, we'll . . . think of something."

Crewman Clement looked at the Com. "Sir, he said. "I don't think we're completely unarmed."

They stepped into the darkened bay. The place smelled of old shot blasts and cordite.

Gwendolyn carefully stepped into the bay and stood near Stenstrom. She looked around in the dark. Crewmen Clement and Allistar also entered.

"I thought you'd want to see this right away," Clement said.

Stenstrom took a breath. "Ok, crewman, what are we here to see?"

In the dark was a gangly, Z-shaped robotic assembly. "This, sir," he said, "is Battleshot Battery number 15, starboard."

Stenstrom took in the sight. It was a large robotic arm about twenty feet tall mounting a sturdy armature and a circular cluster of fifteen rotating barrels mounted at the top, ten feet long, each. There was an empty belt feeding the armature and what appeared to be a well-worn track leading out toward the closed doors.

Gwendolyn looked at it. "Please go on, crewman."

"It's an old-style HArM-6 long barrel Battleshot battery. They used to be the Fleet standard for short-range, ship-to-ship combat until the Sar-Beam sort of put them out to pasture."

Though big and looming, it looked quiet, asleep.

"This baby can unload upwards of 200,000 rounds a minute."

"Taara, I thought all the Battleshot batteries aboard the *Seeker* had previously been removed for retooling," Stenstrom said.

"They were, all except for this one," Clement said. "This gun has been used so much over the years that the bolts holding it to its run-out platform are fused in place. The craftsmen who removed all the Battleshot batteries previously couldn't get it out and they were going to cut the gun out of the position with laser torches during the *Seeker's* refit. It's all in the Com report."

Gwendolyn ran a finger up the length of its armature. There was a red label affixed to its housing. "No, no, Clement look at this—this gun has been condemned by Fleet Engineering."

Clement was a little embarrassed.

Stenstrom studied the towering, silent gun. "Oh, come now, Gwen," he said. "Let's think creatively for a moment. Has this gun been branded defective because it's actually broken, or simply because a regulation in a manual says it's defective due to some time limit being met and expired? Do we have any ordinance for it?"

"I found a drum containing two-hundred, fifty-four rounds in a bin marked DEFECTIVE," Clement said.

"Defective?" Gwendolyn replied.

Stenstrom winced. "Two-hundred, fifty-four rounds? At the rate of speed these long-barrel Battle Shot batteries fire, two hundred, fifty-four rounds will last about a fourth of a second."

Taara gave the battery a rap. "Yeah, but that'll be a fourth of a second of pure hell. If we line it up right, we can saw the *Heade-on-the-Hearth* in two."

"Provided the ammunition works and doesn't explode in the chamber," Gwendolyn said, shaking her head.

"Yes, of course. Have a bit of faith."

"It won't do that," Allistar said. "This is a great gun—a classic. My father was an armorer aboard the *Grayfox*. He used to tell me that the old long barrel was a gun you could count on. It was a gun that would get you home."

Stenstrom looked up. "Navigation, what is our ETA to the *Heade*?"

"Fifteen minutes."

Stenstrom smiled. "Let's load her up and run her out."

14

—Chance Drury—

The *Seeker* covered the distance fast. Clearing the debris field surrounding Cronyn World, she sprinted into a vast area with Onaris' star, Ole Scrub, shining dead ahead.

Far off, tumbling slightly, was the *Heade*.

She was grappled onto the boxy, ribbed form of a rickety *Merci* liner, holding it in the manner a praying mantis would hold a dying fly. The robotic armature mounting the cassagrain cannon was pointed at the liner's belly.

Stenstrom took in the scene in the holo-cone. "Looks like he's gripping her tight."

"Sir," crewman Clement said. "Incoming message. It is Chance Drury."

Over the Com came a sinister voice.

"Paymaster Stenstrom, you are full of surprises, a-heheh. *Vous m'ennuyez beaucoup.* But, look here. Looks to be 400 souls on this wretched tub, all miserable Xaphans seeking to change their fortunes in the League. I've got my cassagrains aimed right at their keel. One or two shots and the ship will break in half and all those screaming souls will be spaced. *Fácil viene, fácil va, no?*"

"What do you want, Drury?" Stenstrom replied.

"I want their engines, as you saw fit to damage mine."

On the ovular monitor screens, a pair of eyes appeared—Chance's eyes. "And," he said, "I want you as well. Put yourself out into space and I shall collect you—as you are a machine as I am, you shall survive without issue. I wish to keep you near me, as a dangerous attack animal. Or, maybe I'll just kill you, stuff you, and keep you in wardrobe as a hated Auto-Icon, getting you out on days when I feel like yelling at something. I shall inform my reconstituted brothers what an inconsolable bore you were. *Vous êtes une maladie sur mon âme bénie!*"

"We are unarmed, Drury. Let the liner go. What have you to fear from us?"

"I am not going to the let the liner go, Paymaster. I am going to hold it here, take its engines, and kill everyone aboard as slowly as I can. I see you put a call out. I see quite a few ships en route at this moment. Too bad I shan't be here when they arrive. Disappeared into the dark, as I do so well. *Wie Spaß das ist?*"

Stenstrom made a cutting motion across his throat.

"Com muted, sir," Clement said.

"Com, what is the ETA of the Fleet?"

"We have the *Exody, Tempest,* and *Coober Peedie* coming in through Kana and the *Danner* en route via Olgolvy. ETA two hours, approximate."

Stenstrom thought a moment. "Two hours—that's enough time for him to up and vanish sure enough. A-Ram, get me a bit closer and give me a full, unobstructed view of the *Heade's* cassagrain assembly. We're going to get close, and I am going to take it out with my NTHs. Then, on my signal, I want you to Slap the Drury-ship hard enough to knock the liner free. Then, we can be ready to deal with them."

He looked around. "Everybody ready?"

The bridge crew nodded.

"Unmute, please."

Crewman Clement pressed a button. "If you want me, Chance, those people aboard the liner are to be set free. It's not negotiable."

"They shall be free, sir, once they're dead—free to float in space. *Leurs morts jetteront des détritus les cieux.* Now, here is how we are going to proceed. In a few minutes, I am going to kill some passengers just to demonstrate my good intentions. To prevent the further killing of passengers, you, Paymaster, shall then exit your ship—you need not don a pressure suit either, sir. At that time, the *Seeker* shall retire, and I shall take the engines of this liner and be off, well ahead of the party the Fleet shall soon be throwing for me here."

Stenstrom walked into his office. In the distance, he could see the *Heade* with its robotic grapples tied up around the boxy, primitive-looking liner. The *Heade* kept the liner out in front of it, rotating around and presenting it to the *Seeker* like a hostage.

The three ships slowly swirled around each other.

A-Ram skillfully got the *Seeker* in closer, bit by bit.

There! There was the robotic cassagrain assembly mounted underneath the *Heade's* nose.

Just a little bit closer.

"So, Paymaster, what's it going to be? *Fait ils vivent ou mourront-ils?*"

He was now close enough to see the rounded nodes and housings of the robotic assembly. He could see the silvery connectors and servo motors, like a musculature of metal. He drew his NTH's and cocked them.

"I have an alternate proposal for you."

"Do you?" came Chance's voice. "You just cost thirty people their lives. I don't have time for games, Paymaster . . ."

There!! There was the control housing.

He fired both NTHs. "Nor do I," he said.

He watched the cassagrain gun go dead, stuck in position, pointing at the liner. Not firing.

"Now, A-Ram, now!!"

A-Ram spun the wheel and the nose of the *Seeker* quickly came around, the ship moving like glass. Desperately, the *Heade* tried to free itself from the liner.

The *Seeker* and the *Heade-on-the-Hearth* collided, the superstructures of both ships momentarily tangling. The passenger liner was released, and the long, clunky ship trundled away as fast as it could, leaving the two warships to battle.

The robotic grappling arms of the *Heade* moved to seize the *Seeker* like an octopus reaching out to grasp a crab. With a bang it locked on.

"Everybody hang on!" A-Ram shouted. He spun the wheel and rolled the *Seeker* in a maneuver Captain Davage himself would have been proud of.

The *Heade* was thrown away with the force. She turned her remaining guns to the *Seeker* and blasted away, trying to pierce her armor.

But, this time, the *Heade* wasn't facing a mostly dead, depowered Warbird. This time, Chance Drury was facing a fully functional ship.

Gwendolyn fired up the newly installed coils into overboost, and the ship jumped to additional life. The Cyclops eye of the main sensor lit up to near full strength.

A-Ram turned the wheel and the *Seeker* Slapped the *Heade* hard, caving in a good portion of its gantry-laced superstructure. Several pieces of odd technology fell off and spiraled away.

The *Heade* then tried to disengage and get away but the *Seeker* would not allow it, and, with her coils glowing, she was much faster than the damaged *Heade*. They rammed her full astern, sending her spiraling. The crew capsules began to vent, spewing jets of vapor into space.

The *Seeker* pulled up a-starboard and Slapped her again, more bits of gantry and hull plating careening away. Grapplers fell off and tumbled.

The *Heade*, in a panic, aimed her small caliber, rim-fired guns at the *Seeker*—the same guns that they mercilessly fired at the doomed men in the water on Cronyn World. In this case, nothing happened, as the guns were far too small to dent the *Seeker's* armor. In some instances, the shots reflected back and punctured the *Heade*.

Locked together, the *Heade* was finally in the correct position.

"Fire!" Stenstrom roared.

The solitary Battleshot unit in Bay 15 came to spinning life and laid a one second barrage full on the broadside of the *Heade*, a galaxy of blinking explosive ordinance dancing on its skin.

The *Heade* fell apart in a cascade of debris and deformed metal. The bridge capsule shot away, containing the Druries and their last remaining shards of foul programming.

"Another day, Paymaster, another day," came Chance's sinister voice over the Com. *"Ce n'est pas le dernier tu vas entendre à propos de moi, diable! Au revoir, salaud!"*

The bridge sped off into the night of space.

Nothing doing. The *Seeker* fell on it, like a hawk pouncing on a squirrel. The capsule burst open, revealing the struggling occupants. Eventually, either by flattening against the unbending hull of the *Seeker*, or by aimed NTH shot, Chance Drury and his brothers met their apparent end, being trampled by the *Seeker*.

With luck, he and his brothers would never rise again

15

—Under the Table—

Stenstrom sat in his office. He still wasn't quite used to lights and the breathing sounds the living ship made. He'd gotten used to the dark and the mumbling quiet. He sat there absently holding Lilly's Locket, feeling the smooth gold in his hand.

In a few hours, they'd be back at Kana, and he would give up the ship and face whatever charges awaited him at Fleet. The charges didn't bother him much. Just like a stout pair of handcuffs, he could get out of those easily enough. He had friends in the right places, he belonged to the right organizations, and he had lots of money to finance his defense.

What he couldn't get away from was the disappointment.

What was he going to say to Captain Davage and to his father? He promised Captain Davage he would make something of this lady again, this old Warbird *Seeker*. He promised him. Being an optimist, he guessed Captain Davage would see the positives and would happily support him again in the reappointment to another vessel.

Davage was always good for that.

And, his father—what would he say to him? *Sorry, father. I annoyed just about every Admiral I could find. I found out I'm some sort of 'It Man' as well and I belong to the Sisterhood of Light—oh, by the by, Lillian of Gamboa, whom we all liked so much back at the manor, isn't really a woman—she was the Sisters' construct made of sand, and I discovered a world full of hideous creatures that actively feed upon us, both mentally and physically. Oh, and I let them go, too. Also, I got into a big fight with the 400 year old Drury brothers, and they were a bunch of robots being controlled by their Kestral masters. Just like me . . .*

And then there was the *Seeker* herself. What would become of her—as Captain Davage had promised, she stood tall against all that had been arrayed before her. She still had all kinds of fight in her—it would be a shame to let her go.

He stared at the locket that once meant so much to him.

Such a shame.

There was a knock at the door and Gwendolyn came in.

"Ship's engineer," he said. "How goes it?"

"We're making good time, *Captain*," she said with familiar emphasis. "The small coils are holding up quite well. I'm very pleased."

She sat down. "You look a little sad, Bel. What's on your mind?"

He smiled at her. "You know, Gwen, we've only been acquainted for a short time, yes, and we're already probing each other's thoughts?"

"Neat, isn't it? So, spill it, Bel, what's got you down?"

"Oh, it's nothing. I'm just sitting here wondering what's it's going to be like to give this lady up. Looks like I blew my first mission and my time on the *Seeker's* chair is done."

She smiled. "Well, I suppose 'blew it' is a subjective term. Look at all the people you've inspired along the way to blowing your first mission. A-Ram would still be polishing silver at the Fleet, Taara would still be guarding nothing down at HQ, the Druries would still have free run, and I would still be a miserable, grouchy person without a friend in the world. I seem to have learned that I'm a pretty mean person when I'm in charge—I don't handle it well. I am much better as an important follower. This mission, I think, was a grand success. Feel like hitting something? Come on, let's head to the gym. Care to go a round or two with the Grizzly Bear? You'll feel better."

"Is the gym in pieces like the rest of this ship?" he asked.

"Don't know. I suppose we'll find out."

Stenstrom laughed. "Maybe later."

Gwendolyn left her seat and sat down on his desk. She took his hands. "This isn't an end, Bel; it's just the beginning. The place doesn't matter, and the ship doesn't matter. Wherever you go, I'm coming with you, or you're coming with me. It's a big Fleet, and I'm happy to tackle it knowing you're nearby. I sound like Morgan-Jeterix, don't I? She's always had a knack for saying things that I was thinking or feeling—but that's over. I'm going to say what's on my mind myself from now on—and guess what's on my mind right now?"

"What?"

"You, face down on the mat, tapping out of a rear naked choke hold that's won me so many tournaments. Come on, let's go let some steam off. Kana and all that can wait."

Stenstrom laughed and set the locket on the desktop. He stood and grabbed his HRN. "Ok, I'm told I'm pretty tough."

"I'll bet."

Gwendolyn put her arm around him and they headed for the door. There was another knock. Taara, A-Ram, and Lady Alesta came in.

"Come on in, everyone; there's plenty of room," Stenstrom said, biding them to enter.

Taara stepped in. "Were you two going somewhere?"

"The gym," Gwendolyn replied.

"The gym? You were going to the gym to fight, weren't you? Were you going to get me, so I could watch? You weren't, were you?"

"Good sir," Alesta said, "I wanted to offer you a present, one that you have well earned."

"Something for me?"

A-Ram spoke up. "I took Lady Alesta to the mess to see if we could scrounge up a snack before we put into Kana."

Alesta smiled and held out a black bottle of brandy. "I found this rolled under a table in the dining area. I'm told that you need this, that it will help you. Please, take it."

Stenstrom took the bottle of Admiral Derlith's brandy, the last remaining bottle. "Well, what do you know?"

"The Star works in wonderful ways. There are no martyrs, and all will be rewarded. None are left behind," she said.

Taara spoke up. "A-Ram, we still headed for Kana?"

"That we are."

"Then let's come about—we've got a party on Bazz to get to, and I think we can just make it."

A-Ram ran out of the office to the helm.

"Thank you, Lady Alesta," he said marveling at the bottle.

Alesta bowed and followed A-Ram out.

Gwendolyn grabbed Stenstrom by the collar. "Come on, Bel,"

"Are you still going to the gym?" Taara asked, tagging along.

"We're going to engineering, Taara, to see if we can squeeze a little bit more speed out of these coils, as Bel has an important date to keep on Bazz. Then we're going to the gym and you can watch me beat him up."

✳   ✳   ✳   ✳   ✳

Several hours later, Stenstrom and Gwendolyn returned to his office. They were both mussed up and sweaty.

"That was actually pretty fun," Stenstrom said. "You are quite skilled, Gwen."

She smiled and seated herself. "What, did you think I'd be a pushover or something? We need proper attire next time—it's too hard to move properly in what we're wearing now." Gwendolyn took a deep breath. "Ah, the first thing I'm going to do when we get a moment on Bazz is change. Goodness, how long have I been wearing these same clothes?"

Stenstrom looked out the window. "How long until we get to Bazz?"

"Seven or eight hours if we can hold this speed. We'll be cutting it close, but I think we'll have a little time to spare."

He seated himself. The golden locket was missing from his desk. He wondered where it had gone when Gwendolyn spoke up:

"What's this, Bel?" she asked.

"What's what?"

"This."

It was a huge package, at least seven by four feet wrapped in gray paper. Its size and general shape indicated that it was a large, framed painting.

There was a tag. Gwendolyn pulled her gloves off and read it. "It says: To Paymaster Stenstrom, Lord of Belmont. From: An Admirer. Well, you needn't wait until Nether Day, Bel. Open it."

He pulled away the paper. Exposed, he recognized the frame—it was the portrait Lilly had been working on years ago, the one she had never let him see.

Had he not been wearing his mask, he would certainly have been in tears.

"A friend of mine made this for me, Gwen," he said.

"Where did it come from?"

"I've no idea. The Sisters, perhaps."

Gwendolyn stood there holding the tag. "Well, can we look at it?"

He put his hands on the sides of the frame and turned it around. They looked at the vast face of the canvas.

There he was, standing tall: Lord Stenstrom of Belmont-South Tyrol, masked, in his green HRN coat. Gwendolyn stood in the background, wearing her Fleet uniform and FEDULA, a tiny scar on her cheek. A-Ram and Taara were there too, as was the *Seeker*, peeking through the clouds. He could also see the Merians milling about in the farther reaches of the garden.

He gave the frame a tap, and heard the slight hiss of sand falling away.

"Hey, is that me?" Gwen asked, looking at the canvas.

"Looks like you."

"How is this possible?"

Stenstrom took a deep breath. "Ask the Sisters. They seem to know everything."

Gwen leaned close to the canvas. "Who's that back there?"

Stenstrom was lost in thought.

"Bel?"

In the far recesses of the painting, was a figure crouching behind a tree. It was a slender figure, garbed in red.

"It's Knife," he said in reply.

"Who's that?"

"My enemy."

16

—The Ball—

They arrived at the wonderful Fleet complex at Teflegar-Martin II, near the calm waters of the Endax Sea, the evening sky a typical Bazz greenish-gray. They landed the ship at Fleet dock and got the civilians and any others who needed medical attention to The Jones at once. The rest, Fleet and Merians alike, headed to the Fleet ballroom at the heart of the complex. It didn't occur to anybody that the Merians were civilians—they, as a group, had become very close in their shared experience on Cronyn World.

The well-dressed attendants at the door saw the odd gaggle approaching and turned their noses up. "Have the lot of you been invited to this private function?"

"Indeed," Stenstrom said. "We are here under the orders of Admiral Derlith and have been commanded into his presence."

The attendants appeared unconvinced. "Have you a paper invitation or a code to offer?"

Gwendolyn stepped forward. "Ajax, Ajax, Endecar-two. That is his current personal code."

The attendant checked a nearby terminal. "Aye, that's his current code. Very well."

The attendants parted and Stenstrom and his band entered. As Lady Alesta approached, the attendants halted her. "You may not enter the ballroom, ma'am."

"And why not?" A-Ram asked, incensed, taking her by the shoulders.

"Because she is not properly shod as is required," he replied dryly, noting Alesta's bare feet.

Stenstrom returned to the attendants. "These people are worthy of all honor. They are shod in dedication and clothed in courage. She and her lot shall have entry to the ball."

The attendant thought about it, and then stepped aside, the rest of the group piling into the busy ballroom.

Stenstrom and Gwendolyn strode through the posh crowd and approached the vast dining table.

There was Admiral Derlith seated amongst his Admiral friends.

They arrived and stood there a moment.

The Admiral looked up at him. "Gwendolyn, are you all right? What is your business, Paymaster?" he asked, knife and fork in hand.

"You should know, Admiral," Stenstrom replied. "I'm here at your pleasure."

Derlith smiled. "Yes, sorry about that," he said. "Losing your chair and all."

"Lose my chair? On the contrary . . ."

Stenstrom waved his hands and produced a dusty bottle of brandy which he thumped down on the table.

"What's this?" Derlith asked.

"Your brandy. You should recognize it. I have fulfilled my mission, at your pleasure. And, with several hours to spare, I might add."

The Admiral scoffed. "One bottle? You had a whole crate to bring."

"Sorry, you didn't say how much brandy to bring to Bazz. Some bottles got smashed in my rough upload to the *Seeker*, and a few were used to comfort a group of civilians from Mallets who were in desperate need of aid. But please, enjoy the final bottle with your peers."

"What shall we do with one bottle? There are over a hundred admirals in attendance here."

"I suggest smaller snifters."

"Balderdash—your Appointment is cost. Gwendolyn, please take this fool into custody, under my orders."

Gwendolyn spoke up. "Uncle, you know I love you very much, but this fine man has fulfilled his mission and is, as of now, the bonded captain of the Main Fleet Vessel *Seeker*, and I will attest to it under tribunal. Along the way, he showed remarkable pluck, great ingenuity, and great courage. He saved not only my life, but the lives of my crew and those of the Merians, who are heroes by any measure, and he put an end to a scabrous band of outlaws operating right under the Fleet's nose. I am proud to stand here at his side."

"Gwendolyn!" Derlith yelled, "you are under orders—arrest this man!"

"I'm sorry, Uncle. I have been duly conscripted by the commander of a Main Fleet Vessel and am in his charge. I am currently not subject to your orders."

"Doing what, if I may ask?"

"Ship's engineer," Stenstrom replied. "By hook or by crook, Admiral."

Stenstrom waved his hands and produced a silver dagger. He gently took the bottle from the Admiral and began slicing away the wax. "You are to be commended, sir," Stenstrom said. "You helped raise a fine young woman, if Gwendolyn vouches for you—which she does—then you must be a good fellow. I'm sorry I offended you and I'm sorry this lone bottle is all that's left of your crate. Be comforted, the rest helped save the lives of League citizens and, therefore, was well-used."

Stenstrom got the wax off and uncorked the bottle. He took a whiff of the contents. "I was wrong about this as well; it smells wonderful, truly a product of fine tending and skill. I shall take my leave, sir, and bid you good night."

Derlith stopped him. "Paymaster, I have been known to be judgmental, and rather stubborn. You inspired my adjutant to insurrection. Josephus . . ."

"He prefers to be called A-Ram, sir."

"Yes, Lord A-Ram then, has never shown that sort of style before, and you have won over my niece, whom I love very much and whose judgment I trust. I may have misjudged you and given ear to bizarre things not of either of our makings. So be it. I hereby acknowledge that you have fulfilled your mission at my pleasure. You are, as of this moment, the bonded captain of the Main Fleet Vessel *Seeker*. I will take care of the pending charges against you, and bade you return the *Seeker* to Dry Dock 186 to begin her refits as soon as you are able to get her there. And please, enjoy the ball, stay and be refreshed, be entertained. I would enjoy a dance with my niece at some point this evening." And please ask Lord A-Ram to join me when he can, I would like to congratulate him on his appointment. I shall greatly miss him."

Stenstrom and Gwendolyn bowed. They turned to make their way from the table.

Stenstrom's special white Holystone, the one that detected the Astral Plain, rattled. Carefully he surveyed the table.

Seated a few place settings down was a black-haired woman in a green gown. She sat there smiling up at him. "Good sir?" she said. "I'm pleased you made it. I was hoping . . ."

Stenstrom stopped, his stone rattling hard. "Madam? Do I know you?"

"Yes," the woman said. "You do. I promised myself I'd never return to Bazz, yet here I am. It's different than it was before, and so am I."

He stood there regarding her for several moments. Finally: "I believe I do know you. I thought you a phantom of my own imagination for a long time. You have tried to kill me as an infant, as a helpless boy, and again as a bewildered young man. Do you deny it?"

The woman fidgeted. "No sir, I don't."

"Are you here to kill me now?"

"I came here to congratulate you for accomplishing something I never could, to offer my thanks for the example you've shown me, and to ask your forgiveness."

"My forgiveness?"

"For everything. For everyone. We are in a closed Circle, the Bazzers say. Time to end it. Time to let old hurts heal."

Stenstrom thought a moment. "I will say that an injustice was done to you once. What you must have felt for my father to be so angry for so long. To put an end to this, to break this curse, I will say that I forgive you, and hold you no further malice. Additionally, I must inform you that I intend to escort you to the authorities and inform them of everything I suspect regarding your former activities. I am also going to inform the Sisters that you have breached their thoughts."

The woman sat there. She considered her response, then spoke. "I was ready, to atone for my sins, to face justice, but then . . ."

She pulled a small envelope from her bag. It was new, freshly written in familiar handwriting; looked like his father's hand, he recognized the letterhead. "Then I discovered it's never too late to begin living again. We all deserve that, don't we?"

"A fine sentiment, but regardless. Shall we?" he said, motioning for her to take his hand.

She pulled something else from her bag and set it on the table. "First, please accept this gift," she said. "I have no further use for it."

Stenstrom looked down. Sitting on the table was a large garnet on a burnished chain. His Astral Plane detectors went wild: it was a Planar Bridge, a key to opening a gateway to the Astral Plane. He'd never seen one up close before.

"Please take good care of my niece," she said.

There was a brief commotion of uncorking bottles out on the ballroom floor. He glanced away for a moment.

When he looked back, she was gone. Her chair was empty, only the garnet and its chain remained.

Gwendolyn was confused. "Who was that, Bel? Where'd she go?"

He looked at the now empty chair and sighed. "Nobody. I don't know where she went, but I wish her luck."

They walked away from the table and made their way across the busy dance floor to where Taara, A-Ram, and Lady Alesta waited. Morgan, still weak, was sitting nearby, alert but a little tired. Taara was standing there with a plate of something. A-Ram fetched a glass of punch for Morgan and for Lady Alesta, who took it and smiled at him, holding her cup. She was so lovely when she smiled—very pretty, and clearly in love.

Good for you, A-Ram. Well done.

Several of the crew stood around, some holding plates from the buffet line, while others had waded out onto the floor, testing the waters, some dancing with other crewmen, others with robed Merians. The bond that had formed between them was clear and well earned.

They waved, and A-Ram and Alesta waved back.

The music picked up and the dancers parlayed about. Stenstrom and Gwendolyn found themselves jostled and pushed in the tight reaches of the floor. Lace and confetti landed on their shoulders and got in their hair.

Soon, they were arm in arm, swirling across the floor, Gwendolyn's eyes locked with Stenstrom's eyes.

He tried to pull away but she held him. She was so strong.

"We've our ship to return to, Gwen."

"Must we, so soon? You heard my uncle—we've the night. The ball is ours. This is our celebration, Bel—we've earned it. If I may make a suggestion, as acting Ship's Engineer the crew's been through a lot, and they've earned a few days of fun, to relax, to put on some clean clothes and get their heads back on, and I'm sure Taara would like to visit her folks while we're here, to show them what she's become. And, I wouldn't mind trying some of this hot Bazz food that I've heard so much about, provided I've good friends to share it with. Now that the ship has a real set of coils, albeit small ones, it'll only take us a day or two to get back to Kana and begin its refit. Let's not be in any hurry. We've much hard work ahead of us, all in due course."

She stood there a moment. "I'm sorry. I forgot myself. I'm only an *acting* Ship's Engineer."

Stenstrom smiled. "There shall soon be an appointment available for ship's engineer aboard the *Seeker*—want the job, for good? I know you wouldn't be in command anymore, but think of the name you could make for yourself . . ."

Gwendolyn stared at him. Stenstrom continued. "And A-Ram . . . I know A-Ram would miss the daylights out of you if you weren't there, and . . ."

Gwendolyn didn't say anything. Instead, as the music grew, she reached up and slowly pulled the mask from Stenstrom's face. As she did so, he felt no pain, no rush of anguish for his lost Lilly. Rather, he felt the thrill of possibilities with this beautiful Lady of Prentiss who stood at his side in the pit of hell. She stood there looking at him with unforgettable eyes. She pulled the mask away. Letting it go slack at her side, the hermelin fell from the folds of cloth and clattered to the floor, forgotten.

"So handsome," she said. For the first time, Stenstrom and Gwendolyn—the man in the HRN coat and the Grizzly Bear—kissed.

Apparently, she did want the job.

Epilogue

Up on the bluff overlooking the grand Fleet complex, a solitary figure crouched down and listened to the sounds of the ball drift up to the heights.

The figure was clad in red and black, wearing wrappings and robes. It was soon time to move on, to renew the chase.

Knife stood and began to make her way back to her little Shadow tech vessel.

As she walked, a storm picked up, and wind and bits of grit flew into her face. Though masked, she covered her eyes and quickened her pace.

Something lifted her up and threw her down. Knife flipped back up to her feet and whirled around. Something was hiding in the wind.

She slashed out with her hands sending out invisible, micro-beams of Shadow tech, deadly and cutting.

She heard something cry out. Not understanding what she was fighting, Knife slashed again and again, sending her Shadow tech into the maelstrom, hearing her unseen adversary wail in misery.

Knife thought she saw something slump to the ground ahead. She formed a Shadow tech harpoon and advanced to plunge it into her opponent's heart.

She fell upon the form, rose up and brought the harpoon into its chest.

There was a scream, and the maelstrom of wind and sand got more and more fierce. Her mask was blown away, and the wrappings around her arms began to tatter. She felt the wind-driven sand scouring into her bare flesh, rending it from bone.

She dropped her harpoon and tried to get away as quickly as she could.

Hands of sand grabbed her from behind.

Knife was lifted into the air, struggling and kicking, micro blades of Shadow tech shooting out in a deadly fan.

She was savagely bent backwards with a sickening crack, her head suddenly wrenched back with her legs, her pelvis snapping in two. Folded up and scoured clean, Knife died in agony.

The storm of wind raged about for a minute or two more, picking Knife's pitiful bones clean.

The winds calmed. A figure formed.

It moved to the edge of the bluff and looked down on the Fleet complex, just as Knife had done only minutes earlier.

The figure lifted a parasol over her head, twirled it about, and sighed. "I'm coming for you, Bel . . ." whispered a soft voice.

Author Information

Ren Garcia is a Science Fiction/Fantasy author and Texas native who grew up in western Ohio. He has been writing since before he could write, often scribbling alien lingo on any available wall or floor with assorted crayons. He attended The Ohio State University and majored in English Literature. Ren has been an avid lover of anything surreal since childhood. He also has a passion for caving, urban archaeology and architecture. He currently lives in Columbus, Ohio with his wife, and their four dogs.

Coming Soon

Coming Soon

PUBLISHER INFORMATION

VISIT THE LOCONEAL BLOG AT

www.loconeal.com

Breaking News
Forthcoming Releases
Links to Author Sites
Loconeal Events

www.ingramcontent.com/pod-product-compliance
Lightning Source LLC
Chambersburg PA
CBHW070303260626
47160CB00003B/700